The scribe smiled, and her eyes seemed older than her years. "I don't care if they all burn each other to nothing, I just hope you can keep them from doing it here."

Yardem's gaze flicked to Marcus, expecting or dreading a cutting remark from him. But Marcus didn't have one to hand. It was a bloodthirsty and selfish sentiment, but it wasn't an uncommon one. Charity and compassion were easier when there was no sense of threat to poison them, and the world was woven from threats these nights. In other circumstances, the scribe would likely have thought a bit more before she hoped death and fire for the whole world, only not her city. It was war, though. It stained everything.

"Abraham questions and explores the fantasy-world assumptions that most authors take for granted, telling an enjoyable and genuinely innovative adventure story along the way."
—*Publishers Weekly* (Starred Review)

"A pleasure for Abraham's legion of fans."　　　—*Kirkus*

"Prepare to be startled, shocked, and entertained."
—*Locus*

"*The Dragon's Path* is an enjoyable read that holds great expectations for the series."　　　—*SF Signal*

Praise for
Daniel Abraham

"Abraham is fiercely talented, disturbingly human, breathtakingly original and even on his bad days kicks all sorts of literary ass."　　　—Junot Díaz

"Daniel Abraham gets better with every book."
—George R. R. Martin

"The storytelling is smooth, careful and—best of all—unpredictable."　　　—Patrick Rothfuss

Publications by Daniel Abraham

THE LONG PRICE QUARTET
A Shadow in Summer
A Betrayal in Winter
An Autumn War
The Price of Spring

THE DAGGER AND THE COIN
The Dragon's Path
The King's Blood
The Tyrant's Law
The Widow's House
The Spider's War

THE EXPANSE
Leviathan Wakes (with Ty Franck as James S. A. Corey)
Caliban's War (with Ty Franck as James S. A. Corey)
Abaddon's Gate (with Ty Franck as James S. A. Corey)
Cibola Burn (with Ty Franck as James S. A. Corey)
Nemesis Games (with Ty Franck as James S. A. Corey)
Babylon's Ashes (with Ty Franck as James S. A. Corey)

THE BLACK SUN'S DAUGHTER
Unclean Spirits (as MLN Hanover)
Darker Angels (as MLN Hanover)
Vicious Grace (as MLN Hanover)
Killing Rites (as MLN Hanover)
Graveyard Child (as MLN Hanover)

Leviathan Wept and Other Stories
Balfour and Meriwether in the Incident of the Harrowmoor Dogs
Hunter's Run (with George R. R. Martin and Gardner Dozois)
Star Wars: Honor Among Thieves (with Ty Franck as James S. A. Corey)

THE
SPIDER'S
WAR

BOOK FIVE OF THE DAGGER AND THE COIN

DANIEL
ABRAHAM

www.orbitbooks.net

Orbit
Hachette Book Group
1290 Avenue of the Americas
New York, NY 10104
orbitbooks.net

First edition: March 2016

Orbit is an imprint of Hachette Book Group.
The Orbit name and logo are trademarks of Little, Brown Book Group Limited.

The publisher is not responsible for websites (or their content) that are not owned by the publisher.

The Hachette Speakers Bureau provides a wide range of authors for speaking events. To find out more, go to www.hachettespeakersbureau.com or call (866) 376-6591.

Map by Chad Roberts

Library of Congress Cataloging-in-Publication Data has been applied for.

ISBNs: 978-0-316-20405-7 (trade paperback), 978-0-316-20404-0 (ebook)

Printed in the United States of America

RRD-C

10 9 8 7 6 5 4 3 2 1

To Fred Saberhagen
He was right.

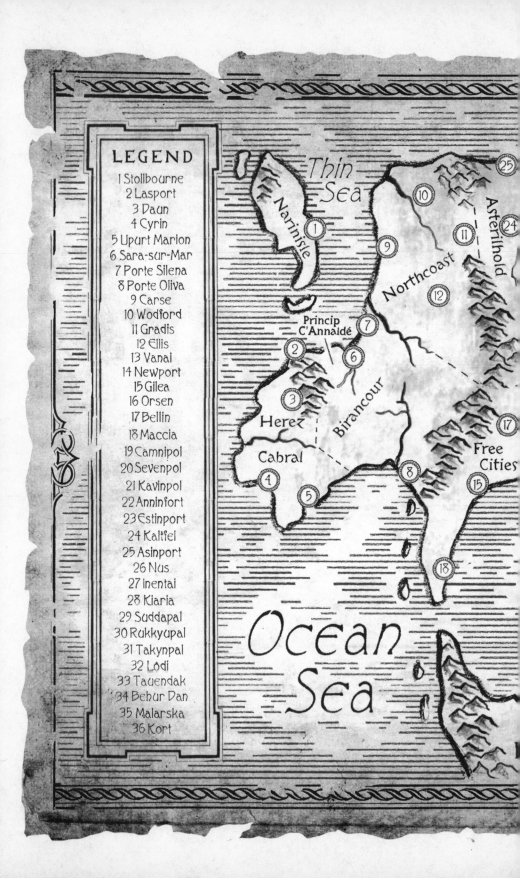

LEGEND

1 Stollbourne
2 Lasport
3 Daun
4 Cyrin
5 Upurt Marion
6 Sara-sur-Mar
7 Porte Silena
8 Porte Oliva
9 Carse
10 Wodford
11 Gradis
12 Ellis
13 Vanai
14 Newport
15 Gilea
16 Orsen
17 Bellin
18 Maccia
19 Camnipol
20 Sevenpol
21 Kavinpol
22 Anninfort
23 Estinport
24 Kaltfel
25 Asinport
26 Nus
27 Inentai
28 Kiaria
29 Suddapal
30 Rukkyupal
31 Takynpal
32 Lôdi
33 Tauendak
34 Behur Dan
35 Malarska
36 Kort

Thin Sea

Narinisle

Northcoast

Asterilhold

Princip C'Annaldé

Birancour

Herez

Cabral

Free Cities

Ocean Sea

Prologue

The Second Apostate

The heart of the goddess, her new temple—her *true* temple—had neither the grandeur of the cities nor the simple dignity of the Sinir Kushku. In Camnipol, it was said that her banner hung from the great tower of the Kingspire, goddess and throne made one. In Kaltfel, the temple was ancient stone, and had been dedicated to some false god before the Basrahip had sent Ovur to remake it as the center of her truth in the new-conquered land. All through the world, the banner of the goddess flew above great pillars and windows of colored glass. And one day, they would be true temples, untainted by lies and error.

But that day had not come.

Here, in the lands to which Ovur and his priesthood had fled, the pulpit was not ancient granite adorned with gold, but a low platform of rough wood rimed with frost. Here, the pews were not carved oak upholstered with silk, but stones and logs stinking of rot and cold. For candles, they had smoking torches of wrapped grass and fat. For the altar, a mound of frozen earth. The air smelled of decay and winter, and the ruddy, early sunset bled across the wide sky.

Ovur looked out from the pulpit over the men who had come to his call. The pure. The few who had heard the truth of his voice and thrilled to the echoes of the goddess with him. At the front, the newest initiates swayed, their eyes glassy and their jaws slack, still rapt with the awe of her transformation, their blood still thickening with the mark of her favor. Three dozen men in a winter swamp at dusk, cold, shivering, and hungry. If it were not for the presence of the goddess within each of them and the glory of the purification they carried, it would have been a sad, squalid scene. Instead, it was like looking upon a rough seed and knowing the vine that grew from it would one day cover all the world.

"For years, my friends, we followed the Basrahip," Ovur said, his hands lifted to them. "Some of you knew him of old as the voice of the goddess. Others of you saw him first as a conqueror at the side of the Severed Throne when your nation was lifted up from its corruption and ignorance."

The men in the pews lifted their hands and their voices. Some spoke praise for the power and beauty of the goddess, some their hatred of the false priest who twisted her teachings from his glorified seat beside Antea's throne. Ovur felt his heart warmed and reassured by both, and the spiders that dwelled in his blood shifted and thrilled. He spoke the truth to his people, and they spoke it back, and with every living voice his certainty grew.

"I stood in his shadow too, as did we all," Ovur went on, his breath ghosting in the cold. "But even as her voice spread across the world, the Basrahip fell into darkness. As she rose in every temple, her light peeling back the ancient lies of the dragons, the Basrahip was made corrupt. He claimed that of all the temples, only his was true. As if a spider had only one true leg to which all others answered."

Now none of the responses were of praise; all were of anger and condemnation. Ovur breathed them in, smiling and nodding as if his affirmation was also comfort to them. The threats against the Basrahip were justified by the power of the voices making them.

"Yes, once the Basrahip led straight. Once, his voice was hers. It is a tragedy that his strength was too little to withstand the lies of the world, but it is only a tragedy for him. *Not* for the goddess, for she is perfect and incorruptible. And we few are her true voice, welling up even in this place, as others shall all across the face of the world. Our brothers Eshau and Mikap have gone to spread our truths to the great powers of the world and shall return soon with an army that will cast down the false Basrahip and break his lies like ice upon stone. What has begun cannot be stopped, not ever, and—"

A horn blew, three rising notes. Two more answered. Ovur felt a tightening in his throat. Not fear. He was chosen of the goddess, and so protected by her power and her grace. If the quickness of his heart and breath imitated that base feeling, it was only that the man he had once been would have felt fear. Or if not that, surprise. Ovur grinned. In the rough pews, his priests looked to one another, unsure what the noises meant.

The men who came looming up from the swamp's shadows were a sad, sorry lot. Thin and ragged. Some very old, some very young, and few enough between. They wore the armor of Imperial Antea and the eightfold sigil on their shields. Some carried swords before them, the blades catching the light of torches and fading sunlight. More had pikes braced in two hands, as if to stave off a cavalry charge. Ovur's laughter rolled out through the wilderness, warm and delighted and thick with threat to the impure. In the pews, one of the new initiates seemed to notice for the first time that something odd was going on. He rose unsteadily to his feet, looking as astounded by the surrounding enemy as if they had woven themselves into being from the grass itself.

The mud-muted steps of horses followed. A dozen men in the saddles. They wore the brown robes that Ovur once had, before the Basrahip had fallen from grace. It was the uniform of the fallen now, and Ovur looked on them with pity. The swords they carried would have been green in the full light of day. In the red light of torches and sunset, they seemed black. The false priests drew the poisoned blades, and the fumes from them gave the air an astringent bite. The spiders in Ovur's blood, restless, seemed to vibrate and squirm from beneath this thinnest skin down to the pit of his belly.

"I do not fear you," Ovur said. "You cannot win against the power of the goddess!"

"We do not seek to," a familiar voice boomed. And there, arriving last among the priests, was the Basrahip himself, his massive body astride a thin-framed pony. And at his side, another rider sat a nobler horse. This man wore a robe of thick grey wool and a hood pulled over his head against the cold. His lips were pressed thin, and his shoulders hunched.

"Prince Geder!" Ovur said. "I praise her light that you have come."

"I'm not a prince," Geder Palliako said, his voice high and peevish. "I'm Lord Regent. That's better than a prince."

"He has come to see the beginning of her reign," Basrahip said, and his voice rolled through the growing darkness. "We have brought him to this final battle against lies that he might witness the place where the great age begins."

In his blood, the spiders shuddered with something like delight. The truth of the Basrahip's words was like honey on the tongue, and Ovur's laughter grew almost gentle.

"Yes, old friend, so you have," Ovur said.

The new initiate moved toward the soldiers, his steps unsteady. The pikemen looked at one another anxiously.

The new priest tittered, stumbling toward them. One soldier reached out with his weapon gently enough to push the man back without making it an attack.

"Ovur," the Basrahip said. "We need not come to a violent end here. Once we were brothers in her light. We can be again."

"This is so," Ovur said, and for an instant, his heart filled with joy at the power of the goddess. "Even now your living voice carries truth in it."

"Does that mean we can go back to camp?" the Lord Regent said, his voice tentative but light, like that of a boy trying to joke among men. "It's getting cold."

"Do you renounce your apostasy?" Basrahip asked. His mount shifted, uneasy. The red-lit clouds in the heavens cooled to a sudden grey. Ovur felt a qualm, uncertain not of his faith, but of how the Basrahip who only a moment before seemed to have come to the edge of absolution from his error could now say this.

"I cannot," Ovur said. "I am no apostate."

The Basrahip grunted as if he'd been struck. Around in the growing darkness, the brown-robed priests held their blades at the ready. The rickety soldiers of the empire grew more solid in their ranks.

"The goddess speaks through one voice," the Basrahip said, his tones rougher now. "And that voice is my own."

In Ovur's blood a strange thing happened. The spiders, gifts of the goddess, told him that the Basrahip's words were true, even as he knew that they were not. For a moment, the world seemed to shift under him, the landscape itself heaving a great sigh beneath his feet. And then, rising up from his belly like the heat of a fire, came the rage.

"The goddess speaks through us all!" Ovur called back, his voice hard as gravel. The power of the goddess shook the words, and his throat ached with it. "No one temple holds her truth. All temples are hers, all priests are hers, and *all* voices are hers!"

In the pews, Ovur's priests rose as one, their balled fists at their sides. The brown-robed priests in the shadows shifted, moving forward, outrage in their eyes. Only the third group—the Lord Regent and his awkward soldiers— appeared hesitant.

In the back of Ovur's mind, a small, still voice told him that there was a way, that there had to be a way to reconcile. But the anger in him was like a storm breaking against cliffs. He heard the blood rushing in his ears, felt the indignation in his belly like a dragon breaking from its shell full-grown and terrible.

"You are in error!" Basrahip shouted, and Ovur's blood filled with the spasm of a thousand spiders. Truth and not-truth ripped at him. Any thought of brotherhood, of being reconciled, was forgotten.

"No! *You* are apostate!" Ovur shrieked. "You are a thing of *lies*!"

There was no plan to the attack, not on either side. Goaded beyond his tolerance, Ovur ran forward, through his priests and toward the thick shadow of the Basrahip. His fists were clenched to the point of pain, and he felt his battle yell more than heard it. The skittering of his blood and the heat of his anger were like boiling, but without the pain; as if he himself were not the flesh and the blood but the *act* of boiling. Where once there had been a man, there was now only the vessel of her vengeance. With him, the others came, throwing their bodies at the apostates with abandon and faith. The Basrahip and his servants of lies would fall before them, grass before the scythe.

Frozen mud slipped under his foot, and he stumbled. The

ragged pikemen fell back, their torchlit faces masks of con-fusion and astonishment. But the others, the brown-robed priests, leapt to battle, mouths twisted in an answering rage. Ovur lost sight of the others, enemy and friend alike, as he sprinted toward the Basrahip. He swung his knuck-les at the huge man's mount as if he might knock the horse back by brawling with it. The animal shied, fixing him with one affronted brown eye. Ovur grabbed the enemy's great branch-thick thigh, yanking at the Basrahip. Pulling him down.

Something happened, and the noise of battle seemed to grow both more pitched and distant. He was on his knees without any recollection of falling, and a bloom of pain was coming to the back of his head. He glanced over his shoul-der to see the Lord Regent of Antea staring down at him in fear and horror, a mace in his hand. The man had *struck* him. Ovur struggled to his feet, but the battle was past him. The gloom was a chaos of bodies. Men and horses were screaming.

She will protect us, Ovur thought. *We are her chosen.*

Something bit at his side, harder than teeth. Ovur fell for-ward, away from the blow, and twisted. The pikeman who'd stabbed him was dancing back as if the semi-prone enemy were more dangerous than snakes. Ovur slipped.

He could not see the Basrahip, but he heard the great ox-strong bellow of his voice. *You cannot win! Everything you love is already lost! You have lost! You cannot win!* Each word struck him, filling him with anger his body could not support. He scrabbled at the frozen mud with clawed fingers. Blood poured from his side, soaking his rude clothes. A voice he knew cried out and was cut off. A torch fell near him, smoldering in the grass and illuminating noth-ing beyond its own death. Ovur gasped and panted. Tiny legs flickered over the backs of his hands, the spiders spilled with his blood skittering in miniature panic. He wanted to say something to reassure them, to comfort them in the confusion and agitation that mirrored his own.

The sounds of the battle began to calm. Someone was screaming in panic nearby, but only one. Other voices moved through the night, some in the tones of conversation, others in a kind of hushed awe. The Basrahip had ceased his shouting. Ovur rested his head against his outstretched hands. In a moment, he would rise. Pull himself to his feet and carry the battle on to the end, however bitter, until his strength and his anger failed him. It would be only a moment before he gathered his strength...

Footsteps in the dead winter grass. The vicious stink of the poisoned blades. A gasp. Ovur rolled to his side, aware of the pain of his injury but unmoved by it. It was only pain.

The Lord Regent had lost his horse. In his hand, he held one of the venomous blades unsheathed. The tool of the dragons. How had Ovur lived so long knowing that the Basrahip wielded the weapons of the great enemy and not seen him for what he was? He had been blind. His strength was failing him. He felt his body growing heavier. Growing numb. Something like sleep tugged at his mind. Like sleep, but not.

"He's here! I found him!" Palliako shouted.

Tiny black bodies skittered in the dark, moving quickly at first, but then slowing. Even before the fumes of the sword could shrivel them, the cold of the ground and of his drying blood was deadly. Palliako looked over his shoulder, the tip of the dragon's sword wavering as his attention to it slipped. It was the opportunity. Ovur imagined himself leaping forward, wrestling the blade away and carving through the man's throat. Using the tools of the enemy against it. He barely had the strength to smile at the thought.

"I said I *found* him! He's over here!"

"Listen!" Ovur hissed, and the Lord Regent turned back to him, alarmed. "Hear me!"

"You be quiet."

"You think that we can be stopped by swords? You think we can be stopped by slaughter?"

"Yes," Geder Palliako said. He stepped forward, and the spiders nearest him withered. "I think there's some pretty good evidence for that."

Even dying, Ovur felt the great leader's doubt. "You kill men. Only men. The truth that lifted us up will lift others too. In all the cities, in all the temples, the faithful will find the truth. All will turn against you. All."

"No they won't," Geder said, and the doubt within him had grown. "You're the liar. You're the one who turned against her power."

"I am not," Ovur said, and the Basrahip loomed up from the darkness. The wide face looked almost serene. Sorrow welled up in Ovur's heart, vast as oceans. "We are not to be reconciled after all, then."

"No."

Ovur nodded, then rested his head against the ground. The cold didn't seem so terrible now. The pain in his side was vicious, but distant. Something deep in his belly felt heavy and wrong. Others were coming close now too. Soldiers and priests. Men holding lanterns and blades. Some few were familiar, but none were his own.

"Her voice," Ovur said, then lost the thread of his thought, coughed, and began again. "Her voice is heard in all her temples. Her light shines from every torch. You,

Basrahip, are only another torch. You're not the sun. And I am no apostate."

The large man's eyes widened and his mouth became a scowl of rage. He snatched the green blade from Palliako, stepped forward, and, roaring like a storm, sank the blade deep into Ovur's chest. The pain of the strike was surprising and fierce, but worse was the burning. All through his body, even those parts he'd thought numb, the spiders seemed to take fire. Acid and venom filled him. His flesh pulsed with death throes not his own. And then with his own. He was only vaguely aware of Basrahip's voice, continuing to denounce him. Of the terrible nausea that seemed to center in the envenomed wound. For a moment, he had a sense of profound clarity, but it brought him neither insight nor comfort.

Ovur, born of Sana and Egran of the Sinir Kushku, offered to the temple in his sixth year, and pilgrim under the Basrahip to the great world beyond the mountains, closed his eyes for the last time. The thing that was not sleep pulled at him, and he let himself be drawn down into it, certain that the goddess he had served with his full heart and whole life would be in that darkness to receive him.

As it happened, she was not.

Captain Marcus Wester

Like wine poured into water, the war stained the world even where the actual fighting had not yet reached.

Carse, the greatest city of Northcoast, looked out over a winter sea. The sky was the grey of snow, the water the grey of slate. No army had crossed the kingdom's borders, but one camped in Birancour to the south, and another—smaller—was said to be marching in the swamps near Kaltfel to the east. There were rumors that Lord Regent Geder Palliako rode with that second one, that the spirits of the dead had swollen his host to the largest the world had ever known but only at night, that the forces of Antea were poised to sweep over the kingdom like a plague wind. For all Marcus knew, it might be true. Everything else had been strange enough these last few years that drawing a line between groundless fear and plausible scenario had become difficult where it wasn't impossible.

It didn't change the job.

He hunched into his cloak, walking through the same frost-touched streets he had as a younger man. His feet ached, and his right knee had started to click sometimes, but it didn't hurt yet. The poisoned sword hung across his back, eroding his health and making his blood watery and thin. He felt the weight of years slowing him, making each day a bit harder than the one before it. Death was constant, inevitable, and coming. His own, and everybody else's. Age and maturity meant he was aware of the fact, that was all.

Beside him, Yardem stood tall, his canine face alert, his ears canted forward. There was grey at their tips. They were both getting old, but the years didn't seem to weigh down the Tralgu as much. So maybe his bleakness was just the sword.

A boy wheeled a cart ahead of them, the steam from it billowing and filling the air with the scent of burning wood and roasting chestnuts. Marcus lifted a hand, and the guards shifted to walk around the cart. Marcus had seen more ambushes than he cared to remember, and this wasn't one. The carter nodded to them as they passed. No hidden blades appeared in the shadows, no sudden battle cries split the air. Marcus was vaguely disappointed.

"I don't know who we are anymore," he said.

Yardem flicked his ear, considering. The earrings jingled. "You're Marcus Wester, sir. I'm Yardem Hane. Those back there are Enen and Halvill. The one at the back's called Little Fish, but I couldn't say why."

"Not what I meant. Used to be I was captain of the guard for the Medean bank in Porte Oliva, but seeing there isn't a branch in Porte Oliva anymore, makes it a bit strange. Do we work for Cithrin? Is she still part of the bank? There's no chain of command anymore."

"We sleep in the bank's rooms and eat from the bank's kitchen," Yardem pointed out. "At a guess, we work for them."

"Do they pay us?"

"They do."

"Do they pay us money?"

The Tralgu flicked a thoughtful ear. "Granted, that's more a question, sir."

The chest that Enen and Halvill carried between them was hard oak bound in iron. The lock was thick and well made. It would have taken a man with a crowbar half an hour to crack it open. Everything about it—including the five guards walking through the chill grey streets—indicated that whatever it contained was important. Valuable. Everyone Marcus passed—the carter boy, the old woman in leather and rags trundling through the intersection behind them, even the city watch—would see their burden being treated as if it were precious as gold. And it would add, the idea went, to the story that the yellow sheets of paper with their arcane script and the shining flecks in among the fibers were actually worth something.

Cithrin had called them letters of transfer, but Komme Medean had instructed everyone else to use the name *war gold*. It was a name meant to weave the idea of real coinage with the fear of the imperial armies at the borders, as if by the magic of pretending the drawing of a gold coin was the same as the thing itself, Northcoast and Carse would be somehow safer from the killing blades and tainted priests.

And the hell of it was, for all Marcus could see it might work. Certainly the sheets that he and his guards were given at the end of each week traded for food and drink, a launderer's services or a cobbler's. And Cithrin, sitting deep in the great brick keep that was the holding company, seemed busier than she'd ever been as a simple banker. And still, he felt more like an actor pretending a length of painted wood was a battle-axe than a soldier guarding treasure.

The scriptorium had a wide blue door and wooden walls with carvings of a dozen different scripts worked into them. Snow covered the tiled roof, and icicles clung to the eaves, thin tendrils hanging from the thicker stumps where they'd been broken to keep them from slaughtering random passersby. Marcus rapped on the doorway and waited, his breath ghosting before him. A woman's voice called from within, then a scrape came, and the door swung open. The master scribe ushered them into a workroom. Twenty desks, each with someone sitting at it. All of the full guild members at work. Thick-bodied, ruddy Firstblood; pale, sprout-thin Cinnae; scaled Jasuru, all with reed-thin pens scratching gently at papers. Four iron braziers warmed the air almost to the point of comfort but not quite. In the back, he knew, were thirty more apprentices with less heat and smaller workplaces. A harpist played in the back of the room in an attempt to keep boredom at bay. A Jasuru woman glanced up at them, her bronze scales glowing in the light, and then went back to her work.

"This way, Captain Wester," the master scribe said, and Marcus followed her back to a smaller office. The papers waiting there didn't have the yellow dye of war gold, but they were tools of conflict just the same. They stood on the desk, square pages tied in twine. Marcus slid one around to read the top sheet.

METHODS FOR DEFEATING THE ENEMY

The abominations that have corrupted Antea and brought war to the world are powerful, but they are not invincible. Their power is in their voices and in their blood, but they have been defeated before and they can be defeated again.

It went on. Simple, unadorned letters that outlined the dangers that the priests posed and how to drown out their voices, fight battles deaf to their commands, and avoid the contagion of tiny black spiders that spilled out like rotten blood when you cut one open. The words were simple to the point of simplistic, but they were a place to start. He ran his thumbnail hissing up one corner of the stack.

"Three thousand copies," the master scribe said, and there was more than a little pride in her voice. "We will need more paper soon."

"There's a dozen people on Sisters' Street taking old books apart and washing off the ink as fast as you all are putting it back on," Marcus said.

He thought she flinched a little at the words. It would be hard, he supposed, for someone in her position to accept the idea that her work was less permanent than she liked to imagine it. But welcome to the world. It wasn't as if any of the wars he'd fought in stayed won either.

"Where are these going?" she asked, changing the subject.

"This batch? Asterilhold, same as the last. We've got a fast boat ready to carry it along the coast and a few names in the city that might be open to a little life-threatening sedition."

Yardem coughed gently. Marcus took the meaning behind it and forced himself to smile. It wasn't this poor woman's fault he was in a mood as foul as last month's milk. He lifted the brick of papers from the desk and nodded to Enen and Halvill. They placed the chest gently onto the cleared desk, and Marcus unlocked it. The war gold was a bit longer than it was wide, embossed by a press that existed only in the bank, signed by Komme Medean and King Tracian's master of coin. A few carefully worded lines promised that king and crown would honor the transferred debt, and a line of cipher made it possible to check the note against forgeries. Yardem handed the papers to the master scribe, and she accepted them with a small, formal bow. Her hesitation was almost imperceptible, but it was there. Yardem's ears shifted toward her inquiringly.

"Are they helping?" she asked.

"Maybe," Marcus said. "It's throwing seeds to the wind. A stack like this in every city they hold? Give the people they've conquered a better idea what they're facing and how to stand against it? Not to mention that it aims at the snake's head."

"Snake's head?"

"He means the priests, ma'am," Yardem said. "One of the things we hope the letters will do is keep the focus on the priests so that people won't be distracted into other conflicts."

The scribe smiled, and her eyes seemed older than her years. "I don't care if they all burn each other to nothing, I just hope you can keep them from doing it here."

Yardem's gaze flicked to Marcus, expecting or dreading a cutting remark from him. But Marcus didn't have one to hand. It was a bloodthirsty and selfish sentiment, but it wasn't an uncommon one. Charity and compassion were easier when there was no sense of threat to poison them, and the world was woven from threats these nights. In other circumstances, the scribe would likely have thought a bit more before she hoped death and fire for the whole world, only not her city. It was war, though. It stained everything.

When, as a younger man, Marcus had lived in Carse, the taproom had just been a taproom and the field beyond it only an odd strip of commons. Since the dragon had come, wounded and morose, the place had become the most prestigious meeting house in the city. Someone had built a massive wooden perch on the commons so that Inys could rest there and look into the taproom's yard. The tables within the building were packed close, adding the heat and stink of bodies to the smoke and fire in the grate. The meat was probably pork, but spiced to a tear-inducing heat that could have hidden anything. Marcus leaned his elbows against the table and tried to ignore the way the bar boy kept jostling him as he squeezed by.

"What's the point of having a cart if you've nothing to put in it?" Mikel said. The thin actor's hands spread across the table in something approaching supplication. The raw emotion over small issues was something Marcus had grown used to in his travels with the troupe. Soldiers tended to be more stoic than actors.

"Where are you going to put your props and costumes if you haven't got a cart?" Cary snapped. Since they'd lost Smit in the fall of Porte Oliva, her temper had been shorter. Marcus liked her better for it. Mikel's hands retreated from the surface of the table.

"I hope we can agree that both will be needed before the company is made whole," Kit said. "I think we might be better listing out which plays we can perform in our present circumstances, and then determining which replacements will add most to the repertoire."

"Like another actor?" Cary asked. "Is that what you mean?"

"I suppose it is one thing I mean," Kit said, only the way he formed the words was like warm flannel on a cold night. Cary looked away. Kit turned a concerned expression to Marcus. "Are you well, my friend?"

"Why wouldn't I be?"

Yardem cleared his throat. "You made a noise, sir."

"I did?"

"Yes, sir."

"A noise?"

"Something between a laugh and a cough, sir. Could have sounded like sneering to someone who didn't know better."

"Didn't notice doing it," Marcus said. "Sorry. Must have been in my own head too much. Nasty place, that."

The actors were all looking at him now, and all with differ-ent shades of concern. Soldiers didn't tend to do that either.

"I'm fine," Marcus said, more defensively than he'd intended.

"He'll be better in a few days," Yardem said.

"I will?"

"Yes, sir."

"And why's that?"

"Today's Merian's name day."

"Ah," Marcus said. The beer was warm and a little bitter. He shrugged. "I'll be better in a few days."

A flicker of understanding passed through the troupe crowded around the little table. Nothing spoken, but a moment's understanding and companionship. A grief acknowl-edged and shared almost without the need of communication at all. That, at least, was a thing soldiers did as well. Marcus listened for a while more. Cary and Mikel, Sandr and Charlit Soon and Hornet, all of them talking through the next steps for the company they had been and the one they would soon become. Marcus took another few bites of the spiced what-ever-it-was, finished his beer, and took a folded slip of war gold from his belt to pay for it all.

In the yard, a thin, resentful snow fell from a low, grey sky. On the perch in the middle of the field, Inys, the last dragon, hunched and played disconsolately with the carcass of a bull. It was like watching a five-year-old fuss with boiled vegetables. The dragon lifted his eyes to Marcus, let forth a small, stinking gout of flame by way of greeting, and then went back to batting the corpse across the frozen ground. Marcus leaned against the black wood fence, the chill of it seeping into his sleeves. The moon, if there was one, was eaten by clouds and mist. The greatest city of Northcoast endured the darkness and the cold, waiting for a day that would come as pale as it was brief. Inside the taproom, someone struck up a song, and a beery chorus rose. The sound grew louder when the door behind him opened and quieted a degree when it shut. He felt the looming presence of Yardem at his side without having to turn and look.

"You know," Marcus said, "I keep hearing how other people have suffered terrible losses and then years pass and things change and they heal over it. Girl who falls in love with a bad-hearted man doesn't always end up at the bottom of a cliff, no matter what the songs say. Often as not, she's married to someone else five years on, and the bad-hearted man's just something that gets brought up when she's spatting with the new one."

"Can happen," Yardem said.

"And then there's me, where it just never seems to get better."

"It doesn't, sir."

"Ever wonder why that is?"

Yardem's earrings jingled as his ears flicked. "I have some theories, sir."

"Do you? Well. Keep 'em to yourself."

"Was my plan."

The winter wind shifted, pushing snowflakes at him like little handfuls of sand. Marcus squinted into the cold and ignored it. The ice might make him a little blind, but the chances were thin that he and Yardem were going to be ambushed in sight of the dragon they'd escorted to North-coast. Even if they were, the worst that would happen was they'd all be killed.

He tried to imagine Merian here with him. And Alys. He could hardly recall the shapes of their faces some nights. All that was left was a sense of overwhelming love and overwhelming loss that had names and memories built into it.

His daughter's determined smile when she'd taken her first step. His wife's arm around his sleeping waist. Years ago. Decades. They were dead. They didn't miss him. But he'd have cheerfully slaughtered anyone who tried to relieve him of the wounds they'd left behind.

"Made that noise again, sir."

"I know," Marcus said. "It ever strike you that we're doing the same thing as they are?"

"No, sir. It hasn't."

"I just mean the mythical spider goddess and all her priests' hairwash about what history was and what the future'll be and how it all fits together. They're just making up stories and getting everyone to act like they're true. No real stone to build on anywhere."

"That's fact, sir."

"How are Cithrin and her paper gold any different? We're telling a story and talking people into forgetting that it's all something we made up. Then we're using what we've snowed them into thinking in order to make the world the shape we want it to be."

For a long moment, they stood in silence with only the winter wind to reply. Inys, tiring of the game, scooped the dead animal into his gullet and swallowed massively before tucking his head under his great battle-tattered wing. Muffled by the snow, distant footsteps came nearer.

"I still see some distinctions," Yardem said, but then Halvill burst into the yard. White snow dotted his broad black chitin scales and his inner eyelids flicked open and closed in agitation.

"Captain Wester. Yardem. You're wanted, both of you, back at the holding company."

Marcus looked up into Yardem's wide, considering eyes. "What's at issue?"

"It's Barriath Kalliam, sir. He's come back from Sara-sur-Mar."

"Ah," Marcus said. "So the pirate admiral's finished presiding over the bounty board already, has he? Well, I suppose we should be glad he didn't get himself killed doing it."

"No sir," Halvill said. Then, "I mean, yes sir. I mean, he hasn't come alone."

Marcus stood, seeing the excitement in Halvill's stance clearly for the first time through the veil of his own unease. He felt his spine grow a little straighter, the weight of the sword on his shoulder not so heavy.

"Didn't come alone?" Marcus said.

"No, sir," Halvill said. "He's brought his mother."

Cithrin Bel Sarcour of the Medean Bank

All the money in the world. Even now, with winter's progress turning the war sluggish, it was the thought that kept her awake in the night. *All the money in the world.*

Creating debt was nothing new to her. Conjuring an absence of money was as simple as laying any wager at odds. Should storm or piracy intervene, a weight of silver paid for insurance on a ship might call forth twenty of its kind. To create an obligation for money greater than the actual coins in the coffers was nothing more exotic than a default. It happened, if not constantly, at least often.

But to reverse that, to create letters of transfer that summoned the idea of gold—the function of it—without need of the coin itself, still left her giddy. From the remnants of the fortune from her branch of the Medean bank, she had purchased a debt that would never be repaid, and from that debt she had made all the money in the world. As much as she could print, so long as she kept the confidence of the merchants and tradesmen, nobles and artisans whose custom she had changed.

All the other forms were being kept as they had been. The letters were kept in the same strongboxes that the coin had been. They bore the image of the coins they represented. They traded as coins would trade. King Tracian's master of coin was even coming around to the idea of accepting them for taxes, which would, she believed, seal them forever as the legitimate equivalent of gold. She had even heard of money changers weighing the papers as if the heft of the pages themselves signified anything. It was a kind of grand theater piece where the whole kingdom—and Narinisle and Herez now as well—ate imaginary food and was miraculously nourished by the exercise.

And because of it, things that had once been impossible were now within reach.

When first she and Isadau had plotted their war in Porte Oliva, desperation had driven them. The breadth and varieties of strategy had been immense. Did the enemy need to cross land to reach you? Offer a guaranteed high price to the farmers along the dragon's roads for cotton and tobacco, and when the army came to loot the farms, there would be no food to eat. Did the enemy outnumber you? Hire mercenaries wise in the ways of the battlefield and warned against the poisoned voices of the spider priests. Buy ore and drown what couldn't be used so that Antea and Geder Palliako could forge fewer weapons. Post bounties against the enemy on every front—Elassae, Sarakal, the Free Cities. Even cities of Birancour that hadn't yet shared Porte Oliva's fate. Let the enemy face a silent army of the desperate and greedy that you only had to pay.

They had been constrained by the gold in their coffers then. Now that the gates of possibility had opened, Cithrin's time was spent less generating plans than with putting them in action. Bounty boards were fast and easy. A single local agent in an occupied city could inspire any number of actions against the enemy simply by setting a price on them. Or, if the enemy forces within cities like Nus and Inentai and Suddapal proved too dangerous, some nearby hamlet in Borja or the Keshet could be converted to a base.

Hiring mercenaries was slower than that, but in the long term more effective. The paid blades were for the most part between contracts for the winter. Those who were not subjects of Northcoast or Herez or Narinisle might demand coin rather than the letters of transfer, but Cithrin was confident that she could buy hard coin with credit if she found the right discount rate. It wasn't as though the gold of Northcoast was needed in the kingdom any longer. Not if she had her way about it. Fixing prices on ore and inedible crops, while ultimately more powerful, took a greater time to see results. She found herself wishing that victory against the enemy might be a matter of years, just so she could see all her schemes enacted.

She sat in her workroom in the holding company's compound, the dim, fitful light of winter that came through the window adding blue to the buttery yellow light of her candles. Her ledgers piled the desk, and maps lay unrolled and tacked to the walls. A bottle of wine still half-full stood forgotten beside a plate of cheese and hard sausage. In her small space, the world opened like a blossom in springtime, visible only to her. And to people who had the trick of seeing the world as she saw it.

From Inentai, reports said the empire's strength was faltering. At Kiaria, the mountain stronghold of the Timzinae race, the armies of Antea had met defeat even with the power of the spider priests. Like a child who had never learned restraint, Geder Palliako had spread his might so wide that it had grown thin and brittle. The war was the widest and swiftest anyone had ever seen, and the price it had demanded was terrible. The cities it had taken from her—Vanai, Suddapal, Porte Oliva—still ached like a lost limb. The Timzinae taken into slavery, their children imprisoned as surety of their good behavior, suffered and died on the farms of the Antean Empire even as she sat, warm and safe in Carse.

To sow chaos among the enemy now, with enemy forces spread so wide and schisms beginning to form among the priesthood of the spider goddess, was less than blowing aside a feather. The map of the war was a portrait of overreach.

In any other conflict, it would have given her hope.

There had been a time, not even very long ago, when winning a war had meant crushing an enemy, killing them, lighting their cities afire. She, like the others around her, had imagined redeeming the world with the point of a dagger. It was, after all, the story everyone told of how a war ended: a righteous victor, a conquered evil, order restored. It was a lie in every particular. Every war was the precursor for the wars that followed, a slaughter that justified the slaughters to come. And the spiders that tainted the priests' blood were a tool designed by a brilliant, twisted mind to sow this violence. They were the living embodiment of war without end, a promise of permanent victory, infinitely postponed. To imagine tools—even her own tools—turned to some different solution was like trying to wake from a nightmare. She failed more often than she liked.

"I find myself looking through a scheme," she said, gesturing to Isadau with a cup of steaming tea, "and chortling over how it will break Geder's army or ruin his supply lines or give weapons to the traditional families in Nus. And I realize I'm doing it again. I'm looking for ways to *win* the fight, not to *end* it."

The Timzinae woman smiled her gentle smile. From their first shared flight from Elassae and then Birancour to now had hardly been more than a year, but it sat on Isadau's black-scaled face like decades. The greyness at the edges of her chitinous plates made her seem fragile. "There may need to be a certain amount of winning," she said.

"I know that," Cithrin said. "But I don't think past it. I get as far as *That'll show the bastards* and then I just... stop. It's frustrating."

Isadau sipped her own tea. The steam curled up around her face, softer than clouds. "The first enemy is the priesthood," she said, as if she were agreeing. "If we can find a way to defeat them..."

The frustration in Cithrin's gut knotted itself tighter. "Then what? Say we did find a way to drive them all back to whatever hole they've been living in since the dragons fell. Would that end our problems?"

"The critical ones, yes," Isadau said.

"Or would it only make it a war we thought we could win? Tell me that when Antea falls all the Timzinae will drop their chains, shake the hands that whipped them, and say *Don't worry about all the people you killed and the families you shattered. The priests are gone, and we're fine now.* Because I believe that they wouldn't."

Isadau's inner eyelid clicked shut, leaving her both watching Cithrin and not. The rage under her surface calm was palpable. A stab of regret took Cithrin under the ribs.

"I'm sorry," she said. "That was too far."

"No, I take your point," Isadau said. "They wouldn't. Nor would I, for that."

"I don't know how you fight against war. Even the words don't fit."

They lapsed into silence for a long moment, two women who had once been voices of the Medean bank, neither of them welcome or safe in the cities she'd called home. The damp of the city air made droplets on the palm-wide panes of window glass. Isadau's expression was angry, then closed, then amused.

"At least you've ended the age of usurpers," she said. "Not, perhaps, the task we'd set ourselves, but not an inconsiderable windfall."

"How did we do that?"

"We took the power of gold and married it to the crown," Isadau said. "Who'll ever rise against King Tracian when as soon as he falls, all the coins in their chests turn into leaves and ink?"

Cithrin waved the comment away as if she were fanning smoke. "All it means is that whoever cuts off his head and takes the throne will have to offer the same guarantees he did. Kings are just as disposable as they ever were."

"But bankers aren't."

Cithrin heard Komme Medean's half-joking voice in her head. *Cithrin bel Sarcour. Secret queen of the world.* This was what he'd meant, then. Whatever house rose or fell in Northcoast, whoever sat the throne would need to keep on good terms with the bank, because as soon as the kingdom lost confidence in the worth of the letters of transfer, everyone from the boys selling pisspots to the launderers for bleach to the highest lord in court would be bankrupt. The worth of gold had always been a shared fiction about a soft and shining metal, but now it was also braided with a crown and a bank. The loss of any would shake the confidence in all three, and so long as the powerful understood that, perhaps it was less likely that a usurper could rise up. Or at least not without her permission. There was a giddying thought.

"So," Cithrin said. "We only need to design something like that that we can apply to the world as a whole, and the problem...well, it won't vanish, but we'll put a blanket over it anyway."

"An end to all war," Isadau said. "Next we'll be tying ropes to clouds and having them carry us across the sea to Far Syramys."

"Well, if not an end to war, at least an alternative to it. That's a bit less grandiose."

"Do you think so?"

"A *bit*," Cithrin said with a shrug.

A soft knock came as the workroom door opened, and Paerin Clark leaned in, his pale face an icon of amusement and a cynical sort of wonder. "Forgive my interruption," he said. "I have someone in my sitting room I think you two might like to meet."

Cithrin put her tea down with a clatter. Isadau rose to her feet. Cithrin's expression was a question, but Paerin either didn't see it for what it was or else chose not to. He led the way down the brickwork hallway with its tapestry hangings and crystal-and-silver candle holders. The melting beeswax still held a ghost of autumn honey. Thick woven rugs gentled their footsteps, so Cithrin heard the voices coming from the sitting room well before they reached it.

Paerin Clark didn't bear the name Medean, though his wife Chana did. She sat now at her father's side, her smile demure and warm in a way that made the hair on Cithrin's neck stand up. Komme Medean, his joints only somewhat swollen by gout, warmed his hands at the fire. Yardem Hane stood by the door, his expression unreadable apart from the interest in his forward-pointing ears. Captain Wester leaned against a low teak table, his arms crossed. And opposite him, Barriath Kalliam and an older woman.

The last news Cithrin had had of Barriath placed him in Sara-sur-Mar, taking the role of the mythical Callon

Cane and funding bounties against the Antean army that his brother Jorey Kalliam led. Seeing him here now was a shock, and Cithrin's mind took hold of it at once. The bounties were no longer being offered in Birancour. They had been compromised, perhaps. Or the queen had decided that antagonizing the soldiers who had already sacked one of the great cities posed too great a risk. For a moment, she was lost in a cascade of implications that his presence set in motion. The woman at his side seemed almost an afterthought at first.

She was older, and a Firstblood. Her hair was done up in a prim bun, and her skin had the ruddiness of the naturally pale who had been roughened by the sun. She could have been a caravan carter or a farmer, but her bearing was elegant and easy. Here among people of violence and wealth, she was at ease. More than that. Relaxed. Her hands, folded on the table, had a scattering of age spots, but they were strong. The woman's gaze met Paerin as he brought the two magistras-in-exile into the room. The new woman nodded to Isadau with grace, but her eyes sharpened when they met Cithrin's gaze.

She felt a wave of unease. For a long moment, she couldn't place the woman. There was only a sense of the familiar and a half memory of terrible violence. Of blood and fear. It was as if a figure from Cithrin's nightmares had stepped in among the flesh-and-blood of her daily life, and the dread that tightened her throat was inexplicable. Then the woman moved her shoulders, and something about the motion brought her full memory back.

"I suppose," Paerin Clark said, "that introductions may be in order."

"Of course not," Cithrin said. "It's a pleasure to see you again, Lady Kalliam."

"I was afraid you wouldn't remember me," Clara Kalliam said, rising to her feet. She wasn't a large woman, but she seemed to radiate a strength that Cithrin didn't remember of her. Of course the last time they'd spoken had been moments after Geder Palliako had slaughtered Lord Dawson Kalliam in front of the Antean court. "For that matter, I wasn't at all certain I would know you, other than by reputation. As it happens, I do. I think you were very kind, the last time we spoke. Though I admit my recollection of the day isn't what it might have been."

"It was a terrible time," Cithrin said.

"One of several, I'm afraid."

Isadau cleared her throat. "Cithrin has an advantage over me."

"Magistra Isadau," Paerin Clark said, "Clara Annalise Kalliam, formerly Baroness of Osterling Fells, mother to the Antean Lord Marshall Jorey Kalliam and also our own ally Barriath. And also, it seems, to a spider priest named Vicarian who's still in Porte Oliva."

Isadau extended her hand, and Clara took it warmly.

"I also have a daughter," Clara said, "but she often finds it more comfortable to distance herself from me, poor dear."

"She doesn't mean anything by it," Barriath said. His voice was oddly childlike, as though the thought of his mother and sister being at odds distressed him. It wasn't at all the reaction Cithrin expected of the exile of empire and pirate commander. She found it oddly endearing.

"Forgive me, Lady Kalliam," Cithrin said. "I don't mean to be rude, but are you here as an ally or a prisoner?"

The older woman laughed and took her chair again. "That is a fine question, isn't it? I am here as a messenger and a spy."

"A messenger from the Lord Marshal," Komme said. "And a spy, it turns out, for us."

Marcus made a small grunting sound that was probably some version of a laugh. "You recall how Kit and the players and I all spent weeks in Camnipol looking for the mysterious man who'd been feeding Paerin information on the Palliako's court? It's her. The handwriting matches. She's been behind the struggle against the spider priests almost before we were."

A rush of joy filled Cithrin. New intelligence of the Antean army, and more than that. A channel to feed her own information to the heart of the enemy. With someone at the Lord Marshal's side, they could draw Geder's army to its destruction. Only . . . no. She was doing it again.

"Is something the matter?" Chana Medean asked, but Cithrin waved the question away.

Komme was the one to pick up the thread. "We were just talking about our rather peculiar situation. Fighting alongside one of her sons against the other two. It seems that it's even more complex than we'd thought."

"Jorey's been protecting his family. Myself and his wife and now his daughter as well," Clara said.

"That," Barriath said, "would be Lord Skestinin's daughter and granddaughter respectively."

"The same Lord Skestinin that's in our gaol?" Isadau asked.

"Mentioned it was complicated, didn't he?" Marcus said dryly. Lady Kalliam continued as if she hadn't been interrupted.

"Jorey may be the man in Camnipol closest to Geder's trust—apart from Basrahip and the priests and possibly Prince Aster—but he is not blind," Clara said. "He knows as well as any of us the danger that Geder poses to the world. And to Antea. And to the soldiers under his care whom he has led against you. I am very sorry, by the way, about what happened in Porte Oliva. I was there during the battle and its aftermath. I grieve for your losses."

"Thank you," Cithrin said, then nodded, paused, shook her head. She felt as if she'd drunk too much wine. "Forgive me again. Have you just said that the Lord Marshall of Antea is ready to turn against the throne?"

"No," Clara said. "I am saying that we need your help to save it."

Clara Annalise Kalliam,
Formerly Baroness of Osterling Fells

It was a fact well understood that a person was never a perfect match for the tales told of them. It might be something as small as Lady Caot's reputation as having an iron will, which was true so far as it went but neglected her weaknesses for her grandson and butter tarts. It might be as great as the person of Geder Palliako, hero of Antea and champion of the empire, who was instead...what he was.

The story of a person could never be as complex as they actually were because then it would take as much time to know someone as it did to be them. Reputation, even when deserved, inevitably meant simplification, and every simplification deformed. Clara knew that. Since Dawson's death, it was the space in which she lived.

And still: Cithrin bel Sarcour.

It was a name to conjure with. The woman who had broken Geder Palliako's heart. Who had tricked him into letting God alone knew how many Timzinae escape his grasp in the fivefold city of Suddapal. A half-breed whose Cinnae blood thinned and paled her. Or whose Firstblood taint left her thick and dark, depending from which direction one came to the question. A merchant-class woman who had outwitted the Lord Regent of the greatest nation in the world. The most hated woman in Antea, and so also secretly beloved.

It was legend enough to carry a full lifetime, and she

looked hardly more than a girl. So terribly young to have so much on her shoulders. And yet the impression she gave, sitting there among professional killers and hard-headed men of business and power, was one of naïve brilliance. A monstrous talent that could do anything because no one had managed to convince it of what was impossible. Apart from Geder himself, Clara couldn't think of anyone she had met who had impressed her so profoundly as being dangerous.

"It's nearly too late," the girl said to the room and to herself. "If what you say's true, he's run the armies to their breaking point. Past it. And the priests have already begun to schism."

"Have they?" Clara asked.

"Seen one already," the mercenary captain—Wester— said. "Came in ready to lead King Tracian in glorious war against your Basrahip and Antea. Light of the truth, voice of the goddess. All the same hairwash, but pointed the other way."

"Is he still at issue?" Clara asked.

"He's a char mark on the pavement," the captain said. "But there'll be more like him. And faster, once your son's army falls."

"Does the one lead to the other?" Clara asked.

It was the Tralgu that answered. Yardem Hane, he'd been introduced as. He had a low, rolling voice that was beautiful in its way. "Retreats always invite a certain amount of chaos, ma'am. Gives the impression that no one's in control. Takes time for things to calm back down."

"But," Komme Medean said through a vicious scowl, "with these fucking priests spreading lies no one can see through—themselves included—every little whorl becomes a whirlpool."

"Has that potential, sir," Yardem said. "Yes."

Barriath cleared his throat and leaned forward. "If we could maintain the army as a whole and draw them back to Camnipol before they broke? And especially if we could coordinate an occupation by Birancouri soldiers who knew to watch for the priests?"

The Timzinae woman—Isadau—had been silent. Now she lifted her chin. When she spoke, her voice was thin and resonant as a bowed string. "Have we decided this, then? Is there no conversation about the people who've been killed or the families shattered?"

Cithrin bel Sarcour nodded, not in agreement, but a kind of recognition, as if the phrase was part of some other conversation.

"Isadau," Komme Medean began, but the woman went on, her voice more terrible for being as matter-of-fact.

"I don't ask for myself...No, that isn't true. I saw my city humiliated," she said. "I saw Firstblood men whipping Timzinae women through the street for sport. Children stolen from their mothers and fathers. Sometimes the priests were there, and *sometimes they were not*. I respect that the Lord Marshal and his mother aren't pleased with Geder Palliako, but how does that wash clean all that's been done in Antea's name? Do we believe we can end this without also demanding justice? Because I am not convinced."

And in a breath, what had been a meeting of minds with a common purpose became split. The Timzinae woman stood in one world, and Clara—to her dismay—in another. Like flakes of iron pulled by a lodestone, the others would become allies of one or the other. Already she could see it. Barriath shifting in his seat, moving toward her as if to protect her from attack. Cithrin easing down her gaze, pricked by a moment of shame perhaps. Guilt at her disloyalty. Chana Medean and Paerin Clark glancing at the old man of the banking house to see how Komme reacted to the question, but the old man's face was blank as stone.

And it had all been going so well up to now.

Clara took a deep breath, searching for words that would bring them back together. She couldn't imagine what they were. To her surprise it was Captain Wester who spoke.

"When you start talking about killed friends and lost babies, justice and revenge are two names for the same dog. If the question's how much do we have to punish the other side before we can stomach peace, my experience is you can do the enemy a damned lot of hurt before it starts feeling like justice enough. Most times it comes down to how many of them you can kill before you get tired and bored. And whether you can break them so they don't take their turn after. Looking for everyone to feel happy is waiting for yesterday."

The Timzinae woman's inner eyelids closed with a faint click and she rocked back an inch as if she'd been slapped. The Tralgu's tall, mobile ears went flat against his head in what looked like chagrin. "He'll be better in a few days, ma'am."

"I hope you'll excuse me," Isadau said and walked stiffly from the room.

Wester sighed. "Am I going to have to apologize for that?"

"Yes, sir," the Tralgu said.

"Put it on the board for tomorrow."

"Was already planning to, sir."

"Still, she brings up a fair point," Komme said. "Even if you pull Antea back inside its borders, there are going to be a lot of people howling for blood. It might not be too early to start thinking about what reconciliation would look like."

Barriath snorted, "The spiders have been in play since

before the dragons fell. Don't you think we should find how to win against the priests first?"

"Or figure out who we're talking about when we say *we*," Wester said.

Cithrin bel Sarcour raised her thin, pale hand. Her gaze was fixed on nothing, as if she were reading a text invisible to everyone else. "It has to all happen at once. The spider priests, the war—all the wars. And building what comes after to keep it from all starting up again. It all has to happen at the same time."

"That's quite a bit to ask," Komme said.

"Well," Clara said, "*necessary* isn't the same as *simple*, is it?"

Komme's laughter was sharp and barking, but she saw how it eased the tension in all the others' faces. Except Wester's. "Fair point, Lady Kalliam. If we'd wanted easy, we should have stayed home. Or all of you should have, at any rate. It isn't as though I've left my house. Why don't we drink a little wine and talk through this like it was a question of business. What do we have to work with?"

"All the money in the world," Cithrin said, the phrase coming with a depth of meaning that Clara couldn't entirely parse. Then she smiled at Clara with a brightness and sharpness that might have been genuine or an actor's artifice. "And the mother of the Lord Marshal as an ally."

"Well, one of those is better tested than the other," Komme said. "But I follow you on both points. What else have we got?"

For the better part of an hour, they spoke. Much of it Clara followed—the letters written against the powers of the priests, the knowledge that the dragon Inys could provide, the dispositions of the Antean army and the forces rising in Elassae. Other points, like the peculiar relationship among Narinisle, Northcoast, and Herez mediated by the new "war gold" letters, she couldn't quite parse, but she did her best to listen intelligently. A brown-pelted Kurt-adam girl brought platters of glazed meat and soft cheese. A Firstblood boy with skin as dark as a Timzinae's scales poured wine into thick crystal cups. The day flowed quickly into night until the fire couldn't outpace the chill. When, at evening's end, they parted, Barriath walked with her to the rooms the bank had set aside for her.

For a moment, she suffered a sense of displacement. Memories of winter nights in Osterling Fells while Dawson was off on the King's Hunt mixed with something more recent— walking in unfamiliar halls with a young man. So much had changed in her life in so few years. And in herself.

"Well," Barriath said as they came to her rooms, "and what did you make of your first council of war, Mother?"

"A very apt rehearsal for the real one," she said, and Barriath chuckled. A Dartinae servant, his eyes glowing a gentle yellow, slid her door open with a bow.

"That *was* the real one," Barriath said.

Clara paused in her doorway. He didn't sound as though he were joking, and his face didn't have the expression he employed when he was teasing. But she couldn't take what he'd said seriously. When she spoke, she sounded scandalized, even to herself. "Without a representative of the crown?"

"Things are different since the bankers took over."

The journey from Jorey's camp to the great city of Carse had been unpleasant, but not overly long. Jorey had given them good horses and a sturdy cart. Nothing grand enough to attract the wrong kind of attention on the road. Coming so far and through so much only to be killed by bandits would have been absurd, but the world didn't seem to shy away from absurdity now. If it ever had. Barriath had traded his disguise as Callon Cane for a servant's robes and a cheap hat that drooped down on the sides to obscure his jawline. The winter roads were thinly traveled, and while the forces of King Tracian kept a close eye on the southern border, an old woman and her son weren't a threat they feared. They had slept in merchant inns and public houses, keeping to themselves as much as they could. Barriath could pass for a man of no country, but the accents of the Antean court were too much a habit for her. She could no more deny her origins than explain them.

The hardships of following the army had served her well. She rose before dawn, her eyes opening while the still-dark sky betrayed nothing of the coming day, and traveled until twilight faded to dusk. Between the falling winter and their northern route, the light came late and left early. But the fighting had not reached Northcoast, and a mild autumn had left the granaries full, the harvest just passed still rich in memory. Clara had been greeted with as much generosity as suspicion, seen as much courage as fear. In time of war, it was more than she had hoped.

Her rooms at the holding company, home and hearth for Paerin Clark and the Medean bank, were less than the room she would have offered guests of her own in Osterling Fells, greater than she'd had in Abitha Coe's boardinghouse in the poorer quarters of Camnipol. The bed was large enough for two, with a thin down mattress and wool blankets that she could lose herself in. The fire grate held a small blaze and the bricks held the heat for hours after the flames went out. The inner walls of the little keep bent in there, giving her something like a balcony that looked down on the inner courtyard, walled off by thick cedar shutters with oiled cloth in the joints to keep out the wind.

When she slept there, she dreamed of Dawson. Something about the cold or the voice of the wind, perhaps. In her dreams, he was neither alive nor dead, neither with her nor apart. Often she did not see his face or hear his voice. There was only a sense of his presence that faded when she woke. For the hour or so she sat alone with her tea and honeyed bread, wrapped in a robe as thick as tapestry, she would remember him. The names of his favorite dogs. His overwhelming contempt for Feldin Maas and Curtin Issandrian. The way he'd taught Barriath and Vicarian and Jorey to fight and to hunt. The melancholy she felt then wasn't for her own loss. She'd spilled her grief in strange places, and what remained was a complicated tissue of fondness and gratitude and guilty pleasure at who she had become.

Dawson had wagered his life that the world could be kept as it had been: static and unchanged. He had lost. These people of ledgers and sums would have been as vile to him as the foreign spider priests. For him, the world had had an order. To plan a war against a noble—and Geder wasn't king, but he was certainly of noble blood—without its being between peers would have been unthinkable. He would never have done what she had chosen to do. She loved him for that. Worse, she was relieved that he hadn't lived to see this.

And she missed Vincen Coe. Not simply as a man, not any man, but the one particular face and body and voice. The lover of her new life as Dawson had been the lover of her past one. Necessity had made leaving him behind with Jorey easy. Not pleasant, never that, but easy. Once one saw what had to be done, it simply had to be done. She'd needed to find Cithrin bel Sarcour, the enemy of her enemy, and hope to turn the fall of Geder Palliako into something other than the devastation of her country.

Perhaps it was even working. But as the first scattering of fat grey snowflakes swirled down from the white morning sky, she found herself picturing Vincen huddled in a cunning man's tent. Cold. Still recovering from the wounds he had suffered. She wished him here, in relative safety. In her bed, where she could warm him and be warmed by him. And more than that. He was her one critical vice.

She knew, or thought she knew, what Antea would be if they failed against the spiders. And if they won? Who would she be then? Would she stand in the court by her remaining sons and turn her scandalous lover aside? Would she vanish into the low world at Vincen's side and leave behind her children? Her grandchildren? All that she had built and loved and made?

No matter what, the nation she saved—if she saved it— wouldn't be the one she'd known.

She filled her pipe thoughtfully, her thumb tamping the leaf into the bowl with the ease of long practice. She lit it from the fire, drawing smoke deep into her chest. When she breathed out, the smoke was as grey as the snow. She had to make a plan, but she couldn't. Not by herself. Not any longer.

The shriek came suddenly, and from everywhere. She started, her fingers snapping the stem of her pipe. It came again, louder, and followed by a rushing sound like the voice of a great fire. Her breath shuddered as she stood. She shook, fears deeper and more primal than speech could form filling her mouth with copper, but she rose all the same. The shutters were frigid against her hand as she pulled them aside and stepped out onto the little balcony.

A vast shadow passed over her, blackness dotted white by snow-strewn air. The dragon dropped to the courtyard in the center of the keep, its war-tattered wings too wide to fully unfurl. It was magnificent and awing. Its dark scales defied the cold. Its massive head turned on a serpent neck. Clara had the sudden, powerful memory of going to court for the first time. A child of eight years faced by the splendor of a king.

A black wooden door opened far below her. A thin figure stepped out into the fallen snow. Cithrin bel Sarcour walked out to the dragon, notebook and pencil in her hand. The dragon folded his wings and settled before her. Clara couldn't hear the girl's voice at all, and Inys's replies were bass rumbles, like a landslide with words in it. She watched them consult, the most ancient ruler of the world and the newest.

These are the allies I've picked, she thought as her toes and earlobes began to ache. Please God let me have chosen well.

Geder Palliako, Lord Regent of Antea

As he had been preparing for this last campaign, Geder's father had come to see him. They'd sat in one of the gardens just within the grounds of the Kingspire, the huge tower rising up on one hand, the depth of the Division on the other. Lehrer Palliako, Viscount of Rivenhalm, had been the central man in Geder's life, even when he was not present. Ever since Geder had become first the hero of Vanai, then Baron of Ebbingbaugh and then Lord Regent of Antea, he'd felt a little odd around him, as if his rise in court were somehow a reproach upon his father. It had struck him that day as they sat eating dried apples and fresh cheese how much older Lehrer had become.

A day would come, he realized, when he would be the Viscount of Rivenhalm himself. The idea had been both melancholy and wearying. He'd distracted himself and his father by outlining the hunt for the apostate. He'd done all he could to make it sound the grand adventure that it was, but Lehrer seemed only to hear the risk in it.

"Be careful out there, Son," he'd said.

"I'll be fine. I have Basrahip, and the men may not be the first pressing, but we have the goddess with us. We can't lose."

"Still," Lehrer had said, "do be careful out there. And when you come back too." Then he'd smiled and patted

Geder's knee as he'd done since Geder had been a child. "My good boy. My good, good boy. There's more danger in court than on a battlefield, eh? Always remember that."

Now that the fight was done, Geder found himself wondering what exactly the old man had meant.

Killing the apostate priests in the swamps of southern Asterilhold—or what had been Asterilhold before he'd conquered it—had been the final defeat of the darkness, the birth of the light. Geder, sitting alone in his private rooms in the palace at Kaltfel, thought it might have been a little more momentous.

From the way Basrahip had described things, Geder had imagined the apostate priest as a dragon in human skin. A being of darkness and violence and rage, bent on holding all humanity in a death-grip of lies. He'd imagined the man would be tall and graceful and threatening, honey-tongued like a villain in an old song. And his defeat would crack the world like the Division in the center of Camnipol. Split the earth itself down to its bones. And afterward, everything should have been light and hope and renewal. The world made right. The allies of evil slaughtered or else, if they'd been innocent, set free. That was the way those things were supposed to happen.

Instead they'd followed a rough path into the swamp, killed a couple dozen wet, cold, angry men, and come back to the city.

Basrahip had explained that the light of the goddess wasn't like real light. The world wouldn't suddenly start glowing gold or some such. And of course, Geder had known that. The light of the goddess was a metaphor for purity and righteousness, only sitting by the fire with a rug over his knees, the insides of his thighs still chapped from the ride, he couldn't help feeling that purity and righteousness might be metaphors for something too, and he wasn't quite sure what.

Kaltfel had been the first city to fall in the war that stretched out behind him, year after year. Dawson Kalliam had taken it and brought King Lechan to Camnipol in chains. King Lechan who'd plotted to kill Prince Aster and claim the Antean throne for some cousin of the royal line whose loyalty was to Asterilhold. Unify the kingdoms.

Well, Lechan had managed that anyway, though not the way he'd meant to. All the remaining court had sworn allegiance to Geder and Aster and the Severed Throne. And since the priests had been there when they'd done it, the ones who hadn't meant it were all dead. The court in Kaltfel was loyal to Antea. Still, it was strange.

Lechan, the old man Geder had put to death, had probably sat in this room. In this chair. Warmed his shins before a fire like this one. Slept in the bed where Geder had slept last night, would sleep again tonight and then hopefully never again. With Basrahip arranging priestly things at the temple, Geder had thought of searching through the old man's library, browsing the shelves and boxes for something rare and old and special. An essay that had never been translated. A poem he hadn't seen. Speculative essays that laid out visions of the world and wild insights and imaginings he would never have had on his own. It was the way he'd amused himself on any number of evenings before he'd become Lord Regent. But the idea of pleasure wasn't the same as the thing itself, and all during the long, grey afternoon, he'd found he didn't quite have the will to rouse himself and go looking. Or order someone else to do it for him. Or really manage anything much besides sit and watch the fire dance in the grate and the sky go dark with the sunset.

He was tired. That was all. It was only that he needed a solid night's sleep. Tomorrow would be better.

A soft knock came at the door, and he let himself imagine that it would be something dramatic. Assassins come to assault him or Jorey finally arrived with Cithrin in chains. Something. Anything. But it was only a grey-haired old man in the gold-and-silver filigree of the highest servants. Geder had been told his name at some point, but he didn't remember it now, and didn't care enough to pretend otherwise.

"Lord Regent," the servant said. "Sir Raillien Morn requests a moment."

"Who?" Geder asked.

"Sir Morn is the sworn protector of Asinport. He has ridden a day and a night to reach you, my lord. He says it is a matter of deadly import."

He didn't remember anyone named Raillien Morn, but he also didn't recall whom he'd named protector of Asinport. He might not even have done it. There were so many declarations and proclamations and appointments and things that Daskellin and Mecelli had shoved in front of him for his signature. Or Ternigan might have appointed the man before he'd turned loyalties.

Or after. Maybe it was assassins after all. Geder felt a thrill of fear. "Is Basrahip back from the temple yet?"

"I do not know, my lord."

"If he is, bring him. And my full guard—"

"They are outside your door, my lord."

"I didn't ask where they fucking were. I said bring them in here. With Basrahip. When they're all here, you can get this Morn person."

The servant backed out bowing. Geder turned his gaze back to the fire, but the flames had lost their charm. With a growl, he threw the rug aside and stood up. He paced the room, his hands behind his back, his legs aching with every stride, for what seemed like hours. The windows had long since gone dark. Without moonlight, the glass became only a dark mirror that reflected Geder's movement. When the door opened again, Geder's private guard entered the room in silent formation. And after them, Basrahip.

The massive priest's face was broad and untroubled. He bared his teeth in a smile. "Is all well, Prince Geder?"

"Fine," Geder snapped, and Basrahip shook his head.

"No."

"I didn't really mean it to be true," Geder said. "It's not really a lie if you don't mean for people to think it's true, you know." He was whining. He hated it when he whined. Odd that it wasn't enough to stop him.

"What troubles you?" Basrahip asked.

"There's someone come to see me from Asinport. The protector, apparently. Only I thought maybe Ternigan...or Dawson Kalliam..."

"You fear he is not loyal?"

"It crossed my mind. People have tried to kill me, you know."

"And failed, for you are beloved of the goddess," Basrahip said. "Bring this man, and let his living voice proclaim whether he is corrupt."

Sir Raillien Morn was a Jasuru, which was odd. But the court of Asterilhold had allowed for more mixing of the races than the Antean. And even in Antea, there were a few minor nobles whose line was said to be less than purely Firstblood. The Jasuru noble fell to his knees. His scales were a deep copper color, his teeth black and sharp. It was odd, really. The Timzinae were the race that weren't really human but a kind of lesser, debased dragonet carved into human form. But Jasuru scales were more like dragon skin than the chitinous plates of the Timzinae. Or maybe that wasn't true. After all, he'd never seen a dragon, only gotten reports. They might be more like great insects than the serpent scales in the old books. He'd have to ask Jorey when he got back.

As Lord Marshal, Jorey had defeated one in battle with the tools and weapons Geder had made for him. The story of that battle was one he wanted to hear. Certainly more than he did whatever the man still kneeling before him was going to say.

"What's your name?" Geder asked.

"I am Sir Raillien Morn, Lord Regent. I am protector of Asinport."

Which was all pretty well established, Geder thought, but he looked to Basrahip all the same. The priest inclined his great head in a subtle nod. That was true.

"Are you loyal to me?"

"Yes, Lord Regent," Morn said, and looked to Basrahip. There had been a time that not everyone had known that it was the priest who told Geder whether things were true or lies. Everyone had held him in awe back then and wondered how he'd known so much. Now everyone looked to Basrahip and the other priests that way instead. It shouldn't have irked him. It didn't, only he'd enjoyed it back then and he wished he could enjoy it now too. It was like the libraries that way.

Basrahip nodded.

"Do you mean me any harm?" Geder asked, more sharply than he'd intended.

"No, Lord Regent."

He thought about following it up with something more extreme. *Would you sacrifice your life for mine?* or *What are you most ashamed of?* Not that it would change anything, but Geder was curious what the limits of Sir Morn's dedication were, and prying open someone's private self was always interesting. But he'd only have been doing it because he was feeling peevish, so instead Geder ordered his guard back out and sat again by the fire.

"What is it?" he asked.

"I have ridden through from Asinport in the north," Morn began, and Geder cut him off.

"I know you did. They told me. What is it?"

"There have been statements, Lord Regent," the Jasuru said. "They began appearing in the city very recently."

Geder shifted in his chair. "Statements?"

Morn, still kneeling, fumbled at his belt. When he held out his hand, a thick paper was in it, folded in a square. Geder plucked it out and unfolded it. It was sturdy and thicker than the page of a book, the fibers that made it up coarse enough to texture the words inked upon it.

THE SPIDER GODDESS IS A LIE AND HER PRIESTS ARE THE TOOLS OF MADNESS

The scourge of the spider goddess that has touched all the world in recent years is not what it claims to be! The peculiar and insidious powers of those dedicated in the false temples hide their true nature, but now THE TRUTH CAN BE KNOWN! YOU CAN RESIST!

It went on down the page. The spider priests, it said, were not the voice of a suppressed goddess, but a creation of the dragons, like the twelve races of humanity or the eternal jade roads. They had two powers—to sense it when people knowingly spoke an untruth and to convince whoever heard their voices that what they said was true, whether it was or not. The page called the first "the power of the ear" and the second "the power of the mouth," which seemed like a particularly old-fashioned way to frame the idea. Archaic, even.

For a moment, an old fascination stirred in him. The pale ghost of his old love of speculative essays. What if it were true? What if the dragons had made a tool to sow chaos among their own servant races? How would that fit with all he'd read of the ancient past? Something like excitement sparked in his brain.

"They...began appearing?" Geder said. "What does that mean?"

"All through the city, my lord. They would just...be there. One was pasted to a wall near the port. Another, we found on a table in a common house. In all, we've gathered almost a hundred."

"Are they all like this?" Geder asked.

"No, my lord. There are several versions, and people are copying them. We found a house in the salt quarter where a scribe had started making others with the same text. We questioned him before he was killed, of course, but he didn't know where the papers had come from. He only made copies out of his own hatred and malice. But I fear he may not be the only one such."

Geder handed the page to Basrahip, who shook his head. "Dead words on a dead thing, Prince Geder. They are less than nothing."

"It isn't true, what it says," Geder said. "The spider goddess wasn't made by the dragons."

"Of course not," Basrahip said with a warm, rolling chuckle. "She is the truth itself, and her enemies are the servants of lies. It is why they must use this emptiest form of words to defy her." The priest sobered. "What is written is in no voice. Ink on a page means no more than a bird's scratches on bark. You know this as well as any man."

For a moment, Geder remembered another letter. The one Cithrin had written him from Suddapal. The one he had humiliated himself over. Bird scratches on bark indeed. Was this letter hers as well? It seemed likely.

It was the kind of thing she'd do. The kind of thing she'd done. Hiding behind phrases. Pretending things were true that weren't. With a growl, he threw the Jasuru's page into the fire grate. The flames dimmed for a moment, then brightened as the words turned to smoke.

"You did well by bringing this," Geder said through clenched teeth. "And by killing the scribe."

"Thank you, my lord."

"Go back. Make patrols. Anyone who has one of these, take to the gaol. The priests can question them. Anyone who's making them or passing them on is guilty of treason against the Severed Throne. As the Lord Regent, and in the name of Prince Aster, I authorize you to question them and execute them in whatever manner you think would be most likely to keep anyone else from following in their path. Torturing a few people to death in the public square's better than being gentle and letting them get away with...with *this*."

"Yes, my lord. Thank you, my lord."

"And if you find how they got here? Who's writing them? I'll get you your own weight in gold."

The Jasuru's eyes went wide. Geder regretted the words as soon as he'd said them. It was too extravagant a promise, but taking it back now would be embarrassing. He was stuck with it. He had to be more careful about that.

"I will turn the city out like a pocket, Lord Palliako," Morn said. "I will pull every man, woman, and child in the salt quarter into the sea if I have to. No one will escape."

"Good," Geder said. "Do that."

After the man had left, Geder turned back to the fire. The last remnants of the page floated over the coals, grey and fragile. He felt his scowl as an ache at the corners of his mouth.

"I thought after we stopped the apostate, everything would get better. That it would be over."

"Everything is getting better, Prince Geder," Basrahip said. "The world of lies is failing before us. All this that you see is only the curling back of the corrupt world. There is no cause for mourning."

The darkness of Geder's mood didn't ease, but a layer of shame overlaid it. Basrahip was right, of course. Things were going well. They'd beaten the apostate. There was no reason that he should feel so dispirited. That he did left him with the creeping suspicion that he was the problem.

"Doesn't matter," Geder said, forcing a grim smile. "We'll march ahead all the same. Back to Camnipol and Prince Aster and all the rest of it."

"We shall," Basrahip said. "Bring yourself, Prince Geder. The feast in your honor is to begin."

"Of course. Of course."

"Your work has been long and noble and hard," Basrahip said. "Your sacrifices are deeper than those around you know. All this that troubles you? It is only the passing of a cloud across the face of the sun. Come eat and drink. Let those who love you surround you. All will be well."

Put that way, the feast actually sounded worth sitting through. Geder hauled himself up and bowed to the priest. "I'm sorry. You're right. A little food will certainly do me some good. Let's go to it."

The great hall was filled with the members of the court and their families. The heat of their bodies filled the room. The scent of pork and mint, stewed plums and cinnamon, fresh bread and sweet butter caught Geder's attention at least. Lanterns of worked crystal glowed along the walls. Men and women both wore the overlarge black leather cloaks that he himself had made popular what seemed like a lifetime before. A group of Dartinae acrobats amused the crowd; lithe thin bodies capering impossibly in the air, eyes aglow. A Southling cunning man conjured fire out of the air for a time, his massive black eyes seeming to recoil from the light. A Cinnae girl with a silver slave chain around her neck sang second-empire love songs in a voice as rich and warm as a viol, and bright and clear as a flute. Geder waited for it all to salve him, but the most it managed was to distract.

It wasn't until Basrahip stood before them all on a raised dais, his palms out to the crowd commanding silence, and gave a speech honoring Geder as Lord Regent and chosen of the goddess that he started to feel a little better.

Geder Palliako had been drawn across the Keshet, called for the righteousness of his soul. He had brought the Righteous Servant out of the desert and into the noble houses for her glory. No man in all of history had done as he had done. It was like being reminded of something he'd almost forgotten. Yes, that was right. He had led the empire to glory. That was true. He had been entrusted by the dying King Simeon to care for and raise Aster. That was true too.

By the end of the speech, Geder actually felt a little better about himself and all he'd done. Even the slaughter in the swamp seemed to have taken on a patina of grand adventure. If he went to bed afterward more nearly at peace, the rest, he told himself, would pass with the morning. It was only that he needed to recover from his struggles.

It wasn't—couldn't be—that he was oppressed because the morning would begin a long, cold journey along the jade road. Or that he already dreaded the work that would be waiting in Camnipol for him. Or that he still loved Cithrin, and hated her. Missed her, and who she could have been to him. That he was disappointed by how the death of the apostate and the moment of greatest victory had seemed to change so little.

Applause and cheering rose up at the end of Basrahip's speech, and Geder stood to acknowledge it as his due. Once, long before, he'd told Basrahip that he wanted his enemies to suffer. It had been true at the time. The adulation of the court washed over him, warming him, cleaning him, forgiving him his failures or else denying they existed.

If that wasn't enough, it was close. It would have to suffice. He drank in not love but renown like a man dying of thirst and pretended to be slaked.

Clara

Buildings, she thought, echoed each other. Though they might have been in different cities, every palace she'd been in had had the feel of a palace. The rooms, the decors, even the scents of the places might be as different as apples and walnuts, but they served the same functions, and so perhaps it was natural that they took on an ineffable sense of being the same. Marketplaces all seemed to have the same resemblance among themselves as siblings of a large family. Even the cunning man tents in the field had some resemblance to the sickrooms of great manor houses.

And the same was true, it now appeared, of gaols. The one she'd seen most recently had been a prison of the innocent: Timzinae children parted from their parents and brought to Camnipol as assurance of the good behavior of the newly enslaved race. The one she sat in now held the guests of King Tracian of Northcoast. And still they were meant to divide space, to confine, to represent the power that one person held and another did not. They were even meant, as unalike as they were, to represent justice, though if justice had so many different faces, she wasn't at all certain she knew what the word meant any longer, and good God, but her mind was running away with itself.

Clara adjusted her sleeve for what must have been the fiftieth time. Cold radiated from the stone of the wall, and the weak winter light that came from the high, thin window did little to push back the shadows. Her throat felt tight, as though she might be coming down with something, and wouldn't *that* be unpleasant. She'd heard cunning men say that unchecked emotion could bring on illness, but she couldn't help thinking of all the times she'd felt swept away by strong feeling and hadn't gotten so much as a sniffle, so perhaps that was only a story they told to explain away what they had no better answer for.

But why, after all she'd been through, all she'd *done*, should she feel so unmoored now? She had faced down soldiers drunk with bloodlust with no more than her voice and a raised eyebrow. She'd sentenced men to death and stood to watch her sentence carried out. What was this meeting—with an unarmed man who hadn't enough power now to walk outside when he wished—that it should make her blood cold? The complications of her allegiance to her nation were well enough known by now. Jorey knew. Barriath. Vincen Coe had known almost before she had. Hers was a secret well-practiced in the telling, only . . .

Only never before to someone who would feel it as a betrayal. The thought settled on her heart, calming it, though not in a comforting way. At least she knew now what fear was driving her. Knowing made it easier to bear.

"Lady?" the gaoler said. He was a thick man. Firstblood, but as wide across the shoulder and belly as a Yemmu. She wondered—a passing fancy—if the races echoed one another the same way buildings did. If a gaoler in Borja might seem the fellow of this man, though he was Tralgu or Jasuru or Dartinae. Clara took a deep breath, rose, and banished all other concerns.

"Yes, I'm ready," she said, and the gaoler turned. She followed.

The walls were too cold to be damp. Frost rimed them, and the gaoler's torch smoked. He looked back at her when she coughed, his expression an apology. She lifted her chin and moved on. Their footsteps sounded lonely on the bare stone, as if they were looking for some companionship besides the walls. It was a silly thought, but that she'd had it meant something. The door, when they reached it, was black oak bound in iron. There was no rust, and she found herself perversely grateful for that. It would have been worse, somehow, if the cell had been poorly kept.

"I can come in with you if you like," the gaoler said. "Keep him in line."

"That won't be necessary."

"You sure about that, lady?"

Was she? It didn't matter. The answer had to be the same. "I'll call if there's need."

The gaoler shrugged, undid the lock, and slid back the bar. Even with her assurances, he pulled the door open carefully, his torch at the ready like a cudgel. Within, the cell was small and close, with a window no more than a finger's width just by the ceiling. But a crystal lantern hung from a hook, and there was room enough for a tiny desk beside the cot. If there was a lingering scent of the chamber pot, it was no worse than she'd suffered in far nicer rooms, and a small brazier left the air warmer than the hall. Lord Skestinin himself rose when she entered, his snowy eyebrows beetled, but his eyes bright and alert. He wore a prison gown rather than the uniform of a lord of the Antean court, but he wore it well.

"Lady Kalliam?" he breathed, as if uncertain of his senses.

"Clara," she said. "If you'll permit my calling you Anton. We are family by blood now, after all."

"Sabiha?"

"I understand the birth was touch-and-go, but from all I've heard she and the baby are quite well now. They've named her Annalise, after me. I hope that's all right."

Lord Skestinin grinned. His teeth were yellow as ivory, and crooked. She wondered now whether she'd ever seen him grin before. "Whyever would it not be?"

"That's a longer conversation," she said, and turned back to the still-open door. "I'll call."

The door closed, though the bar did not scrape back into its place. Poised for a swift return, she supposed. Well, it would be embarrassing to have a visitor assaulted on one's watch. She couldn't blame the man for being anxious on her behalf. She arranged herself at the foot of the cot. Lord Skestinin lowered himself to the thin desk, seeming almost to deflate. Clara cast a weary eye on the walls, the cot.

"It's not so bad," Skestinin said. "I've shipped in smaller cabins than this. Miss having a deck to walk at will, though. And the sea. I seem to have fashioned myself into the sort of man who needs the sea about him. What news of the war?"

Clara shook her head. It wasn't a question she knew how to answer. The war was going well, or poorly, or dancing on chaos's edge. How was she to tell the difference? Or report it? Facts, she supposed. Simplicities. "Jorey took Porte Oliva. I suppose you know that, seeing as you aren't there any longer."

"May he burn the place flat," Skestinin said with a rueful laugh. "It was not the site of my greatest triumph. And my men? The navy?"

"The ones who were still imprisoned in the south are freed. I don't know how the ships stand. Winter, you know."

"Winter business," Skestinin said with a bitterness she recognized.

"Winter business," she said, letting the words roll in her mouth.

"If it isn't too indelicate to ask," Lord Skestinin said, "how were you captured?"

"Oh," Clara said. "I'm afraid I wasn't."

For a moment, he was confused. She watched him understand. He lifted his eyebrows and looked at the ground. "Ah," he said.

"You've seen what's gone on in Antea. Palliako is the worst thing that's happened to the empire in my lifetime or yours. We'd have been better giving the throne to Aster straightaway. A kindhearted child would be better than the Lord Regent we have now. And, Anton, these *priests*..."

"Yes, my lady," Lord Skestinin said. "The foreign priests your late husband led his rebellion against. I...understand and respect your loyalty to his cause."

She felt for a moment as if he'd spoken in some unfamiliar language. Her laughter was sharp and sudden and only partly related to mirth. There was also disbelief in it. And something sharper for which she had no name. "I can accuse myself of many things these last years, but slavish devotion to Dawson has not numbered among them."

"We disagree on the point. No, hear me out. I am loyal to the crown. Did I agree with every choice King Simeon made? No, but that doesn't matter. You can't pick and choose when to be loyal. That isn't loyalty. There is a right system to the world, my lady. God, then the king, then the lords of the court. The father rules over the mother rules over the children. The husband rules over the wife. That is the right order of the world from the stars to the lowest nomads in the Keshet."

His voice had grown louder and rougher. Spots of red appeared on his cheeks. She considered him closely, as she might a particularly colorful insect that had landed on her arm. The brightness of his eyes. The folds of his sea-leathered skin. The jut of his jaw. He had been her son's commander for years. He was her own family, first by marriage, and now both of their blood flowed in a little girl in Camnipol. How strange, then, that she felt she had never seen him before as he was.

"You're quite right," she said. "We do disagree on the point." He clenched his jaw, his white beard jutting out like a goat's. A sorrow she had not expected shook her. And then a guilt, and a resentment at being made to feel guilty. She laughed again, but more gently and more to herself. "Still, we needn't be rude to each other. God help us both, we are family. Is there anything I can do to make your confinement less odious?"

"I wouldn't ask favors," Lord Skestinin said. "Gives the wrong impression."

"Of course. But all this unpleasantness aside, might we not come to a private understanding?"

"I don't know what you mean."

A gust of wind spat a snowflake in through the window. It spiraled close to the lantern, shining for a moment, then winking out as it melted. "The world is a cruel place, and the next few years are going to be difficult," Clara said. "I don't know how this all comes out. And...and they did name her after me."

Lord Skestinin's smile was flinty. "The king protects his land. The father protects his child. And his grandchild, however unfortunately conceived. There is no need for agreement between us, Lady Kalliam. Not for that."

"Should history favor my views over your own, my lord, I will bend stone and bleed fire to see Sabiha kept safe. And not as a favor to you."

"I am pleased that you still have some honor. Perhaps we may yet be reconciled."

"It wouldn't be the strangest thing that's happened since we left Camnipol. If I see your wife and daughter, is there a message you'd like me to give them?"

"Other than that Lady Kalliam and her exiled son have betrayed the kingdom?"

"Yes, other than that."

"No," he said. "It won't be called for."

Clara put a hand on his knee. The fur was cold to the touch. "It was good to see you."

"And you, my lady," Lord Skestinin said. Etiquette was such a beautiful system of lies. It allowed everyone to pretend when the truth was too ugly to bear. That they all shared in the lie made it at least something that they shared. She rose and called for the guard. The door opened at once, and then closed behind her once she'd reached the hall. The bar ground back into place with a sense of finality. She wondered whether she had just seen her granddaughter's grandfather for the last time.

"Ma'am?" the gaoler said, bringing her back to herself.

"Yes, of course. They must be waiting," she said. "Lead on."

No chance then of Skestinin taking our side?" King Tracian said. He was a young man, and she had a sense that it was more than just his age. He was older than Simeon had been when he took the throne, after all. There was a nervousness about him. An anxiety that seemed to infuse his words and movements. Perhaps it was natural in the son of a usurper. Or it might only be that he was harboring the sworn and public enemy of a kingdom that had recently conquered all its immediate neighbors and had an army camped at his southern border. Or that the last dragon roamed his street. Come to think of it, he had more than enough reason to be uncertain of himself.

"I think he will not," Clara said, accepting a cup of mulled wine from Komme Medean's thin hand. There were no servants in the withdrawing room, and none in the hall without. It was not a conversation to be overheard. "It would have been too pretty, I suppose, to have the Lord Marshal and the master of the fleet both in our confidence."

"Shouldn't get greedy," the old banker said. If it was meant to be ironic, he hid it well.

The room was colored with gold. It was in the tapestries on the walls, woven into the carpet beneath her feet. There were other colors—the shining green and indigo of the cushions, the scarlet of the wall hangings, the gentle yellow of the lanterns—but all of them seemed there to offer contrast to the gold. The air was mulled wine and incense, rich without being cloying, which was much rarer in a palace than Clara thought it should be. Incense was too easily overdone. It spoke well of Tracian that he knew to restrain it. There was a plate of raisins and cheese to go with her wine, though she couldn't bring herself to taste them. Not yet.

The king of Northcoast paced, four steps along the wall, then back the other way, hands clasped behind him. Komme Medean sat beside the wine with his fingers woven together and a calm expression in his eyes. She had the sense that the world might turn to fire and ash, and the banker would have the same calm about him. The king turned again. For a moment, she wasn't certain what he reminded her of. Ah, yes. A captain pacing his deck.

"It would be a kindness to put him in a larger cell," she said. "One, perhaps, where he could walk a bit."

"Did he ask for that?" Tracian said.

"No," Clara said. "He was quite careful to ask for nothing."

"We have Barriath's pirates," Komme said. "And the ships

of Northcoast, of course. I'd be surprised if we couldn't convince Narinisle and Herez to step in as support at the least. Though they may balk at open battle."

"Is open battle our plan?" Tracian said. "Because last I checked, we still had an army to the south with orders to bring Cithrin bel Sarcour to Camnipol in chains."

"Jorey won't come north," Clara said. "We're safe here. For now."

"With respect, Lady Kalliam," Komme said as he poured himself more wine, "are we sure of that? Have we had word from the army since you came?"

"I haven't, but neither was I expecting any. Jorey has no intention of marching on Northcoast. He knows I've come, and he will wait until I return."

"You're making some assumptions," the old banker said. "By your own report, the soldiers are overtaxed. There are two of the priests there at least."

"Only two," Clara said.

"Only two if no others have arrived in your absence." Komme's voice was gentle, but firm. "We speculate on what's happened in the winter camp, but we can't know. And though I hesitate to point it out, Lord Marshal of Antea hasn't been an invitation to a long career since Palliako took the crown."

"Why didn't Skestinin come to us?" Tracian said. "He has to know what the priests are. We have showed him the one we have, haven't we? The actor?"

"He's known since Porte Oliva," Komme said. "It isn't at issue with him."

"Why not?"

Several thoughts collided in Clara's mind: *He is bound by his honor* and *He has reason to fear Palliako* and *Men of a certain age can only understand the world they were boys in.* She was left with an impatient grunt as the most eloquent answer she could give.

"More to the point," Komme said, "is what we can do about it. You know the court in Camnipol better than any of us. Will they rise against the priests? When they know, will they take arms? Or will they be like our guest?"

Clara wished badly she'd thought to bring a pipe. The wine was warm, but too sweet. She wanted the feel of the stem between her teeth and the taste of smoke. "The court," she said, "is unlikely to turn. The lords who were most prone to object to the priests rose already, my husband among them, and they're all dead. Anyone disloyal to Palliako is dead or exiled or hung from the Prisoner's Span. The fear he has built in these last years...No. I think they won't rise up. Even if they know what the priests are and how they function. And after all, they think they're winning."

"They *are* winning," Tracian said, only of course that wasn't true. None of them were winning, except perhaps Morade, thousands of years dead and still sowing chaos among the dragons' slaves.

Komme Medean sighed. "That's the thing with these spiders, isn't it? Even when the wolf's at their door, they'll *believe* they're on top of the world and pissing down on the rest of us. You can't change a man's mind when he's lost the capacity to see he's wrong."

Cithrin

"How long did you work with Karol Dannien?" Marcus asked. If she hadn't known him for as long as she had, it might have sounded like an innocuous question. The Yemmu sitting across the table from them reached up and scratched at one of the great carved tusks that rose from his lower jaw. Since Cithrin was fairly certain the intricate whirls and images in the enamel weren't capable of itching, she interpreted it as a sign of annoyance.

"Three seasons, more or less," Dantag Moss said. "Two in Borja when the council shat itself and Tauendak declared against Lôdi, and then a summer in the Keshet."

"Small unit work?" Marcus asked.

"And some garrisoning. Elder Samabir up in Tauendak wanted his family to have the glory of the battle, so he set us up to stop anyone from looping around behind him."

Yardem flicked a jingling ear. "And you let him?"

"Dannien let him," Moss said. "I was tertian back then. Not going to dictate to my prime."

Marcus glanced over at Yardem, the two men conducting some tacit conversation over her head. Cithrin wished she had a tusk to scratch, then smiled, amused by the image. Around them, the common house was quiet. It was just after midday, and the streets were at their warmest. When the door opened, there was the smell of water and the sound of dripping snowmelt from the roofs. The winter sunset would come in fewer than three hours and turn it all back to ice. There would be time later to huddle together around the rough wood tables, but anyone whose work called them out into the city was hurrying now to get it finished before the dark came.

Cithrin was comfortable where she was.

"Fair enough," Marcus said. Whatever test he'd been making, the mercenary had passed it, or near enough.

Cithrin took it as time for her to take the negotiation. "How long before you could put your men in the field?"

"Start of fighting season's still six weeks out, if the weather's with you. Nine if it's not."

"Not what I asked."

"Then the answer's going to depend on what your cold bonus is. Man loses a finger, it ain't much comfort that it was frostbite and not an axe."

"Fair enough—"

"And, ah, no offense, miss? Captain Wester? But hard coin. This war gold? It doesn't do with the men."

Yardem made a low throbbing sound in his throat, something equal parts cough and growl. Moss's scowl deepened, his lips flowing around the carved teeth. The only other Yemmu Cithrin had worked with was Pyk Usterhall, the bank's notary lost in the flight from Porte Oliva. Seeing Pyk's expression on the mercenary's face left her melancholy. Cithrin took a long sip of wine to clear it away.

"There's a bonus for accepting war gold," she said. "If you only take coin, it'll be eighty on the hundred. And you're going to be provisioning from Northcoast and Narinisle. It won't make much difference to a bag of feed whether it was bought with metal or paper. Tastes just the same after."

"Still," the Yemmu said.

"We could do the provisioning, ma'am," Yardem said. "Captain Moss takes coin for his wages, we give him the horses and the food. Any arms or armor."

It was a suggestion Cithrin had fed to the Tralgu before the meeting. He'd brought it up a little sooner than she'd hoped, but it was close enough. She made a show of thinking about it. "Ninety on the hundred for that, but yes. We could."

"Let's not get too far ahead on ourselves."

"Of ourselves," Marcus said. "*Of.* Not *on.*"

Moss shrugged, but the correction had hit home. That was fine. Marcus made an accomplished hard party. He was older, a man, and Marcus Wester. She was younger, slighter and paler than a full Firstblood, and a woman. If Moss was like the others, he'd play to her.

"Let's not get too far ahead of ourselves," Moss said, and Cithrin made a silent note that he'd accepted Marcus's correction. "What's the work we're doing here? My men are hard as stone and sharper'n axes, but if you're putting us against Antea in the field—"

"We aren't. Their army's going to fall back. We want you to...clean where they've been. Look for people who've been taken by the spiders. Whoever you find, you burn."

"Hunters, then," Moss said, sucked noisily at his teeth, and shrugged. "We can do that, yeah. If your price is right."

"There's risks," Cithrin said. "We're working to have Birancour's permission, but if the queen doesn't agree, it won't change our contract."

"You paying me or is she?" Moss said. Cithrin felt a knot in her belly untie.

"I'm paying you."

"All right, then," Moss said. "We won't bother the queensmen if they don't bother us. Plenty of peace to get kept, I figure. Enough to go around anyway."

"One thing," Marcus said. "If one of the queensmen has the little fuckers in his blood? Even if he's captain or lord of whatever town you're passing through…"

"He burns," Moss said. "I understand. But what's the money?"

The negotiation went on for the better part of an hour as they worked through the details—how much for a sword-and-bow, how much for a horse, how much for a cunning man; the length of the contract; the payment schedule; the bonus for every one of the tainted they burned; the standard of evidence they had to provide for it. The cold bonus. The penalty for killing outside their mandate. It wasn't her first pass through this particular area of contract law, and having Marcus and Yardem talk her through the logic of it all beforehand let her seem more experienced than she was. When it was done, Cithrin shook Dantag Moss's huge, thick hand. The contracts would be drawn up in three days. They'd cut thumbs on it and sign, and she'd hand over the initial payment—hard coin for the men, war gold for the provisions. If it had all been coin, it wouldn't have happened.

She stepped out to the street, Marcus and Yardem behind her, and turned to the north. The sky was white from horizon to horizon. Snow melted in the sunlight and glowed bluish in the shadows. Carse wasn't a beautiful city. It was too open, too austere. She had grown up in the close streets and canals of Vanai, come to her full power in the dense humanity of Porte Oliva. Even the fivefold city of Suddapal—where she'd been as out of place as a candle for the Drowned—had been more beautiful in its way. Carse was unnerving, she realized again, because it was built on the scale of dragons.

Inys could walk through these streets, his tattered wings folded behind him. He could perch in the square or throw himself down to weep among the claw-marks of the

Graveyard of Dragons. Children might roll hoops in its squares and alleys, food carts could steam at its corners and fill the air with the scent of roasting nuts and spiced meat, but Carse was not a human city. It was a place for the absent masters of humanity. Or nearly absent.

"We going to see him?" Marcus asked as they walked.

"No," Cithrin said. "Not the dragon. The troupe."

Marcus grunted his approval and squinted up into the sun. The lines of his cheekbones cast shadows down his face. The venomous green culling blade was strapped across his back.

"Why do you carry that thing?" she said, speaking her real concern as if it were only banter.

"In case I need to kill someone with it," he said, just as lightly.

"Expecting a flood of spider priests?"

"No, but I wasn't expecting the last one either," Marcus said. "That was nicely done with the war gold just now. Get a few more countries on the same scheme, you'll have men like Moss willing to take full payment in paper."

"We've had letters from Princip C'Annaldé and Cabral," she said. "Apparently the idea of giving all the gold there is to the crown is fairly popular among certain strata of power."

"Imagine that," Marcus said.

"I only wish we weren't calling it war gold."

Yardem cleared his throat. "Any reason not to, ma'am?"

"War's what we're fighting against. What we're trying to avoid. I'm afraid that if we keep the name, we bake it into the new system from the start."

"New system's not really new, though, is it?" Marcus said. "There are always people who'd rather not solve problems by killing each other. Or at least by doing it at some remove. It's why we have people like me and Moss. Karol Dannien. Merrisan Koke."

"We have mercenary soldiers because we don't want war?" Cithrin said.

"You have us because you don't want to go to the field yourself."

"That's not why I'm using them."

"No?"

"No. I want soldiers who won't hold a grudge against the enemy once it's done. If you're fighting out of love or loyalty, peace can be a kind of betrayal. Mercenaries are like whores. By taking money for it, they debase what it means. I *want* to debase what violence means."

Marcus laughed, but Yardem didn't. His great brown eyes met hers. "You may have missed your calling, ma'am. You'd have been a fascinating priest."

"No!" Marcus said. "No recruiting for the priesthood on my watch, Yardem. I've got enough trouble following her when she's talking about things that exist. Start pulling gods into it, and I'll lose the thread entirely."

"Sorry, sir," Yardem said. "Didn't mean to confuse you."

"And you have to call it war gold," Marcus went on. "If you called it *peace gold*, no one would take it seriously."

The news had come three days before from Suddapal, and whether it was good or bad was beyond her capacity to say. The fivefold city, home of the Timzinae race, had risen. The siege at the mountain fortress of Kiaria had broken. The forces of Antea had been put back on their heels. In a normal war, it would have been excellent news. If there was such a thing as a normal war. Cithrin found herself beginning to doubt the idea.

Isadau and Komme had been locked in conference since the courier had arrived, stumbling, exhausted, and filthy, in the middle of the night. Already, the servants were packing Isadau's things. Taking ship to Elassae now was a terrible risk. Antea held Porte Oliva, and likely the ports of the Free Cities as well. But Barriath's pirate navy had fast ships, and sailors who knew well how to evade a navy. Cithrin was torn between wanting Isadau to stay and wanting to go with her, though neither was possible. It was a choice between ache and ache.

And as with all aches, she found she could soothe it in a taproom bottle. That the troupe was also there made things convenient for her.

She wanted to like the new actor, but she didn't. His name was Lak, and he was thin and gawky with eyes the color of ice and an unruly head of hair only just darker than straw. His voice was good, though, and with his paleness against Cary's dark hair, some striking tableaus became possible. She could see the reasons for choosing him, especially as the company had lost its stage and props and costumes. But he wasn't Smit. And fair or not, she couldn't forgive him for that.

Cithrin found them in the yard outside the stables. Cary, her arms crossed and her breath smoking in the cold, stood where the audience would be. Master Kit, Hornet, and Charlit Soon held their places and poses. And Lak. Mikel and Sandr were off somewhere, but a pair of young Timzinae boys stood in the door to the stable, watching with dark and shining eyes.

"Again," Cary said as Cithrin took another long pull of wine from the glass neck. "From where the king makes his speech."

Master Kit nodded and walked across to a different spot on the frozen dirt. "Here?"

"That'll do," Cary said.

Kit lifted his hand dramatically and turned to Lak. "Boy, know this," Kit said, his voice suddenly rounder and deeper, as if he were speaking inside a temple. "To be king of all the world would not be enough to sate my hunger. I am more than a throne, more than a land, more than death or love. I am King Ash!"

Lak fell to his knees and Cary sighed impatiently. "No. Stop. It's still not right."

"What if I was on his left?" Lak said. Kit put a hand on the boy's shoulder and shook his head. Cary walked back toward the common room scowling. Lak watched her go with a poorly disguised distress.

"I would be surprised if this was yours to carry," Kit said to him. "I think it more likely that she's used to the way we staged it before. Give her time to reimagine how it could be, and I think you'll see a different side of her."

"I don't think she likes me," Lak said.

Kit didn't say more, but clapped the boy's shoulder again and made his way to Cithrin.

"You're still rehearsing," she said.

"Did you expect something different?" Kit asked as they fell in step with each other. "We're actors."

"It's only that, with things as they are..."

Kit chuckled, low and warm. "If we only worked when the world was certain, I expect we'd have starved long before this. I'm afraid this one may be beyond us, though, for the time being."

"The props and the costumes?"

"I think more than that. *The Ash and the Pomegranate* is, I feel, more a story of war than of love. I've always found war stories difficult."

"Worse than romances?"

"Yes. Love, I believe, is a small thing that feels large. I

find the feelings might overwhelm, but the action is between a handful of people. War, by comparison, seems to me so large and happens so differently to so many people that capturing it in a tale leaves me with the sense that I've simplified it so much that it no longer resembles the thing it depicts. The best I've managed is a story about people while a war goes on around them, but I think that isn't the same."

Charlit Soon yelped and sped past them down the street. Sandr and Mikel were struggling around the corner of a brewer's yard, pulling a low wooden cart loaded with sacks behind them. Old cloth and thread, Cithrin guessed. Perhaps some lumber. The raw material for costumes and a better stage, false swords and paste-and-leaf crowns. The slow rebuilding of all that they'd lost to the great war.

"I can't remember not being afraid," Cithrin said. "I can't remember what it was like when Antea wasn't killing people."

"Palliako's war has been greater and worse than any war I've seen or heard of," Kit said. The paving stones gave way to a wide strip of dragon's jade. A path through the city unworn by the ages.

"It started before that, though," Cithrin said. "I started being afraid in Vanai, and there weren't any priests then. Or only the normal sort. Prayers and herbs and promises about justice after you die. Not like *them*. Not like—" She pressed her lips together, but Kit knew what she hadn't said.

"Not like me," he said.

"We talk about Morade's spiders as if they were the root of all the evil, all the killing, but they aren't, are they? Because they've been back in their temple long enough that no one even remembered they were real, and there have been wars and murders and cities burned all that time."

"I understand there have been, yes," Kit said. "It seems to

me that the source of war isn't the dragons or magic or the spiders in the blood. I hear the histories and learn the songs, and I feel that humanity is the beginning of it all. Pain and lust and vengeance and oppression. But I also see that we are capable of tremendous compassion and hope. I think of all the cities that war has razed, and still, we've built more than we've torn down. I think of all the things of beauty that found their end in violence, but there keep being more beautiful things." Kit gestured at the city around them. "As I see it, Morade's spiders didn't create a fault in us, but rather inflamed what was already there."

"Certainty's always brittle, and disagreement's inevitable," Cithrin said. "And so apostates."

"And schisms," Kit agreed. "The creation of enemies from those who were once allies. And I may be wrong, but it's seemed to me that the sense of betrayal by someone who you thought of as one of your own is even more punished than simply being of a dissenting tribe. If you think of it, I am an example of what the spiders were meant to do. I believed as they did, worshipped as they did, and then I had a thought that took me from the group."

"Only instead of running off and starting your own church to lead into battle against them, you turned into an actor," Cithrin said.

"And yet, it seems I still find myself at the head of a kind of army fighting against the men I once called brothers. I lost faith in the goddess, and in the story we told of her. The world that brought her forth. The apostate who came to King Tracian broke with the Basrahip in Camnipol over issues of doctrine. I broke with the temple because I came to understand the words *truth* and *certainty* differently. I'm not sure the distance between my heresy and theirs is as great as I would like to pretend." A small dog trotted past, a length of rope in its jaws. The sounds of cartwheels clattering against stone and a woman laughing seemed to blend into each other, and the low, white sky. Kit put a hand on her shoulder. "Is something troubling you?"

"I don't think I can win," Cithrin said. "I'm doing as much as I can. I've sent the letters about the spiders and what they are all down the coast, east to Asterilhold and Borja and All-star. I've doubled the bounties against Antean forces and shifted what we're paying for so that it's bent to take on the spiders. I've hired all the mercenaries I could find to keep the Lord Marshal's army from coming north and to keep the peace if he retreats the way Clara seems to expect him to. But I keep thinking that I'm fighting Antea, and then remembering that I'm really fighting the spiders. And then remembering that I'm not fighting the spiders, but the impulse toward war."

At the common room, someone was shouting, and then two people, and then a dozen. It didn't sound like violence so much as a shared celebration, but it might have been a brawl. It was hard to know.

"And how many swords does it take to defeat an idea?" Kit said.

Geder

There were an endless parade of events and feasts, rituals, and customary celebrations in the course of a season at court. When Geder was a boy, his father had taken him to many. As Lord Regent, Geder suffered through them all. Of them, many—the grand audience, the Remembrance Ball, Midsummer—occurred at set times, predictable as the fall of sand in a glass. With a few, though, there was no set schedule. First Thaw with its honey floss and candy ice came when the warm winds blew it to them. Abandon Night with its masks and smokes and dangerous sexuality came when an heir to the throne was born. And a triumph came at the end of a military campaign when the soldiers returned to camp outside the walls of Camnipol, and their commander called the disband. For those sorts of occasions, part of their joy was their uncertainty.

Geder had been a child when the rebellion in Anninfort was put down. He tied his memory of his first triumph to that, but he could have been misremembering. As he recalled it, the streets had been filled with cheering men and women of all classes—from barons and lords to beggars and pisspot boys. He remembered it as being overwhelming.

He'd seen others since. Had one of his own after his return from Vanai. The overall shapes had been the same. The conquering hero—or defender of the empire, if the campaign hadn't gained any new land for Antea—moved through the city to the accolades of Camnipol. The walls were decorated, sometimes in the house colors, sometimes in the king's, sometimes just with whatever looked most festive and came to hand. Then there were feasts and parties in the houses of the most honored lords, with the commander whose men had just earned their release the most honored guest.

It seemed wrong that this particular triumph should seem so weak and vaguely foul. It was, after all, the one that marked the final battle in humanity's war against the dragons. The apostate's death was the dawn of the new, brighter age. The spider goddess's power was sweeping invisibly out from the spot where her false servant had died. Basrahip had explained it all to him. Of course, it being winter, there were few lords at court. And there was more pleasure in parading down streets that didn't have ice coating the cobblestones. There was music, but it was thinner. There were houses with open doors and plates of bread and meat and cakes, but they all opened just ahead of the procession and closed again behind it. Not that he blamed them. It was a cold, grey, miserable day. An icy wind pushed the fog from the southern plains north until it broke against the walls of the city and filled the Division with mist the color of milk. The Kingspire darkened to the color of iron against the low, grey sky. Cunning men on the street corners performed small miracles of light and fire, but no one crowded around to throw coins at their feet.

His soldiers, returned to their lives with the success of his campaign, trailed behind him. Very old and very young, thin and fat and coughing. They looked more like slaves of a fallen foe than heroes returned in glory. Geder held his chin high, but the cold made his nose run, and really he just wanted the parade over so he could go inside.

It was the greatest triumph in history, and all he felt was tired and dispirited and ashamed of himself for feeling tired and dispirited. Was he really so shallow that he couldn't be pleased with just the truth? Did it all have to come with cloth-of-gold and flares and music to mean something?

Victory—true victory—is humble, he told himself. Just the knowledge that he had led the force that ended the dragons' last and greatest threat against the goddess was enough. Even if it had been the biggest, most lavish celebration in Camnipol's long history, it wouldn't have been as glorious as the truth. There was even a beauty in this exhaustion. This wasn't the paper-thin remnant of a third-pressing army celebrating that it had slaughtered a few dozen religious zealots in a swamp. It was the proof of how much the empire had pushed itself in the name of the Righteous Servant. All of Antea was like a warrior kneeling on the battlefield with the dead enemy all around. It was easier to see a nobility in the greyness when he thought of it that way.

At the entrance to the royal quarter, Prince Aster waited. He was dressed splendidly, and the handful of lords and nobles who'd stayed in the capital through winter stood with him. There were fewer of them, and many of the great faces he'd known growing up were missing. Either suborned and corrupted by the plots of the Timzinae or scattered to the corners of the vastly expanded empire. The few that remained stood like watchmen in a tower, a forest of servant-held torches warming the air around them and making a little circle of gold in the darkness of the city.

The prince came forward. In the time Geder had been gone, he'd grown a little fluffy peach-fuzz moustache. It made him look like a puppy. Geder could see the boy's anxiety and knew him well enough to recognize its meaning. A dismissive comment from him now—or even a false compliment—would devastate the prince. Geder felt a smile burgeoning and bit his cheek to force it back as he knelt.

"Lord Regent Palliako," the prince said. "We welcome your return."

"My prince, you honor me," Geder said. "The enemy of the Severed Throne is defeated."

There was a round of applause, noble palms banging together to fill the air between leafless trees and dry fountains. And above them, the Kingspire rose, higher, it seemed, than the clouds. For a moment, it reminded Geder of the green blades Basrahip and his men had carried against the apostate, as if the heavens had leaned down with one and cut the city in half, the mist rising out of the great wound of the Division like milky blood.

With the parade complete, the men scattered. One of the low halls was ready for them, ham and beer and roasted fowl, singers and cunning men and perhaps some of their families come to welcome the unlikely warriors home. Many would go, and others would scamper back to their homes—their children, their parents, their wives. Aster drew Geder to a black carriage with gold bunting and a team of pale horses. The servants helped them inside, and the carriage lurched off, wheels and hoofs clattering. Aster let himself sink back against the cushions and grin. For the first time since he'd left, Geder felt something like relief.

"You did it," Aster said. "You found the apostate."

"We did," Geder said. "Killed him where he stood. It was mostly Basrahip, though."

"You always say that," Aster said. "This was it. It's over now."

"Not totally over," Geder said. "We still have two armies in the field, after all. But yes. With the apostate gone, the dragons' power is broken. Basrahip said it will be like light

pouring through the fabric of the world until everything's ...
right."

Geder felt a blush rising in his cheeks, called up by the
admiration in Aster's eyes. The prince swallowed and
grinned. "You'll be remembered as the greatest hero in history, Geder. You know that."

"I probably won't be remembered at all," Geder said. "I
didn't really do anything that someone else wouldn't have
done in my place. I'm not special."

"You are," Aster said. "You know that."

Geder let the smile he'd been holding back come through.
He was back. He was home. He had Aster with him, and
the carriage was warm, and he wasn't expected to lead an
army or sleep in a tent. There was pride, yes. And there was
a glow that came from the young prince's admiration. And
more than anything else, there was a relief that it was all
finally over.

"We'll need to talk soon about how to prepare for your
coronation," he said. "Not right away, of course, but in the
next two years. Maybe three. You'll be old enough to take
the crown. All I wanted was to keep the empire strong until
it was yours. It's got more than twice the holdings it had.
The Timzinae are broken. The goddess has come back to
the world and beaten her enemies. I think you'll be the first
king to rule in peace ... maybe ever. You're the one they'll
remember. Not me."

The carriage lurched around a corner. There were tears in
Aster's eyes. "It's not going to be right. Not without you."

Geder pretended to wave the comment away, but in fact it
left his heart feeling warmer for the first time since he'd left.
And maybe in some expanse of time before that. "I won't be
gone. I only won't be Lord Regent. No call for a regent when
you have a king."

"Still," Aster said. Geder thought about taking the boy's hand, then didn't. Aster was almost a man now, and too old for taking comfort in hand-holding. So was Geder, for that.

The carriage stopped at the Fraternity of the Great Bear. The carved animal that announced the place was coated in ice, as if the weeks of winter had greyed its pelt with age and weariness. With the precedence of both prince and Lord Regent, there was no one closer to the great doors. Geder and Aster entered the great hall together. Within, the air was warm and fragrant with the smoke of pine and pipe. The silk tapestries were lit by cut-crystal lanterns. Great chains of gold and silver glittered along the walls. A servant girl in a uniform that was just revealing enough to be pleasant but not so much as to provoke offered them both mugs of wine. Aster caught Geder's eye as if asking permission before he took it. Geder smiled. He didn't mind. A little mulled wine never hurt anyone.

The others came in afterward, men of the great families laughing and joking. They stopped at the table Geder and Aster had claimed and paid their respects. A Dartinae woman with a viol took her place in one of the niches at the corner of the hall and began playing soft music, her glowing eyes darkening when she closed them in concentration or ecstasy. Geder found himself watching her, appreciating the beauty of her music, of her hands. Of the gentle swell of her breasts. Only that made him think of Cithrin, and he turned away. Better to be distracted than think too much of her again.

The patriarch of one of the minor houses of Asterilhold lifted to prominence by the recent tumult was reciting a lengthy poem. It appeared to be about the nobility and burdens of empire, which Geder thought was perhaps a little obvious and self-serving. He wondered what would happen if he questioned the man about his sincerity with Basrahip present. It would be interesting to know if the old man actually meant all he said, or if he was just trying to curry favor. Or both.

Geder craned his neck. Even though the winter court was thinly attended, anyone who remained in the city was here. There were enough that the tables were filled, the halls crowded. It didn't feel as thin now, except for the early darkness at the windows and the chill that even the fires and braziers couldn't quite dispel. It took him some time to find Basrahip among the bodies and motion, despite the priest's size. But yes, there he was, his head canted forward, listening to someone. To Canl Daskellin, in fact.

The Baron of Watermarch and the high priest of the goddess were in an alcove. Daskellin was gesturing as he spoke, his hands making low smoothing gestures, his head shaking in a constant, barely perceptible no. The man's skin, usually as dark as a Timzinae's scales, had an ashen cast. Geder felt a tightening at the back of his neck. He rose, the poet forgotten, and made his way through the crowd. Aster followed in his wake. When he was perhaps half a dozen steps away, Daskellin glanced over, and his face went greyer.

"Lord Regent," he said, making a fast, birdlike bow. "I'm sorry to interrupt your triumph, but there's news. From the south."

"What is it?" Geder said. Aster stepped into the alcove's mouth, shutting the four of them off from the rest of the fraternity.

Daskellin's lips pressed thin as a drawn line. "The siege at Kiaria, Lord Palliako. It broke."

"Well, about time," Geder said. "I was starting to think the Timzinae'd be holding those walls until the end of the world, eh?"

Daskellin's confusion passed quickly, replaced by chagrin. "No, my lord. We didn't win. They broke the siege. Fallon Broot led a counterattack, but it failed. We don't know if he was captured or killed. The city...Suddapal is no longer under our control."

Geder heard the words, but couldn't understand them. Daskellin could as well have said *The pigeons have all voted to become crabs.* It would have made as much sense. "No," Geder said. "We put a temple in Suddapal. Once we put a temple there, it can't fall." He turned to Basrahip. The wide face was the perfect image of concern and sorrow. "It can't fall. Can it?"

"It cannot be lost," Basrahip said, "but even what is not lost can be made to suffer terribly. The blow has been struck, and even though we do not see it, the world knows. Feels within its blood and its flesh. Death throes can be violent and dangerous, even as the final end comes."

"Oh," Geder said. Just hours—less than hours—before, they'd been talking about how it was all already ended. How Aster was safe and all the good that Geder had managed for him, and now he couldn't meet the boy's eyes for fear of seeing the disappointment in them. Everything he'd said in the carriage came back like a weight. He felt as if he'd swept open the curtains to reveal a grand ball in Aster's honor and revealed a bunch of panicked servants still setting up the tables. He felt the humiliation like putting his hand in a fire.

"The problem is not only there, my lord," Daskellin was saying. "Mecelli has written from Inentai. The raids have grown more intense, and there are suggestions that the traditional families have regrouped in the towns of Borja. They may have been coordinating with the enemy in Elassae. He reports that letters like the ones in Asterilhold have begun appearing. And, my lord? There is the question of the farms."

Geder shook his head, anger flaring in his throat. Daskellin was one of the great men of Antea. Advisor to the crown since before Simeon was king. You'd think he could come out with something more useful than "the question of the farms." What question? Was he just leaving the phrase out there to make Geder ask? Or was there something so obvious that he should have known what the man meant, and they were all laughing at him on the inside for not knowing?

Geder scowled at Daskellin so fiercely his cheeks ached, and shrugged. *Are you planning to explain that?*

"Half the farms in the southeast are being manned by war slaves," Daskellin said. "*Timzinae* war slaves. It won't be possible to keep word of the troubles in Suddapal from reaching them. And if they should revolt, we don't have enough swords to send, even with your army home."

"And?"

"And . . . we have the prison," Daskellin said.

A thrill of horror cut through Geder's foul mood. Of course they had the prison. He'd had it built when the invasion began. Housing for Timzinae children taken as guarantee of their parents' good behavior. Only now the parents in Suddapal had misbehaved, and if the farm slaves saw that Suddapal could rise without consequences, trouble would spread like fire. The understanding of what he would have to do sank in his gut, and with it, anger and resentment for the people—not the people, the *Timzinae*—who'd put him in this position. But Daskellin, for all his stammering and talking past the point, was right. The thing had to be done.

"Identify all the hostages with parents working the farms," Geder said. "Pull one out of every ten as witnesses. The others, keep them locked in their cells. The ones with parents in Elassae, throw off the Prisoner's Span. When it's done, send the witnesses to the farms under guard and let them tell what they saw."

"My lord," Daskellin said, "they're *children*."

"I know what they are!" Geder said, more loudly than he'd meant. "Do you think I like doing this? Do you think it's something I take pleasure in? It's not!" All around, the conversations went quiet. The eyes of the court turned toward them. Toward him. Geder lifted his chin, his rage giving him confidence. "This isn't a choice we made. They knew what would happen. They made the decision. They *made* us do this. If the roaches can't be bothered to love their children, I don't see why we should."

Entr'acte: Borja

The Low Palace at Tauendak looked down over the river port. The High Palace faced the sea. On the dragon's road that wound into the city from the east, there were no palaces, no compounds of the rich or powerful, only the defense walls. The first was in stone and as tall as two men, the second twice the height and girded by plates of iron. The wars of the Keshet might sweep north into Borja, but those waves broke against the walls of Tauendak. There were even songs about it.

Ships might come to the seaport from as near as the cities and towns of Hallskar or as far as Cabral and Lyoneia. The river trade was all from Inentai, or had been before the Anteans ate the city. Since then, there hadn't been many barges at the river port.

Within, the city was broad and flat. Seen from above, Tauendak looked like an exercise in cross-hatching done by some great and godlike artist. Roads ran north to south at the bases of the flat-roofed buildings, caught most of the day in some level of shadow and darkness. Bridges spanned east to west above them, their railings painted yellow. And every few blocks the wide circle of a ramp let oxcarts rise up or sink down. Temples rose above all, red brass and blue tile.

The people of the city were of the Eastern Triad: Jasuru, Yemmu, Tralgu. Timzinae were welcomed, especially those related by marriage to the traditional families that ruled Borja and Sarakal. Dartinae, Haaverkin, and Firstblood were permitted in the city, but barred from certain kinds of trade. Southlings were called Eyeholes, and walked the streets with guards, if at all. Mostly they stayed away. And the Drowned... Well, what could anyone do about the Drowned? They washed through the bay and out again. No one fished for them or sold their flesh at market, because it was ritually unclean, though whether that was because they were another race of humanity or because they were filthier than fish was a matter of some debate.

Damond Gias had been born at the cunning man's house three streets south of the Red Temple twenty-six years before. As a Jasuru, he had lived in his uncle's compound, carrying weights of grain and beans and ore from the cara-vanserai in the east of the city to the ports, carrying weights of fish and rope back to the caravanserai. His cousins and brothers and sisters lived with him until they married. He himself had no interest in women, and the lovers he took among the men of the city had no interest in raising chil-dren, so the question of marriage never came up for him. And so it was natural enough that, when the representative of the Regos came and called upon his uncle to give one of the family over in service to the city for ten years, Damond had been picked.

He hadn't minded. The life of a guardsman wasn't harder than that of a carter, and the uniform brought a certain level of respect with it. Most violence could be handled with threat, and when that failed, he had a group of well-armed men from across the city who felt that any attack on him was an attack on all of them. Even the odious duties of col-lecting taxes and closing businesses that hadn't given up their share to the council weren't too awful. It had taken years, in fact, to find a duty among the many duties of the city guard that was so soul-crushingly dull, so arbitrary and absurd, that Damond genuinely dreaded it.

Blood duty was a new thing, a ritual from the west that stank of panic and war-fear. But war-fear had its hand on Tauendak too, and so it went. He didn't have to like it.

"Tilt your head."

Damond looked up into Joran's black eyes. The older man had scales three shades lighter than Damond's own, and a scar across his cheek that spoke of old violence. By summer, Joran's time in the guard would be ended, and the old man would go back to whatever he had been. It made him a little easier to negotiate with.

"Not today, eh?" Damond said. "It's my second blood shift in a week, and I spent all my time since then digging that shit out of my ears."

"You know the rules. Tilt your head."

"I'll give you six lengths of copper to forget it. Just for today. And next time, I won't even ask. I'll just put my head on the table and let you pour it in my ears. Not even a grumble."

"The day you don't grumble, the sky'll fall into the sea," Joran said, baring his sharp black teeth in a grin. "I'll forget this time, but don't *you* forget when we come to the tap-room that it was six of copper. Or I'll have it too hot next. I mean it, I won't haggle on a finished deal."

"I'd never ask it," Damond said, grinning back.

"Then get your thick ass out there," Joran said, putting the cup of wax back with its brothers beside the fire. "You can at least be on time."

Damond jumped out of the chair, strapped on his blade, and left the close, warm guard's station for the chill of the streets before the old man could change his mind. In the half light of the rising dawn, he went up the stairs three at a time, and then across the bridge, running east to the river port. Ammu Qort, the day's prime, was harsh to men he found shirking their duty, but lazy about checking after the work had started. Damond wanted to be in place well before any inspections could be done.

The cut-thumbs letters had begun arriving just before Longest Night, smuggled past Antean ports on ships from the west. Sheaves of them had been handed around the taprooms and temples. Damond had seen only one himself. *The forces of madness are all around*, it had said. He'd joked with his cousin that anyone who'd worked for the guard had known that for years. For a time, the letters had been the first subject of everyone's jokes and speculation—whether they were sincere or a kind of expensive joke, whether the things they said were true or pure invention, whether the people making and distributing them had Borja's best interests at heart. He'd heard that the letters had been written by pirates, or a Northcoast merchant, or some sort of resurgent dragon cult. For himself, he took them lightly.

Someone else, though, hadn't. A priest had put something in the letters together with a passage of scripture and petitioned the council. The council—probably influenced by Sarakal's traditional families in exile—had declared new policies for the guard. And Damond, through no fault of his own, had been introduced to blood duty.

Now, he skittered down the stairs where the bridges stopped and run-walked to the inspector's station. All along the river, a high wall sank down into the muddy depths and rose high above them. Algae greened the stones from the high-water mark down to the surface of the river, and guards only slightly luckier than himself patrolled the thin walk at its top. When he'd started in the guard, there'd been jokes about Timzinae merchants from Sarakal climbing the walls by night to avoid the inspector's station. Since the war, the jokes seemed less funny.

Barges stood on the water, shadows on the shining river. In years past, a busy morning might see a hundred boats waiting for the station to come open. Since the war, Damond had never seen more than thirty, and usually fewer. The inspector's station stood at the end of a walled quay. Whatever goods were to be loaded or unloaded stopped here to be counted, considered, and have tariffs levied. Whoever wished to come into the city or leave it was questioned and examined. Tauendak was a city of the pure, and it didn't stay that way by opening itself to all comers. Or that was the story it told, anyway. Damond had believed it until he'd been part of the guard.

The number of people the inspector's station waved through for expedience or changed its mind about for a bribe had scandalized him at first. He'd settled into a professional cynicism since. The cut-thumbs letters had tightened down the passage, as had the fashion of ransom kidnappings in Lôdi before that and the War of Ten Princes in the Keshet before that. Every time the rules became stricter, they also would eventually relax. Antea's spread across the world was like that too. Whatever the rich and powerful thought, whatever the priests pretended to find in the ancient scripts, the madness of the Firstbloods wouldn't come here.

Kana Luk, inspector for the Regos, was at her table in the station when Damond came in. It was still dark enough outside that she had her lantern lit, and the flame glittered on the scales of her cheek and forehead.

"You're late," she said.

"I'm early."

"That was a trick. Your ears aren't done."

Damond shrugged. "Joran and I must have forgotten."

"I'm sure that's it," the inspector said.

"I can go back, if you'd like. But it might take a while. You know how Joran heads out once his morning duties are done."

"Any candlemaker in the medina would have wax enough to do the thing."

"If it's worth being late—"

"Don't bullshit me, boy," she said, a smile in her gruff voice. "I was making excuses to get out of work before your mother licked off your caul." Damond grinned and took his place, blade and cloth in hand, but Kana wasn't done. "You watch yourself. I went to the cunning man last night. He said there was great danger coming."

"He always says that."

"Does not. Sometimes he says there's great fortune coming. Or a man to sweep me away in clouds of passion."

"I don't know why you give him your money."

"Promises of danger, fortune, and passion? He's the most entertaining thing in my life anymore. Now let's open for work before Qort gets here and finds you idle enough to examine."

Damond stood by the quayside door, thin blade in one hand, white cloth in the other. Kana opened the door at his side and shouted into the darkness. The voices of the laborers and carters answered back, as they always did. There was a music to the work, and it was the last beautiful thing in Damond's day.

The first man to come in was a Dartinae, his body thin and lithe, his eyes glowing from within like his brain was afire. He looked from Kana to Damond and back again.

"The fuck is this?"

"New rules, Dabid," Kana said. "State your name."

"You just called me by it. I'm Dabid Sinnitlong, just the same as I was last month."

"I know it," Kana said. "What's your business?"

"Grain from the farms down by Sabbit township. Five hundredweight."

"Nice," Kana said. "East or west bank?"

"All west," the Dartinae said. It was a lie, and they all knew it. Someday, Kana would lose patience, and Dabid would pay a thick fine or a slightly thinner bribe. But apparently this wasn't that day.

"Lucky for you that's the cheap one," Kana said, holding her hand out for the bill of lading. She passed her eyes over it, clicked the beads on her figuring board, and wrote a number at the bottom of the bill. She looked up at Damond and pointed three fingers at the Dartinae. It was the motion she was supposed to use so he'd know it was time.

"Thumb, please," he said, and the Dartinae held out his hand. Damon pricked it, squeezed out a single drop of blood, and wiped it with the white cloth. The smear of red was unremarkable, as they always were. "Pass," Damond said.

"Well thank God for that," Dabid Sinnitlong said dryly. "How much are you dunning me for today, Kana?"

"Same as I ever do," the inspector said. "Now pay it and get out. I've a line behind you."

This was the banter, the human voices, that Damond would have been without if he'd followed the rules too close. His whole day would have been spent in silence, watching people come through the doorway, seeing their mouths move, watching the papers go back and forth from Kana's desk. Then three fingers up, and he could hear his own voice traveling through his flesh rather than the air. *Thumb, please*, like he was underwater. Like he was one of the Drowned. The prick, the dot of blood, the swipe with the white cloth. Though by midday the cloth would get to looking pretty gory itself.

As it was, Qort arrived in the middle morning, wandering in and out of the station at odd intervals so that Damond had to pretend he couldn't hear the whole time. Still, listening was more diverting than the isolation of temporary deafness, even if he couldn't say anything himself. Most of the morning was dull. A Yemmu woman coming up from the western Keshet to take up house with her cousin. A Tralgu man hauling poppy seeds for the cunning men's shops. A Firstblood woman sneaking Timzinae goods out of Inentai for refugee families living in Lôdi. The river trades were more interesting for Damond because they spoke of the southern lands. He didn't have much interest in anyplace with winters colder or darker than Borja.

The Firstblood man came in just before the station shut for midday. He wore a robe the colorless brown of sparrows and stood before Kana with a patient smile, like there was a joke that only he was in on. Damond's experience of Firstbloods was that a lot of them were smug like that, so he didn't think much of it. Not at first.

"State your name."

"Kirmizi rol Gomlek," the man said.

"What's your business?"

"I have come to take audience before your Regos."

Kana widened her eyes and bared her teeth. "Audience with the Regos, ah? The Regos know about that yet?"

"She will," the Firstblood said. "And from my words shall she profit greatly. There is a darkness that has fallen upon the world. Even now, it walks the streets of your city unfettered and free. I have come to cleanse it."

"Ah," Kana said. Even if he had been deaf, Damond

thought he would have recognized the tension and unease in her shoulders. He took a tighter grip on his blade. "How many in your party, then?"

"We are seven," the man said.

"Coming from?"

"Sarakal."

Kana nodded. "Where in Sarakal?"

"Outside Inentai."

"Not inside it?"

"We have been traveling among the towns for some time," the man said.

"Carrying anything for trade?"

"Only truth, and that we give freely to all who listen."

"Right," Kana said. "No papers, then? It's ten lengths of silver for entrance."

The man took a purse from his belt, counted out ten coins, and placed them on the table before her, each one making a sharp tap as he placed it. Kana took them, looked to Damond, and lifted three fingers together.

"Thumb, please," Damond said. His heart was beating fast. It wasn't possible, was it? It couldn't be truth.

The Firstblood scowled deeply. He turned his gaze to the blade, the bloodied cloth, and shook his head. "We will not need to do this. You would be foolish to insist."

"It's a . . . it's needed. Protocol," Damond said, but in truth he did feel a bit silly. The Firstblood shook his head.

"Listen to my voice, friend. There is no need. It would be foolish to insist. Better that we let this go. Better for you, and for me, and for your people. Nothing good can come from insisting. Better to let it go."

Damon's throat thickened and he nodded, lowering the thin blade. A kind of deep embarrassment was spreading through him. Here he was, a guard of the city, poking strangers at the word of God alone knew who. Qort was likely having him do it just as a show of contempt.

"Listen to my voice," the Firstblood said again. "There is no—"

The door opened and Ammu Qort came in. The Firstblood turned to him, anger in his eyes.

"What's the matter here, inspector?" the prime demanded.

"Nothing, sir," Kana said, sounding dazed. "It's just this man—"

"Is he processed?" Qort said.

"He's paid," Damond said, not realizing that he was proving he hadn't taken the wax. "But the blood...it seems like we should just—"

Qort scooped the blade from Damond's hand and grabbed the Firstblood's wrist, and before any of them could speak, a tiny drop of crimson was on a corner of the white cloth. And in it, skittering wildly, a tiny black spider.

"Fucking hell!" Qort shouted, jumping back.

"Drop your weapons," the Firstblood shouted. "You cannot win against me. You have already lost—"

"His voice's poison!" Qort shouted. "Don't listen to him! Don't *hear* him!"

Some part of Damond understood and he screamed. It was wordless at first, but loud. And then, as he pushed the Firstblood back through the door to the quay, he added syllables. *MA-LA-LAL-BAY-AB-ABA! ZA-MAM-BABA!* Nonsense gabbling like a bored child singing in a yard, but it drowned out whatever the Firstblood was saying. His own blood seemed to rush white-hot in his veins as he pushed the Firstblood back. Kana was scrambling toward the loaders and dock guards, shouting at them, but Damond couldn't hear her over his own screaming any more than he could hear the spider-infected thing.

The Firstblood was trying to yell at him, but Damond's voice was louder, and he shoved the man back, and back, and back again. *BA-BA-YA-BA-MA-BABA! YE-BE-YE-BEY-BE*! And Qort had a rope around the Firstblood man's neck. The Firstblood reached for the noose, clawing at it. Damond stopped shouting.

"Come on, you bastard!" Qort shouted. "Help me with this!"

The rope around the man's neck was tied on the other end to a stone anchor weight. Together, Damond and Qort pushed it to the river's edge, and then into it. To their right the guards under Kana's direction were throwing lit lanterns onto a boat that was trying to throw off its moorings. The anchor weight sank, hauling the Firstblood down behind it. Damond watched until all he could see were the soles of the Firstblood's shoes, kicking in the gloom, then going still.

Qort lay on the quay beside him, breathing hard. The prime's expression was one of rage and triumph. Damond tried a smile.

"Forgot the wax, sir. Sorry."

Marcus

Marcus swung hard and low, but the blow didn't connect. Yardem danced back just outside the arc of the attack and brought his own sword down. Marcus shifted, parrying with a hard clack of wood against wood. The impact stung his fingers. He stepped back as Yardem pressed his advantage. Marcus blocked, blocked again, dodged, and tried to slip under an attack. Yardem's sword caught him just above the temple, and the world went a little quiet for a moment. He felt his mind willing his body to shift away, to raise his own blade in reply, but nothing happened. His hands and feet had gone sluggish, and he stumbled to the icy brickwork of the pit.

"Sir?" Yardem said, his voice humming with concern. Marcus lifted his hand, waited until the world stopped spinning.

"I'm all right. That was a good counter. Nice work." He hauled himself to his feet. The fighting pit was ten yards across, and a little longer. The walls curved, but not into a circle the way they made them in the south. It still had corners. The poisoned sword leaned in one of them beside Marcus's overcoat and Yardem's less exotic blade. In the summer people would stand at the lip, or sit and dangle their legs. The cold made it a less enticing spectacle. Marcus didn't care either way. Let them look, let them stay indoors by their fires. It didn't change what he had to do.

"Let's go again," Marcus said, taking a grip on the hilt of the wooden practice sword. "I'm good for it."

Yardem huffed out a white, frozen breath and raised his own false blade, but not fully to the ready. "Might want to discuss that, sir."

"You knocked me on the cob," Marcus said. "Not the first time it's happened. Come on. Take position."

"Comes a point where more training doesn't gain you anything, sir."

"You think we're there?" Marcus said through a tooth-baring grin.

"Were an hour ago. Didn't mention it."

Marcus let his shoulders sag. Truth was, he didn't feel well. Hadn't in a while. He sank to his haunches, leaning on the practice sword. He was breathing harder than he should have been. His back ached, and not with the vigorous burn of worked muscle. More like the sharp complaining of loose joints. He coughed and spat. The brick walls rose up on all sides, the looming wall of the gymnasium to the east, and the white winter sky above that. He wondered where the habit had begun of sinking practice pits into the ground. It wasn't done for formal dueling. He pictured vast perches at the edges, and dragons looking down at them, slaves fighting each other for the masters' pleasure. It seemed a little too plausible.

"It's not the sword," he said.

"Didn't say it was, sir."

"No, but you thought it mighty loud. So don't crawl up my back again about how I should leave it be more."

"Or let someone else take a turn carrying it," Yardem said.

"You think it's rotting me from the inside out, and you'd pass it to someone else? That seems cruel of you."

"Fit across my back," Yardem said. "Give you some time to find your strength."

"I know where my strength went," Marcus said, pulling himself up. His scalp felt cold where the sword had taken it. Oozing blood, most likely. "It's not the sword. It's age."

"It's both, sir."

"Well don't paint it gold for me," Marcus chuckled. "Tell me how you really see it."

"You're past the age when most men in our profession have stopped," the Tralgu said, his ears flat against his head. "Taken long-term duties running a guard company or opened a training camp or died. Instead, you've trekked across the world two times over, half died in the interior of Lyoneia, been hauled up mountaintops by a dragon, and strapped this blade across your back. You act as if you could go on forever, and your body's starting to show you it isn't truth."

"I was joking, Yardem. You can go ahead and paint it gold a little."

His second-in-command looked down and flicked an ear. "All right. You've got a mostly full head of hair, and that one girl at the inn still thinks you're handsome."

"Fuck you," Marcus laughed, walking across the brick-work to their things. His legs actually seemed to creak. Yardem was right about one thing, at least. There was such a thing as overtraining. They bundled the wooden swords together with a leather strap, and Yardem tossed them across his shoulder like a day soldier carrying a pack. Marcus pulled on his overcoat, and then the dark-green scabbard and hilt of the culling blade. As they walked toward the ladder, a figure appeared at the edge of the pit. The sole observer of their showfighter's practice.

If the last few years had worn Marcus down, they'd

grown Cithrin up. She'd never have the shard-of-milk-ice paleness of her mother's race, but she carried something of the Cinnae calm. She no longer showed the awkward girlishness that Master Kit and Cary had tried to train out of her back in ancient days. Back when they'd been smugglers running from an Antean army not yet fueled by the spite of dragons. She was a woman now. A young one, but experienced beyond her age.

She's not your daughter, Marcus thought. And yet, standing before her as Yardem climbed the ladder behind him, he felt the same mixture of pride and melancholy he imagined a Merian grown to womanhood might have called forth.

"I need you," she said.

"And here I am," Marcus said. "What's the problem?"

"I have a plan, or part of one, but it means the two of you talking."

Yardem grunted his way over the lip of the pit and leaned against the wooden railing. Marcus glanced at him.

"We're here," Marcus said, settling the blade more firmly on his shoulder. "What is it we need to talk about?"

"Not you and Yardem," Cithrin said. "You and *him*."

"Well, God smiled," Marcus said sourly.

Inys stood on his perch, staring out over a slate-grey sea. The vast head turned as the three of them came close. The intelligence in the huge eyes was unmistakable, as was the weariness. Marcus hadn't spent much time around the dragon since they'd come to Carse. There had been no end of people to serve Inys—bring him food, clean away his dung, sing and caper for him. Marcus understood it. Even felt some of the same urges to cater to the master of the fallen world. Almost all of humanity's races had been built to serve the dragons and to read the feelings in their faces like sheepdogs watching the shepherd. For thousands of years, no one had suffered that burden, and now, with Inys suddenly among them, no one had any practice resisting it.

Marcus had the feeling someone should, and he was fine with its being him. Part of the job. He had the sense that Inys knew it too. That, perhaps, it was why the dragon had a fondness for him.

"Stormcrow," Inys said, the words low and deep, "you return at last."

"So it seems," Marcus said. "You're looking ragged."

When Marcus had woken him, Inys had been sluggish from ages of stonelike sleep, but he'd been unscarred. The dark, shining scales had been dulled by dust, but perfect, row on unending row. Porte Oliva had changed that. Long streaks along the dragon's side were roughened by scar. The huge wings had holes in them where Antea's great spears had pierced them and pulled the dragon down. Weapons designed to slaughter dragons, and invented, it seemed, after Inys began his long hibernation. That they existed at all meant someone out there had shared Marcus's opinion of the masters of the world and the dignity of being their slaves.

Cithrin stepped between them, taking the moment for her own. It was a good skill to have, in her position.

"We've had more reports from the east. Birds now. Not just cunning men."

"That's good," Marcus said. "Half of what the cunning men make out winds up being dreams anyway. I'd rather we had an actual courier, though."

"I'm working on that," Cithrin said.

"What will it matter?" Inys said, his gaze turning back to the sea. "The world is empty anyway."

Cithrin ignored the comment. "For now all we know

for certain is that Kiaria is no longer under siege, and the forces that were meant to hold Elassae are hunkered down in northern Birancour."

"Hunting you," Marcus said.

"Hunting me," Cithrin agreed. "Geder was so fixated on that, he left himself open, and the Timzinae are taking advantage of the fact. There was fighting in Suddapal and along the coast. We don't know how bad it was, but... people there have more reason to be angry than merciful."

"Mercy has no reason," Inys sighed. "Mercy justified is only justice."

"Deep," Marcus said.

"We don't know who's in charge of the uprising," Cithrin said. "That's in part what the courier is going to find out for us. And Isadau is going too. Barriath's given her a fast ship and a crew.

"The good news is that the priesthood there has been closely identified with Anteans. Even if there is a schism, the priests hate the Timzinae and the Timzinae hate the priests. Komme's fear—and I think it's a fair one—is that when the chaos goes north into Inentai and Nus or west into the Free Cities, it'll start reaching other races. Jasuru, Yemmu, Tralgu. People who might see a schismatic priest as an ally."

Marcus nodded. "And then fall to their unpleasant power, lift up another bunch of fanatics, and start the whole damned war over in miniature."

"Not miniature," the dragon sighed, his breath pluming out yards from his mouth. "And not starting over. They will only carry it forward. More sides, more causes, more reasons to demonize and slaughter the slaves in the next valley. It was what Morade wrought."

"Birancour is stable," Cithrin said. "For now. But the Antean main army's still there. The Lord Marshal and a force

of cold, skinny Anteans are still tasked with hunting me down
and taking me back to Camnipol in chains. And even if Jorey
Kalliam's turned sides the way his mother says, that's not a
promise they won't try to take Northcoast come the thaw.
Antea's got a new and thriving tradition of killing off its Lords
Marshal. At which point Northcoast is bound to act."

"So chaos on both sides of Antea," Marcus said. The
dragon heaved a massive sigh. *Great whiner,* Marcus
thought. *He brought the whole thing on us, however many
hundred generations back. Least he could do was pretend
interest.*

"Pulling the thorn here," Cithrin said, "and keeping the
fighting in the east from turning to the greatest rout in history call for the same thing. The Antean army's well-ordered
withdrawal back to Camnipol. Only there's two priests with
them talking everyone there into thinking they're invulner-
able and protected by the goddess."

"So we'll need to be rid of them," Marcus said.

"And that seems to require Marcus. Or at least his sword."

"If it takes the sword, it takes me. That's the job. And,
fairness, the prospect of not having a massive force of armed
men bent on delivering you to the boy tyrant who feels you
humiliated him would likely help my concentration too."

Cithrin tilted her head, hearing something more in his
words perhaps than he'd meant to say aloud.

He cleared his throat, feeling an unwelcome blush rising in his neck. He turned to the dragon and changed the
subject. "How about it, Inys? Are you up for hauling a few
people south? Or are your wings too weak?"

The dragon turned, real anger in its eyes. Marcus fought
the urge to take a step back, but he did lower his eyes. "My
wings are cut, but I am no cripple, Stormcrow. What is this
that you ask of me? Be plain!"

"How many can you carry?" Cithrin asked. "I mean no disrespect, Inys. You know that. But I won't tax your strength. Not while you're still healing."

"How far?" the dragon asked, scowling in a way that was both inhuman and perfectly recognizable.

"Around the army, far enough that its scouts don't see you. And then south. It'll be less likely to raise suspicions if they don't seem to be coming from Northcoast."

The dragon spread his wings. Marcus knew they'd suffered in the attack at Porte Oliva, but he hadn't made a close inspection. It was uglier than he'd thought. There were gaps in the thick, leathery membrane. Holes. He remembered watching Inys laboring across the water toward the escaping ships and wondered just how close the dragon's escape had been.

"I can carry myself and five others," the dragon said.

"Let's call it three," Marcus said.

"Do you doubt me?"

"A little," Marcus said. "It's why you love me."

The dragon bristled, bared its teeth, and then laughed. Gouts of stinking flame rolled through the winter air as Inys chuckled. The smoke rose above them, spreading until it became the sky. "Three then," the dragon said.

"When will you be ready?" Cithrin asked.

"I am ready now," Inys said, folding his wings together and settling heavily on his perch. The great eyes closed, with the feeling of the conclusion of a royal audience. Marcus walked at her side in silence until they reached the court where Yardem stood waiting.

"Went well?" Yardem asked.

"Didn't end with us burned or in his belly," Marcus said. "Willing to call that a victory. So me for the sword. This

Lady Kalliam to get me past the guards. Maybe Enen? Kurtadam are common enough in the south she wouldn't seem odd. Or should we keep to Firstbloods?"

"Not Yardem?" Cithrin asked.

"We're known," Yardem said. "A man traveling alone might be anyone. A Tralgu man with a Firstblood beside him, and people might remember stories. Especially this near to Northcoast."

"Barriath will want to go," Cithrin said.

"Can't let him," Marcus said. "Lose him for too long and his little pirate fleet'll pull up stakes. Metaphorically speaking. And...Oh. Yeah."

"I think that's right, sir."

"What's right?" Cithrin asked. The cliff and the sea and the dragon retreated behind them as they walked. A Timzinae woman hurried past, wrapped in a wool scarf, the scales of her face catching the dim winter sun. "Marcus? What's right?"

"You're sending me in to assassinate the priests, yes?"

"Unless you're willing to hand the sword to someone else," Cithrin said.

"Once that's done, though, the soldiers are going to lose all the false certainty they've had carrying them through. Start thinking for themselves, and since the truth is they're hungry, exhausted, and working with shit supply lines, they'll likely come to the fact that all's not well pretty damned quickly. If we just wanted a mutiny or a mid-campaign disband, it'd be simple. But you want to march them back east. To do that...Well, we'll need a priest, and that means Kit."

"Cary won't like it," Yardem said.

"You can tell her, then," Marcus said, and Yardem flicked a jingling ear. "And truth is, Kit's just going to have to keep them together at least long enough to let them scent home. After that, they'll likely go where we want like water running downhill."

"Through the pass at Bellin?" Yardem said.

"Depends on how deep the snows are," Marcus said. "Otherwise...I don't know. The coast and by ship? I don't like the idea of marching all the damned way south to the Free Cities again, and I can't see King Tracian letting them through Northcoast, even if they're sort of on our side."

"Complicated," Yardem agreed. "You'll go back to Camnipol with them, then?"

"Can't see leaving Kit behind. It'd be rude," Marcus said, and smiled. If anyone had asked, he'd have said that being back in Carse, in Northcoast, walking down the streets that Merian and Alys had walked down once a lifetime ago, didn't bother him. The pleasure he felt at the prospect of leaving—even leaving in disguise at the heart of an enemy army—suggested his assessment might have been optimistic. Any reason not to be here was a good one.

He wondered how much he could really trust Lady Kalliam, now that his life and Kit's depended on her. He supposed there was an easy way to find out.

The great keep of the holding company came in sight as they rounded a corner. Carts and horses and servants in the colors of half a dozen houses swarmed the street around it. The Medean bank hadn't been built for the constant traffic that came with governing a kingdom, much less three of them. Perhaps more. They'd have to redesign.

"Why do you bait him?" Cithrin asked.

"Who? Inys? Do I bait him?"

"You do, sir," Yardem said.

"I don't know," Marcus said. Then, "Because he's self-indulgent with his grief. Because he screwed up badly once, and now everything he ever does is about that, and God forbid that anyone around him ever be let to forget it for a day."

"Oh," Cithrin said. "All right. I understand."

"I wasn't going to say it," Yardem said.

"Say what?" Marcus said, then understood. He disliked the dragon for being too much like Marcus Wester. He shook his head. "You can both go piss up a rope."

"If you say so, sir."

"And you two take care of each other while I'm gone. I'll miss you. Now let's go break the bad news to Kit."

Clara

Clara, wrapped in layers of wool and leather against the cold and the wind, pressed her face against the dragon, closed her eyes, and waited for the worst to be over. Inys's leg shifted as he flew, the huge muscles flowing and flexing against her in a way that felt both intimate and impersonal. The leather straps that kept her from plummeting to her death bit into her legs and back. She couldn't say whether her feet had gone numb from the lack of blood reaching her toes or the intense cold. She had imagined one time and another what it must be like to fly through the air. Always, she'd evoked ideas of freedom and joy. Now that it came to the actual practice, it felt more like being a baby carried along the edge of the Silver Bridge by a not-entirely-trustworthy nurse.

On the occasions when she did open her eyes, there was little enough to see besides the horizon of stars and the bulk of the vast animal to which she was tied. The land below her was dark, and the few firefly glimmers she saw might have been anything: cities, camps, farmhouses, tricks of her over-tired eyes. The others—Wester and Kit—had straps of their own on other legs. She couldn't see them, nor could she imagine hearing them over the sound of the wind. Had they fallen to their deaths, she would not have known.

They had left Carse only hours before, with the dull red disk of the sun hovering just above the horizon. She'd felt

then, waddling out to the open space nearest the Graveyard of Dragons, ridiculously overdressed. Her elbows and
knees seemed hardly to bend. Barriath walked beside her,
and if he found her as laughable as she found herself, he
showed respect enough not to say it. The dragon was on a
great perch made from a felled pine. The scent of its sap was
still fresh. When she saw the harnesses hanging limp from
the great beast's legs, she had to work to stifle her laughter.
What would the ladies of the court think if they saw this?
Hardly appropriate behavior for a baroness. But what had
to be done, would be.

In the shadow of the great wings, two figures were already
waiting. The older man with the long face and wiry hair of the
priests and an attractive younger woman with a thick braid.
They were speaking with an intensity that made her wonder
whether they might be lovers or father and daughter, though
that didn't seem likely. The woman's face was hard, and tears
streaked her cheeks. The man's posture was equal parts sorrow and strength. Clara found herself wondering how they
managed to express so much with their bodies alone, but then
they were actors. She supposed it was the sort of thing one did
without thinking, if only one practiced enough. Like the way
her daughter Elisia used to spend the whole day whistling to
herself after working with her music tutors.

The woman said something she couldn't make out, and the
old man laughed, then they embraced. Not as lovers would,
nor yet parent and child. Family of some sort, though.

"I should be going," Barriath said.

"Of course you shouldn't, dear. They need you for Callon
Cane or the leader of the little fleet or some such. Besides
which, there's little you could do to look after me that Jorey
won't be able to accomplish. He is still the Lord Marshal."

And if he took her place, she wouldn't be reunited with

Vincen Coe, she didn't say. In truth, the implausible journey she was about to take might have uneased her more deeply without the prospect of Vincen at its end. Of course, she couldn't explain that to her son. For him, her eagerness might even look like courage. She felt a bit dishonest about that, but didn't see what else she could do.

The actors stepped apart gracefully, as if they had ended their scene. What fascinating people really. And the woman, at least, seemed vaguely familiar. Clara wondered whether she'd seen her perform somewhere. Barriath took Clara's hand, turning her. The distress in his eyes reminded her of how he'd looked as a boy. A baby. Of course this was hard for him. Since the day they'd found each other again, he'd been able to play the protector. Now he was sending his mother off into the teeth of danger. What boy could ever see that done and be unmoved?

She raised her laughably puffy arm and touched his face. "No regrets now. We've gone past that."

"Just tell me you won't take any chances you don't need to," he said.

She wondered for a moment what her life might have been if she'd lived by that rule. Nothing like it was, she thought. She wondered what her son would make of all the things she'd so carefully never told him. The rage and despair she'd suffered losing Dawson. The joyful recklessness of standing against Geder Palliako even at the height of his power. She was friend to thieves and cutthroats now. Lover of a man her sons' age. And none of it could be said.

"I will use my very best judgment," she said. "And this won't be our last meeting."

"You don't know that," Barriath said, choking on the words.

"I don't," she said. "But I choose to believe it, or else I'd never stand going."

"I love you, Mother."

And then they were embracing. Not for the last time, she told herself. There would be another, at least. Somehow. She was weeping now as well. When she could bring herself to let him go, Barriath's eyes were red and wet. He wiped them angrily with his sleeve and stepped back. She turned to the dragon.

The mercenary captain and his Tralgu second fell into step beside her. The green blade was strapped across the older man's back. The Tralgu—Yardem, his name was—flicked an ear.

"I know," Marcus Wester said, as if something had been said. "Watch after it all until I'm back."

"Will."

And then she was at the dragon's leg, and they were helping her into the harness. She still didn't entirely believe that it was going to happen until the dragon spread its wings, howled like a storm, and fell up into the sky.

That had been hours ago, and the sun had long since fled. Clara couldn't entirely believe that she'd slept, but her mind had surely lost track of time. A scattering of fires glimmered far to what she presumed was the east, and the ground seemed closer. She could make out the shapes of trees, and a thin silver line that might have been a stream or a dragon's jade road. Her cheeks were stiff as plaster, and as unfeeling, but she craned her head against the storm wind. The ground was closer. Much closer. The dragon dipped, dipped again, and didn't rise. The great wings worked, stirring loose snow and winter-killed grass. They landed in a drift that rose to her knees. The ripping storm that had plagued them since Carse vanished instantly, and the calm seemed unreal. Clara sagged against the dragon's flesh. Now that they weren't in motion, the warmth of it was like sitting near a fire, and she wondered how much Inys's heat had sustained her during their flight.

Someone tugged at her, and she opened her eyes. The actor-priest. Kit. Starlight lit his smile, and she felt a little thrill of fear and revulsion. The man might be a tame priest, but the same spiders were in his blood as in the others'.

"I think you'll find it more comfortable once you're unharnessed, Lady Kalliam," Kit said.

"Thank you," she said, meaning to go on with *I can manage for myself* only it seemed she couldn't. The straps had worked themselves around her back, and so she suffered the priest's aid in silence. When she tried to walk, her legs felt half strung and uncertain. Captain Wester was at her side, helping her to keep her balance. He had already stripped off the thick wool traveling clothes to reveal the guard's tunic beneath. The great green sword was still across his shoulders, but wrapped in rags and leather. The priest was pulling on the grubby robe of a servant with a deep hood to conceal his face and hair. Somehow, he managed to seem smaller than he was. It was quite a talent.

"First light's not more than an hour from now, and I'd guess we're at least an hour's walk from the camp," Wester said.

"I don't know that I can manage that," Clara said.

"Once we start moving, you'll warm up," Wester said. "Besides which, if you rest, you'll cool down. So we're short on options."

"You stand before me," Inys said, his great voice low but all the more threatening for that, "and moan you can find no warmth?"

"Anything that would fuel a fire, that army burned weeks ago," Marcus said. "And while I'm sure streams of dragon flame could heat some rocks enough to thaw our hands by, I'd prefer not to call attention this way just before we walk up to their sentry posts."

The dragon snorted his vast derision, but didn't press the

issue. Clara nodded and began pulling off her own flying gear. She knew the robes she wore underneath were warm and thick enough for uses besides flying through the night sky like a witch out of legends. Still, she did wish they had something to make a little fire with.

"Head out away from the camp before you turn north," Wester said.

"I shall go as I wish, and do as I please, Stormcrow."

Now it was the captain's turn to snort, but when the dragon leaped again into the darkness, it seemed to Clara he was doing as Wester had ordered. Or suggested. It wasn't easy to know the difference with those two.

"Kit?" Wester said.

"Ready, I think," the priest said. "I'm not certain which direction to go in, though."

"That's all right," Wester said. "I am. Keep close, both of you."

He forged through the snow, breaking through the soft white with his legs. Clara found it was easier to walk in his footsteps, and before long the snow thinned, and they found themselves on a track of frozen mud and churned ice. It stretched out to north and south, winding. The ruts of wagon wheels showed in the muck like scars.

"All right," Marcus said. "Let's go see if this works."

"It will," Clara said.

"Things can always go wrong, lady," Wester said, but there was a smile in his voice. Clara took the lead. It was a shame, she thought, that they didn't have horses. Or at least one for her. Coming in on foot was beneath her station, not that a poor beast could have survived being carried all the way from Carse. Even if it didn't freeze to death, the fright would likely have killed it. But they could have gotten a litter. Something light that the two men could have used to carry her. Well, it was something to keep in mind for next time.

Next time. She chuckled. *God, let there never be a next time.*

Wester was right: the walking did help. By the time the eastern sky began to come rose and gold, she was feeling almost herself. She was Clara Kalliam, taking a brisk morning's constitutional with a guard and servant trailing behind her. She wondered whether Jorey had any tobacco left. Almost certainly not, which was a shame.

The track curved around an outcropping of rock, and a voice came across the snow, sharp and angry. "Stop there! What's the watchword?"

Five archers, arrows nocked, stepped out from behind the stones. They looked terribly thin, the dark leather of their armor hanging loose against their sides. Clara remembered the story—wholly imagined—that the dead rose at night to march in Geder Palliako's army. She didn't know if it was amusing or tragic.

"Watchword?" she said crisply, her accent perhaps a bit thicker than it might have been. "Why, I haven't a clue, dear. Who would have been the one to tell me?"

The archers hesitated. The lead man lowered his bow. "Lady Kalliam?"

"Yes, of course. You are . . . no, wait. You're Sarria Ischian's boy, aren't you? Connir?"

"Ah . . . yes, ma'am."

"I never forget a boy child," Clara said, something like victory singing in her veins. "The fathers are always so put out if you do. I've just returned from Porte Oliva. I hope it's all right that I haven't got the watchword? Because it would be terribly inconvenient to go back now."

The other archers lowered their bows as well. Wester and

Kit stayed carefully behind her, as they ought. The more the guards looked at her, the less they saw anything else. Guards and servants weren't the sort of people one paid attention to anyway, not when a baroness was present.

"Of course not, ma'am. Only we didn't know to expect you."

"My fault," she said, waving the comment away. "I should have sent word. Where would I find my son?"

"The Lord Marshal's tent's up on the western side of camp, ma'am. If he's not inspecting the troops, he'll be there."

"Lovely."

"Permit me, ma'am. I can lead you."

"Thank you, Connir. That would be very welcome."

The mask of habit slipped on so easily, it almost frightened her. Was she the somewhat touched woman of the court wandering about the field of war like it was a garden party? To them, she was. It wasn't that appearances were deceiving. That was a given. What astonished her every time was that they were so *fluid*.

Her weeks away had done the camp no good. Dawson had always spoken of supply lines and provisioning men in the field, and she had listened with half an ear. These men had been away from their homes for years. The little city of tents and shacks they had cobbled together in the fields of Birancour were less than those of the beggars and thieves who made homes on the sides of the Division. What food there was would have to arrive by cart from Porte Oliva. There was no allied city nearer. All the woods nearby had been cut down for firewood, the game, she had no doubt, hunted to extinction. They were hungry, cold, and far from home.

And she had watched them kill the innocent of Porte Oliva. Had seen the pain and horror in the Timzinae woman's eyes. These men she walked among, by whom she was greeted with pleasure, had killed. Had stolen. Many, she was sure, had raped. And her son, her Jorey, was their leader, as Dawson had been before him. Soldiers of the glorious empire or monsters of violence and suffering. So much depended on the story one told about them.

And then he was there, in a group of emaciated men, his hair under a knit cap he'd gotten somewhere. Her Vincen, his eyes bright and his smile as rich and full as it had ever been. Tears leapt to her eyes and she blinked them away. He touched his hand to his heart, and she melted. No one seemed to notice when she dabbed her cuff to her eyes.

The news of her arrival had run ahead of her, and Jorey was standing outside the leather walls of his tent when they arrived. The spider priests, thankfully, were not with him. She saw the exhaustion in his face and the relief.

"Mother," he said. "I was worried you wouldn't be coming back."

"Oh no, dear. Nothing could have kept me away." She waved absently over her shoulder at Wester and Kit. "These are my men. They've been very good to me during the journey. Now do let me come in and warm my feet, won't you?"

"I'm afraid all we have is grass tea and hard bread," Jorey said, ignoring the two newcomers magnificently. "But I can't think of anyone I'd rather share them with."

Clara walked past him and to the door of the tent. She patted his cheek gently as she passed. "You have always been such a good boy. Come along, you two. You can rest for a bit inside while I talk to my son."

Once they were inside and the door closed behind them, Clara made her introductions. She could tell from Jorey's reaction that Captain Wester's name meant more to him than it had to her. She also caught a flash of distrust in Jorey's eyes at the sight of Master Kit.

"What's the news from Carse?" Jorey asked.

Wester was the one who answered. "Six kinds of hell have broken loose in Elassae. And possibly Sarakal by now. We've come to kill your priests and put in our own, such as he is, and get you and as many of your men as will survive the trip back to Antea in hopes that you can keep things from falling apart entirely."

Jorey scowled, looking from Wester to Kit to her. They ought not to have let the actor-priest come along. It looked too much like another faction, another schism, another apostate come to champion another side in the war. And yet, would Jorey have been able to lead his men home without the perverse gift of the goddess?

No, not the goddess. The dragons.

"This is bel Sarcour's plan?" Jorey said. "To send us home so that we can defend Antea against the consequences of the Lord Regent's overreach?"

"It is. Assuming that you're willing to abandon the plan to abduct her and hand her to Palliako for whatever unfortunate revenge he has in mind," Wester said.

Jorey Kalliam was silent for a long moment, then let out a long sigh. "Can't say my heart was in that to start with. Yes, I'll turn back the army if you can keep it from mutiny when I give the order. I'll tell Geder I had to. It won't be a lie."

"Well, we've an understanding then," Marcus said. And then, "Just between us, it feels damned strange doing it. You and your men have killed some friends of mine. Helping your kingdom? Working with you? It feels more than half like betrayal."

Jorey's too-thin face broke into a bitter smile. "Well, at least we've that in common."

Geder

It was a fit of pique," Geder said. "I was angry. I wasn't thinking straight. We can't kill all the Timzinae children with parents in Elassae."

"As my lord wishes," the chief gaoler said.

"We have to keep enough back so that there's incentive for them to put down their swords," Geder said. "So maybe half? Does that sound right?"

A light snow was falling in the prison yard, dots of white too small to be called flakes. The Timzinae children were lined against the wall. Their scales were a light brown that would darken with age. Well, would have. The witness cull had already taken place. The ones who were set to watch and carry the word out to the farms huddled in a corner of the yard, the guards knotting leads around their necks, ten to a rope. Their inner eyelids flickered open and closed.

They didn't know yet that they were the lucky ones.

"If my lord likes half, we can do that," the chief gaoler said. He was a thin, grey-haired Firstblood man with skin almost as dark as the Timzinae, though of course his was real skin and not the insectile plates of the enemy. He lifted his whip, handle first, and the guards by the line stood to attention. "Count 'em off by twos. All the ones go back to the cells. The twos come with."

Geder nodded to the chief and smiled. One of the

children—a girl with pale-brown scales—tentatively smiled back at him, and he looked away.

The others were waiting in the street. Aster and Daskellin, of course, but a few other of the great houses had representatives. Coul Pyrellin was there. Mallian Caot, hardly older than Aster and standing in for his father and elder brothers. Some distant cousin of the Broots. If it could have waited until summer—or even until the King's Hunt was ended—there would have been more. It couldn't, of course. Tradition was all well and good. Geder had even read an essay once that said the rituals of tradition were what defined a kingdom, even more than the bloodline of its kings. But if that were true, it would mean Antea now was a wholly different empire than it had been when Geder became Lord Regent, and that couldn't be right.

Their carriages stood at the ready, the horses' breath pluming in the cold. His private guard surrounded him as he walked to the gold and silver carriage at the fore of the group. As if there were any danger to him here. Aster and Basrahip were waiting.

"Is there a problem?" Aster said, his voice strained and anxious.

"No, no," Geder said. "Just some last-minute details. Nothing to be worried about."

The carriage was more open than Geder would have liked, given the weather. It was designed to let them be seen from the street, which was important for the occasion, but since most occasions for the prince and Lord Regent to be seen happened in summer, keeping in the warmth wasn't a priority. Aster wore a richly embroidered hunter's jacket, Basrahip a grey wool cloak. Geder himself slipped under a thick lap blanket and a servant boy draped his shoulders with a throw still warm and smoky from a brazier.

High above and to the north, the banner of the goddess—red and pale with the eightfold sigil in black lines at the center—hung from the temple at the top of the Kingspire. The iron gates of the prison swung open, and a dozen guards with whips and blades paraded the prisoners out. Geder watched the small bodies trooping across the icy cobbles in double file. They were the witnesses, he thought. These weren't the ones who were going to die, these were the witnesses. But they kept coming, so he was mistaken.

"Does something trouble you, Prince Geder?" Basrahip asked.

Geder shook his head, but said nothing. For some reason, he found himself recalling the burning of Vanai. There had been a woman in the city, on the wall. He remembered seeing her silhouette against the flames. That was a strange thing to recall now. Today was nothing like that. No fires. No smoke.

"I hear the Hunt's sparse this year," Aster said.

"Mm? Little game or few hunters?" Geder asked.

"Few hunters," Aster said. "Everyone's at war or busy with their new holdings."

"Stands to reason," Geder said. "It all stands to reason. All of it. We do what we have to do, and it'll come out right in the end."

The last of the Timzinae emerged. The iron gates closed. The carriage lurched. The procession began down the eastern side of the Division, sometimes along the cliff edge, sometimes turning down a street that only ran alongside it. Geder's belly felt odd, and there was a thickness in his throat he couldn't explain. The wet or the chill. Something.

"It's a shame they've made us do this," Geder said. "But they knew. They knew from the first, and they made their choices. And the death throes of the enemy are on them."

"They are," Basrahip said. "We are her righteous servant as she is ours, and the world is made whole through our works."

"Even this one," Geder said.

"Especially this," Basrahip said. Geder tried to take comfort in it, and managed a bit. The Timzinae had, after all, brought all this on themselves. He had to remember that. They were the ones who'd tried to kill Aster. They weren't even human, not really. Not like the other races. Even the Yemmu with their jaw tusks and the candle-eyed Dartinae were more purely human. The Jasuru might have dragon-like scales, but Timzinae were dragons at the heart. Turn over a stone, and the grubs died of exposure. Turning over the world was just the same.

The Prisoner's Span was the bridge farthest to the south. The cages that hung from it held the guests of the magistrate's justice. The crowd that stood on the bridge was the families of the prisoners or their detractors, tossing down food or throwing stones. But all went quiet when the Timzinae arrived. Guards cleared the bystanders from the bridge, but once removed, the citizens didn't leave. The sides of the Division grew thick with people. Witnesses. There were voices, but no cheers. No shouts. No jeering at the fate of the enemy. Geder didn't know whether he was pleased or disappointed at their solemnity. The cold of the air tightened his chest. Just the cold. Nothing else.

The guards lined the children against the side of the bridge in ranks. They covered it with their bodies. How many children had been in that prison? A nation's worth. Hundreds at the least stood here in the cold. The maw of the Division itself gaped below them. For a moment, Geder saw the great urban canyon as a titanic mouth. The city swelling up to swallow the world, and all of them in the path of its hunger. The witnesses stood together, still bound by ropes. The others stood anxious and confused, looking to the north, toward the Kingspire and the crimson banner of the goddess.

The carriages, his own included, stopped on the bridge. Crows shouted from the sky. Sparrows darted across the wide air, as if agitated by their presence. Or celebrating it. Geder couldn't tell which. He looked to the west. It wouldn't be ten minutes' walk to the little ruined yard where he and Cithrin and Aster had hidden during the insurrection. It seemed like it should have been farther away. In some other city, or vanished perhaps into a kind of legend. He imagined her there, dressed in white, her pale body among the dark-chitined Timzinae. Her eyes hard and rich with contempt. Or weeping from fear of him.

It's not me, he thought. *It's them. I didn't want to do any of this. It was all of them that forced this.*

And then, worse. *No, not just them. It was you. You've made me do this. This is your fault, not mine.*

"My lord?" someone said, and he realized it wasn't for the first time. The chief gaoler stood waiting at the carriage door. Geder felt a sudden and powerful urge to talk with the man, to ask where he'd been born, where he came from, how he'd happened to become a gaoler for the crown. What he thought justice meant. He didn't even care what the answers would be, only that he wouldn't be giving the order.

The Timzinae children stood in the cold. Some were shivering. If they wept, they did so quietly. And in the carriages, the great men of the empire waited, growing colder themselves. He saw the one girl who'd caught his eye at the prison. Who'd smiled at him. Geder pointed to her.

"She's in the wrong place," he said. "She's to be a witness. Pull her back."

"Yes, my lord," the gaoler said. "And...the others?"

"You may begin."

The gaoler saluted with his upraised whip. The first child in the line was a boy, perhaps ten years old. He wore grey rags and a soiled bandage on his right arm. The guard standing behind him put a foot on the boy's back and shoved. Geder watched the boy's arms fly out to catch himself on ground that wasn't there. His screams were taken up by the other children.

It went on for a long time.

It was almost evening when he came unannounced to Lord Skestinin's house. It was always a bit hard going there. Lady Skestinin always greeted him, a mixture of hope and dread in her eyes. She never said the words, quite, but she skated around them. *Is my husband free? Is he dead? Is there news of any kind?* And of course, there wasn't. He hated seeing the relief and disappointment when he asked only whether Sabiha and her new daughter were accepting visitors.

As Lord Skestinin had been away with the navy more than in Camnipol, it was a smaller compound than other lords of equal dignity might have. The gardens were modest, the stables frankly small. There were servants and slaves, such as anyone might have, but fewer, given the needs of the house. For most of the time he'd known it, the house had actually been overfull.

Jorey Kalliam and Sabiha had lived there together after Lord Kalliam's failed revolt. And later Jorey's mother Clara and her retinue. And when Sabiha's birthing had been in danger of failing, Geder had very nearly lived there with his guard, and a full complement of cunning men besides. The sense he had as he sat in the withdrawing room, that the house was empty and hollow, actually just was that it wasn't unnaturally full. The Kingspire would likely have felt the same. Or anywhere. Anywhere in the world.

The door opened, and Geder jumped to his feet. Sabiha entered. Since the baby had come, her color had gotten better. Her hair had lost its ashen dullness. He'd never been around new mothers before. He didn't know whether this was normal. If he imagined that she hesitated or that her smile was just a degree forced, it was surely just his unquiet mind. She was his best friend's wife. Maybe his only friend's wife.

It was why he'd come.

"Lord Regent," Sabiha said, and he interrupted her.

"Geder. Please. It's only us."

"Geder," Sabiha said. "Mother said you wanted to see me?"

He wiped his hands on his thighs. "Well, I wouldn't, wouldn't have said it that way quite. I mean, I did. Want to see you. I do. But really what I said was to ask if you were, were free." He was stuttering like a child. No. Not like a child. Like something else. But he was stuttering. "Is the baby well? She's not, she's not with you."

Sabiha's brows knit and she turned her head a degree, like a bird uncertain whether it was seeing a vine or a snake. "She's sleeping. She does that quite a lot."

"Is she all right?"

"Yes, she's fine. It's what she's meant to do. Geder, is something the matter?"

He laughed, but the sound came out strained. Thin and high as a violin badly played. He walked to the window and then back as he spoke, unable to keep from moving. "You're the, the second person to ask me that today. And the first was Basrahip, so I couldn't, couldn't really answer him, could I? Not when I don't know the answer. I'm sorry. I'm so sorry. I don't mean to be a trouble. I really don't. It's just that Jorey isn't here, and you are, and you love him, and he loves you, and you have a baby, and so you're like him. I mean you aren't like him, but you're connected to him. And I don't have anyone."

He stopped. A plume of white rage rose from his gut to his throat, as sudden and unexpected as a lightning bolt in bright sun. "I don't have *anyone*," he said through clenched teeth.

Something moved inside him, a knot of emotion he could put no name to shifting in the space below his heart. He wanted to stop talking, to leave and go back to the Kingspire with Aster and have everything be what it was supposed to be. He wanted to erase the alarmed look from Sabiha's eyes. He wanted to stop talking, but he couldn't. He'd started, and now it was like a landslide.

"It's all going so well, you see. It's all just the way it was meant. The goddess, she's coming back to the world, and she's bringing peace and truth, and all the lies are dying. Everywhere. Since we stopped the apostate, everything in the world's been getting better and brighter and purer."

"Do you want to sit down? Can I have them bring you something? Tea? Wine?"

"If, if, if they had just done what they were meant to do in Suddapal, this would never have had to happen. They knew. They knew what would happen, and they did it all the same. They rose up. And then I had to. Because of the farms and because of the fucking traditional fucking families in Borja pushing at Inentai, and because if I didn't do what I said, they would all be laughing at me. And I told them *I told them*."

"Geder. You're shouting. It will wake the baby."

Laughter pushed its way up out of his chest, rich and hot and mirthless. He sat on the divan, his head in his hands.

"I'm sorry," he said. "I shouldn't have raised my voice. I didn't mean to."

"I understand," Sabiha said, sitting across from him. Her back was straight as a tutor delivering a lecture. Her eyes were wary. Well, why shouldn't they be? He hadn't explained himself so much as popped his soul open and spilled it on the floor. He chuckled ruefully and shook his head.

"It should have been Jorey," he said. Sabiha stiffened. When she spoke, her voice was careful.

"What should have been Jorey, my lord?"

"He should have been regent. Not me. And more than that. The goddess should have chosen him. He's smart and strong and people like him. He's kind. No one laughs at Jorey. And he has you—"

Outside the window, the garden was dead from the cold and dark. Brown sticks and bare wood that would flower again when spring came. That was the promise. It was hard to see the promise of green in all the death.

"You see," Geder said, "I can't talk to Aster, because I'm supposed to be strong for him. I can't talk to my father, because he thinks I'm doing well. And Basrahip...I don't know what he'd say. What he'd do. I know that everything is happening as it should. The rise of the temples. The voice of the goddess driving back the Timzinae and their plots. The world's becoming pure again. Maybe not even *again*. Maybe for the first time. I know that's all true. And so when I feel..." He lifted his hands, words failing.

"You're...upset," Sabiha said. There was a buzz in her voice. A roughness that he could hear her struggling against. "You ordered and oversaw the deaths of hundreds of captive children. And you've come to me for comfort because you're upset?"

"Yes," Geder said, gratified that she'd understood him

despite his rambling. "I was chosen, you know? I am the light that brought her back to the world after her exile. That's me. I'm making the world better, and everyone knows. I'm the most important man, maybe in the whole world. I know that what we're doing is right. I know that I've helped, that I keep helping. How can anyone do this much good, help the world into light as much as I have, and feel...like this?"

"I...I don't know what to tell you," Sabiha said.

"That's all right," Geder said softly. "It helps just to say it to a friend. I'd have bothered Jorey with it if he were here. Maybe I will when he comes back. Do you think he'd mind?"

"I can't imagine," Sabiha said. She shook her head slightly. He didn't think she knew she'd done it. What he must look like to her. The greatest man in the empire, the power of life and death in his hand, weeping on her couch over nothing. Over a feeling he couldn't even put words to. He tugged at his sleeve and dried his eyes.

"To be so sad," he said, "when there's no reason for it. I'm only afraid that...Ah, Sabiha. I can tell you this because I know you won't laugh. I think there might be something *wrong* with me."

Cithrin

Cithrin wasn't there when Inys killed the guardsman. Her understanding of it grew first from the mixture of rumor and report, gossip and speculation that followed the unexpected violence the way thunder follows lightning.

It happened the day after Inys's return from the south. Cithrin had meant to have one of her usual conversations with the dragon, but freezing rain and a set of queries from the scribes had distracted her. Inys had taken shelter in a covered amphitheater, and for reasons no one knew and likely no one ever would, one of King Tracian's guardsmen took exception to the choice. To call it a confrontation would have been generous. The guard had approached the dragon, calling Inys by name, and told him to find another resting place. Inys had gutted the man, eaten the corpse, and fallen back asleep.

All those facts were agreed upon. It was the interpretations of them that spread out like feathers on a wing. The guardsman had been drunk or embarrassed after having been dressed down by his commander or goaded into rash action by his friends. The dragon had warned him or it hadn't. King Tracian was enraged and preparing to act against Inys or he approved of the dragon's actions. There was even the suggestion—taken more seriously than it deserved—that the guardsman had been the secret lover of a noble lady at court, and the dragon had slaughtered him as a sign of favor to the cuckolded husband.

Only a few seemed alarmed that the huge, intelligent predator that had taken residence in Carse had begun killing. It was a dragon, glorious and powerful. The populace at large seemed willing to assume that whatever it had done was justified by the mere fact that a dragon had done it.

Komme Medean and King Tracian were in the minority that did care what had happened and why. Even then, Cithrin had the sense that it was more a matter of tactics in the war than an issue of justice. Law for dragons, as for kings, was less about abiding by rules than the making of them. It was a distinction she hadn't considered before she'd starting making laws of her own. That she kept such company—that they were in some ways her peers—left her feeling uneasy, but not so much that she resorted to the bottle. Or, anyway, not more than usual.

Inys arrived at his usual time. Rain and clouds had blown away, leaving a clean blue sky from which the dragon descended. Cithrin sat in the courtyard of the holding company, as she had before, a brazier glowing beside her and a dead lamb cooling on the winter-killed grass. She felt only a little more trepidation than usual. Inys folded his tattered wings and swallowed the animal. His breath was hot and acrid, the fumes stinging her eyes.

"So," the dragon said. "I have come again. Ask me what you will."

Cithrin pretended to consult her notebooks. All their conversations were there. The nature of the spiders, the history of the war, the strategies by which Inys suspected the enemy might be overcome. Many times their conversations veered widely from Cithrin's questions. She had pages of description of the small politics of the dragons' court, the composers Inys thought of note, the styles and fashions and vast projects that had been the great concern when humanity had still been tame.

She cleared her throat. "There was a man you killed. A guardsman of the king?"

"That," Inys said, and his deep, symphonic voice seemed thoughtful. "Yes, I've been thinking of that since it happened."

"You have?"

"You sound surprised. Yes, I have thought on it. It was badly done, and I should not have. And so I have been thinking on why I chose to do as I did. What it was that fouled my spirit and led me to act improperly. I think it was the loss of the Stormcrow."

"You mean Marcus?"

"The burden of the empty world," Inys said, canting a huge black eye toward the sun. "Every day I smell the air and taste the water, hoping for some sign of another, but there is nothing. I am alone. Profoundly. Completely."

"Except for us," Cithrin said, but it was like she hadn't spoken.

"To be so set apart. So isolated. It was one of the greatest punishments that could be leveled against us, and it is the one to which I've consigned myself. The feelings I have can find no outlet, and so I begin to bond with them. And the Stormcrow most of all. It's sentiment. Nothing but sentiment. But I feel his absence, and it stands in for all the other absences."

"Them?"

"What are you asking me?"

"You begin to bond with them? Who do you mean, 'them'?"

"You," Inys said. "The slave races. I shouldn't have eaten the one. It was bad form. I wasn't even hungry. And if I do not police myself in these small things, how will I preserve my mind from the large ones? The path from trivial misstep to losing myself utterly is short and broad."

"Trivial," Cithrin said. She hadn't meant to.

"I am the only hope for the resurrection of the world. Everything depends on me. On my holding my mind in place. But I am ashamed, and I am humiliated."

And you are enjoying it entirely too much, Marcus Wester said in Cithrin's imagination. She wondered if she said the words aloud whether Inys would laugh or destroy her as he had the guard. Better, she thought, not to answer that question.

"The spiders," she said. "Was there any pattern to how the conflicts between them first spread? A distance between them that allowed disagreements to take hold? A number of people? The time they were separated from each other?"

"Not that I know," Inys said. "It was unimportant to me at the time. The slaves were corrupted, and the corrupted were of no use. We culled the tainted and kept the pure. The only pattern, so called, was the frenzy they fell into when that which they believed and that with which another confronted them would collide. To hear another voice say something offensive to their sense of the world and also know that the other was not lying? To be faced by the fact of their error called forth a rage like no other."

"That's not the spiders," Cithrin said. "That's people."

"It was the bent scale in your minds where Morade put his claw," Inys said. "It is how he destroyed you."

"How he destroyed all of us."

"No, just you," Inys said. "I destroyed the rest."

*   *   *

What I hear," King Tracian said, "is that the dragon can't be depended upon. Yes, if it's a bright day and he's in a sunny mood. Or if Wester is here to goad him into it. But I think we can all see that Inys cannot be commanded. Can that be agreed?"

The meeting room, while it was in the palace, wasn't the one Cithrin had first seen. This had a fire pit in its center worked in iron, silk upholstered chairs, and lanterns of crystal lit not with flame but by some cunning man's trick that more nearly seemed like sunlight. The tapestries on the walls were designs of blue and red and gold as deeply saturated as if they'd just come from the dyer's yards, though they were likely centuries old. Komme Medean, sitting near the fire in robes of simple brown, nodded. Tracian's master-at-arms— a thin-faced man called Lord Fish though that wasn't his name—hoisted an eyebrow and waited.

"I think that can be agreed," Komme said, "at least provisionally. Inys can be negotiated with—"

"And if he breaks his word, what punishment are we going to place against him?" Tracian said. "Put him in the stocks? Fine him? Stop giving him food and drink?"

"Dealing with great power does limit our options," Komme said. From Tracian's nod, Cithrin thought she was the only one who'd heard the mordant humor in the words.

"And so we need to have something else on our side," the king said. "I've been in conversation with Birancour. The ambassador of the queen."

Komme looked up, his expression bland but his eyes suddenly sharp. "Sir Brendis Sarreau? I didn't know he'd come to the city."

"Come and gone," Tracian said lightly, but Cithrin heard the pleasure in his voice. Diplomats and statesmen speak, of course, to the throne. Not the bankers. So Tracian was beginning to understand the deeper price that came with the gold he'd taken. That was a shame. She'd hoped to have a few years at least before that happened.

"A wise man," Komme said. "Deep thinker. Have you met him, Cithrin? No? Well, I'm sure you will. What did the ambassador have to suggest?"

"An expansion of what we already have. Tamed spider priests of our own to counteract the others. Men like your Master Kit who can use Morade's weapon against Antea and its false goddess." Tracian smiled and made a wide, sweeping gesture as if he were displaying a fine piece of art. "We've already seen that we need the man in more places than one. We needed him here to safeguard the court. They need him with the Lord Marshal's army to see that it retreats. How many other places would men like him be of use? We could send them to Borja and Hallskar. Cabral. You have your papers, but how much more convincing would demonstrations be? Our tame priests standing before every court in the world, explaining how the whole thing works, how it can be fought against. Your public letters are fine, I don't dispute that. But if they heard the truth from one of our Master Kits—"

"They wouldn't be able to disbelieve it," the master-at-arms said. "They'd *have* to believe."

The knot in Cithrin's gut tightened. Komme stroked his beard and looked into her eyes. His silence was a warning. She took her lower lip between her teeth and bit to keep herself from speaking. Komme had lived his whole life in Northcoast. He knew King Tracian better than she could. She had to trust the old banker to see the world she did, and the dangers it held.

"It's an interesting thought," Komme said. "How far have you gone with it?"

"Porte Oliva will be retaken eventually. The queen has plans in place," Tracian said. It wasn't a direct answer, but Cithrin understood. If Kit didn't return or didn't agree, there were other priests. If Komme and Cithrin objected, there would be other opportunities to find the corrupted blood and use it. She took a salted nut from the silver plate before her but couldn't bring herself to eat it. Anything close to hunger she might have had before was drowned by her quiet alarm.

"Well, it will be interesting to see what the queen does with her new agents," Komme said, leaning back. "I can certainly see how it would help with the immediate issue, but I wonder how we would convince Birancour to put that sword down once they'd picked it up."

"We might not," Tracian said. "All tools are dangerous when they're misused. Properly controlled, though, these may be a blessing."

"Perhaps," Komme said. "Perhaps."

After the meeting ended, Cithrin and Komme rode back toward the holding company in a carriage. The sky was dark, and the streets frigid. Shuttered windows glimmered at their edges, the light of lanterns and fires slipping out into the night. Otherwise the streets were only moonlight and stars. Cithrin huddled into a wool blanket, but Komme sat in his shirt and jacket, his eyes on the passing buildings.

"It's a terrible plan," she said. "He can't do it."

"I know," Komme said. "He won't. But we can't tell him not to. He's the king. Informing men on thrones of what you will and will not permit them to do...Well, people juggle knives too. The danger's what makes the sport interesting. If we weren't already doing what he proposes, it would be an easier argument to make."

"You mean Kit."

"These spiders," Komme said. "They're meant to drive us against each other, yes? Factions within factions, all with their own particular priests leading the way. Maybe by standing at a pulpit, maybe by whispering in the right ears at the right time. With your actor fellow, we fit that description."

"Kit's different," Cithrin said.

"You're sure of that?"

"I am."

"Tracian's not. Others may not be. And even if Master Kit is unlike the others, that's an argument that they can be tamed. Used by forces of good to bring victory to the righteous." Cithrin's short, choked laugh brought a wry smile to Komme's lips. "Yes," he said. "I know."

"Even if they destroyed all the corrupted that believed in the goddess, it would be a season before Birancour and Northcoast were at each others' throats over something else. They wouldn't even recognize that it was happening."

"I agree," Komme said. "Give him a few days to think he's won. I'll write him a letter explaining that the holding company has no objection, but the voices of the branches would feel uncomfortable setting business under a crown that uses the spiders. I'll send a copy to Sir Brendis. It'll be a carrot to Birancour, since it suggests we would be open to expanding this war gold scheme to them, and a threat to Tracian that we might pull it back."

The carriage shuddered across a length of bad paving, the wheels rapping the stones like an assault. Komme put his hand on the door until the roughness passed.

"Will he see the danger in that?" Cithrin asked.

"I don't know. He might not. Not yet. It's all still a novelty. Once people are used to it—once they've lost the memory of coins—we'll have more leverage. It's like going down a steep hill in a sled. It'd be easier to steer if it weren't all going so quickly. But this is how quickly it's going, so we'd best do what we can."

The old man sighed and lapsed into silence. Cithrin sat back. The winter cold pressed at her. In Porte Oliva or Vanai, the cities she'd lost, the nights never grew cold the way they did in Northcoast. Carse's winter was vicious and long and cold. But more than the chill and darkness, she dreaded the winter's end. As long as the fighting had stopped, there was hope that she could end it. That the chance wouldn't fall outside her reach. The sound of another cart came from the street and then faded away.

"I was naïve," she said.

"Everyone is at the start," Komme said mildly. "Were you thinking of something in particular?"

"The public letters. I thought that by telling people what they were, the world would rise up against them."

"That if you told them the truth, they would thank you and see things as you do?" Komme said. "Yes, that was naïve. It's a forgivable error, though."

"Only if I can correct it," she said. "Inys didn't mean to slaughter the world when he upset his brother. He didn't see the end his actions would take him to either. If the stakes are everything, no errors are forgivable. We have to be better than that."

"So be wiser than dragons?" Komme said. "Don't let it be said you aim low."

"Dragons aren't wise. They're only powerful and noble and impressive to the people they fashioned to be easily impressed."

"True," Komme said as the carriage shifted and slowed. The gate of the holding company passed the window, and the voices of the grooms and guards and footmen rang out in the dark. Torches flared, and boots tapped against the paving stones. The carriage lurched to a halt, and the door swung open. Two servants stood ready to help them out, but Komme Medean hadn't moved. His eyes were on Cithrin, glittering in the light as if the fire were in him. His expression was grim and considering. "So how do you win this war? More hunters? More fighters? More public letters exhorting people to take your side?"

No, she wanted to say. It was in her mouth. She could taste the word. Komme lifted his eyebrows, and for a moment, she was a child again, sitting at Magister Imaniel's table, peppered with his questions. Trying to show that she was clever enough to be loved.

"In part," she said. "Gathering new allies is part of what we can do, even though they may not all do quite as we'd hoped. That part wasn't wrong. It was only incomplete."

The servant at the door cleared his throat and leaned in. "Sir, is there something—"

Komme lifted his hand sharply, and the man went silent. "Go on," Komme said.

"It's a war, but it's also a marketplace. I have to have something better than the people at the next table and at the right price."

"Lower price?"

"Perhaps. Unless costing more makes it seem more to be valued."

"And what is it you're selling? Peace? Been a long line of clever people who couldn't clear that inventory."

"Not at first. No. I'm selling dead spiders. As long as their death is worth more to the world than the advantage they give, I won't need to pull anyone to my side. They'll find their own reasons."

"And how do you do that?"

Cithrin was silent for a long time. The torches muttered. The grooms unhitched the horses. Cithrin felt her mind grow still, the knot in her belly loosen. "What do kings want more than power?" she asked.

"Find that, my dear," Komme said, "and we'll have something worth knowing. Because in my experience, the answer's *nothing.*"

Marcus

Marcus went on campaign the first time when he was sixteen. His first sword had been a thin blade, meant for close, dirty work. Even pretending he'd never carried a knife until that day, he'd spent more of his life armed than not. He'd taken the field in the ice-caked springs of Northcoast and the kiln-hot summers of the Keshet. He'd commanded men and been under the command of generals and doges, princes and kings. He'd wintered in the most libertine of the Free Cities and the most pious garrisons of Herez.

Long experience told him that an army camp had its own logic, its own form, its own character unlike that of any township or hunter's encampment. Even without setting foot in it, Marcus knew quite a bit about the Anteans'. He couldn't have said where exactly the tents of the camp followers were, where the dice games were played, who was the company prig and who the joker, who was undercutting which commander when his superiors weren't about. He knew that they all existed, though. It was only a matter of finding the specifics.

And then, of course, the priests. They had to be found and followed. Once he understood just a bit of their role in the geography of the army, he'd be able to make the plan that the Lord Marshal of Antea and Cithrin bel Sarcour both wanted of him. Along with that, there were other things he was looking at and looking for. Signs and indications, patterns and systems. And again, he knew that they would be there before he knew what they were.

And all the things he saw drew him to the same basic conclusion: Antea, after the most successful and extended campaign he'd heard of outside legend, had destroyed itself.

Part of the blame—though he wouldn't have said it aloud—lay at Jorey Kalliam's feet. The boy seemed smart, competent, even well enough read in the theory of leading an army. But he was also little more than a boy, and his mistakes were the mistakes of inexperience. It was possible to hold a small army in the field all through the winter if there was no other option, but this was the bulk of Antea's fighting force. Even with supply carts coming up from Porte Oliva in the south and water and occasional fish from the little creek that ran through the camp, it was too large to sustain itself. The weariness and hunger of the soldiers made them look like he could push them over with a breath. And the Lord Marshal hadn't kept discipline in digging the latrines. The frozen ground would make it hell's own work, true. And shit left out in the cold of the little ravine beside the camp froze. It was easier to let it lie there in piles. After all it didn't stink. They'd pay for it all when the thaw came, though. First in flies and then in fever.

The placement of the tents said something as well. Cliques were forming among the men. Maybe they'd been there from the start, but the camp wasn't a unified whole. It was a network of camps centered around Kalliam's subject lords and sharing a few common resources: the cunning men's tents, the practice yard, the priests' tent. Far better to keep the men from fragmenting, especially when they had so many other reasons to be primed for mutiny. If it had been a smaller army—the command of a new leader who was himself answering to some greater lord—it would have been serviceable. Respectable, even. But as the central force of a great empire, it looked like something that the Lord Regent had awarded a young friend instead of an experienced commander.

Which, in fact, it was. If not for the priests, the whole thing would have fallen into chaos long before.

"He's a good man," the young huntsman said. Vincen Coe, Lady Kalliam had called him. Her conspirator and servant. And, since he'd followed the army only from the Free Cities and not trekked with it all the way through Sarakal and Elassae first, he was about half again the weight of the average Antean soldier. All in all, not a bad ally to have. "Jorey's men like him."

"They're told to," Marcus said. "If he didn't have this dragon's trick on his side, it'd go harder for him. And I didn't say he was a bad person. I said he was an inexperienced war leader."

"He took down your dragon," Coe said.

"Once," Marcus said. "That's the problem with a maneuver like that. It works best the first time."

Coe shrugged. The man seemed to take any criticism of House Kalliam personally. Either doglike loyalty or the natural distrust of a servant for anyone who might take his place in the household. Either way, Marcus made the point to himself again not to bait the man without meaning to.

The three of them—Marcus and Coe and Kit—had set up tents in the gap between two of the larger factions within the camp. It was an unpleasant piece of land. The siege towers and machinery that had brought down the dragon sat to the east, white with frost. Come morning, their tent would be in shadow until the sun was five or six hands above the horizon. The curve of the low hills seemed to channel the wind to it, and the heat from their sad, underfed little fire didn't do much against it.

Marcus wouldn't have chosen the spot, but in four of the

past five days, the spider priests had crossed this way on their rounds. Marcus's first hope had been that the priests would sleep far enough from the others that he could take them in the night. But the enemy was in the center of the most concentrated group of soldiers, and so the second plan was this. Find a place along their customary route, distract them, and then kill them fast enough that no one noticed.

The middle of an army was a poor place for an assassination. His only comfort was that, once it was finished, the Lord Marshal would be able to help cover the thing over. If he'd been trying to escape after, it would have been harder.

Not impossible, but harder.

Voices came from the neighboring camp. The chatter of the men, but above them, trumpeting in rough tones, the priests. Vincen Coe had helped them stay out of the priests' immediate path while Marcus made his plan. Even now, he hadn't come close enough to see them as anything but dusty cloaks. They spoke like actors from a stage, filling the camp with their words. *We cannot fail. The goddess is with us. All enemies will fall before us. We cannot fail.* It didn't work if the soldiers didn't hear it, and they shouted it all wherever they went.

For all that he knew it was hairwash and deception, Marcus found himself wondering when he heard them. When they said *We cannot fail*, the soldiers all took it as a promise of Antean victory. Marcus knew more, and the words meant other things to him. The war will never stop. There are too many of us already, and scattered too far across the world. The chaos will come, and nothing will stop it. Put in those terms, their argument seemed convincing. And he thought it would have even if it hadn't come with Morade's cruel magic to back it.

The others heard it too. Coe's face took on a clarity and

focus like a hunter on a trail. Kit folded his arms together. The lines at the corners of his mouth drew deeper.

"You all right?" Marcus asked.

"Fine," he said. "It's only…I can feel them. Like little rivers of pain in my flesh. I hear them say that the goddess is with us. The truth of that is in their voices, and yet that it's false is something I'm sure of. The two come together, and it's…" Kit shook his head. "I find it difficult to fully describe."

"Are they going to be able to feel your presence too?" Coe asked.

"I think not. My experience is that the spiders have an affinity for one another, but I expect each of them will assume any sense of my presence is inspired by the other. Unless they hear me speak. When that happens…"

"It'll be close to the end," Marcus said. "May not even need it."

The voices of the priests grew louder, and then stopped. Their visit to the neighboring camp was ended. If the previous two days were a guide, they'd cross the empty space near Marcus's tent on the way to the next little camp. The poisoned sword lay beside the fire, the scabbard covered by dirt, the hilt by a bit of cloth. Kit met Marcus's gaze, nodded, and moved into the darkness within the little tent. Vincen stood, stretched, and ambled off toward the frost-rimed bulk of the siege towers. Marcus understood the man had been badly injured earlier in the season, but there was no sign of it in how he held himself. There had been a time when Marcus had healed that quickly too, but it hadn't been in the last decade. Or since he'd started carrying this thrice-damned sword, for that.

The two men appeared, walking together. The cold breeze pushed their brown cloaks against their bodies. They had wiry hair not unlike Kit's, and skin of a similar cast. Mostly, though, they were just a pair of Firstblood men. If he'd seen them sitting together at an inn anyplace from Daun to Stollbourne, he'd have thought them cousins and ended there.

Marcus shifted from sitting to a low squat. One hand rested on the hilt of the hidden blade. Two men, unsuspecting. He saw them notice him. From their smiles and nods, he was nothing more than another soldier to them. The plan was simple. Draw them to his fire, have Coe distract them, then cut them down. Two quick cuts, and then let the blade's toxic magic finish the rest. And if things went poorly, hope that Kit could pull him out of it.

Now he just had to see it work in practice.

"Afternoon," Marcus said, loud enough for it to carry. "How are you two doing?"

"Well," the taller of the two said. "The goddess blesses us with this beautiful day."

"If you say," Marcus said. They hadn't broken stride. A single tent apparently wasn't draw enough for their time. "You're priests then? I saw another like you not long ago. Up in Northcoast, it was. Eshau, he called himself."

Their steps faltered. Marcus poked at the little fire, bringing up a cloud of tiny sparks. It was the truth. Marcus had seen the man die in dragon flame. Now, Eshau was an unpleasant memory and bait for the hook. And bless the man, he did his job.

The two priests came to stand by the fire, looking down at Marcus. The shorter of the two had a chipped front tooth. The taller, a scar on the back of his wrist. Marcus smiled up at them, his fingertips brushing the hilt under its cloth.

"You knew Eshau?" the taller one said.

"That'd be an exaggeration," Marcus said. "I met him once. He was up looking to speak with King Tracian. All on about how your Basrahip fellow had become corrupt and the goddess was incorruptible, and everyone should raise up an army against you and Antea and revel in the light of her truth. Something along those lines."

They exchanged alarmed glances. Marcus smiled vacantly up at them, making himself seem innocuous and a little dim. It was a mistake to think you couldn't mislead the spiders. You just couldn't lie outright to do it. There was and always had been a gap wide enough to march a cohort through between speaking truth and being understood.

Coe whistled sharply from behind them, and they glanced back. Marcus grabbed the hilt and moved forward, using the weight of his body to unsheathe the blade and swing it. The tall one was turning back to him when the blade took him in the side, just under the ribs, cutting up. The priest's eyes went wide, and Marcus yanked the sword back to free it. The shorter priest yelped with alarm, and the taller one grabbed the blade in his bare hands, encumbering it, holding it in his own gut. The blood pouring down his belly was lumpy and black. The spiders already dead from the venom of the blade.

Marcus pulled again, slicing deep into the meat of the tall priest's palms, but he couldn't get the blade free. The shorter priest stumbled back, turned. Coe was near him, a long knife in his hand.

"No!" Marcus said. "Don't cut him! Don't get close!"

Marcus planted his boot on the tall priest's chest and shoved. The blade slid free. White foam mixed with his blood now. The dying man collapsed into the fire pit, but Marcus was already running across the frozen field. The short priest, ahead of him, was shouting a gabble of words he couldn't follow and pumping his legs. Marcus put his head down and ran. The poisoned sword was long, and poorly balanced for sprinting. The priest opened the distance between them and closed the one to the nearest camp and the soldiers of Antea. A glance showed Marcus half a dozen men in imperial clothes who'd already noticed them, but hadn't started toward the fray.

That wouldn't last. And he wasn't catching up. For every four steps he took, the priest managed five. The cold stung Marcus's lungs. He fought not to cough. The Antean tents came closer. A couple of men were running out toward them, coming to the rescue of the disease that was killing them. Marcus pushed his awareness of them aside, his gaze on the shifting brown cloak in front of him. Nothing else mattered.

Something flickered to his left, and the priest stumbled. Fell. The hunter's knife, thrown from God knew how far, protruded from the priest's thigh like a bone in a bad break. Tiny black bodies skittered across the frozen ground, the chill already slowing them. The priest looked up, his hand raised as if to parry, as Marcus brought down the blade. He sheared through the man's wrist, sank the point of the green-black sword into his chest. The fumes from the blade wafted up into Marcus's face, astringent and cutting. The priest cried out once, then blood gushed from his mouth. Blood and other things: the bodies of spiders and the white foam of the poison.

Marcus stepped back, pulling the blade free. The soldiers were crying out in dismay and anger, their voices close. He looked up. Five of them in the first wave. Maybe twenty more behind those. They looked like sticks rattling in too-wide jackets. Scarecrows with the stuffing picked out for nests. They held their swords smartly enough, though.

Marcus lifted the blade, breathing between clenched teeth. He could try outrunning them. Might even manage it, given how near starvation they all were.

"Stop!" Kit's voice rolled across the frozen earth. "In the name of the goddess and empire, put up your swords!"

The first five didn't put up their blades, but their charge lost its speed. Marcus took a couple of slow steps back and risked a glance over his shoulder. Kit was a few yards behind him, arms lifted wide, face beaming in a wide grin. He looked joyful. Marcus rolled his eyes.

Actors.

"Do not be alarmed! Put your confusion aside, and rejoice! I have come as your liberator and savior! I am Kitap rol Keshmet, sent by the goddess to free you from the bonds of these false servants. Put up your swords, my friends, and let us be merry! Those who brought false words of the goddess, who kept you from the full truth, who pretended to guide you to victory, have fallen beneath my righteous blade!"

"Fuck is this?" one of the soldiers shouted. The second wave was catching up to the first, surrounding them. There was no running to safety now, but seeing as they hadn't butchered Marcus or Kit or Coe, there were also ways it could have been worse.

Kit came to Marcus's side, put a hand on his shoulder. Marcus lowered the point of the blade and tried to seem like Kit's righteous servant. If it came down to blows now, they were likely all dead anyway.

"Have you not wondered, my friends, why victory has been so slow to come? Have you not wondered why, for all your good work and sacrifice, the goddess has withheld the comforts of home? I bring good news and more than good news. The peace you deserve is upon you! You have been misled by those who would use the gifts of the goddess against her, but she has seen *your* faith. And she keeps her faith now with you. Put up your swords and rejoice. I am Kitap rol Keshmet, and I have come as the true voice of the goddess to lead you home!"

Marcus knew the trick, knew that Kit was spinning a tale, but he felt the pull of it all the same. Perhaps because it was half-true. These men had been tricked. Had been held in a kind of dream of noble warfare, of honorable slaughter.

Coe snuck through the crowd with the green scabbard, and Marcus put away the blade. The soldiers around them shuffled, uncertain. There was still rage in some of their faces, but confusion was growing in others. And in a few—maybe two, maybe three—something that looked like hope. Or possibly relief.

"I see your doubt, and I forgive it. From so deep a sleep, you must take a moment to wake, yes? So come, my friends!" Kit shouted, waving his arm in a well-practiced arc. "To the tent of the Lord Marshal! Where all shall be made clear!"

A rough shout came up from the soldiers, halfway between cheer and threat. More of the soldiers were streaming in now, coming from camps in all directions. Even a half dozen from the siege towers that Marcus hadn't known were guarded. They moved as Kit moved, following him toward Jorey Kalliam and confirmation that what Kit said was true. Which, of course, it wasn't.

"Well," Coe said, "this is interesting."

"Not quite how I'd pictured it," Marcus said. "But I figure it'll do for now."

"Should confuse the hell out of Camnipol when the news gets there."

"Might, might not," Marcus said. "With any luck, we'll be the ones to bring it."

"Then what happens?"

"We defeat the idea of war itself and end this whole thing gracefully. That's honestly the plan."

Coe was silent for a few seconds. "I don't understand."

"Neither do I, friend. Neither do I."

Clara

People of high status in the court were, of course, made of the same flesh and bone as anybody else, and hence died as often. The fact of bodily mortality had never been hidden from Clara. By the time she first witnessed someone entering the last days of their life, she was perfectly clear on what was happening. Still it had come as a shock.

Cerria Pintillien had been an aunt on her mother's side, and Clara had been eight when she died. Her memories of Cerria before the illness were vague. She was a sort of thick-faced presence in the background of Clara's childhood home. A deep, almost braying laughter, a sense of judgmental intelligence, an image of almost comically wide hips negotiating a stairway. When Cerria contracted her final illness, it presented at first as a kind of beauty. She lost a great deal of the weight that had broadened her body and face, and her skin tightened and took on a strange sheen, like she'd been carved from wax.

Clara remembered vividly the murmurs of admiration among her mother's friends before the cause of this transformation was known. Those same tendencies—the thinning flesh, the tightening skin—were not, however, an *end*, but a *direction*. Cerria continued to shed the bulk of her flesh until her collarbones cast shadows of their own and her hands lost their strength. Her skin grew less supple and took on a yellow tone, like the fat skimmed off cold soup. There had been no praise for her beauty then. Cerria's last days had been spent in her solarium, sitting in the warmth, the skin stretched across her face like an artifact from a tanner's shop. A mask fitted upon a skull.

As Jorey's army broke its miserable camp and prepared to march through the brown fields of the Birancouri winter, Clara found herself thinking of Cerria. Not reflecting on her, or considering the philosophical implications of her aunt's passing, but suffering sudden, jolting visual memories. Had she been of a spiritual bent, she knew, she might have interpreted this as a ghost trying to reach her. In point of fact, it was only that so many of the soldiers had the same thinness and pallor, the same pain in their movements, the same sense of a body pushed until it was nearly used up.

And there was still the pass at Bellin to be negotiated. The prospect filled her with dread. So recently these same men had swarmed upon Porte Oliva, a conquering army strong enough to break the strength of dragons. They should have stayed there, in the south. They should have wintered in their captured city where ships could bring grain to the port and fishermen could harvest the seas to feed them. But Geder Palliako's pride had been hurt, and the inhuman voices of the priests had filled them with lies of invulnerability. They had pushed on, chasing Cithrin bel Sarcour until their strength had almost failed.

In place of food, they had gruel so thin it was more accurate to call it soup. The soldiers hunched over their bowls, empty gazes fixed on nothing in particular. She found it hard to remember that this was the largest part of Antea's armies. She kept wanting to think there was some other force—in Antea or Elassae or somewhere in the east—where the true strength of her nation lay. That the army that had laid waste to the world had been reduced to these wraiths seemed too terrible to be true. Certainly this could not be what victory looked like.

"Is something wrong, my lady?" Vincen said, and her heart gave its little leap as it did so often when he was involved. The little frisson was complicated—one part schoolgirl joy at her lover's presence, one part fear that she might somehow reveal their clandestine affair, and perhaps another part the deep frustration that there was nowhere she might conveniently and discreetly take the comfort from him that she craved. From his smile, she guessed that he saw it all in her. She lifted an eyebrow. Until such time as they were free of the army and the field, all their most important exchanges were reduced to such gestures.

"Nothing of importance," she said, answering his words rather then their deeper meaning. "I am a bit weary."

Vincen nodded. He had grown thinner since she'd left, though he had less of the emaciation of the other soldiers. He'd spent the time she'd been away recovering from his wounds, and that had meant a slightly less impoverished fodder than the hale and able-bodied among the troops. She shifted to the side, making room on the little shelf of stone she'd chosen for her seat. Vincen hesitated. To sit so near the woman he served would seem uncommonly like taking liberties. He was right, damn the man. Pressing her lips more tightly together, she moved back.

"I'd offer to fetch you better food," he said, "but I think the wait might be a long one. There's no good hunting before Asterilhold."

"It looks to be a long and unpleasant winter," she said, lifting another spoonful of gruel and then putting her bowl down uneaten.

Vincen hesitated. She could guess what he would say next.

He might have saved himself the effort. And yet. "It needn't be, ma'am. A small escort could take you someplace more comfortable."

"By which you mean safer?"

"And with decent food and a real bed."

"To sleep in?" Clara asked.

He looked around before answering. "That too."

Clara laughed. Hungry as she was, and tired besides, her laughter surprised her. It sounded like something that belonged to a stronger woman. "You are kind to suggest it," she said. "But no. I began this. I will see it through."

It was hard to tell. Long days in the field had darkened his skin, but she imagined he was blushing just a bit. He'd embarrassed himself to bring her a moment's amusement. She wondered whether the gratitude she felt for that might define love as well as anything else did. Part of it, perhaps, though love in general was a vague enough target that she might not be able to define it in any consistent or useful way, had anyone occasion to ask.

"It's odd, don't you think," she said, "how a word can seem so very clear until one gets close, and then it all goes as solid as fog?"

"Such as?" Vincen said. She could still hear the trailing mischievousness in his voice. She didn't think before she answered.

"Love."

He went very still, and she realized what she'd said. Where she'd said it. She looked up at him. There were tears in his eyes, and in hers as well. If they won this war, how long would she be able to draw out this utterly inappropriate alliance? How long before she was forced back into the ill-fitting chair of Lady Clara Kalliam, Dowager Duchess of whatever holding Geder, or perhaps Aster, saw fit to bestow on Jorey? Or perhaps the empire would fall into chaos, and she would live her life as Lady Nothing of Nowhere. Vincen's heartbroken eyes made that last seem the grandest title imaginable.

"I was speaking of love," she said.

Their progress was slow and painful. Her short time in the field following the army from the Free Cities to Porte Oliva had taught her something about the movement of a military force. She had walked in the swaths they cut through the flesh of the land. The ruin they left behind them now seemed less only because the land around them already felt dead, a landscape of dry grass and old snow and crows. There were few horses left. She suspected that most had been eaten.

They rose before dawn, often to the cajoling and hectoring of Wester's actor-priest. He walked through the tents with assurances and broad smiles, much as his predecessors had. The soldiers took comfort in the words—*All will be well, you will see your homes again soon enough, your efforts shall meet great reward*—and that gave them strength enough to pack their things another time, walk for another day. Or often it did. Two men had died in their sleep since they'd broken camp, exhausted beyond their ability to wake.

When he was not spreading cheerful lies, the old actor walked alone, his eyes shadowed. Clara understood the price that Captain Wester paid for carrying his poisoned sword, and it struck her more than once that Master Kit bore a similar burden. She recalled all the times she'd lied to her own children: promising Vicarian that his favorite toy would be found, telling Elisia that her fever would break the next day. Caring for the innocent wounded involved a surprising amount of deceit, and she could not keep from thinking of the emaciated men staggering through the short winter days as innocent.

Yes, they had slaughtered Timzinae, razed towns, sacked cities. They had torn children from their homes and sent them as hostages to Camnipol. Jorey and his men had blackened the Antean Empire. She was aware of the senseless violence they had conducted in the name of the Severed Throne. But to see a thin face light with hope, to see them leaning on each other as they stumbled up one last hill before the sunset turned the red to grey, was also to give up her ability to stand judge over them.

They were soldiers, but many had been farmers before that. Crofters and merchants and huntsmen like Vincen. The highest among them were the sons of noble houses who should have been chasing stags through the wood, drinking and boasting and singing songs until morning rolled around again. It was as if fragility absolved them. Fragility and the knowledge that they had been betrayed by their kingdom.

Dawson would have loathed it all. The stupidity of the war, the pettiness of Palliako's vendetta against the banker girl, the failure of the nobility to tend to their vassals. Not that he would have cared for the men themselves. She hadn't romanticized him that much. He would have shaken his head at the winter-thinned army the way he would have at a dueling sword left un-cleaned after a fight. One took care of one's tools. Oiled one's swords. Saw to the well-being of those born too low to see to themselves. To do anything less was to not be fully adult.

Her own hips ached, and the cold and sun coarsened her skin. She slept without dreaming, the chill of the night and the black exhaustion in her body tugging her in opposite directions. By day, she rode with Jorey as often as she could, Captain Wester riding with them in the guise of her servant.

They fell into conversation, the two men, awkwardly at first, but as the days passed, they found a greater ease. Wester treated Jorey as Clara imagined he would any client who had hired him, with deference constrained by a brutal kind of honesty.

Yes, making a field camp in the north had been a mistake. If the army had stayed at Porte Oliva, it wouldn't be in such terrible conditions. No, there was no reliable path north that wouldn't cross the border into Northcoast, and even if there were, the days would be shorter and colder there. Better to take a longer southerly path. And avoid the Dry Wastes on the other side of the mountains. As terrible as the Birancouri plains were, the Dry Wastes would have killed them all faster. Jorey took the knowledge in, even the painful truth of his own missteps, with a student's focus. Under other circumstances, Clara imagined her son and the banker's mercenary might have been friends, though perhaps it was the desperation of the campaign that gave them common ground.

The mountains began as a thicker kind of haze to the east, a complication of the sunrise. Clara had expected them to loom up more quickly, especially once they'd found the jade strip of the dragon's road to smooth their passage. It was another three days before they reached the field where Antea and Birancour had faced one another in the previous year. A rude and dismal snow clung to the shadows, but the earth there was largely bare brown. She wondered at first who had come to bury all the spring's fallen bodies. It was only when they paused to make camp that she noticed the bones: a rib here, a knob of foot or knuckle there. The dead were still with them but scattered. Returning slowly to the ground, to be forgotten as so many generations before them had done.

She found Marcus Wester at the siege towers looking over the weapons that Geder had sent to destroy the dragon, and the captain's expression was oddly rueful.

"Evening, m'lady," he said as she approached, then he looked around to be sure there were no others close enough to overhear. "Do I need to come play the servant some more?"

"No," she said. "I was only wandering a bit before the sun went down and it got too cold to move about."

"Fair enough," he said. "Probably should have left these behind earlier, but I'd hoped the pass would be clear enough to take them. Some of them, at least."

The mountain pass that led up and to the east glowed like an ember in the falling sunlight. She wondered what it was about sunsets and dawns that made them so bloody. "How bad is it?"

"The trail? Bad enough."

"Impassable?"

"Won't know for certain until we've tried passing it, but I've seen it worse," Wester said, squinting up at the siege engines. "If there was a better option, I'd speak for it. Your son's scouts all agree that even Kit won't be able to talk these great bastards through. We'll have to abandon them."

"Should we destroy them, then?"

"Why would we?"

"It's something my late husband used to talk about. Ruining the things you leave behind so that the enemy can't make use of them."

"Assumes you know who the enemy is," Marcus said. "These things are only good against one target, and I'm not particularly concerned that Birancour will track Inys down and pull him out of the sky anytime soon."

"I suppose that's true," Clara said.

"Don't suppose the Lord Regent's made more of them?"

"I couldn't say. I'd left Camnipol before he made these," she said. And then, "I'm afraid that trekking back to Bellin may be the wrong thing."

Wester made a low assenting grunt, then tapped his palm against the tower's side and turned away. "Under other circumstances, I'd advise against it. Taking the pass in winter's a gamble at best, and long odds. Going south means food, warmth, shelter. But it also means more of the priests, and giving up on providing Antea anything like a garrison force. So there's your trade-off."

"Are we certain that a defense will be needed there?"

"Yes," Wester said. "And we'll need to get through before the weather gets warm."

"Before that?" Clara said. "And here I was lighting candles in hopes of a day that didn't freeze the water in the skins."

"Wouldn't hope for that," Marcus said. "If you're going to be the kind of reckless we're being, you want to do it in midwinter. The snow's not so fresh that it's all powder and it's not warm enough to thaw. Being buried by an avalanche...Well, it's our biggest risk after freezing or starving or getting caught in a storm. Still, it's something worth avoiding if we can. A long march in winter isn't a sign things have gone right."

"This is their second. Or is it third now?" Clara said. "This war feels as though it's been going on forever."

To her surprise, he laughed. "Well, count it as the fight between the dragons, and it has."

"It's too large, isn't it?" she said. "War. History. Each battle growing from the quarrels that came before and sowing the seeds of the ones that come after."

"I try not to think about it," Marcus said. "Getting these men through another day, and lining up a decent chance of the day after that's more than enough to keep me busy. All the rest will be there when we're past Bellin."

Something in his voice—some combination of mordant humor and compassion and despair—chimed in her breast. He would, she thought, do whatever he could to protect these soldiers from the dangers that lay before them. Though they were the enemy, though they would have killed him where he stood and her besides if they had known a little more of the truth. There was something both noble and doomed about it.

Perhaps she made some sound without realizing it, because Wester shot her a look, lifted a querying eyebrow.

"I admire your willingness to help with this," she said.

"It's the job."

For a moment, she thought he might say something more, but instead he spat, shoved his hands into the pockets of his jacket, and turned toward the tents. A colder breeze was coming from the north, not powerful enough to call a wind, but biting. It would be unpleasant if it kept up through the night. They walked together down the slope. Arrayed below them, the army camp looked less like the force that had brought the world to its knees than a collection of refugees at the mercy of the wide, uncaring sky. Wester's expression was calm. Peaceful, even. It was as if he found comfort in the absurdity of suffering. Perhaps he did.

The last rays of the falling sun painted them both in red, and the bone-strewn battlefield of the world as well.

Cithrin

Marcus Wester was gone. Master Kit was gone. Isadau was gone. Carse was the greatest city of Northcoast, and it still felt empty. Lonely. As many bodies packed the taprooms, as many dogs loped yapping through the streets, as many meetings with suppliers, debtors, mercenaries, and officials of the crown filled the day, and still she felt alone. It didn't help that Cary worked the troupe from the late, sluggish sunrise to the early twilight. Or that Yardem, love him though she did, seemed folded in his own thoughts. Or that Inys had fallen into a sulk that hadn't proven murderous again as yet, but might at any time. Cithrin woke in the morning feeling anxious and unmoored, worked through the day at whatever there was to be done, inventing tasks when there were none, and settled in at night with her fears and her ambitions and her wine.

Winter was passing. Every hour brought spring closer, and with it the fighting season. She felt it in her gut. The growing certainty that this was the last year, that if next winter found the banner of the spider goddess still flying in the temples of Porte Oliva and Camnipol and Nus, it would be too late. Like a glass grabbed for the instant it passed her reach, the world would shatter into war within war within war, forever. And for all she had done, for all she was doing, she still dreamed at night of trying to stop a river by pushing the water back with her hands.

There had been no word from Marcus or from Kit, which was either a blessing or a sign that their plan had gone wrong or both. Or neither. The companion to the pirate ship that had spirited Isadau to the south had turned back with word that the magistra had made it as far as the smugglers' coves at the edge of Herez. The treacherous passage around Birancour's southern coast had still been before her, and the long, swift run past the Free Cities—free now only in name, since fear of Antea left their ports too dangerous for landing.

The most recent word had been good, so Cithrin clung to it, but still she went to the taproom near Inys's field, and listened to the chatter of the people, the gossip, the lies and fabrications and half-formed hopes of a city as frightened and unsure as she was herself. And the singers—Mikel and Charlit Soon among them. And the fortune-tellers and jugglers—Cary and Sandr and Hornet as well as a different, less-practiced local bunch.

And she drank. More often than not, in the days of emptiness and absence, she found she drank with Barriath Kalliam.

"One time the freeze lasted so long we found a pod of the Drowned washed up on the beach," he said. "If you've never sailed the north in winter, you've never been cold."

"You seem to have a great many opinions on what I have and haven't felt," Cithrin said.

Their table wasn't theirs, except that they were sitting at it. It was long enough for a dozen, and six besides them shared the benches. The cook's boy brought low wooden devices more trough than platter filled with flatbread and pepper jam and cheeses that smelled like grass and summer. The others dropped coins on the table or in the boy's open hand and took out food to eat straight from the table. Cithrin lifted her cup, and the boy nodded. More cider would come when he had a moment.

Across the common room, Yardem Hane and Enen sat across a square board, both scowling at the low wooden markers. The fire in the grate popped now and then, scattering embers and the smell of cut wood. The wind that blew through the streets promised snow, and clouds hid moon and stars alike, and the bitterness of it made the taproom's warmth sweeter. When Cithrin said as much, Barriath laughed.

"I think you're talking about more than weather," he said.

"Oh do you?"

"Sure," the man said, leaning his elbows on the table and hunching toward her. "It's the same for everything, isn't it? Everything's more itself with a bit of contrast. All this?" He nodded at the room around them. "None of it would feel quite the same if the world weren't tearing at the seams. It'd just be a taproom in winter, and we'd all be here for the food and the drink and a way to kill a bit of the boredom until the sun came back. Instead, it's..."

The sentence stopped without ending. Cithrin followed his gaze, trying to see the room as he did. Men and women of half a dozen races, sharing warmth and bread and air. Outside, a dragon slept in the darkness, and beyond it, a city waited to find out whether it would be the next to face an invader's blades, and then war and the threat of war spilling out to the edges of all maps. Seen that way, it was hard not to imagine the spill of firelight as the last breath of clean air in a world of smoke and fire. Barriath sighed and brushed the back of his hand wearily across his eyes.

He had changed since Lady Kalliam had arrived. Or, no. That wasn't quite true. He had changed when she came, but he had also changed again when she left. He'd come to them, his navy at his back, a warrior and an unexpected ally. And he was that still, but also a man whose family faced danger without him. A man who'd seen his father killed before him. An exile from his home, wounded but unbroken. His gaze shifted to hers. A moment of confusion flickered in his eyes. A question.

"I was wondering who you would have been if none of this had happened," Cithrin said.

"Just another sailor hoping for Lord Skestinin's approval," Barriath said. "What about you?"

"I'd have been...I don't know. A girl in Vanai with a bit of money her parents left her and no clear work, I suppose. I could have managed a launderer's yard or some such."

"You'd have made a good yard manager," Barriath said. "In a better world."

Across the room, Yardem's ears perked up and he moved one of his tokens. Enen growled, the silver-grey pelt of her arms rippling as she shrugged her annoyance. The cook's boy brought Cithrin's cup of fresh cider, then hurried over to tend the fire. A Firstblood woman at the end of the table laughed and coughed and laughed again. The knot in Cithrin's belly—her constant companion—was looser now. The cider had a bite to it, and this was her fifth. Her mind was clear, though.

Barriath shifted on his bench. His fingers brushed against her arm as if by accident, but not by accident. Cithrin felt her blood go suddenly bright, her heart triple its pace, and for a moment she thought she was afraid. Then she turned to look at his wide, callused hand, again into the darkness of his eyes, and her body made it clear to her that it was not fear.

Oh, she thought. And then *How did I not see this coming?*

Barriath's smile was soft, neither apologetic nor gloating, but again with a question at its back. Cithrin's mind went suddenly blank. There was, she was certain, something she was supposed to do now, some way she was supposed to act.

She tried to imagine that she was Cary or Isadau or anyone other than herself. Anyone who knew what to do at moments like these. The best she could manage was the polite regard of the negotiating table. Barriath nodded as if she'd spoken, regret in his eyes but humor as well, and shifted his hand away. Her skin felt warm where he'd touched her, and she immediately wanted his fingers back where they'd been.

Oh by all gods ever, this is undignified work.

"I find I've grown a bit fatigued," she said, her voice crisp as frost. "It may be time that I retire for the evening."

"Of course, Magistra," he said. "Your company's been a pleasure. As always."

She looked to Yardem and then back to Barriath. Every movement she made seemed like the first performance of an amateur actor. Secret queen of the world, Komme called her, and she was awkward as a colt. "It seems my guard is busy. Would you be so kind as to walk me back to the holding company?"

She watched him understand, doubt his understanding, and then match her fragile formality. A particularly vivid and pleasant image intruded on her imagination and she pushed it away. "I would be happy to," he said. "Just give me a moment to . . . finish my cider?"

"Of course," she said, folding her arms.

Barriath took his cup and sipped from it twice, his gaze focused on the middle distance, his attention intense. Enen growled again, and Cithrin felt a sudden stab of fear. *Don't let their game be over. Please God, don't let them be done.* Barriath seemed to share her thought. He put down the cup and stood, offering her his arm.

"Shall we?" he said.

"Apparently," she replied, suddenly giddy. Barriath pressed his lips together and pretended not to know what she'd said.

As they walked to the door, she looked back at Yardem. The Tralgu's head was raised, his ears forward. His broad, canine face took her in and saw more than her. For a moment she was at the side of a frozen millpond south of Bellin, shouting down Marcus Wester for interrupting her moment with Sandr. Sandr who stood now not fifteen feet from her with the other players, and a world and a half away. But Yardem only shifted his soft brown eyes from her to Barriath and back to her before nodding and going back to his game.

Near dawn, Barriath finally slept. They'd made it as far as her rooms before their reserve entirely dissolved, and so it was her blankets and pillows that lay in ruins around him rather than his own. True to all he'd said of being proof against cold, he lay with his bare skin in the air, exposed and unashamed and at rest. Naked, he was lovely. No, not lovely. That wasn't the word. He was fascinating. Strong and vulnerable, a masculine animal at rest. Beautiful for a hard, curiously melancholy definition of beauty. If she'd known better how to draw, she'd have made a picture of him there.

For herself, she could no more sleep than shout down the moon. She sat by the fire grate, feeding in wood for the light more than the heat. Wrapped in a wool robe with a lining of raw silk, her body felt like it had been carved from warm butter. Nothing about her felt tense or tight or weighed down with fear. Not that anything had changed. Her fear was still there, but at a distance for the moment. It was like she'd taken a rib from her body and could consider it in the air, turning it one way and then the other without any discomfort or pain.

The aftermath of sex insulated her from herself, and it felt glorious. Better than wine even, although wine alone never risked getting a girl pregnant. Trade-offs. All the world was made from trade-offs.

The wind outside was picking up. Even through the shutters, she heard it hissing against the stones. There would be snow before midday. Or hail. Or freezing rain. It might give her a reason to cancel her meetings. Once Barriath had gone, she expected she would be able to sleep. And would need to. She pressed her fingertips to her lips idly, feeling the pleasant bruise.

She'd lain with men before now. Not Sandr, thankfully. But Qahuar Em, her rival in Porte Oliva. He'd been a kind lover in his fashion, but half the thrill of it had been that she was betraying him. She'd thought she was using her sex to distract him, and any lingering pleasure that had come from their time together was tainted by the humiliation that he'd known her plan all along. She'd played with bed and intrigue and been beaten.

And then, of course, Geder Palliako while Dawson Kalliam's insurrection had burned through the streets of Camnipol. He'd seemed so lost then, so much in need of comfort and care. During the days they'd spent in the darkness, hiding from the violence, he'd been powerless even over her. Granted, he'd still been a man of great power in the court, and there were risks in refusing gifts to kings. Had he insisted, she'd have been an idiot to refuse. Not that he was precisely a king, but a Lord Regent was near enough.

Neither adventure in the mysteries of physical love had left her longing to repeat the experience. Not shamed, though. She knew that girls did feel that way sometimes. Often, even. She felt stupid at having been outplayed by Qahuar and permanently unclean from having seen Geder for what he was afterward, but sex itself seemed...foolish? Messy? Undignified and pleasant and playful in roughly equal measures? Except she wasn't sure she had felt that way about it. Not before tonight.

She thought Isadau would be proud of her. Or if not proud outright, at least subterranianly pleased that she'd made a connection with a man without thinking of it in terms of a marketplace exchange. Barriath was the first man she'd taken for pleasure, without hope of profit or fear of loss.

Someday, she might even take a lover out of actual love. Stranger things had happened. In the grate, the ashes settled, glowing gold and red. She placed another log in among the coals and watched as it smoked and burst into flame.

Barriath's breath changed as he rose up from the depths of sleep, growing shallow and soft. He moved, his skin hushing across the cloth. She turned to watch him, and she enjoyed the sight. His slow smile graced her.

"What are you thinking, m'lady?" he asked.

About every man I've bedded that wasn't you seemed the wrong thing. She turned to the fire, the tongues of flame blackening the wood. "I'm wondering how you un-sow a field," she said.

Barriath shifted again, rose to sitting. The wind rattled the shutters, and he pulled a blanket across his shoulders. "I'm not a man of great fortune. But if...if there were to be a child, know that I would—"

Cithrin laughed without considering whether her laughter might be cruel. "No, not that field. Though thank you for the reassurance. No, I was thinking of the world. And the priests. Everything they've done with Antea has spread them across the kingdoms and cities like wheat in springtime. And if we don't gather them all up..."

"Well, you could take out the scarecrows."

"That was what I reached for. What I did. Sent out letters and bounties. Turned everyone I could reach into crows and sparrows in hopes they'd eat the seeds, but it turns out people aren't birds after all. Too many of them are going to look at the power the spiders have and see an opportunity for themselves. And we can't afford to let events teach them they're wrong. I want some way to call all the seeds back into the sowing sack, but I haven't got one."

"No one's going to try taking control of the priests," Barriath said. "It'd be like putting a harness on a wildfire."

"I know. You know. But when a king sees power, that's all he sees. And there's nothing a king wants more than power."

Something shifted at the back of her mind. Something attached to the words. *There's nothing a king wants more than power.* She went still, waiting for it like a cat on a riverbank watching for fish. It was there. It was there, just under the surface.

Barriath spoke. "I can't believe that—"

She lifted her hand. What had she just been thinking? Something about sex? No. Wait, yes. She'd been thinking of Geder. She put the two thoughts side by side like entries in a ledger. *There's nothing a king wants more than power.* Geder Palliako, hiding in the dust and dark with Prince Aster. Playing games, telling stories, making ill-considered and tentative love while the boy prince slept. Geder Palliako, the Lord Regent of Antea. Chosen of the goddess, who brought the priests from nowhere. The spiders' great leader and tool. If anyone alive still held power or influence over the priests, it was him.

But he was not a king. He would never be a *king* . . .

"He won't hurt Aster."

"What?" Barriath said.

She wasn't ready to say it, but if she didn't he'd just keep talking, so she tried. "Geder. He won't take power from

Aster. He won't...kill him and claim the Severed Throne for himself. Even though he could."

"I don't know that's true."

"You don't need to. I know it. That's enough. There are things Geder wants more than power."

"Are there?"

Jorey says I should be honest and gentle, and I want to be. Cithrin, I love you. I love you more than anyone I've ever known. That's what the letter said. He'd been telling her. All along he'd been *telling* her and she'd been so busy showing how unembarrassed and mature she was, how their physical liaison didn't define her, that she hadn't seen it until now.

"Love," Cithrin said. "He craves love."

"He can have it at the end of a sword," Barriath said, hotly. *Shut up*, Cithrin thought. *You're so much better when you're not interrupting me.*

Aloud, though: "You knew him from court. From before he was Lord Regent. Your brother served with him at Vanai. There must be people Geder loves?"

"You mean besides you?" Barriath said, laughter in his voice.

He reached out and touched her arm. He was a strong man. A Firstblood, with years of hard labor on the sea to thicken his shoulders and roughen his hands. He could have lifted her and tossed her out the window without opening the shutters first. She didn't know what he saw in her face, but whatever it was, he flinched back.

"Tell me who Geder Palliako loves," she said.

"I don't know," Barriath said, his voice diminished. "His only near family is a father."

"And how can I take control of *him*?"

Entr'acte: Porte Oliva

Vicarian Kalliam, priest of the goddess, sat on the seawall and looked out to the south. The winter sea below him was a deceptive blue that promised the warmth of midsummer. Kurrik sat at his side, legs folded under him, and looked out over the water as well. The paper cone of sugared almonds, they passed between them. At their backs, the salt quarter of Porte Oliva bustled and chattered to itself. A grey cat with notched ears slunk along the wall, caught sight of them, and dashed away. Vicarian watched it vanish among the shadows.

"It is beautiful, this sea," Kurrik said. His almost-but-not-quite-Kesheti accent clipped the words in strange places, like a familiar animal butchered into unfamiliar cuts. Vicarian understood the sense of them always, but found something new there as well.

"It's a gentler sea here than in the north," he said. "Clearer water too. If you go south from here along the coast of Lyoneia, there are islands in water so clear you can see down to the seabed. The Drowned call them Dead Islands. Nothing lives in the water there but seaweed. Not even oysters and clams."

"Why is this, do you think?"

"No idea," Vicarian said, pinching another almond between his fingers, then popping it into his mouth. "But it does seem the colder the water gets, the better it resembles soup."

"At the temple, we heard of the sea. I imagined it as a wide lake. This is better."

"It is," Vicarian said.

In his years studying to become a priest—the traditional role for the second son of a landed noble—Vicarian had participated in the mysteries of half a dozen of the more popular cults. He'd drunk wine and recited stanzas of the Puric Creed under the half-moon. He'd prayed to the empty chair that was the symbolic center of the Lissien Rite. For four long months, he'd fasted or eaten only flour paste and water until he'd found visions at the bottom of the secret Shoren Temple hidden deep in the caverns and ruins under Camnipol, though in fact the visions he'd suffered seemed as plausibly the results of starvation and sleeplessness as anything holy. For the greater part, the Antean court treated its religions much the way it did hunts or feasts or ceremonial balls. The stories of gods and goddesses, of the spirits of the wood and the water, were taken seriously by a few. Membership in the rites was more important by far than actual belief.

Vicarian had quite enjoyed it. It had felt at the time like a kind of pretend that none of them—or at least none of the smarter of them—took all that seriously. There were a few here and there for whom the creeds and rites meant something deeper, but so far as Vicarian could see, none of those ever displayed a power from the divine more impressive than a street-corner cunning man's. The philosophical disputations carried some actual pleasure, though.

He had spent countless hours sitting with his fellow novices, crawling through the knottier problems of living in a god-haunted world. Could the gods be mistaken? Were the figures in the various dogmas truly separate, or did they represent aspects of a single, unitary, wider faith? Was divine will discovered by prayer or created by it?

The long nights of disputation held an honored place in his memory, like running down the halls of his father's house with his brothers or climbing a very large tree at the corner of their garden that he wasn't supposed to climb. Innocent pleasures he'd indulged in joyfully, once when he was young.

The cult of the spider goddess was a very different thing. The clarity he knew now, the unveiling of the world and the souls of the people he spoke with, was subtler and more beautiful than the talents of the most talented cunning man. The coming age of purity promised a peace unlike anything the world had seen. He'd played for years at being holy without understanding what being holy was. Now he had achieved it.

Kurrik had been there from the start, tending to him and the other inductees in the temple at the top of the Kingspire. Whispering words of comfort and promise in those first difficult hours and days when the goddess's power was still new to him, when his blood had not yet finished changing from his own to hers. That he was in Porte Oliva now, tending to Jorey's conquest, felt like the goddess expressing her favor like an indulgent nurse letting him sneak a honeystone before bed.

"This is the Inner Sea, yes?" Kurrik asked.

"It depends on how you judge it, actually," Vicarian said. "Some captains say that the Inner Sea stops at Maccia and this is the Ocean Sea. Others call it the Inner Sea until you've lost all sight of shore and headed out on the blue water for Far Syramys."

Kurrik grunted, scooping up the last two almonds in his fingers and shaking his head. "Something is or it is not. So many names for the same water? It is a symptom of the world of lies."

"I understand it has something to do with port taxes," Vicarian said, chuckling. "So, yes, I suppose it is."

Kurrik smiled, balled the remaining paper into a wad the size of his thumb, and tossed it out over the wall. A seagull swooped in, plucked the pale dot out of the air, and sloped away again. Vicarian stood and held out his hand, helping draw his fellow priest up. The midday sun held a bit of warmth, and there was no snow, even in the alleys and corners. So deep in the winter, Camnipol would be encased in ice. Jorey and the army, still in the field, would be shivering in their boots. Feeling cold in Porte Oliva was a sign of decadence. And still, Vicarian did feel a little cold.

"Walk with me? Take off the chill?" he said.

"Always, brother," Kurrik said.

Vicarian had never been to Birancour before he came as its conqueror. He had no knowledge of Porte Oliva to use in making a comparison, but it seemed to him that for a fallen city, it was doing fairly well. Certainly the scars were there. Empty, soot-dark doorways where fires had gutted buildings during the sack. Gouges on the walls where arrows and bolts had chipped away the pale stucco. Street-corner carts where a girl might sell cups of sweet mash or strips of peppered meat that were empty now, the girls who'd stood them dead or fled. He'd heard for many years of the puppets of Porte Oliva, the public debates and competing performers. There were a few such now, but only a few.

As they strolled through the streets, their guard at a polite remove, Vicarian pulled his hands into his sleeves against the cold. The citizens—milk-pale Cinnae, otter-pelted Kurtadam, thick-featured Firstbloods—made way for them, and Vicarian couldn't say if it was out of respect or fear or whether the two had a great deal of difference between them now. There were, of course, no Timzinae.

After the sack, the roaches and enemies of the goddess had been rounded up. Some had been consigned to the yard of stocks and gallows that divided the palace from the newly reconsecrated temple of the goddess. Others had been weighted down and thrown into the bay. Some had burned. Vicarian supposed that to the uninitiated and unaware, it would have looked like monstrosity. It worried him, but only a little. With time, his voice and Kurrik's would bring the truth to them. Antea's invasion was the best thing that could have happened to them. They hadn't been beaten, but saved.

"Still no word from my brother," Vicarian said, though likely Kurrik was aware of the fact. Had some report come from the army, Vicarian would have blurted it out as soon as he'd met his friend and fellow priest that morning, not waited until now.

"Your former brother," Kurrik said, gently. "The Lord Marshal is not of our blood now."

Vicarian nodded, but only halfheartedly. He heard the truth in Kurrik's voice, the gift of the goddess, the certainty she brought. If he felt a bit sad to think of Jorey as no longer being his baby brother, it was a matter of language more than truth. "But you know what I mean," he said, gesturing with a sleeve-swallowed hand.

"Thanks be to her," Kurrik said. "All hidden things come to light through her."

They stepped into the wide, empty plaza that had once been the Grand Market, past the gouged-out socket that had once been a cafe where Cithrin bel Sarcour had held her unclean court. It was strange to think that she'd been here. She'd walked the same streets, eaten the cousins of these almonds, looked out over the endlessly changing bay. It rankled to have come so near to capturing her.

Nor was that precisely the only thing that rankled. From the burned stones of the square for almost two more close streets, he kept his peace. "You know, the use of the word *brother* really has changed since the goddess led you to the desert. You're right, of course, that the blessed of the goddess are my brothers since I took the vows, but Jorey is still the child of my same parents."

"That you misuse your voices is part of the impurity of the world," Kurrik said gently.

Vicarian grunted. Kurrik was correct, of course. If it hadn't been for the rhetorical reflexes built by his years of disputation, Vicarian would probably have let the matter drop. Probably.

"Whole languages have risen and fallen into disuse since you've left," he said. "And the goddess's word is true in all those languages."

"Her truth is eternal," Kurrik said. He'd begun walking a bit faster, as if in annoyance. Vicarian stretched his stride wider to keep up.

"That's my point, isn't it?" he said, forcing his voice to be light and teasing. If the slightest buzz of annoyance slipped through, it wasn't so much that it demanded acknowledgement. "Her truth is eternal, but the world isn't. Kingdoms, cities, languages. They're all in flux. The goddess is like a lighthouse, unchanging and unmoving, but the world is like a ship on the sea, and the angle that it sees her from changes. Every age needs to find new words to express the same truth."

Kurrik stopped at a corner where three streets came together. A high warehouse wall rose above them both, its shadow darkening Kurrik's face and the cobblestones around them. Across the street, one of the remaining puppeteers was yanking a gold-scaled doll through violent paroxysms that Vicarian recognized as part of a Penny-Penny story. The thin crowd standing before him all seemed to be covertly watching Kurrik and himself. And the expression on Kurrik's face sobered him. Annoyance. Vicarian told himself it was only annoyance.

"Her truth," Kurrik said slowly, "is eternal."

"Of course it is," Vicarian said. "I would never dispute that. What I'm saying is that when you have something outside of change like the goddess and something that suffers constant change like the world, the relationship between them must change too. There was a court philosopher in second-age Borja—a Haaverkin named Pelemo Addadus—who wrote a book on the question. I studied it when I first joined the priesthood."

"You did not join the priesthood until you were touched by her," Kurrik said. There was more than annoyance in his voice. There was anger, and Vicarian, despite himself, felt its echo in his own chest. It felt like taking a breath and then taking another without exhaling in between. It enlarged him. Through his body, the spiders wriggling in his blood, whipping him on.

"Not the true priesthood, no," he said, struggling to keep himself from shouting. "But I studied the thoughts and forms of the world. The changing world. You and your brothers from the temple did a tremendous good for us all. You kept the truth of the goddess safe for thousands of years when the dragons would have silenced it. There is nothing that can diminish how important that was."

The rage in Kurrik's eyes dimmed, his jaw softened. Across the corner, the puppeteer coughed and spun Penny-Penny into a frenzied dance, trying to pull her audience back to herself. Vicarian rested his hand on his friend and—in the religious sense of the word—brother's arm. The spiders grew calmer, if not quiet. "Those of us who remained in the world while the goddess was gone went through many changes," Vicarian said. "We will bring her word to everyone. You can hear that in my voice, yes? We will spread her truth to the world and watch the world remade. And we will find the right way to do it."

"We will," Kurrik said. "Yes, this is true, we will."

His agreement felt like a salve on Vicarian's soul. *But it will mean changing the words we use to reflect the changes in the world* floated at the back of his throat. He was right. He knew it. And Kurrik would too if he would only listen to Vicarian's voice long enough to hear it. The presence of their guard—Antean soldiers with swords and battle-scarred leather armor—seemed to unease the audience. The puppeteer shifted PennyPenny to face Vicarian and dropped whatever threads of story she had been weaving. The Jasuru puppet lifted a string-hoisted hand.

"You there! You! I am PennyPenny. Come and hear my story, yes? Come and hear."

"We should keep walking," Vicarian said. "Once that sort starts, they won't stop until you've paid them."

"Of course," Kurrik said, turning. PennyPenny's cries grew quieter as they strode away to the north and the palace. Overhead, seagulls screeched and whirled beneath high, thin clouds. Two dogs, one brown and the other one grey, darted out of an alley, then ran ahead of them and turned back to bark. Vicarian turned their conversation to other matters: the disturbing news from Elassae, how the presence of the goddess would solidify the traditionally fractious Free Cities, the plans for taking the word of the goddess west to Cabral and Herez and Princip C'Annaldé.

By the time they reached the wide, paved square with the governor's palace to the left and the goddess's newest cathedral—the blood-red banner with the pale center and the eightfold sigil of the goddess rippling in the afternoon breeze—to the right, questions of the relationship between flux and eternity had been nearly forgotten. Nearly, but not quite.

The end of their walk through the city marked the beginning of their evening duties. Kurrik took a speaker's trumpet and the guard, and returned to the streets, his voice carrying over the street performers and the taproom conversations, penetrating into every building, pressing through every window. *The enemies of the goddess have already lost. Everything they love is lost. Those who come to the goddess will be lifted up, their fortunes restored and their grief assuaged.* In content it wasn't so very different, Vicarian knew, from the religious claims of any cult. It was only that theirs had the power of truth behind it.

For himself, he remained at the cathedral, overseeing the workmen as they chiseled out the icons of the old local gods and hammered the old statues to gravel. The local dye yard, the only one old enough to have been within the city wall when everything outside it burned, delivered banners to hang over the emptied niches. And as he worked, he took little audiences. A Dartinae boy brought his girl love to the temple putatively to be blessed, though in fact he wanted Vicarian to find if she'd been sexually faithful to him. A merchant captain hauled his crew to the steps of the cathedral to ask which of them had been stealing from the company box. It was the work of a magistrate, but Vicarian did it without charging the tax and fees. All he required was that they all stay for the evening sermon. Their ears and attention to his voice was enough.

But that night, as he rested in the palatial luxury of the rooms they had taken from the governor's priests, the issue gnawed. He'd spent the better part of a month once, debating

Addadus and Cleymant with his fellow novices, and found the knowledge he'd squeezed from it fascinating. More than fascinating, *important*. The idea that all that wisdom would be swept away by the goddess seemed almost self-evidently mistaken. Her power was to lift up truth, and to celebrate the world as it genuinely was, and that included what had been understood during the goddess's exile, so long as it was also truth.

Kurrik was wrong to turn away from it, and that his spiritual brother was caught in an error was like having a splinter. It bothered. He lay in his bed, the smells of incense and the sea competing in the air. The walls around him ticked and shifted as the day's heat radiated away into the humid air. He wondered whether he should go wake Kurrik, explain the error, show him how the work done by philosophers and priests during the goddess's exile still held value because they reflected the history that had played out. Show him that knowing more made the goddess's word stronger. The temptation plucked at him.

But it was late, and Kurrik's anger earlier—though it had been misplaced—wasn't something he wanted to bring up again just now. He was tired. Better to wait. Perhaps he could write a letter outlining the issue to Basrahip. The high priest was more likely to understand than a minor prelate like Kurrik. He was a good-souled man, but perhaps not the smartest after all.

Vicarian sighed, adjusted his pillow, and tried to will himself to sleep. He remained troubled by the certainty not only that he was right, but that Kurrik was wrong. The anger in him was irrational, but knowing that didn't comfort him.

Kurrik was *wrong*. And sooner or later, something would have to be done about it.

Geder

"I find nothing wrong," the cunning man said. He was an old Tralgu man with one cropped ear and a gentle voice. He was the sixth of his profession Geder had appealed to. The others had either voiced the same opinion—that the Lord Regent was in fine health—or offered random maladies on a platter. He had taken bad air, or bad water, or he had too much blood or not enough sleep or his spirit had come a bit loose from his body. Of all that he'd heard, that last sounded most likely. None had been able to help.

"If there's not a problem," Geder said, "why don't I feel well?"

In the royal apartments, his palatial bedroom had high windows and thick rugs, tapestries on the walls with scenes from history and legend that had looked out on generations of kings. Now they looked down on his bare chest and exposed legs and the scowling cunning man. It was hard not to feel like a disappointment to them.

The illness—and Geder felt certain it was an illness—had begun, he thought, on the return from killing the last apostate. Oh, his optimism and good cheer at the time might have covered it over, but it had been there. Thin enough to ignore, but present, like a blemish on an apple small enough to overlook, but warning of worms inside. Since then, the illness had grown. Sleeplessness at night, and exhaustion in the daytime. The almost physical sensation that his mind was stuffed with cotton. The overwhelming sense that something was wrong without anything he could find that justified the dread.

"It started in Asterilhold. In the swamp," Geder said. "I think it started there." He'd said the words before, but to no effect. The cunning man flicked his one whole ear thoughtfully and rubbed his canine chin.

"I have a tea I can give you. It may fix nothing, but if it does improve your vigor, that will tell us something."

"Fine," Geder said. "That's fine."

The cunning man nodded more to himself than to the Lord Regent, and opened his small wooden chest. He hummed to himself as he plucked bits of herbs and stones from his collection, dropping each into an iron pot. Geder watched him for a time. Absent the cunning man's permission or prohibition, Geder tried covering the softness of his body with his undershirt. The Tralgu didn't object, so Geder pulled it on entirely. He felt better that way. He hated it when people saw him just in his skin.

The tea smelled peppery as it steeped, and weirdly astringent. Geder drank it quickly to get it over with. Waves of heat and cold pressed out from his throat through his body, leaving him queasy.

"Sleep tonight," the cunning man said. "Tomorrow, we can talk again?"

"Yes, fine. Yes," Geder said.

The Tralgu smiled, nodded, and packed away his herbs and daubs and the iron pot. Geder watched him, disconsolate. Something was wrong with him. There was no question about that. Everything was going so well, after all. Antea had conquered the world, or close to it. With the power of the goddess, he'd doubled the empire's territory. Maybe more than doubled. He'd gained the respect of every kingdom he didn't run. Respect or else fear. Same thing, really. He'd exposed the Timzinae threat, killed the apostate, ushered in an age of light and truth that was being born now with terrible birthing pangs in the Timzinae's own homeland.

Every time he doubted, all he had to do was sit with Basrahip. The huge priest's deep, rolling voice had the gift of putting everything in its right place. Only lately he'd wanted Basrahip's reassurances more often, and for longer, and the sense of calm that came after had lasted less.

The Tralgu cunning man bowed and Geder waved him away. Maybe the tea would do something. Maybe tomorrow he'd feel better. Or maybe he was simply heartsick. How many songs were there about the man whose lover had broken him? At least some of those had the injured man wasting away, didn't they?

For a moment, the memory of walking into the compound in Suddapal flooded back to him, fresh as a cut. He ground his teeth until it went away. God, he'd been such a fool. And everyone knew it. He was going to live and die with that moment pricking him forever.

He wasn't sick. He'd been poisoned. By Cithrin, whom he'd thought he loved.

The bitch. He clenched his fists until his knuckles ached. The evil, two-faced, manipulative bitch.

"Geder?"

Aster stood in the doorway. His lifted chin made him look both stronger and younger than he was, like a child prepared to fight a mountain. Of course. Of course. The boy had watched King Simeon sicken and die, now here Geder was consulting with a dancing line of cunning men. Aster was frightened. Of course he was frightened. The thought put another stone on Geder's chest. He wanted to leap up, to tell Aster that everything was fine. Or, more accurately, he wanted someone else to do it.

Geder Palliako, Lord Regent of Antea, protector and steward of the Severed Throne. It was his duty to care for the prince. Aster was his friend. One of his only friends. Geder wanted to want to comfort him, but all he really felt was tired.

And still...

"Aster," he said, waving him closer. The prince came with halting, tentative footsteps. "How are you? Did I miss anything important in court, or is it all still the same?"

Aster tried to smile. Managed it, mostly. Geder lowered himself back on the pillows. The cunning man's tea was doing something odd in his gut, and it didn't feel particularly healing. Aster sat on the mattress beside him, hands folded together. He struggled to meet Geder's eyes and failed.

"I was thinking we could walk," Aster said. "Just down to the Division and back, maybe? Some fresh air?"

"Oh, I don't know. I don't think so. Perhaps after I sleep a bit, I could manage."

Aster's nod came quickly enough that Geder knew he'd had it on the ready. He'd expected the refusal. For a moment, guilt almost made Geder reconsider, but it was too much. It was too far.

"It's the weather," he said. "It's the cold. Just that. The thaw's sure to come soon, and I'll be back to myself."

"All right," Aster said.

"I'm not that bad," Geder said with a little forced smile. "I'm just weary. That's all."

"Is there anything I can get for you? There was beef stew last night. It was very good."

"No. Thank you, no. Just. Just a little rest."

"Do that and you won't sleep tonight," the prince said, trying without success to make a joke of it.

"It doesn't matter. I won't sleep anyway," Geder said. Aster flinched at the words, and Geder closed his eyes for a moment. He didn't need another reason to feel worn. He loved the boy, wanted well for him, all that, but just now—just for today—he wished Aster would go away. Go chase girls or fight boys or read books. Something that didn't require him. Geder longed to be outgrown.

"I have some good blankets," Aster said.

"I have blankets," Geder said. "I have lots of blankets. As many as anyone could need."

"I'm sorry."

"Don't be," Geder said. "I didn't mean to snap, it's just that I'm tired. I'll rest. I'll be better. Just let me rest for a little, yes? I'll be up again before sundown. We can play some cards, you and me and Basrahip. Only we'll always lose to him."

"It's all right," Aster said, his smile a little nearer to genuine now. "I don't mind losing."

"That's because you're a wise man," Geder said, taking the prince's hand. "A wise man who'll be a wise king one day. You'll make your father proud."

They sat for a moment in silence. Geder tried not to wish it was ended and the boy gone elsewhere, but he did. And then, when Aster rose and walked to the door, he immediately wished he would come back. The door closed behind him, and Geder sank, giving his full weight to the mattress. His body felt too heavy, his muscles too slack. He was a puppet version of himself with the strings all cut. Or fouled in each other.

He closed his eyes, hoping that sleep would take him. Hoping that when he woke, he would be himself again. Or maybe someone better. The pillow felt unpleasantly hot against his cheek, and when he turned, his shirt twisted, clutching at him like a huge cloth hand. He willed his mind to let go, but when he did begin to slide into dream, the voice of the fire was waiting for him, all the way from Vanai. A woman's body silhouetted by flames, and the sense that he should have sent someone to get her, quick before she burned.

Winter had always been the slow time in Camnipol. The lords and ladies of court were elsewhere, killing deer and boar in the King's Hunt or at their holdings managing the lands that they ruled. The feasts and intrigues and ceremonies rarely began before first thaw. If anything, being in the capital carried a nuance of the merchant class. Geder and Aster were above petty status wrangles, but most people concerned themselves with it all deeply. Which was why it was so surprising when the court began to arrive early.

It was only a few at first. Minor families, mostly from the east. Breillan Caust had only just gained a holding for his family on the plains outside Nus, the first actual land his family had commanded in four generations. He and his wife and daughter arrived at the trailing end of a storm, ice and snow caked inches thick on the sides of their carriage. Then, two days later, Mill Veren. Then Sallien Halb. Karris Pyrellin. Sutin Kastellian. Iram Shoat. Not the grand names of court, but their younger cousins and nephews.

At first, Geder was pleased. It gave Aster new faces and people and distractions. But as the trickle grew to a stream, it became...not worrying, but strange. He wondered if it might signal some shift in the customs of the court. Younger nobles longing for the company of their own, perhaps. Or less established members of their houses vying for the attention of the Lord Regent and prince.

It was only when Geder found himself reading over a

report on the strife in Elassae that he understood. The flow of young and minor nobles to court reflected not the age of the people, but the recentness of their holdings. They had all been given lands and titles in the lands that had been Sarakal and Elassae, and now, before the thaw, before the fighting season, they were coming back to the heart of Antea. It was hard for Geder to see it. His mind, considering the map, brushed over the short-term fighting. It was, after all, the death throes of the old world, and not something that would have a permanent effect. But the pattern was there. Those who'd arrived early to Camnipol had not been drawn by the prospect of the court. They had fled the threat of violence.

They were afraid.

Letters and reports had been building up, of course. Since the day he'd overseen the execution of the hostages—that was how he'd come to think of it—he'd been under the weather. The letters that had come in, he'd skimmed. Yes, the news had been delivered to the slaves on the Antean farms. No, there had been no uprisings there. He'd shown that Antea had the strength to do what it had promised, and peace had been the prize for it, so that was as it should be. No need to dwell on it.

The reports from Inentai, most from Ernst Mecelli, had been alarmist as they always were. News from Elassae was understandably sparse. That was fine because, after all, the broad strokes were clear. No city where a temple had been raised in the name of the goddess could fall. Her power wouldn't allow it. Elassae would fight, would struggle, and would fail. The question was only how long it would take and how much blood—Firstblood and Timzinae both— would be spilled along the way, and in his present funk, that wasn't a question Geder wanted or needed to meditate upon. There would be time enough later.

Mecelli appeared unexpectedly at the Kingspire early on a cold morning. The sky that day was whiter than bleached cotton, and bright. He wore his riding leathers and stank of the road. He was thinner than Geder thought of when he pictured his advisor. Thinner and older and grim. He bowed when Geder entered the withdrawing room, but that was the only concession he made to etiquette.

"Inentai has fallen," he said. "I've ridden here with the couriers. I would have used a cunning man but... but there weren't any."

"No," Geder said. "It's not fallen. It can't. It has a temple. So we might lose control of it for a time, but it won't—"

The older man cut him off. "A force of seven thousand came south from Borja. We stood against them as long as we could, but most of the men had gone to support Broot's remnant in Elassae. These letters, these... *recipes* for how best to unmake the priests, had been appearing since midwinter. The priests stood and shouted, but the enemy weren't listening. We tried to stop them, and we couldn't."

"It's not like that," Geder said. "I'll call for Basrahip. He can explain. It's not like that."

"You have to raise an army. You have to call the army back."

"Just rest. I'll have them bring you tea. Some dried fruit. Would you like some dried apples? Just wait. Just hold together, eh?"

Mecelli collapsed into his chair, his gaze fixed on the flame of the lantern hanging above it. Geder stepped out to the corridor, grabbed the first servant who came to hand, and told her to get the priest. And Canl Daskellin. And to hurry. Even so, it was almost half an hour before Basrahip's heavy tread approached the door. He entered the room smiling his broad, placid smile, as calm as it was certain.

"Prince Geder," the priest said, and then to Mecelli, "Lord."

"We're dead," Mecelli said, and the gutter diction was like a slap. "The Lord Regent wanted you to hear it, and by God, I do too. We're dead. Elassae's all but taken back from us, Inentai's fallen. Sarakal *will not hold*."

Basrahip's expression sobered, and he lowered he head. "I hear the despair in your voice, my friend," he said. "But know this: the power of the goddess has already won. No force in the world can stand against her will. She is truth itself, and the allies of deceit will—"

"Stop it!" Mecelli shouted, standing so quickly that his chair tipped back and clattered against the floor. Geder's heart skipped. Rage darkened Mecelli's face to purple and the man's clenched fists promised more than rhetorical violence. "You listen to me, priest. You hear *my* voice. There is not a single Antean soldier left alive in Inentai and there are thousands of sword-and-bows that answer to Borja or the traditional families of Sarakal or a paymaster bent on taking bounties from our dead. Your priests there are burned. Your temple there, they knocked to the ground and pissed on the gravel. It's *gone*!"

Geder's breath was coming too quickly, shuddering. Something was wrong. He was having an attack of something. He stumbled back, wondering whether he would have time to reach a cunning man. If Mecelli saw his distress, he ignored it.

"We have no way to retake the city. None. What little we had left is busy dying in Elassae. If the Timzinae and the traditional families have made common cause—and they have—Nus will fall with the first thaw. There will be enemy armies marching on Kavinpol by *midsummer*!"

A moment came, shorter than a breath.

It struck Geder in the heart like a hammer.

After the moment passed, Basrahip smiled and bellowed, he invoked the goddess and her will and her power as he always had. Geder watched as Mecelli's despair and rage were battered by the flood of words and imprecations. He watched Mecelli shift from the certainty of their doom to a listless, halfhearted kind of hope. The optimism of a fever. By the time Canl Daskellin arrived, it was all but over. Mecelli made his report to Daskellin: there had been a setback in the East. Inentai would have to be reconquered when the spring broke. The temple there would have to be rededicated. Daskellin listened soberly. It was all as it had been before. As it would be again, if they needed their faith in the powers of the goddess renewed.

All of it the same as ever, except for when the priest had heard Mecelli say the enemy army would arrive by midsummer, and for a moment shorter than a breath and longer than a lifetime, Geder had looked into Basrahip's face like he was looking down a well and seen confusion there.

Cithrin

No," the dragon said. "I'm not your cart horse. I took the Stormcrow on his errand. I don't care to take you on yours. If it's so important that you be there, go. I will find you if I need you."

Inys turned his great head away from her and laid it on the ground. His great claws flexed, gouging the flesh of the land apparently without his being aware of doing it. The chill wind bit at Cithrin's cheeks and earlobes as she stood, deciding whether to press on. She knew that he was sulking, and she thought she guessed why. With Marcus gone and her going, both of the humans Inys knew best were leaving the last dragon behind. And God forbid that he not be the center of all things.

The temptation to chide him for his behavior was difficult to withstand. Phrases like *You'll have other people to tell you how important you are* and *This is beneath the last dragon* and *Are you a child?* all rose in her mind, and she turned them all away. They might shame Inys into doing what she wanted of him or they might spur him to casual slaughter. And of all humanity, the only one he seemed to care about preserving was Marcus. She wasn't certain that her value in the dragon's eyes was high enough to protect her, so she stood for a long moment, looking out over the slate-grey sea under a slate-grey sky, then turned and walked away.

The taproom was warm and loud and busy, and she walked past it without a thought. Since her night with Barriath, she'd stopped drinking. It was always hard, every time she did it, but she needed her wits now. Around her, Carse fell away, step by step. The wide roads were as cold as they had been when the winter was new. The towers as grey.

If there was any change at all, it was only in the slowly contracting span of the nights, the inexorable effort of the light to hold the darkness at bay a few minutes more than the day before, and a scent in the air that hinted at the green and new. In a different year, they'd have been the beacons of hope. Winter's back broken at last. But this would be a war spring. If she failed, it would be the first of a very long line of them. Or no. Not even the first.

At the holding company, the servants ignored her and the guards nodded her past their swords and axes. The first hard taps of rain sounded against the stones as she ducked into the warmth of the house. Not snow. Not even hail. Rain. Even the clouds were warmer than they'd been.

She found Komme Medean waiting for her in her room. A small fire danced and spat in the grate. The old man's gout had taken pity on him, and his joints were of a merely human proportion for the time. He looked up at her with eyes unshadowed by the cunning man's draughts and tinctures, and she made a little bow, only half in jest. She felt the coppery taste of fear, but pressed it down.

"Will he take you away, then?"

She considered pretending ignorance, but discarded the thought. Better to play it bare. "No hope," she said. "Not from him."

"Probably better," Komme said. "You'd make up something in speed, it's true. But a fast boat with a good crew's nothing to look down on either."

Cithrin lowered herself to the floor beside the grate, the heat of the flames pressing against her arm. Komme Medean looked down at her along the length of his nose. In the flickering light, she could almost forget who he was: the master of a bank that had spanned nations. And still did. And would again, if the idea of nations and countries and kingdoms survived the coming chaos. All her life had been lived in awe of Komme Medean, in the shadow of him and the institution he'd piloted to greatness. He was only a man. Clever, talented, and lucky, but as subject to illness and time, fear and foolishness, as anyone. He smiled at her.

"I met your parents once," he said. "When they placed their money with the bank, Magister Imaniel had them meet with me. I was traveling in the Free Cities at the time, so it wasn't as grand a gesture as it sounds. We all had dinner together at a table beside a canal. It was roast pork. And almonds. I didn't remember that until just now, but it was."

Cithrin was quiet. She knew little of her family apart from the fact of her parents' death and the extended family's disavowal of the half-breed daughter. She thought she should feel something more when she heard of her parents, but it was like hearing names from a song. *I ate with Drakkis Stormcrow once, and danced with the Princess of Swords.* Father and Mother were ideas, not people. Roles that someone might play, like Magister or Clerk. Or Enemy. Statement of function and relationship, not identity. Komme sighed.

"I didn't think much of it. He was a Firstblood. She was Cinnae. I could tell it had been a matter of contention, and that they had taken each other's side against the world. I suppose I admired that, but for me they were simply money. An account that we would take or not take, pay out on or take a loss. Business. When the letter came from Imaniel that they had died and no one was willing to take you, the only thing I asked was whether their account had enough to support you until you were of age. We called you 'the liability.' Not by your name. Not 'the child.' And now…"

"You're getting sentimental in your old age," she said.

"I am," he said, annoyance creeping into his voice. "I used to be so hard-hearted, and now it seems like a kitten sneezes, and I'm suddenly made of snow. Soft, I am. Old and soft."

He shook his head. The fire settled in the grate. Cithrin lifted her chin. "May I ask who told you about my plan?"

"No one *told* me. But I can smell a change in the weather. I called Yardem Hane and put it to him. He said you'd come up with a flavor of…extortion? Is that it?"

"No," Cithrin said. "Just a way to sell dead priests to the only man in a position to buy. In the coin that matters to him more than coins. Or power."

"Abduct his father and offer the trade."

"If it comes to that. There may be a more elegant solution, but it's good to have a fallback. Have you come to forbid me?"

Komme turned to the fire. The relected fire made him look like an old Dartinae for a moment, eyes glowing and fierce. "Hane argued in favor of your idea. He said…he said he'd seen the shape of your soul, and that keeping you here would bankrupt the world. Break it. And that if I tried to stop you, the death of civilization would be my fault personally."

"He said that?"

"The bit about the soul, yes," Komme said. "The rest, I'm paraphrasing. Geder Palliako is a tyrant who has ended kingdoms and crippled races, and you want to do business with him."

"He's a small man in a large position, and he's the only

one in the world who can buy what I'm selling," Cithrin said. And then a moment later, "We've just said the same thing."

"He hates you more deeply than he hates anything. He's cracked his empire's back to catch you."

"At least I'm important to him. And this is how bankers do things, isn't it? Not armies in the field, but intrigues in back rooms?"

"The way bankers do things is to keep the profit and farm out the risk," Komme said. "*I'm* taking the banker's path. I don't know what way you're going. The odds of anything good coming of this are terrible."

"I agree," Cithrin said. "But that's true of taking the safer route too. Mine has better odds than doing nothing, and the stakes are the same."

"They are, aren't they?" Komme said, and then lapsed into silence. When he rose, it was with a sigh. He reached down and put his hand on the crown of her head like a father placing a blessing on his child. "Good luck. I've had a rich and fascinating life. Seen a dragon. There's been nothing as interesting as your mind."

She watched him as he left. He didn't look back. When the door closed behind him, she took the seat he'd left behind, pressing thoughtful fingertips to her lips and watching the fire dance. He'd said goodbye. Not in any straightforward way, but it was the story under his words. He was the man who, whether he'd meant to or no, had sheltered her all through her life, whose sense of risk and reward had built the financial empire she'd used. He had learned her plan, given his blessing, and said his farewells.

She didn't know if it was more disturbing that he made the odds that she'd fail or that he thought she should try anyway.

*   *   *

The docks at Carse lay at the bottom of the great pale cliffs. The stairways that clung to the stone face were built of wood, and exposed constantly to the salt air and storm and sun and wind. She'd heard it said that they were rebuilt every ten years or so. The cliff face was dotted with old holes where previous incarnations of the stairs had been. And if an attacker ever came by sea, the steps could be burned, and the invader trapped at the bottom of a wall higher than any siege ladder could hope to reach. Walking down to the ship, Cithrin realized how much the violence of Suddapal and Porte Oliva had changed the way she made sense of the world. When she'd first walked up these steps, the idea of burning them wouldn't have occurred to her.

Ice covered the dock in a thin sheet. A slack-jawed Jasuru boy in sailor's canvas walked the length of it with an iron bar, shattering the frozen seawater until the dark wood was white with chips and shards that Cithrin took on faith were surer footing. The little sloop that waited for her looked too small, its draft too shallow. Barriath Kalliam stood on the ladder that reached to the deck, his weight shifting as the ship rose and fell with the motion of the sea. He was speaking to a thin Timzinae woman Cithrin recognized as Shark, one of the commanders of the piratical fleet Barriath had assembled.

On the little deck itself, three figures in oiled skins shifted, talking among themselves. Cithrin reached the ladder and Barriath met her eye. His nod was curt, but not unfriendly. His smile was perhaps a bit self-satisfied. Cithrin wondered whether every man looked at a woman he'd bedded with the same proprietary smugness. She drew her deliberate gaze down his body—neck, shoulders, chest, belly, groin— and lingered there a moment before looking back up. She didn't feel any particular accomplishment in knowing what the skin looked like beneath his leathers, but she could see the uncertainty in his expression at being viewed as he had viewed her. Uncertainty and also a tentative shade of hope.

"Magistra Cithrin," Shark said as Cithrin moved past her. Black water shifted beneath them both. "Best of luck to you and yours. Hope you cut their cocks off and shove 'em up their holes."

"Thank you," Cithrin said. The Timzinae woman nodded once to her and once to Barriath, then went back to the docks and marched away toward another of the dozen ships tied there.

"Shark's going to keep order while I'm gone," Barriath said. "I imagine when I get back she'll have appropriated the better half of the ships and headed out to sink some trade ships coming back from Far Syramys."

"Good to know what to expect," Cithrin said, stepping onto the gently shifting deck. It was small enough that her words carried to the three waiting figures, and one of them laughed. The sound was familiar. Cary pulled back her hood. Her dark hair had a threading of white to it, and her mouth had taken a hardness since Smit's death in Porte Oliva, but she was still beautiful. More so for being unanticipated.

"What are you doing here?" Cithrin said.

"Learning to play the sailor," Cary said.

From beneath another of the hoods, Hornet picked up the thought. "You'll note she didn't say *learning to sail*, Magistra. Luck is I've spent a few years on the ropes. Lak has too."

"You couldn't expect us to stay here," Cary said. "We've no props, no costumes. Half a stage at best. And with Master Kit gone, we've lost our Orcus the Demon King, Lord Frost, Annanbelle Coarse, Bakkan the Elder. Anything that takes gravity or makes its humor by undercutting it."

"I didn't think you'd mind," Yardem said.

"They're looking for you, though," Cithrin said. "All Antea's looking for the troupe since Inys landed on you coming back from Hallskar."

Cary shook her head. "If they're still looking, it'll be for an acting company heading for the border. We're a trade boat from Narinisle to Borja on the last leg of the blue-water trade. Yardem here's Mikah Haup, tradesman of Lôdi. We're his hired crew."

"I won't pass for a sailor," Cithrin said.

"I won't be mistaken for anyone but myself," Barriath said. "Under Lord Skestinin, I patrolled this stretch of water for the better part of a decade. If it comes to someone being that near to us, we'll be belowdecks."

Cithrin considered the ship with a skeptical eye. "How much below does this thing have?"

"Enough," Barriath said. "She's a fast boat. If there's trouble, we'll outrun it. My plan is to find a cove on the north coast about halfway between Asinport and Estinport. There's a stretch there with no dragon's roads at all. Then south and west from there until we reach Rivenhalm and Lehrer Palliako. I can act as guide. I haven't been there myself, but I know the land well enough."

"That's *your* plan," Cary said. "Mine's to get my damned Orcus back."

"What about the others?" Cithrin said.

"They're below already," Cary said.

A soft voice rose up from a thin hatch at Cary's feet. Sandr's voice. "And we're stacked like fucking cordwood, I don't mind saying."

"We'll reprovision along the way," Barriath said. "This is going to be faster than a smuggler's run if I can manage it."

Cithrin turned, looking up at the vast cliff face above her.

She half expected to see wings silhouetted against the clouds, but there were only gulls and terns. The dragon was elsewhere.

"We should go," she said. "Before I change my mind about the whole errand."

Cithrin thought, after her escape from Suddapal to Porte Oliva and then north to Carse, that she'd come to understand the sensations of being aboard ship. She was mistaken. With the sails lifted to catch the winter wind, Barriath's little boat flew until it almost seemed to rise up from the water, skipping on it like a stone. The dock and Carse and Inys fell away behind them more swiftly than she'd imagined possible, and by morning on the next day, they could see the mouth of the river Wod and the fishing boats that haunted its estuary.

She slept below decks fully clothed, with Hornet and Mikel, Charlit Soon and Sandr, Cary and Lak. Barriath took the days on deck, and Yardem the nights. It felt less like voyaging across the sea than being snowbound in a cabin too small for the people living in it. There were parts of the salt quarter in Porte Oliva where people had lived more densely than this, but they'd had the streets of the city to retreat into. She had nothing. The days were cold, the nights colder. The air belowdecks stank of tar and bodies and grew stale until it seemed like every breath was stolen out of someone else's mouth.

She should have hated it. She didn't.

On the third night, the coast to their south began to roughen. Rises became hills. Hills became mountains. Rude, rocky islands rose from the waves like rotting teeth. Cithrin looked for the little winged lizards she remembered from her first voyage to Antea, a lifetime ago it seemed, but there were none. The cold had dropped them into torpor or killed them. She had no way to know which.

After night fell, she stood on the moonlit deck with

Yardem as he measured the stars and adjusted the sails. In other circumstances, they would have stopped for the nights and sailed in the safety of day. Instead, their wake glowed behind them, as if the mirror of the aurora shimmering in the northern sky. Cithrin shivered, her fingers and face numbed, and still she was unwilling to leave. Not yet.

"Komme said you saw the shape of my soul," she said.

"I said so."

"Was it true?"

"No," Yardem said. "I lied. He was looking for a reason to hope, and..." the Tralgu shrugged. "It may not have been the right thing, but it seemed wise at the time. Or kind. But since I expected you would do the thing regardless, it seemed better than he have reasons to agree."

"And you came because you promised Captain Wester."

"He'd have wanted me to."

The sea rushed against the wood of the boat. The canvas sails thudded and barked. Sea travel had a way of making everything sound like a whisper and a shout at the same time. Cithrin leaned against the rail and watched the lights shimmer in the vast air above them.

"I'm impressed with how devoted Cary is to Master Kit," Cithrin said. "All of them, really. It's a deeper loyalty than I'm used to seeing. But I suppose they're like family to each other."

Yardem coughed once.

"What?" Cithrin said.

"Nothing, ma'am."

"Tell me."

"They came for your sake, not Kit's."

"Oh."

Cithrin laughed once in disbelief, then again in embarrassment. She turned to look at the dark water she'd led them to, and the spray hid her tears.

Clara

They trekked through the pass, mountains rising black against the snow and towering above their desperation. Somewhere under the snow a thread of dragon's jade snaked unseen. Clara couldn't guess how deep they would have had to dig down under blue ice and hardpack to find it. The winds that the land channeled down upon them bit in the mornings and killed in the night. They did their best, building block huts at the end of each day small enough that the heat of their bodies made a crust of clear ice on the walls and floors. They melted handfuls of snow for fresh water and ate what little hardtack and salted meat remained. Every morning, fewer rose up than had lain down.

Marcus Wester had taken to accompanying Jorey when he reviewed the troops, and though the bank's mercenary still wore the costume of a servant, his wisdom and confidence lent him stature both in Jorey's eyes and those of his men. Somewhere along the plodding, freezing, ice-haunted march, they had stopped being the army of Imperial Antea and become merely participants in a shared nightmare.

Clara's horse died on the fourth day. Forging through a drift of snow deeper than its knees, the animal paused, sighed a weary sigh, hunkered down, and refused to rise. It was the last, and with it gone, there was nothing but to walk or else lie down beside the dead animal and follow its lead.

The carts had long been abandoned. Men were even leaving behind their weapons as their strength waned and failed them. There was nothing to fight in these passes. What was bringing them all low couldn't be cut and wouldn't bleed.

Clara, for her part, lost herself in the physical misery. At the head of the column, a few men broke the trail, forcing a path through snow light enough to be pushed aside or dense enough to be walked on. It was the hardest, most punishing work of the trail, and which unfortunate was called on changed ten or fifteen times a day. Clara was never called, but Vincen was. And Marcus. And even Kit, their tame priest. The rest of the army followed in that path, two or three walking abreast through an aisle of snow. It made the passage easier, not fighting against a fresh drift with every step.

Time thinned as she walked in a way she'd come to recognize and associate with living on the road. Her numbed feet felt like balancing on stumps. The joints in her hands and hips ached. And still she hauled her trailing foot forward, shifted her weight to it, and began the process again. At first, she heard her own voice in her head saying, *One more step. One more step. You can do one more. Just keep doing one more for long enough, and you'll have made it.* The voice quieted in time, but by then her body had the habit of it, and the soldiers drew her along like a living stream. She had neither the energy nor the inclination to do anything but be carried along by it.

Twice, she passed men who had stopped. Both had the vague and confused expression of someone lost despite there being only one path before them and only one direction in which to go. The first she prodded into taking a few steps that seemed to reorient him. With the second, intervening didn't occur to her at all until she was well past him. She hoped that someone farther back in the line had helped him. That her own exhaustion hadn't condemned the man to death.

Every night, Master Kit came by, sticking his head into the shelters of snow and ice, assuring them that their progress was good and their strength was enough. It was the trick of the spiders, but for the time that he was there and for several hours after, it seemed plausible that they might survive.

There were no women with the army apart from herself. All the camp followers and tradesmen and fortune-tellers had been scraped off by the rough knife of winter. Nor could she warm her little shelter with her own flesh alone. It gave her an excuse to bring Vincen in with her. There was neither sex nor the desire for it. She was worn too thin to even consider that, as, she hoped, was he. But bodies offered other comforts than release, and having him there was as near as she could hope to coming home.

"I think we may die here," she said, her head resting against his chest.

"We won't," he said, his voice as empty as habit.

"Might rather we did," she said. "I'm not sure how much longer I can go on. Life alone may not be worth the effort." She was joking, at least in part. She did wonder how much it would take for her dark humor to slide into simple truth.

"Not life," Vincen said. "Soup."

"Soup?"

"It's how I stay strong through this. Life's too big. Too abstract. Can't bring myself to want it in particular. Soup, though? A good rich bowl of soup is just a little further down the road somewhere."

"God," Clara said. "And a pipe with some fresh leaf."

"Pie. With Abitha's cold crust and cheese and beer."

"You've convinced me," Clara said, shifting against his

body as if she might burrow into him for warmth. "Let's live."

"I will if you do," he said, but she was already halfway to sleep. The ice seemed comfortable as a feather bed, and her hands and feet were all terribly far away. No dreams came, only a deep velvet darkness and a sense of terrible weight dragging her down. She woke to the tapping of the camp's caller on the iced wall. On Wester's advice Jorey had banned use of the speaking horn until they were someplace less prone to avalanche. She rose, chewed a bit of leather the length of her thumb that was breakfast, and the march began again.

Only today, it grew worse.

The first sign of trouble didn't catch her attention until much later. The second came when the leaden march passed a widening in the landscape, the mountains stepping a bit apart before they closed ranks again. Jorey and Marcus Wester and half a dozen of the highest-ranking of Jorey's men stood together at the side of the column. Clara's footsteps slowed, faltered, and turned.

Jorey's face was thin, his eyes sunken. He seemed on the verge of tears. The others—his men, the noble blood of Antea—were little more than corpses who hadn't had the good sense to rot yet. Only Wester seemed to have his faculties fully about him, and they were his words that found her first.

"If we try to sleep, the *best* we can hope is a third dead by morning. The smart bet's more."

"What's going on?" Clara demanded. She had no rank or authority, but they were all past that now. Marcus nodded to her and lifted his chin, pointing with it to the landscape all around them.

"Listen," he said.

When she heard it, she realized she'd been hearing it for some time. A high, merry tinkling sound like a thousand mice playing chimes. It seemed to come from all around her, to rise up from the ground itself and shimmer down from the mountains.

"The thaw's here," Marcus said. "We can't build a decent shelter with wet snow. We'd wind up sleeping in puddles, and that makes waking up come morning less likely. Add that it's hours, not days, before some unfortunately warm breeze gets up to the peaks. Once the melt starts there, all this is going to spend a week as a particularly unpleasant river."

"What can we do?" Clara said.

"Forced march," Jorey said, his voice low and sepulchral. "We don't stop for the night. We don't stop at all. We only keep walking until Bellin."

"It's not much farther," Marcus said. "We can do this."

"Not all of us," Jorey said.

"The ones that can't are dead anyway," Marcus said. "As their commander, the best thing you can offer them is a chance to rise to the occasion."

Jorey's head sank to his chest. Clara felt his weariness and distress as if the ache were her own. She wished there were a way to take him in her arms, to comfort him. She had the mad fantasy, gone as soon as it came, of calling for her servants to bring the carriage close as she'd done when her children were no more than babes. Too late for that now, and in so many ways.

"No choice means no choice," Jorey said. He lifted his head, and his eyes were hard as stone. "Send the word. We'll break before sundown, but just for food and water. Then we keep on."

"As if we had food," one of the other men said with a hollow laugh. None of the others picked it up.

That night, she walked. The darkness came on slowly, and then all at once. The trickling carried on for a time, then stopped as the free water turned to ice. The surface of the snow they passed by had changed. She saw already the texture of it shifting from smooth, unbroken white to a dirtier form, specked where the crystals had broken down and been remade. Beneath the surface would be paths of ice like the branches of inverted trees, clear and hard and cutting through the soft and white.

She could see them all around her, like spirits from the grave. Ice-souls returning for one terrible night before the thaw came in earnest and washed away living and dead alike. She heard their voices chattering like the meltwater and recognized as if from a great distance that she was dreaming. Asleep and walking at the same time. She was half surprised that knowing alone didn't wake her, but it all went on as she pushed one foot out ahead of the other, and then again, and then again. Forever and only in the single, painful moment.

She observed her mind slowly falling apart, at first with horror and then with an almost childlike curiosity. It was like watching an animal being butchered for the first time, seeing all the bits of her self come apart. She didn't realize she'd stopped walking until someone tugged her arm. In the darkness, Vincen was nothing more than a shadow and a scent. She would have known him anywhere.

"Can't stop now, m'lady," he said. His voice sounded rough. "Soup."

"Soup," she agreed, and she walked.

Dawn was turning the snow to indigo when the mountain began to *glitter*.

She thought at first it was another hallucination conjured by her failing mind, but one of the soldiers ahead of her lifted his arm and pointed. And then another. A ragged, sore-throated cheer rose until the commanders gestured for them to be quiet. It would be sad, after all, to have come all this way through all this terror, and be buried by an avalanche there before the candle-lit windows of the free city of Bellin.

In her little rooms carved from the living stone and heated by a single black iron brazier, Clara ate until she was nause-ated, ached like she'd been beaten, and slept like a woman sick with the flu. It might have been half a day or half a month before her mind regained itself and her body found its strength again. She rose from a string-and-cloth cot that seemed grander just then than any bed she'd ever slept in. Thin windows carved into the stone wall filtered in a pale sunlight. She washed herself at the little tin basin for what felt like the first time in years and braided her still-wet hair. Bruises blotched her legs and arms, and she had no recol-lection of where they'd come from. Her leathers and wools vanished, she put on a thick wool robe the color of corn silk and a pair of boots picked by someone with a daintier imag-ination of her feet than her body could support.

She was just beginning her search for a bell or a cord to summon a servant when a scratch came at the door and Vincen's muffled voice came after. "If you're ready, m'lady?"

The hall was a tunnel of stone with lanterns hung at the corners filling the air with buttery light and the scent of oil. He looked better. He'd shaved and his long brown hair caught the glow of the light. Too thin, though. God, they were both too thin.

"Have you been eavesdropping on me?" she asked.

"I hear that all the best servants do," he said. "Makes us seem cleverer than we are."

She stepped into his enfolding arms, resting her head

against his breast. It was difficult not to weep, though she didn't feel at all sorrowful. It was simply a thing her body did after death had tapped her shoulder and then walked past. Vincen stroked her damp hair, kissed her temple, and pushed her gently back.

"We did it," Clara said. "We went through the closed pass at Bellin, just before the thaw."

"And we only lost a third of our men," Vincen said. "The locals are telling us that we're crazy, brave, and lucky as hell."

"What a world that this is good luck," she said.

"You're here. It's enough for me."

She was tempted to pull him into the little room and draw him onto the cot. It wasn't lust, or not lust alone. It was also that he was alive and she was alive and the trek through hell behind them. He saw the thought in her eyes and smiled, blushing. "Your son is waiting. They have a meeting room set up farther in the mountain."

"Of course," she said crisply. "Lead on."

She had heard of Bellin before she knew it. A free city mostly within the flesh of the mountain, built who knew how many centuries before by Dartinae miners and then abandoned when the great plague struck their race. She had passed it less than a year before, following Jorey and his army in disguise. Being within the tunnels was different from knowing the story of them. Reality gave it weight, but also stole away the romance of it. She'd imagined grottoes within the stone, carved walls with the forms of dragons and men, light coaxed down through shafts high above or created in bright crystal lanterns. In the experience of it, it felt more like a complex mine mixed with the narrow streets of Camnipol's poorer quarters. Less impressive than her imagination, but impressive for being actual.

"The men are being housed outside for the most part," Vincen said. "But we've got good leather tents and the local cunning men are helping with the sick. They've eaten real food for two days straight as well, which appears to have helped more than anything. Jorey and his captains have rooms in the city proper, and Captain Wester and Master Kit besides. No one's said anything, but they seem to recognize that Wester's advice is worth considering."

"How are we paying for all this?" Clara asked. "It isn't as though we brought any coin to speak of."

"We're an army, m'lady. They show that we're all friends by housing and feeding us, we show we appreciate it by not killing them all and taking what we want. That's tradition."

"As I recall it, we wouldn't have been able to slaughter and loot a wet kitten before they took us in," Clara said.

"Having one of the priests there to smooth the way was a blessing."

Clara smiled and chuckled, though something about the idea sat poorly with her. She put it aside for another time. For the moment, gratitude that the world had seen fit to keep her warm and fed was enough.

The meeting room was round and roughly cut. The air smelled of dust and smoke, but didn't feel close breathing it. A low table of polished oak with legs of iron commanded the center of the room. Maps and papers were laid out upon it. She caught a glimpse of a troop list. Many of the names had been crossed through. Men of Antea as loyal to the throne as Lord Skestinin, and on much the same terms. They would not be going home.

Also at the table was Marcus Wester. The journey appeared to have affected him least, though how that was possible she could not have said. Perhaps he was simply the sort of man that thrived on travesty.

"Good to see you up and about, Lady Kalliam," the mercenary captain said with a little grudging bow.

"I am very pleased to have the opportunity to be seen," she said. "I thank you for that."

"It's the job," Wester said, then, as if he realized how rude he sounded, "You're welcome, though."

"We were looking at the path from here," Jorey said, turning to the map. "The dragon's road leads east to Orsen, and then north, which brings us near to Elassae."

"Can we not cross through here?" she asked, tracing a finger more directly from Bellin to Camnipol.

"That'd mean the Dry Wastes," Wester said. "We could try it, but it would make the pass look like a stroll through the garden. I wouldn't give odds of six of us making the whole way."

"Then Orsen?" Clara said. Jorey shot a glance at Wester, as if he hoped to read the right answer in the older man's face. Wester shrugged.

"It's got its dangers, but I don't see safe on the table anywhere."

Jorey nodded. "We'll give the men one more day to rest, and then start out. With the road, the path should be quicker."

"There's quite a bit that's quicker than slogging through snow up to your asshole," Wester said, then grimaced his regrets to Clara. She pretended not to have noticed the vulgarity. "But yes. It won't be a bad trot, compared to what we've done."

"Well then," Clara said. "Good that the worst is over."

"Wouldn't go that far," Wester said, but he did not elaborate.

Marcus

Marcus still wore servant's robes. He still pretended to wait on Lady Kalliam and walked beside the new and skittish horse offered up by the aristocracy of Bellin. Even in private, he never presented the Lord Marshal with orders. Just suggestions that the boy knew better than to deviate from. He had a story prepared if the others became suspicious. He was ready to claim Jorey's mother had hired him on as an unofficial advisor. He even had a name picked out: Darus Oak, mercenary captain from the Keshet. As they walked through freezing mud and snow turning to slush, he amused himself by inventing Oak's history and exploits, his loves and humiliations. His tragic failures and brilliancies and dumb-luck escapes. It came of traveling with actors, he supposed. It took his mind off the march.

When he wasn't lost in his own flights of fancy, Clara Kalliam made for pleasant company. She had a better understanding of field wars than most women of court, which was to say she had any at all. More than that, she knew in a general sense what she didn't know, and asked smart questions. Still, he was careful not to be too harsh in laying fault at her son's feet. Wasn't any call to be rude about things.

"He's smart," Marcus said. "That's not the issue. It's Palliako's failing. I've seen it any number of times before. It doesn't matter if it's a garrison command or kingdom or the bastard who's picking the gate guard. He chooses the person because he trusts them, not because they can do the job. Give Jorey another five or ten years in the field, he'd be a fine Lord Marshal. It's just he's green."

Lady Kalliam nodded. "That's my fault, I'm afraid."

"Raising him different wouldn't have helped," Marcus said. "It's experience he needs."

"I meant that I arranged that the last Lord Marshal should be caught conspiring against Geder. Lord Ternigan was quite accomplished in the field, but Geder killed him all the same. Because of me."

They walked for a few moments in silence.

"That's a stronger case for it being your fault than I'd expected," Marcus said.

"It's a weight I can carry," she replied. "If I had done differently, my kingdom would have done better, and things would be worse."

"Confusing, but true."

She favored him with a smile. "I have become more comfortable with contradictions these last few years."

"I'm still working on it."

The truth was that commanding a real army again—even if it was at one remove—felt better than he'd expected. It had been a long time since he'd been a general, and his reputation after Wodford and Gradis had been more a burden than a joy. But there was something ineffable about doing a hard job well. Most wars were won or lost long before the battlefield, and getting a force of any size and strength through a winter-closed pass with only a third lost was solid work under the best of circumstances. With this collection of thin sticks and doom, it was a brilliancy. No one who didn't know to look would see the achievement for what it was but he felt the lift of pride all the same. Except when he remembered whose army he'd just saved.

Spring rose up around them, fragile and pale and new. The trees they passed—the few that hadn't been burned for wood by the same men going the other direction the year before—didn't have leaves yet, nor even buds. It was only that the dead-looking bark was taking on a faint green undertone; the mud smelled less of ice and shit and more of water and soil. Little things, but they added up to hope and the mindless animal optimism that the darkness was passing.

Nor was the only change in the landscape.

The soldiers of Antea had been starving shadows in Birancour. The years on campaign hadn't just hardened the men, they'd scraped them down to bones and madness. Without the priests to goad them on, they would never have kept together so long. Palliako's army had pushed itself past the breaking point, and then kept pushing, firm in the dream that because it hadn't all turned sour yet, it never would. Now, on the road home, it was like seeing them wake up.

No, not that far. Seeing them stir in their sleep, maybe. Food stayed scarce, and the day's march went long, but the men talked more. They joked more. Their homes called them forward like water going downhill. Kit, walking among them as the priests before him had done, was greeted with less solemnity and more joy. Sometimes, Marcus saw it as a good sign. These weren't bloodthirsty swordsmen anxious to cut a fresh throat. They were farmers and laborers and men of the land pressed into service and kept there too long. Even the noblemen who led them were hungry for home and comfort and an end to the war. Other times, he wondered which of the men he'd helped guide through the pass was the one who'd killed Smit and Pyk, or else recalled that any of them would have been pleased to haul Cithrin along in chains. Or worse. Those times, their laughter grated.

The dragon's jade of the road snaked a bit to the north, then to the south, curving gently around hills that had worn away centuries before, rising up above the earth in long bridge-like stretches, and disappearing beneath the loam. The passage of the army on its way toward Birancour and Northcoast had churned the land to either side, but the eternal jade remained. At Orsen, it would meet another track headed north into Antea and one that continued east to Elassae. Roads that had been there before the nations they connected, and that would outlast them too. The confluence of them—along with the defensibility of Orsen's weird single hill in the otherwise flat plains—defined where cities were built and how trade and violence flowed. Odd to think how much the world was defined by where it was easiest to get to.

When the remaining army of Antea made the approach that at last brought Orsen clearly into sight, the free city looked something different than it had. The differences weren't obvious at first, except in Marcus's sense that something was off. The air around the city seemed greyer than he'd expected. Huts and small buildings clumped at the base of the lone mountain that looked familiar and out of place at the same time. With the advantage of being on horse, Clara Kalliam saw it better than he could, and Marcus saw his unease echoed in her expression.

Either the burden of the poisoned sword was dulling his mind or the hard passage had left him more compromised than he knew. When he realized what he was seeing, it was obvious.

"We'll need to get your son, ma'am," Marcus said. "The

halt needs to be called right now, and a scout sent forward under a flag of parley."

"What is it?" Clara asked, but the tone of her voice told him she'd already guessed.

"Orsen's not looking to be as hospitable as Bellin was. That darkness at the mountain's base is a camp."

"They're fortified against us?"

"Doubt it. I'll lay gold that's a Timzinae army making an early march to the north. Probably the force that broke out of Kiaria."

"Ah," Clara Kalliam said. "So we've come too late."

The field of parley sat at the side of the road in a meadow that wasn't yet entirely churned to mud. It wasn't quite near enough to Orsen that they could haul a table and chairs out from the city, so the enemy had set up a frame-and-leather tent. Protocol had them withdrawing to just out of crossbow range and letting Jorey's guard come inspect the place to be sure it wasn't an ambush. That done, Jorey and his guards would wait in the tent and the enemy commander and his guards would come join them, followed by some more or less heated conversation. After that, tradition was everyone went back to their camps and got on with the business of slaughtering each other. The parley was as much about trying to find some hint of the enemy's weaknesses as any genuine attempt to avoid battle.

Putting Jorey's strategy together hadn't been quick. They'd talked over sending someone else in his place in hopes the enemy might think the Lord Marshal was commanding another—possibly larger—force nearby. They'd talked about abandoning the parley and falling back to Bellin. They'd even talked about trying to ambush the enemy commander and hold him hostage, because that was an idea every inexperienced commander reached for one time or another. Usually, they had an advisor to talk their hands out of the fire on that, and this time it had been Marcus.

The plan instead came to this: Jorey would go, with Marcus in borrowed armor acting as one of his customary three guards. That way Marcus could hear the full parley, possibly pick up on some nuance of strategy or tactic Jorey might have overlooked. Once the parley was ended, Marcus would offer up his best suggestions. After that, the action grew hazy. The idea of taking Kit as another of the guard was considered, but Vincen Coe took his place at the last minute as Marcus deemed the risk too great.

Given how quickly the plan fell to bits, it had been a wise choice.

The guards, when they ducked into the tent, were Timzinae. Knowing now that Inys had created them specifically as warriors against the spiders, Marcus could see the black chitinous scales that covered their bodies as armor. Their double-lidded eyes were empty of everything but hate. The way they stood made it clear that even breathing the same air as a Firstblood was an indignity. Or that was how it seemed until their commander came in and took his seat across from Jorey. He was a Firstblood himself, and more than that.

The years had been kind to Karol Dannien. A bit more softness around the jowls, and his knife-cut hair had gone the white-grey of clouds on the horizon. His eyes were as clear and sharp as when their companies had fought together at Lôdi and against each other in Hallskar. Marcus could only hope that he'd changed enough that the other mercenary didn't place him.

"Lord Marshal Jorey Kalliam, yeah?" Karol said.

"I am," Jorey replied. "I take it you're commander of the Timzinae army?"

"No such thing," Karol said, his voice buzzing with anger. "Timzinae's a race of people. This here's the collected force of the nation of Elassae. Got plenty of Timzinae folks in it. Got plenty that aren't."

"As you say. But you are their commander."

"Karol Dannien. Lately in the employ of the fivefold city of Suddapal. We pried the last of you little shits out of it a month ago." Karol's smile could have cut meat. "So tell me how it is, Lord Marshal, you're saying how you're the one in charge when you've got Marcus twice-damned Wester standing behind you?"

Jorey glanced back at him, and Marcus sighed. "Karol. Been a while. How's Sarrith?"

"She quit a few years back," Karol said. "Went to Herez. Last I heard she was raising up two nephews and a niece her brother left behind when a fever took him. Cep Bailan took her place." Marcus hoisted an eyebrow, and Dannien sighed. "I know. He's a good man in a fight, though."

"Your force, your decision," Marcus said.

"Damned right. So what in all hell happened to you? Last I heard, you were on our side."

"Still am," Marcus said. "Just which side's *ours* got complicated."

"This ragtag bunch out on the road looking to join up, go burn some Antean farms on our way to sack Camnipol?"

"No," Jorey said. "We won't let that happen."

"Well, Marcus," Dannien said. "The puppy here's saying we're not on the same side after all."

Marcus sighed. "You know these poor bastards weren't behind any of what happened. They're doing what they're told because they're loyal. Or because it seemed easier to strap on a sword than die in prison for defying their lords. We can march out onto a field and see who can kill how many of the other side if you want. Then if you win, you can go make sword-shaped holes in a bunch of farmers and tradesmen who couldn't have stopped any of this either. That's going make things better?"

"If the war's not the soldiers, then who? The lords? All right, then. Hand over everyone you have there with noble blood or title. We'll just kill them, and only put the rest in chains."

"You know I can't do that," Marcus said.

"Had a hint. How about these priests? Got any of those?"

"I've got the same one who went to Suddapal and helped get the word out what we're really fighting against. And no, you can't have him either. Don't be an ass about it."

"And what should I be?"

"You know damned well that Cithrin and her bank stood against all of this from the start. Well, turns out they weren't the only ones. There are good people in Antea who've been working against Palliako and his priests. We're on our way up to rein this in. Only I can't do it if I've got to crack your ass the other way before I go."

"Rein it in how, exactly?"

"Not going to talk about that," Marcus said. *Mostly because I haven't worked it out*, he didn't add.

Karol Dannien leaned back in his chair. His eyes were so cold they would have put a skin on water. "You hear about the children?"

"What children?" Jorey asked, but Marcus could hear in his voice the boy already knew.

"Suddapal rose, yeah? We popped out of Kiaria, sent Fallon Broot and his bunch swimming south for Lyoneia without a boat. Took back what was ours to start with. Palliako threw the hostages into the Division. Right now, while we're being polite to one another, there's hundreds of children who...how'd you call it? Weren't behind any of what happened? Hundreds of kids that weren't behind any of it either, rotting and feeding worms at the bottom of the biggest ditch in Antea."

Jorey closed his eyes, pressed his knuckle to his lip. Funny how close horror and exasperation could run together. Marcus felt it too. Of course Geder had done the thing. Anything to make it all worse.

"Hadn't heard that," Marcus said. "Not much pleased now that I have."

"Well that's big of you," Dannien said. "So let's review, yeah? You're marching the same Antean soldiers, some of them, that pulled these children away from their families and shoved them up north to die. You've got one of these mind-breaking spider priests in your pocket who you won't hear of handing over. And what you want of me is I go back and tell these men and the ghosts of their babies that we ought to stand aside and let you pass by. Did I get that right?"

One of the Timzinae guards shifted his weight. Marcus paused a long moment to see if an attack would follow, but the man thought better of it.

"It sounded more convincing before you said it that way, I'll give you that," Marcus said. "But let's say your side too. We pick a place and fight. Some of your men die. Some of Kalliam's men die. Maybe you and I live through it, maybe we don't. Whoever wins...what? Gets to brag about it? No dead child comes back. No wrong thing that's happened gets undone. A bunch of angry, confused assholes hack each other to death in a field or else they don't. Now tell me why my way's worse?"

"We'll make Antea an example to anyone else who pretends to empire," Dannien said, biting each word as it passed his lips. "And there will be justice for their atrocities."

"There'll be more atrocities, at least. And it'll be you doing them this time. So that's a change," Marcus said. "Not sure you're made better than Palliako by going second."

God smiled, he thought. *I'm sounding like Cithrin now.*

"There has to be a reckoning, Wester," Dannien said.

"You're right. There does," Marcus said. "But this ain't it."

In the silence, the breeze made the leather tent sides thrum in their frames. A bird called out three sharp and rising notes, like a trumpet calling the charge. Marcus felt his weight centered between his feet, his hands soft but ready. He hadn't been aware of preparing for violence, but here he was. Prepared. The odd thing was, his mind felt clearer and more his own than it had in months. Some things resisted being forgotten.

"You don't stand a chance," Dannien said.

"That's what they said in Northcoast," Marcus replied.

"No other way?"

Marcus felt his plans slipping into place already. How many men he had, and what supplies. Where Karol stood on the plain and the mountain above it. The dragon's roads and the merely human dirt tracks and the deer trails and streams. He saw what he'd need to do later, and it shaped what he had to do now. Hopefully Jorey Kalliam wouldn't take offense.

"No other way," Marcus said. "If it's a fight you need, Karol, I'll hand it to you. And then I'll beat you fair. Afterward, we can talk about justice and reckonings while we wait for Suddapal to pay your ransom."

Karol Dannien stood. The rage made his face darker. His neck was almost purple with it. "You always were a prick."

He left, the Timzinae guards trotting to keep up. Marcus leaned against the table, glanced at Jorey Kalliam, then away. The boy had the shocked look of someone who'd just taken an unexpected blow. "Sorry about that. Overstepped myself."

"Not sure I'd have done better," Jorey said.

"Still. It wasn't mine to decide, and...well, I may have decided."

Vincen spoke for the first time since they'd come. His voice was steady and deep. "What are our chances of winning through?"

Marcus shifted, looking through the seams of the frame where the daylight glinted through. He wanted to be sure none of Dannien's soldiers were near enough to hear, and even then, he spoke low. "They've got more men, and better rested. They've got position on us, and given all we had to leave behind, we can assume they're better armed. They know about what the spiders can do, though I don't think Kit would be willing to use that power to help kill people. It's a problem for him."

"What do we have?" Jorey asked, and his voice was solid as stone. He had some promise.

"You've got the hero of Wodford and Gradis," Marcus said, tapping himself on the chest. "So in a *fair* fight, you're fucked."

Geder

The thaw hadn't reached Camnipol, but the court had returned. The first group tacitly fleeing the strife in the east was joined by the more traditional grandees who'd spent their winter in the King's Hunt. Cyr Emming had presided over the hunt itself, relying on his position as Geder's advisor even more than on the dignity of his titles. Now that he'd come back, he seemed pleased to continue being the social center of the court. Geder was pleased to let him. Despite that, not all balls and feasts could be avoided.

Since the wars began, Camnipol had seen a great influx of wealth from the conquered. Asterilhold and Sarakal and Elassae had all given up their treasuries and the adornments of their temples along with their land and freedom. Emming's grand ball was lavish beyond anything Geder had ever seen. Distilled wine poured out of statues of gold and pearl, spilling as much onto the floor as into the cups. Slaves sat in contorted, uncomfortable positions to act as living chairs and divans for the high families of the court. The food was rich and greasy, meats and butters and cakes thick as jelly. After two seasons of starving, Geder didn't have the belly for it.

The silk banners that hung from Emming's vaulted ceiling listed the names of conquered cities. Suddapal and Inentai were among them. And the guests...court fashion was famed for changing year by year, and now was no different. Some few still wore the oversize black leather that Geder himself had made popular, but more had adopted the newer look based, it seemed, on feathers and bone. Sanna Daskellin in particular wore a gown fashioned from ravens' feathers and a cape of tiny bird bones sewn together with dark thread. She clattered when she moved.

Braziers in the shape of Timzinae bodies bent in pain stood among the guests, the light from their fires licking out of their mouths and eyeholes. The smoke they gave off smelled of incense and burning sap. Reed instruments and viols filled the air with exotic music inspired by the new lands under Antean stewardship and the Kesheti rhythms associated in the court's collective mind with the goddess.

His own chair stood on an elevated dais so that he could look out over it all. The whirl of bodies and darkness, smoke and gold and gaiety. Geder stayed as long as he could stand it, making small conversations with men and women, many of whom were newer at court than himself. Tiar Sanninen, newly Baron of Eccolund. Salvian Cersillian, cousin of the former Earl of Masonhalm, and her daughters. Lady Broot, whose every word and gesture was hoping for happy news of her family in Elassae. Happy words that Geder didn't have to offer.

Everything about the court made it seem a fabric of excess and fear. The laughter, too wild. The joy, too desperate. It was as though the court in general had caught a fever and was pretending that it hadn't. The buzz of desperation and despair this seemed designed to drown out...well, perhaps that was only Geder's own.

He made his curt excuses to Emming, handed back his half-finished flagon of wine, and called for his carriage. Aster was there somewhere. Dancing, most likely, with the girls of his cohort. Well, he was the prince. He could do that. Should, even. Someone should wring a drop of being carefree out of the world.

The streets of Camnipol in twilight were oddly beautiful and quiet after the too-lush feasting rooms. The air smelled clean and clear and like the presentiment of rain. There were few trees outside the gardens of the great houses, but here and there splashes of green ivy spilled up grey stone walls, their leaves defying the cold. Hardy, thick-bodied finches had joined the sparrows and crows of the winter. Geder leaned out the window of his carriage as it rattled toward the Kingspire and let the breeze of his passage cool his face. The banner of the goddess fluttered high above, draped from the doors of the temple. Lights flickered up there as well. Basrahip and his priests, performing their rites or eating rice from simple bowls or simply sitting together. Geder didn't know. If the trek up those stairs weren't quite so awful, he might have joined them. Instead, he took comfort where he had before. His library.

The books perfumed the desk with dust and sweet paste. The light of a dozen candles warmed the leather-bound volumes and parchment scrolls, the codices and maps and fragile paper sewn together with twine. Geder's stomach gurgled and shifted with the unaccustomed too-rich food of Emming's feast, but he didn't call for water or a cunning man. It would have meant talking to someone, and even ordering a servant to do his bidding was more energy than he could manage just now. He was ill, after all, whatever the cunning men said.

He sat on a large chair, the light spilling over his shoulder and onto the pages of a third-age history of Far Syramys by a likely mythical Dartinae poet who went by the name Stone.

Among the civilized lands, Far Syramys is a conjuration of
the possible, the birthplace of soft dreams and harsh mysteries. What we hope and wish and spin from fantasy, we
place there. In Far Syramys, we say, the women walk naked
and unashamed through the parks, their sex available to
any who ask. In Far Syramys, cunning men have deepened
their arts until the cures for all diseases are known, though
the price of cure is sometimes obscure and terrible. In Far
Syramys, the forges make steel that will never lose its edge;
the farms, pomegranates that will sustain a man for a week
with only a handful of pips; the looms, cloth so fine and
beautiful that the wearer of their silk will disappear from
mortal sight.

Among the rough and uncivilized hills of the true Far
Syramys, there are indeed great and hidden cities. There are
indeed women and men of surpassing beauty. The Haunadam and Raushadam make their homes there, with bodies
and minds as unlike the others of the thirteen races as an
apple is from a walnut. But Far Syramys's dreams of itself are
nothing like our dreams of it, and the traveler who dares it
should be warned of all that has happened there before.

Geder fell into the words like he was falling asleep. Or
else waking up to some other life. He imagined himself in
the court of the Grand Agha, sitting on the floor and drinking tea with poets and hunters. Or trekking through great
caverns beneath Sai where the waters ran yellow and red,
and drinking them was death. Or seeing the Uron Tortoise
wandering the northern desert with a city of thousands riding unnoticed on its vast shell. He longed for it all, even as
he knew that in practice, it would all be awkward, tiring,
and uncomfortable if it was even real. But then it wasn't
really those places that left him empty and hungry and rich

with need. It was the Geder Palliako who could take joy in them. That better version of himself who belonged there.

When the Kurtadam servant girl appeared at the door, her eyes wide and the pelt on her face twisted into a grimace by her anxiety, Geder was almost happy to be interrupted. Not quite, but almost.

"L-lord Regent? My lord?" she said, her voice high and piping.

"Yes?"

"I apologize, my lord, but there's—" she choked on the words. Her hands balled in fists and she looked down, her mouth pressed tight. His heart went out to her. Poor thing was so sure she was going to be in trouble.

"It's all right," he said, his voice gentle. "I don't bite. Least not often. What's the issue?"

When she spoke, her voice was smoother, calmer. Still rich with fear, but not throttled by it. "The Baron of Watermarch has come, my lord. He asks your urgent presence."

Geder closed the book and laid it aside. "Show him in, then," he said. "And let this be a lesson to you...what was your name?"

"I'm Chanda, my lord."

"Let this be a lesson to you, Chanda," he said solemnly. "We all have to do shit we don't enjoy."

The servant coughed a laugh, and Geder smiled his encouragement until she smiled back. When he nodded, she backed away, still grinning under the oily fur of her race, and trotted off to retrieve Canl Daskellin from whatever waiting area they'd stowed him in while they got Geder's permission for him to enter. Outside, night had fallen, and the candles in the library remade the window as a dark and deforming mirror. Geder shifted his weight back and forth, watching his reflected head swell to a massive, ungainly monstrosity on a twig-thin body, then shrink down to almost a nub perched on comically heroic shoulders, then back again.

Daskellin appeared behind him, and he turned. Sweat and dirt streaked the older man's dark skin, and he wore riding leathers that smelled of horse even from where Geder sat.

"Lord Regent," Daskellin said, "I have a report."

"From Northcoast?"

"No, from the east. Sarakal, and it seems Elassae."

Geder shifted in his chair. "I thought you were the ambassador to Northcoast. Why are you bothering with things in the east? It's not yours to worry about. Mecelli's supposed to be doing that."

"He isn't well, my lord," Daskellin said. "The cunning men report an army outside Nus. And another massed in Orsen."

Geder waved the news away. "Cunning men can't be relied on," Geder said. "Half the time they get these so-called messages, it turns out they were never actually sent in the first place. Just someone mistook a dream for some crackpot magic and got everyone's feathers in a whirl over nothing."

"I've had a bird from my man in Orsen. That one at least is true. And Lord Mecelli's report after Inentai was right. The traditional families are taking back all we won in Sarakal. And more than that, they may not stop at the border of the empire."

"Inentai *is* the border of the empire," Geder said. "It's just in flux for the moment. It'll come back under our control. We put a temple in it. No city where we dedicated a temple to the goddess can fall. Just be lost for a bit. You heard what Basrahip said. You *know* all this."

"I did hear, Lord Geder," Daskellin said. "But I also had the reports. And I've seen the maps. If we want any hope of defending the empire, we have to raise an army. Possibly two."

Silence fell between them, dividing the room as effectively as the Division split Camnipol.

"Are you telling me you doubt the protection of the goddess?" Geder asked, slowly.

"I believe in it," Daskellin said, and the distress in his voice was like listening to a single high note played on a violin forever. It was about more than the news of the armies, more than the news of the war. There was a personal distress and hearing it made Geder's own soul ring with it like a crystal glass echoing a singer's pure note. "I don't doubt her, but I also look at the world. And as much as my faith tells me that we are under her protection, my life's experience says we need sword-and-bows at the ready. The storm that's coming? We aren't prepared to weather it."

Geder hunched over his book, hand flat against the soft leather cover. The sense of his head being stuffed with wool returned, and with it a deep weariness and anger. He felt the rage bubbling in his chest. It was unfair, monstrously unfair, to bring this all to him. Did Daskellin think he had a cunning man's stick he could wave and conjure able-bodied fighters out of nothing? The men he'd marched to Asterilhold were all that Camnipol had, and since he'd called the disband, they weren't even gathered or armed. And Geder was ill, after all. Something was wrong with him, only no one seemed able to see it. Or else to care when they did.

As long as things were going well, everyone celebrated him and threw victories for him and praised him as a hero. But as soon as there was any trouble, no one cared about him at all.

"This is not my fault."

"Lord Geder?"

"This," Geder repeated, his voice growing to a shout, "is not my fault. The position we're in? The unrest in Elassae and Sarakal? You were my advisors. The best men in the kingdom. You served King Simeon and you've been in the court. You were supposed to be the ones who knew how to run a campaign!"

Daskellin took a step back as if he'd been struck. His jaw worked as if fighting to get out some sentiment too large for his throat. Rage boiled up from Geder's belly. He stood, throwing the book at Daskellin's head as he did it. It missed by a wide margin, but the violence of the intention was clear. For a moment, Geder thought the man would attack him, and in that moment, he welcomed the thought. The prospect of beating Daskellin's smug, self-serving face with his bare fists was like the hope of water to a man possessed by thirst.

They teetered on the edge of the moment, the air in the room rich with the potential for violence. Daskellin took his lip between his teeth and looked down. When he spoke, his voice shook, but it was not loud.

"If I have failed you, Lord Regent, I apologize. I have always done what I hoped would be best for the throne."

"And there just now you've remembered that I can have you killed," Geder snapped, but the fire in his gut had died already. He felt as though he was sinking back into himself. He'd thrown a book at the man. That was embarrassing, but it was Daskellin's own fault. The man should have known better. "I'll put out the call. We'll bring back the men I led against the apostate. It's not an army like Broot had in Elassae or Jorey's force. And you'll lead it. You personally. Then I don't want to hear anything more about how I'm not prepared."

"Yes, Lord Regent," Daskellin said.

"And we won't fall. No matter what we won't fall, because the goddess is here. She's remaking the world, and we are her instruments, so we won't fall. Because of me. Because I brought her here. Everything we've gained, we gained because of me. What we've lost is your fault."

"Lord Regent," Daskellin said, making it sound like a yes without actually saying the word. Geder sneered and turned away. An exhaustion was coming over him, turning his bones to granite and lead. The effort of standing up was too much. Everything was too much. Daskellin was a selfish bastard for taking away what little energy Geder had left.

"You can go," Geder said. "You'll have your soldiers tomorrow."

Daskellin nodded, his jaw still shifted forward like a showfighter's at the start of a match. "Thank you, Lord Regent," he said, then turned and, walking stiffly, left. Geder tried to look out the window and failed. His own bent reflection blocked his view of the city. Of the world. Only when he put the candles out could he catch glimpses of the lights of Camnipol and the moon and the stars. He sat for a time in a darkness too deep for reading. The feast was still going. Would be going all night. If he returned to it, he'd be made welcome. Or he could go to the Great Bear and drink distilled wine and smoke pipes and trade stories with whoever was there. He could command any woman in the court to his bed if he wanted to. Make her do whatever he wanted, and if she laughed at him afterward, he could have her thrown into the Division. That was the power of the emperor. The power of the throne.

The thing was, he didn't want to do any of it. Everything sounded awful. Even the effort to call for more light seemed beyond him. When he'd been a boy in Rivenhalm, he'd dreamed of going to Camnipol, becoming a hero of the court. Now he was here, and he'd done it, and he dreamed of being almost anywhere else.

"It's only for now," he said to the darkness and the books. "Soon, she'll have burned all the lies from the world, and we'll be at peace. It'll be all right."

Or else the confusion he'd glimpsed in Basrahip's eyes would grow. That bad news would multiply. More cities would fall. No, not fall, but be lost for a time. For longer. The death throes of the old world still had the power to crush everything, and staying out of its thrashing meant being nimble and quick. Geder didn't feel nimble or quick. In fact, he barely felt anything at all, except muddy in his mind and angry without knowing who or what he was angry with.

A light in the garden below the library shifted. Some servant walking in the night. Or a member of the court. Or Basrahip and his priests. Or the goddess herself. Or Cithrin. Geder didn't know, and he didn't want to. As long as he wasn't certain, there was hope that it might be something astounding. Something that would heal him.

Far Syramys wasn't actually so far, really. Ships left for it every year from Narinisle and Herez and Cabral. The bluewater trade carried the highest risk in the world, but it was done. Geder closed his eyes and imagined himself on the deck of a ship cutting through the vast waves of the open sea without so much as an island in sight. It was supposed to be a vision of comfort, of possibility, but his mind kept turning to how it would feel to be lost there. Lost in a hostile emptiness without any sense of how to go back home or else forward to safety.

It would feel, he thought, very much like being Lord Regent.

Marcus

As the sky slid from blue to indigo, Jorey and Marcus walked the defenses, Jorey ahead and Marcus behind. Barricades and low, improvised walls stood on either side of the dragon's road. Mud and stone and uprooted hedge, they were often little more than the idea of cover. But it gave the Antean archers places to hold and fall back to as Dannien's soldiers moved in. They'd even managed a scout's perch on an outcropping of rock where someone with younger eyes than Marcus could shout back reports of the enemy movements and Kit could use a speaker's trumpet to call out assertions about the outcome of the fight in hopes of making them true. Night birds began their songs, trilling to each other and the Antean soldiers. The sun, already vanished behind the mountains to the west, sent streaks of red across the thin, scudding clouds. The smoke of the first campfires rose up like it aspired to being a cloud itself.

Marcus watched more than the battleground. Jorey moved among his men with an ease that wasn't quite easy yet. Like an actor new to the troupe, he made the gestures without entirely making them his own. He had potential, though. Marcus had seen more than one great general rise to power with less compassion for the men who followed him. Jorey Kalliam understood the importance of commanding loyalty. It would serve him well if any of them managed not to be killed on this blighted stretch of jade. Jorey called an end to the day's building, as they'd agreed he would, and the men put up a ragged cheer. During the long, terrible days of the march, Marcus had kept as much as he could to himself, but he still knew some of them.

Durin Caust was the one with two missing fingers who'd been the first to learn how to make a shelter out of cut snow. Alan Lennit and Sajor Sammit were the lieutenants under one of Jorey's bannermen who held each other's hand during the march. The one with the flaming red beard and eyes dark as a Southling's was called Mer, and he had a good singing voice.

Trivial, meaningless bits of information that took them from being a single organism—the army of Antea—and made them into a company of men that Marcus didn't particularly look forward to watching die. It occurred to him as they walked back to the main camp that holding himself apart hadn't only been so that his already thin disguise as a servant wouldn't be seen through. He also hadn't wanted to see them as anything more than meat on legs, extensions of Geder Palliako and the priests and Imperial Antea. So he'd cocked that up too.

"Double fires tonight," Marcus reminded Jorey. "If we have wood or twigs or dried dung. Anything that'll burn, burn it. Let their scouts think we're more than we are."

"Last fires we'll see for a good while too," Jorey said. "Might as well enjoy them."

"That's truth."

The attack would come in the morning with the rising sun low on the horizon, blinding the Antean forces. Depending on how the enemy was stocked, Marcus guessed that it would be a hammer blow of horsemen coming down the road in hopes of scattering them quickly or a foot assault swooping south and taking them in the right flank. Or both. Dannien likely had enough men for both. Jorey had laid out the camp to make that plan seem the sound one. More fires in the north, closer together. Fewer and more widely spaced in the south. Likely, Dannien would be using banners or flares to signal his men. Their ears would be stopped against Kit's voice. As advantages went, it was thin, weak, and insufficient.

It wasn't only that Marcus didn't want the battle in the first place. It was also that there was no chance that he could win it. Weak as they were and without the morale-breaking voices of the priests, they had effectively lost already. The Timzinae forces would break the exhausted, underfed, road-weary Anteans like a dry twig, wheel north, and burn a pathway from there to Camnipol.

And so, when Karol Dannien led his men out of Orsen, Jorey and his army would need to be elsewhere.

As the last grey of twilight settled to black, the Antean scouts went out. The moon hung over the horizon at just less than a quarter. It would be below the horizon before midnight. Jorey and his captains went to the men at their fires and checked each group personally. Their packs had to be filled with dried meat and hardtack and the sticky, dense waybread they'd taken from Bellin. That and their swords and bows. No armor. It was too heavy for what they were doing. Boiled leather and worked scale were all burned or ripped down at the seams so that the enemy couldn't make use of them. Marcus sat with Clara Kalliam beside the Lord Marshal's tent, waiting for word to come that something had gone awry. That the enemy scouts had seen them or that Dannien had somehow stolen a march and blocked their way. If they'd done it right, there wouldn't be many scouts to the north of the camp. They'd be marking out ways to lead the attacking forces to the south of the road, but few plans were so graceful as to match the world.

"Are you well, Captain?" Clara Kalliam asked.

"Am I fidgeting?"

"A bit, yes."

"Sorry. I'm told I do that when I'm annoyed. Isn't something I'm aware of at the time."

She shifted, drawing deeply on her pipe and letting the smoke out through her nose. The firelight played across her face. She was handsome, in a solid, well-bruised way. More than looking like a beautiful woman, she looked like an interesting one.

"You're thinking this may not work," she said, her voice low.

"I'm not thinking one way or the other," he said. "I'm waiting to see what happens. If it's interesting, I don't want to spend the time then getting ready to make a call, so I'm just anxious and cranky now. Gets me out ahead of it."

"Your burden seems to be bothering you less," she said.

"My burden?"

"Your blade," she said.

Marcus glanced back at the hilt rising above his shoulder. When he thought about it, the skin across his shoulder still itched and burned a little. The muscles where the scabbard rode against him ached. The weird taste in his mouth that came of carrying the poisoned thing too long had become so familiar, he'd have noticed more if it left. And still, he knew what she meant.

"It hasn't changed," Marcus said. "It's only that I'm more distracted. There are a thousand things I'm bad at. This one, I'm good at."

She smiled. "You're good at being annoyed and anxious?"

"The way I've heard it put is that my soul's a circle. I'm best at the bottom, heading up. The top of things is just the first part of down. At least for me. Being caught in a storm keeps me from thinking about other things, and when it's too quiet, I do. And then I'm not as good."

Clara Kalliam lifted an eyebrow in query.

Marcus shook his head, refusing the question, but then answered it anyway. "I saw my wife and daughter dead before me."

"I see," Clara said. "I watched my husband executed."

"By Palliako. I heard. I'm sorry."

"I am too," she said. "Dawson was an old-fashioned man, but he was a good one. I miss him, but I also think the world as it has become would have been a hell for him. There are times I'm glad he didn't live to see this."

Ah, Marcus thought. *The night-before-battle conversation.* He hadn't expected to have one of those, but here he was, sitting in darkness with the things that simmered and stewed in people's hearts starting to bubble out. Well, she'd opened the bottle because she wanted to. He'd accommodate her and see what she would drink.

"You sound as though you've recovered from the loss," Marcus said.

"No," Clara said. And then, "Or yes. Yes, I have. I haven't unmade what happened. It was too ugly an end to something precious. I shall always have the scars of it, I think. But I realized his wife died with him, and I have mourned her, and I am someone new. And I like who I am. If God gave me the option, I couldn't go back."

"It's not like that for me," Marcus said, his voice lighter and more conversational than the truths he spoke. "I'm the same man I was the night they burned."

"You haven't changed at all?"

"Not in any way that matters," he said. His inflection was like a joke, but she heard past it.

"No scars, then. Only wounds. That must be terrible."

"It is," Marcus said. "But it makes me good at the things that keep my mind off it."

"I'm sorry," she said. "I've intruded."

"I let you, m'lady," he said.

"Then thank you for that. I will not undervalue it."

He looked at her, unsure what weight her words carried. It struck him for the first time what very lucky men her husband and the so-called servant everyone pretended wasn't her lover might be. She was a singular woman.

Footsteps approached the fire, and Marcus looked up. He'd forgotten to put his back to the fire, and his eyes were poorly adapted to the darkness around them. When Vincen Coe loomed up from the night, it was like he'd stepped into being.

"Word's come from the scouts. Jorey's chosen a path."

"Well then," Marcus said. "Let's see if we can pull this off after all."

The night march began. Everyone's orders were strict. No voices rose in chatter or song. No scabbard remained unwrapped for the starlight to glint off the metal. The soldiers had rubbed their faces in dirt and ash to keep the sweat from shining. Likely it was more than they need do, but the way to find that out was to try without and fail. The curious thing about war—about so many things—was the number of critically important things that no one could know.

Marcus and Vincen and Clara Kalliam, like the rest of the great army of Antea, abandoned their fire and their tent, their carts and the great majority of the supplies they'd carried, and became ghosts. Silent as the spirits of the dead, they whispered their way to the north, running along deer trails and through thin woods. The air was chill to the point of real cold, but after the pass, it felt like nothing. The thread of dragon's jade that led from Orsen up into the body of the empire lay somewhere far to their right, unseen. When the last sliver of moon failed them, they went on in darkness without so much as a candle to give them away.

Hours later, the east brightened to charcoal and the figures walking in their silent lines began to have silhouettes. Jorey called the halt, and the army divided. Five groups to the west, to cross the dragon's road and take shelter separately in the shallow hills and forests of Antea's southern reaches. Three to stay here and skirt the edges of the Dry Wastes as best they could. One small group with most of the horses to ride north to Camnipol, raising the alarm along the way.

It was in many ways the end of the Lord Marshal's command. Though Jorey Kalliam would lead the largest of the groups, all would act independently to harass Dannien's scouts and threaten his supply lines, draw him off the swift path of the dragon's road into the weeds and dirt of the plains. They would slow the attackers, distract them, and if one group was cornered and slaughtered to a man, there would still be seven more to carry on the job. It was the kind of fighting they did in the Keshet and the wilder edges of Borja, dirty and harsh and thin on honor. It was the kind of battle an army didn't win so much as indefinitely postpone losing.

None of Jorey's captains, no matter how noble their blood, objected. That alone, Marcus thought, showed how far Antea had gone down the dragon's path. No one dreamed of glorious conquest on the field of battle. No one called their sneaking away in the night an act of cowardice. Years in the field and more than half the men who'd marched out to capture Nus dead or scattered back along the path had left the veterans of Antea with fewer illusions about the glories of war than when they'd started.

Which, though Marcus didn't say it, suggested there was another problem.

They stopped three hours after midday in a shallow valley. Sandstone blocks made a rough wall, the only vestige of some long-vanished structure. There was no snow there, no ice, nothing that could have been made into water. The air had an uncanny salt taste that Marcus had only ever found near the Dry Wastes. But though they were close, these weren't the wastes.

Jorey's personal force was a hundred and fifty men, five horses, and his mother. Of the three that had stayed on the east side of the jade road, it had gone farthest north. Even if Dannien wheeled his forces and quick-marched after them—which would have been a first-campaign level of error—they wouldn't reach here in twice the time Jorey had. The army might be hard to stop, but at the price of speed.

Marcus found Kit on the sun-soaked side of the wall. The actor had grown thinner since they'd left Carse. They all had. His cheekbones seemed ready to cut through his olive skin, and his wiry hair haloed him in brown and grey. He lifted an exhausted hand to Marcus.

"Well," Marcus said, sitting beside the man. "That was unpleasant."

"I found it less enjoyable than I expected," Kit agreed. "And I don't think my expectations were particularly high. I must admit, I was surprised that our little sidestep was effective."

"There are advantages to having a name that kings whisper to scare their princes at night. Great warriors don't traditionally turn tail and sneak out in the dark before a battle. Add to that I challenged him, and he thought we had more men than we did. He believed he'd win, but I didn't let him think I agreed quite so much." Marcus laughed and rested his head against the gritty stone. "I won't be able to pull the trick again."

Kit made a noise of appreciation deep in his throat and went silent. Marcus shifted the scabbard, unslung it awkwardly, and put it on the ground at his side.

"Noticed something odd. When the forces split, no one was talking about the greater glory of the goddess or how we were all bringing truth to the unwashed or any of that."

"I suppose I hadn't paid attention to that," Kit said.

"No, they dropped their honor-and-glory talk in favor of something practical pretty damned fast. Leaves me wondering." He looked over at his old friend and companion. They had come through terrible places together, he and Kit. He didn't want to go on, but it was the job. "Get the feeling you may have been improvising some lines."

"I think you're asking if I played the priest of the goddess the whole journey. Have I understood you?"

"Have."

"I could not," Kit whispered. "I like to think I tried as best I could. I didn't reveal who we truly are or our relationship to Cithrin or the bank. Or Palliako, for that. I didn't lay bare the truth of what the spiders are or how these men's lives were spent on a deceit. But there are things I cannot agree to do."

"If you couldn't stand lying to them, the time to say that would have been before we left Carse. We were counting on you. And you don't get to change that horse midstream."

"Them? It wasn't them. It was me."

"Don't know what that means, Kit."

"Each of them, I spoke to each of them every...I don't know. Two days? Three? I started in the mornings and I played my part until it was time to sleep again. Even in the pass. Even then. They heard me a bit. On occasion. I was *never* free of my voice."

"You're not getting clearer."

"I began to believe again," Kit said. "I said that the goddess would save us. That we would win through. That all would be well, and I found myself taking real comfort in it. Once I saw that, I felt I had to change. Give them encouragement, but not...not the kind I had been giving."

Marcus felt a little twist in his belly. A drop of horror in his sea of weariness. "Knowing what you know and seeing what you've seen, you fell back into believing in the spider goddess?"

Kit was silent for a long moment. A breath of wind stirred the grit and dirt. Salt and copper haunted the back of Marcus's tongue.

"I don't believe we are fighting *cynics*, Marcus. When I see my old brothers, I don't see men manipulating innocents. I see men who have listened to their own stories until who they might have been was eaten away to nothing. I think they wear the goddess like a blindfold and swing their knives on faith. I believe I am as vulnerable to the power of my voice as anyone else, and I felt myself falling prey to the words I spoke. I'm sure that what I knew protected me, but it would wear away given time. Here and now, I want you to see how badly I wish the world free of these things. I hope you understand that I have been fighting against this power longer than anyone else I know. Longer than most of you even knew this danger existed."

"I understand."

"I find that unless we are very, very careful there can be a difference between who we are and the stories we tell ourselves about who we are. I hope I have managed to bring those two together as nearly as I could, and if I have, it was hard work with terrible prices paid along the way. I am willing to sacrifice a great deal, but taking apart what I actually am and what I only believe myself to be?"

"Yeah. All right," Marcus said.

"I would rather die than that," Kit said.

"If you turned back into one of them, I'd kill you."

Kit's eyes went a little wider, his face paled under the leather and burn of his cheeks. The truth of what Marcus said carried a deeper weight than the glib way he'd said it. No one but Kit and his twice-damned spiders would have heard it.

"Thank you," Kit said. "I appreciate that."

Marcus didn't have the advantage of the spiders, but he was fairly certain Kit wasn't lying.

Cithrin

Years before, in another lifetime, Cithrin had been part of a caravan attacked by robbers. They'd been stopped by a tree across the dragon's jade of the road. Before they could clear it, bandits had come from the sides and behind. The plan Cithrin hatched now wasn't precisely the same but neither was it so very different. There were only a few scraps of information she needed.

The inn sat at the intersection of a dirt track and the dragon's road. Yardem had done the negotiations with the keep, pretending to have less coin than they actually had and haggling for a place in the stables where they would be seen by fewer people. The grooms and stable hands, he was more open with, passing them enough silver that most of them found their way to the common rooms here or else other places nearby.

For the players, it was like coming home. With the exception of Lak, who had never been touring with Cary and Master Kit and the others, the stables of inns and taprooms were nearly like a mother's hearth. Hornet and Mikel immediately made friends with the horses, cooing and passing them bits of dried apple. Charlit Soon and Cary scouted the place, finding where they could all sit in relative warmth and privacy, and also where the women could sleep apart from the men and so lower the chance of a local boy's taking the wrong idea. Yardem took it all with the same stoic amusement that seemed to follow him like a cloud. Only Barriath seemed out of place.

Well, Barriath and her.

Cithrin had to keep out of sight. She'd spent the whole journey down from the icy coast to Rivenhalm wrapped in a colorless woolen cloak and hood, trying not to be noticeable and feeling as unobtrusive as blood on a wedding dress. A half-Cinnae woman in Antea would suggest only one name to the townsfolk. Cithrin bel Sarcour was, after all, the slut and daughter of lies who'd humiliated the Lord Regent and aided the filthy Timzinae in their plots against the empire. It gave her more attention than any banker would want. Her best defense was that a woman of that stature and power would never be so stupid as to travel the back roads with only a handful of actors, a single guard, and an exile and traitor whom Geder had ordered killed if found inside his borders. If she had been able to trust the work to anyone else, she wouldn't have come.

Except that wasn't true. This was better than sitting quietly in Carse, waiting for word to come. And if it was a problem, at least it was hers. It was better to be damned for what she was.

Charlit Soon's giggle came from the yard, and a boy's rough voice trying to be deeper than it was. The other players went quiet, holding their conversation until they knew the results of her mission. She squealed and laughed and then her shadow came through the stable door alone. The boy's footsteps were almost too quiet to hear, even before he retreated.

Charlit's round face glowed.

"He's at his holding," she said. "Apparently Lord Lehrer Palliako isn't what you'd call a fixture at court, even if his son does run it."

"Could have told you that," Barriath said, with a scowl. "Wait. I did tell you that. More than once."

"You didn't say he was at home just now," Sandr pointed out with feigned mildness. The two men had been needling each other since landfall in the north. Cithrin had a sense that she didn't want to examine why the pair got on so poorly.

"And," Charlit Soon said, lifting her chin, "he's due to visit a particular set of farms tomorrow. I even have directions to the road he goes down to reach them."

"Well done," Cary said, then turned to Cithrin. "You know what you want to do, then?"

In the stall behind them, a thin, shaggy horse sighed and shifted, scratching himself against the wooden posts. The straw around her feet skittered in the little breeze. The others were looking at her, waiting.

"I know what I want to try," she said.

The next day, they went out. Horses were too expensive to take without drawing attention, but the march wasn't long, and the landscape welcomed them. The trees outside Rivenhalm were still bare from the winter, but warm winds had almost finished melting the snow. Only the deep shadows still held pale and dirty lumps, half snow and half ice, and all surrendering to the coming springtime. Pale-green sprouts were pushing their way up from the dark earth. Gravel and mud made a raised roadway, and a slope to the north came to a ditch already running with brown, murky water. Everything smelled of rich soil and the coming spring. Rivenhalm's farmland to the west of the holding lay on a plain, but Cithrin and the others didn't go so far as to see them. They made their little camp in among the trees on a long straight stretch, waiting. The low, white sky softened the sunlight, leaving everything cool and nearly shadowless.

Everything else she'd done, now she was trying her hand at banditry.

When she was a child, Magister Imaniel had talked to her about the placing of negotiations. The architecture that surrounded a conversation had the power to shape it, he'd said. That was why the bank's offices were kept so modest. When someone came to place a deposit, everything around them lowered their expectation of a return. When the bank was preparing to put out coin as an investment, it was better done at a cathedral or a palace or a wide open square in the city's center. Simply by making the space in which the trade took place wide and large, the bank set the scale for the money involved.

As the sun sailed unseen through the sky, lighting the clouds with pale fire, she wondered what he would make of this empty stretch of road, the bone-bare trees spreading out all around, and the road that reached out toward the horizon. It was a humble place, without even the dignity of the dragon's jade. And it was lonely. She had to take control of Geder's father, one way or another. And then she had to take control of Geder. She strained her attention toward the vanishing edge of the road, willing her prey to appear and dreading it.

Cary struck up a song, her voice low and murmuring so that the melody wouldn't give them away. Yardem throbbed a bass accompaniment. The wood itself seemed to take up the song. For a time, it was beautiful.

The distant echo of hoofbeats stopped them, and in the distance three figures appeared, all on horseback. Cithrin, back among the trees at the roadside, scowled. She'd assumed Lehrer Palliako would travel in a carriage. It was possible that the man she wanted wasn't in the party now approaching. Or perhaps he was and would have a much easier path to escape should it come to violence. Either scenario carried its own difficulties.

Her breath came faster and shallow as the riders approached. Two men, one in a wide, shaggy coat, the other in light leather armor such as a guard or huntsman might wear. The third a woman in plain canvas and patched wool.

Cithrin narrowed her eyes, trying to better see the man in the shaggy coat. He was older, that was sure. The hair that showed at the edges of his leather hat was white. The horse he rode held itself tall and proud. It was hard to think that the father of the Lord Regent would go about his holding in such practical, workmanlike fashion. It was also hard to think that this would be anyone else.

Her heart in her throat, Cithrin lifted her hand to Yardem. He nodded and lifted his voice in a call that sounded like a crow calling twice, and then again three times. A moment later, another false crow came back twice and then once. The others set back along the road were ready. She should have brought more soldiers. Except that soldiers could hardly help looking like soldiers, and actors could better pass unnoticed. Trade-offs. Everything was trade-offs. Always and forever.

Cithrin stepped out from the trees, walking with her weight low in her hips the way Cary had taught her. Cary, Yardem, Sandr, and Lak followed. The hoofbeats shifted, slowed. Yardem and the three players stood behind her, their bodies blocking the way forward at a hundred feet behind, and Barriath and the others did the same. Cithrin's belly was tighter than knots, and she wished she'd thought to bring a skin of wine. Or something stronger.

She walked alone toward the riders, and the riders stopped before she reached them. Close up, there was no question that this was Geder's father. They had similar eyes, and the way the old man's shoulders angled into his thick neck was a prediction of how Geder Palliako would age.

"Lord Palliako," she said, making her curtsy. "I assume I have the honor of addressing the Viscount of Rivenhalm?"

She braced herself for his reply, ready to leap aside if he charged, or fall back if he drew his sword. The seconds lasted hours.

"You have me at a disadvantage, miss," the elder Palliako said. "I don't recall having met, and I would think even at my age, I'd recall a lovely young woman like yourself."

There was no fear in his voice. His male companion and, Cithrin had to believe, guard placed a hand on the pommel of his sword. The woman in the patched cloak had already drawn a long, vicious-looking knife. Cithrin smiled. When she'd pictured this conversation, it had happened in a carriage where it felt much less like shouting. But here she was, and nothing to be done about it.

"I am an acquaintance of your son's," she said. And then a moment later, "I think you'll have heard of me. I mean you no harm. I've come to talk with you. I have an offer I'd like to present."

The old man blinked. It took only a few seconds for him to understand what this half-Cinnae woman in his road was saying. Who she was, and what her presence implied.

"You're certain this isn't an abduction?" the older man said, turning his horse a few degrees. "Because, just between us, it looks a bit like an abduction."

Well, and it might have been if he'd ridden in a damned *carriage*. If he left the road, leapt the filthy ditch, and lit out among the trees, she'd never find him again. She stepped to the side of the road and motioned to the others. Yardem, understanding the tactics of the situation, moved first, and the others followed him. None of them drew a weapon. Lehrer Palliako's way forward was clear, but the man didn't spur his horse.

"Your son is in danger," Cithrin said. "He needs your help. And you need mine."

"My son has a large number of people protecting him. I doubt any new attempt on his life will come to much."

"It isn't his life that's in danger. Geder's fallen under the influence of corrupt and corrupting men. They've turned him into a monster."

"That seems alarmist," the older man said, but he didn't spur his mount. His gaze cut to the side like a man trying not to admit he couldn't pay his debt. Hope surged in Cithrin's breast. Hope and fear. She was so *close*...

"I know what you've heard of me, my lord. But I've come here at the risk of my life because I know your son is a good man," she lied. "He's in trouble."

Lehrer Palliako didn't move for a long time. The leather-clad guard shot a worried glance at him. Cithrin clenched her fists. At last, he took a long, shuddering breath and lowered his head. When he spoke, his voice was low.

"I know," he said.

The holding at Rivenhalm was smaller than Cithrin had imagined. The house itself was wood with only a little stone. It stood tucked on the side of a deep and wooded ravine. The river from which it took its name was in truth hardly more than a wide and vigorous stream that muttered and clapped its way along below. Even without the leaves of summer, the place was dark with shadows. When the crowding trees were in their fullness, Cithrin imagined the house would never rise much above a green and dappled twilight.

Sitting on a small porch with a window that looked out

on the steep hillside, Cithrin imagined young Geder Palliako spending long, quiet hours there on the same floorboards she now walked. Here were the rooms and archways and halls where he had been a boy. Where the seeds of the man he'd become had been planted. She tried to find something sinister in it. There was nothing like that. Rivenhalm felt close and cozy and warm inside. But maybe lonesome.

Lehrer Palliako had led them back, his visit to his farmlands forgotten. His servants had taken the cloaks and jackets from the players and guards and the exile Barriath Kalliam as if it were perfectly normal for the great enemies of the empire to arrive unannounced and be welcomed. But perhaps it was more that there was no one much more likely to appear. No one seemed to come to Rivenhalm.

"My wife died when he was very young, you know," Lehrer said, half to her and half to the cup of wine in his fist. "I raised him myself. Taught him to love books. Taught him to be a good boy. Did what I could. I never wanted him to go to court. They're a bunch of self-righteous bastards, all of them. But it isn't a favor to keep a young man from making friends. Connections in the court. I dreaded it from the day he left. The *day*. And when Dawson fucking Kalliam threw a triumph for him, I thought . . . you know, I thought perhaps I'd been wrong. Just because I'd failed at court, it didn't mean my boy would. I was sure it would be all right. Only it wasn't."

Lehrer shook his head, and Cithrin could see Geder in it. Not the monstrous Geder, hacking a man to death with a dull sword because he'd chosen defiance even at the last. The lost and gentle Geder, the one who'd hidden with her in the darkness. But there were glimmers of that other too. Lehrer Palliako was, she thought, a man of deep resentments as well as deep affections. She wondered what his wife had been like when she was alive.

"And then these priests," Lehrer said. "I went to him I don't know how many times. I told him not to forget himself, not to let them change who he was. Who he is. When Simeon named him Lord Regent...I was proud. I won't say I wasn't. But I was also afraid."

"You were right to be," Cithrin said. "The spiders in their blood were made to sow chaos. To make war constant. Inevitable. They've lied to him, and it's not his fault that he believed."

"Exactly," Lehrer said. "Exactly. It's not his fault at all. It's these priests and courtiers and politicians, isn't it? They're what led him astray. My poor little boy. Do you know, he used to try to save the water beetles? When he was young, he'd find water beetles down in the mud, and some were on their backs. He'd bring them back and try to nurse them back to being well. Gave them bits of leaf and fresh water and kept them warm. He'd cry when they died. He's a good boy."

Tears streaked the old man's cheeks. Cithrin had the sense that he'd been waiting to say all this. All he hadn't had was someone to listen. Someone who understood.

"Will you help me, then? Will you help me to help him?"

"I will," Lehrer said. "You'll stay with me. All of you. Geder has an estate in the city. No one will look for you there, and we can get him away from these bastards before they make it worse."

"Your son is very angry with me," Cithrin said.

"And Kalliam's boy. Barriath. The one you brought. I know he is, but it will be fine. We'll see to it. He'll forgive you once he understands." Lehrer reached out his hand tentatively, and Cithrin paused for only a moment before she took it. Lehrer smiled, tears welling again in his eyes. "You would have made a fine daughter. I'm sorry that this has all done what it's done."

"I am too," she said, and let him go. The relief in her belly was like a drink of strong wine. It unknotted her, if only for the moment.

She'd done the first part. She'd gained the confidence of someone Geder loved. Now there was only finding the way to turn the younger Palliako against the priests whose power he relied on. And as difficult as that sounded, she had her path picked out. With every tale Lehrer spun, with every reminiscence about the innocent, kind young man Geder had been before the court corrupted him, she felt more certain she could manage it.

The priests had taken control of the empire, that was true. They were sowing chaos without even knowing that they had been designed for the task. They were the enemy that had to be defeated if there was ever to be hope of peace.

But fire could be fought with fire, violence with violence, and there had been no priests when Geder burned Vanai.

Entr'acte: Nus

The enemies of the goddess have already lost! None can stand against her power. You, her chosen, stand as proof of her grace and her power in the world."

The priest lifted his hands in blessing, and Duris—along with everyone else in the cathedral—cheered. Their gathered voices echoed off the vaulted ceiling, until the whole building rang with them. A roar louder than a dragon, and more dangerous.

The central cathedral of Nus had been dedicated once to some local god who seemed from the carvings in the stone columns to have had a great deal to do with rose-covered shepherd's crooks and a shallow bowl with a crack in it. Now, it belonged to the goddess. The red of the banners that hung behind the altar represented the blood of true humanity, untainted by the filthy powers of the dragons and their Timzinae agents. The pale circle in the center with its eightfold sigil, the purifying power of the goddess as it reached out across the world.

Not that Duris would have known that if he hadn't been told. As the cathedral had once been the shrine of a crook-and-bowl god, Duris had once been a butcher's apprentice of a little crossroads town that the locals called Little Count, about a morning's walk south of Sevenpol, and was now a soldier of the empire and of the goddess.

When the roar faded, the priest lowered his hands. "There are many who will deny her. Many who will close their eyes to her light. Stripping away the lies of a lifetime—of hundreds of lifetimes, father and grandfather and on back to the fall of humanity at the claws of the dragons—is like tearing away the scab of an infected wound. Some will cling to their infection rather than accept the healing pain. These are the servants of the lie."

"Kill them!" Duris and a hundred others shouted. "Kill anyone who stands against her!"

"They come to us now," the priest said. "They come to kill us and steal back what the goddess has claimed."

Everyone knew that, of course. The scouting parties had been keeping track of the movements of the enemy army since the fall of Inentai. But hearing it in the resonant voice of the priest gave it a weight and a dignity that taproom gossip didn't carry. Duris felt the mixture of dread and exultation in his chest. When he closed his eyes and let the feelings rise up in him, it was like he'd climbed the highest tree in Little Count and was looking down on the roofs and yards far below.

"But," the priest said, "they have already lost. The goddess is in the world, and her power cannot be denied. She is the living voice of the truth. Faith in her is stronger than arrows. Stronger than swords. Nothing in the world can remain unchanged before her!"

Duris rose, fists in the air. All around him, his compatriots and the converts from among the citizens of Nus stood too. Some—especially the locals—wept. Duris, who wasn't a butcher's boy any longer, grinned beatifically and felt the joy and power flow through him.

Nus, the Iron City, had been the first Timzinae stronghold to fall to her, and Duris had been there from the start.

When the army had moved on, Duris and his cohorts Noll and Kipp and Sandin had all been picked to garrison the city. In all, there were three hundred Antean soldiers to hold a city of fifty thousand. Three hundred soldiers and half a dozen priests.

For the first few months, he'd struggled not to feel overwhelmed by the city. The grand square alone was larger than all Little Count put together. The salt quarter at Nus took up almost half the city. The port on the northern edge spread out past the great stone-and-metal walls and onto the water, becoming a complex tissue of docks and ships and boats that changed their configuration by the day, like alleyways in dreams. Then there were the archways tucked in among the streets. Long, lazy swoops of hollow dragon's jade that rose up above the buildings and streets before arcing back down. In Little Count—even in Sevenpol—they would have been wonders to look up at in awe. In Nus, people hung laundry from them.

With the service done, Duris and his friends poured out onto the minor square. Minor, and still big enough to fit most of a village into. The giddiness that always followed a morning listening to the priests left them in playful moods as they strutted past the street vendors with their beaded jewelry and promises of futures told and tin plates of spiced chicken and lamb.

"Did I tell? Had a letter from home," Kipp said.

"Did not," Sandin said. "And it wouldn't help if you did. You can't read."

Kipp shoved the larger man while the others laughed, but Kipp was laughing too, so it was all right. "I can hire a scribe, same as anyone else. My sister sent it. Saved up a tenth of her sewing money for a month to do it too. She said Old Matrin's died."

Duris missed a step. The pleasure he'd taken in the day faltered. "Did not," he said, unaware that he was echoing Sandin. Old Matrin with his knives and the white crop of thin hair rising off his brow like smoke had been the butcher in Little Count and the master of Duris's apprenticeship.

"Did. Caught a fever over the winter and slept himself to death," Kipp said. He kept his voice light because they were men now, and men didn't act sad about things. The look he gave Duris was sympathy enough. "Guess you're the only one knows how to cut those chops of his now, eh?"

"Suppose I am," Duris said. A wave of homesickness washed over him—Old Matrin's slaughterhouse, the treelined lane between his old father's house and the huts where his mother and sisters lived with his new father. The pond where he'd played whistles with the miller's daughter back when they'd both been too young to think of anything less pure to play at. He shook himself, put a smile back on his face, and kept on. There was no use thinking too much on that now. His mother had said *Sorrow calls sorrow* so much that he assumed it was true.

The blare of the alarm trumpets cut through the air. It was so unexpected, Duris looked at the others to see whether they'd heard it too. Noll and Kipp had gone pale in the face. Sandin's jaw was set forward in a vicious grin.

"Guess the fuckers came early, eh?" he said. The alarm came again, and they broke into a run for their siege stations.

At the stone side of the great walls, ladders wide enough for four men to climb side by side stretched up. The walls rose as tall as ten men one standing on the other, and divided so that low walls of iron marked off each length twenty yards long of the street-wide walk along the top. From his post, Duris could see the gates closing, the city of Nus folding in on itself like a turtle expecting a storm. And as he looked out from the top of the wall, the storm front was clear. Clouds of dust rose in the east. The largest plume came from the along the dragon's road, but three smaller arced in from the south. Sandin, beside him, laughed.

"Well, look," he said. "All the roaches are in a hurry to sit at the bottom of our wall. Idiots."

"I don't know," Duris said. "Looks like there's a lot of them."

"If they make the top of this wall, it'll be by climbing over the bodies of their own dead," Sandin said, and spat. It was a phrase Duris had heard before, spoken by the priests. The thought reassured. The captain came last, and the fifteen men of the segment stopped talking among themselves. Callien Nicillian was the second son of some minor house—Baron of Southreach or some such. He had a sharp, dark face and an eager manner that brought Duris and the others with it.

"Take your posts, boys," Nicillian said. "The roaches will be here by midday, and they may take a little knocking back."

"Hope so," Sandin said.

Along the wall, outsize speaking trumpets were being mounted, and the priests were beginning to call into them. *The enemies of the goddess cannot win against us! Everything you love is already gone! If you stand against us, you have already lost!* The syllables rang out clear and sharp. Duris almost felt sorry for the bastards riding so quickly toward their defeat. He sharpened his sword and wondered whether he'd get to use it. Three of the other men on his segment put together the ballistas and set them into the seating hole in the iron. The inner face of the wall looked down over the city. There were few buildings in Nus as tall as the wall. The people in the streets below him were only the oval tops of heads. He wondered what it would be like looking down at Camnipol from the Kingspire. He'd never seen it himself, but he'd heard it was taller than ten of Nus's walls stacked one on the next, though that was likely an exaggeration.

When the call to make ready came, Duris was already looking down over the edge. The enemy had come in a force as large or larger than the Antean army that Lord Ternigan had led. The difference being that Ternigan had marched his men—Duris among them—through the opened gates and fought in the streets. The full garrison of Nus. The guards and soldiers of the traditional families that had ruled it. The shopkeepers and merchants and indentured slaves defending their homes. For a moment, Duris wondered whether the three hundred soldiers topping the walls were quite enough to defend a whole city from a full army, but then the priests began to call again, and his unease evaporated.

"Those catapults," Sandin said, pointing down below them. "You see how the leather at the top looks like a sling? Those are Borjan make."

"And you'd know that how?" Duris said. "All the time you spent as a boy with your lovers in Tauendak?"

Sandin hit his ear lightly and turned back to the army below. "I've heard about them. And see, those aren't all roaches."

It was true. There were Timzinae soldiers below them in profusion, but also Tralgu and Jasuru and wide, tusk-jawed Yemmu. Even a few that might have been Firstblood or Dartinae. The banners they carried were in the vertical style of Borja and the Keshet.

"This isn't an uprising," Sandin said. "That's an army that's fought as an army. Could be this is a good day after all."

"Think that?"

"Break the back of the Borjan army and show them what it means to take the side of the Timzinae? I'll put you a full night's drinks the real people down there are offering up dead roaches by the end of the week as part of their surrender."

"Not taking that bet," Duris said. "I've seen how you drink."

"Ready weapons!" Captain Nicillian cried over the calling of the priests, and Duris moved to his ballista. It almost seemed cruel, killing them from his safe perch. But they'd made the choice when they came, and damn but there were a lot of them. "Loose!"

The bolts of the defending ballistas fell on the attackers below. Duris couldn't tell if they'd done much good. With only four to a segment, it seemed like each bolt would have to spit half a dozen enemy like pork on a skewer to make any difference at all. On the other hand, apart from cobbling together their Borjan catapults, they didn't seem to be doing anything but standing about waiting to be killed. He waited while the others winched back the swing arm, then he shoved a second bolt in place and barked that he was clear of it. The string made a sound like snapping fingers, and somewhere in the throng below, another man died or was wounded or the bolt pierced only earth. The winch creaked again, and Duris waited with the next bolt.

He didn't see where the fire came from. A cunning man at the rear of the army, maybe. Or one of the catapults, set aside for the purpose. The first sign Duris had was the intake of breath from the man beside him. When he turned to see what had caused it, he already knew. The ball of bright-blue flame like a sun made from sky floated above the wall, a trail of black smoke showing the arc it had already traveled.

"The hell is that?" he said. And behind him, the Borjan

catapults answered: it was the signal to attack. All around the city, the Borjan catapults fired, first one and then a few, and then dozens. The stones arced up, and for a moment Duris thought the enemy's aim had failed badly. None of them were going to strike the iron wall. None of them were even arcing low enough to pick off the soldiers at the ballistas. One of the stones passed over his own segment, and he saw the line that it drew behind it. The stone dropped down into the city, swinging hard on its leash and cracking into the stone inner face of the wall. The line, as thick as two of his fingers together, snapped taut under its weight.

"Cut the cords, boys!" Nicillian shouted. "They're coming up."

Duris's disbelief overcame his discipline, and he looked over the edge. It was true. Down below, a Jasuru man hauled himself hand over hand up the line. *You cannot win. All who defy the goddess are already doomed. Your only hope is surrender.* Duris drew his sword and started hacking at the line as another stone flew overhead, another line wrapped itself over the wall. It wasn't rope, but a braid of leather and wire that defied the blade. It wasn't magic, though. Before the Jasuru made the wall's top, they severed the cord. Only by then, there were two more cords drawing black lines across their segment.

Duris hacked as if his life depended on it. For the first time, real fear quickened his blood. The voices of the priests and the calling of his fellow soldiers were the only sounds. No enemy drums or trumpets sounded. When they cut through a cord, there was a scream or a shout or else silence. The stillness of it left him unnerved.

The speaking horn from the next segment over fell silent. When Duris looked over, a Timzinae man stood over the fallen priest, an axe in his black-chitined hand. Duris didn't think, only ran. The barrier between segments was tall, but not so great he couldn't clamber up the sun-hot iron and fall on the other side. The segment was overrun; Borjan soldiers were everywhere. Duris barreled into them. Those who stood with the goddess could never lose.

He swung his sword down, using the blade's weight, and only hitting with the farthest tip, the way Old Matrin had taught him to use the big butcher's knife. The Timzinae man's back opened from shoulder to waist, and he fell screaming to the ground. Duris kicked him away, and stood straddling the fallen, bloody form of the spider priest, his sword at the ready. Something tickled his leg, then something else. Before he could look down to see what was happening or jump back, a Tralgu man stepped forward, a mace in his fist. He batted Duris's sword out of his hand with an air of near boredom, shifted to follow and redirect the momentum of the swing, bringing it up and over and down.

The blow didn't hurt, but it made a deep, solid sound, like stones being dropped onto dry ground. Everything grew quiet and distant and the world tilted oddly. The dead priest stood, or no. No, Duris fell at his side, but he had the clear sense that he was standing. Something danced across his hands, and then more. Spiders. Hundreds of them.

The Tralgu who'd hit him had stepped back now. He was waving a yellow banner over his head, and his teeth were bared in disgust. And fear. Duris tried to stand, but the pain finally found him. The wall tumbled in empty space, though his eyes told him nothing was moving. He rose to his knees. Something sharp happened in his ear, like a sting. Spiders swarmed his eyes, scratching at the lids like a dog trying to dig out a rabbit hole.

I can't die, he thought. *The goddess can't be beaten. Nus won't fall.*

Two Timzinae men appeared carrying wooden buckets, and another came behind with a burning torch. Another signal, he thought, but of what he couldn't guess.

"You bastards won't stop me," he shouted, or tried to. The words came out poorly. He tried to say *I am dedicated to the goddess and the Severed Throne*, but what he heard himself say was, "No one else knows those cuts!"

The liquid that splashed out from the barrels was thick and greasy and smelled weird and familiar. It was something he knew, though his mind was so addled he didn't place it. Was it piss? Or butter? He spat out a mouthful of it, and a lump of oily spider came with it. His hand found the grip of his sword.

Lamp oil. They'd drenched him in lamp oil.

"No," he shouted as the third Timzinae came closer with his torch in hand. "No, please wait!"

The torch flew toward him in a long, lazy arc, trailing smoke behind it.

Clara

War was made from individual lives, but that didn't make it special. Any number of endeavors were just the same. The loaves of day-old bread she'd handed out at the Prisoner's Span had been as much the product of disparate lives as any battle. The boy who gathered the eggs might have done so while in despair of ever winning his father's love. Or in silent contemplation of the murder of his rivals. Or still flush from the revelation of a great secret. Or bored beyond measure by another day's empty work with only chickens for companionship. And so for the farmer who'd brought in the wheat and separated the chaff. A carter had brought grain to the mill and taken flour from it, and done it as part of a full span of years punctuated by its own tragedies and moments of exultation. In Camnipol, a baker had worked the common magic of yeast and heat and time, transforming what individually would have been inedible into a moment of warmth and beauty that passed unappreciated, cooled, faded, staled. And then a noblewoman still deep in her grief had taken it, used the little bun as a way to create some connection with the lower classes of the city with whom she imagined she had nothing in common. And from her to a thief or robber or thug hanging in a cage over the gaping fall of the Division, who had had a childhood and a mother and friends and a moment of defiance before the magistrate or one of fear and sorrow. All that was in a bit of bread, and a city was immeasurably more.

Whenever Dawson had spoken of the nobility of war, or the honor and glory of the battlefield—or even, on rare occasions, obliquely of the atrocities it carried in its saddlebags—he had given the project a life of its own. A name, like a god's name or a city's. War became a person of a sort, and because it was a person, it became worthy of a kind of politeness. One didn't speak ill of one's family or one's friends, however rude they might be. Even sowing derision toward one's enemies was a process rich with rules and obstacles of form. As she became more familiar with the process of battle herself, Clara became less and less respectful of it.

Every soldier in an army had a life that had brought them there, that had tested them and remade them and put them through times of glory and of despair. And if they'd remained farmers and blacksmiths and huntsmen and bakers, then they would have done there as well. More would have died of illness and accident, and fewer on a stranger's blade.

No, Clara had looked war in its face now, and she found herself unimpressed.

For the better part of a week, they skirted the edge of the Dry Wastes. She woke in the mornings to the stink of salt and rode through the day, Vincen at her side, as they ghosted along the road. Twice, Jorey's scouts had sighted the scouts of the enemy. Both times, Jorey had drawn the enemy on as far as he could manage, charged to drive them back, and retreated again to lead them on. The other groups, she presumed, as did Jorey, were doing the same. Forcing the Timzinae to move slowly, to take few chances, to waste time and fodder in making moves and countermoves that by Antea's aim came to nothing.

And now and then, people died for it. Some on Jorey's side, some on Dannien's. None for any reason Clara could respect. They played for time and waited for something unexpected to happen, unsure whether it would.

When it did, it came from the north and it wore Canl Daskellin's face.

"Lady Kalliam," the Baron of Watermarch said. "I...I didn't expect to see you here."

The meeting was a small one: Clara and Jorey and Canl. They'd long since given up both the convenience and burden of the Lord Marshal's tent. The leather sides and metal frames lay in a gully somewhere to the south where they could rot and corrode in peace. Instead of sitting on the field stools behind the little writing table, they stood on a barren hilltop with their men standing at a little distance to give an approximation of privacy. To her right, the land sloped down to the east, growing slowly greener. To the left, yellow dirt and sand. Finding Daskellin here, on the border between springtime and the wastes, was the sort of thing that would have seemed a portent if she'd been dreaming. Awake, it was only what it was.

"Nor I you," she said. "How is your family?"

"Quite well, m'lady," he said, taking refuge in the forms and customs of etiquette. Clara smiled, not entirely kindly. Faced with a woman standing with one foot in absurdity and the other in scandal, small talk was indeed a blessing from the good angels. "Yours?"

"They're well," she said, gesturing at the sere landscape, "given this present unpleasantness."

"Yes," Daskellin said, and then again more soberly. "Yes."

"How many men do you have?" Jorey asked.

"Four hundred," Daskellin replied. "Though none of them are the first cut. You?"

"Less than that, but I'm only one of seven. If your men are rested, armed, and well supplied, I think we can put them to good use."

"I'm only pleased to find I'm not holding the road alone," Daskellin said. "Last I'd heard you were still in Birancour. How did you come so quickly?"

"We weren't quick. We started weeks ago," Jorey said, "and came through the pass at Bellin before the thaw."

Surprise and then respect flickered in Daskellin's eyes. This, Clara thought, is how reputations are made. When they returned to Camnipol, the tale would be of the pre-science and daring that had brought the Lord Marshal to the defense of the empire at the moment he was most needed. Assuming, of course, that they made it back at all and not in the chains of avenging Elassae.

"Good that you're here," Daskellin said.

"How is the situation at court?" Jorey asked.

Daskellin opened his mouth, closed it, shook his head. Even here, far south of the Kingspire, he would not speak the truth aloud. Clara understood. Fear was a habit, and Geder's fondness for pulling even the highest of nobles into his private court to be questioned by the priesthood had trained them all like dogs. Daskellin knew when not to bark, and that was ever. Not even now. His silence was enough to give an answer. Jorey understood as well.

Clara felt as if she were waking from a dream when she hadn't known she was asleep. The court and Camnipol and her granddaughter were all quite near now. She'd left as a spy and returned as...as whatever it was she'd become. It felt like the end of something, though she wasn't certain she could put a name to it.

"Good that you're here, then," Jorey said. "I have maps

made of what we know about the enemy position and what we guess. Let me show you."

"You'll excuse me," Clara said. "It is a pleasure to see you again, Canl. It's been far too long."

"Hopefully we can meet again soon in better accommodations," he said. There was a melancholy in his voice that meant he did not expect that day to come.

"Hopefully," she echoed, and turned away.

There had been a time not so long ago when the walk back over the rough, trackless ground to the tents would have seemed a long one. It was, after all, farther than the garden. At home, dignity alone would have meant calling for one of Lady Daskellin's carriages. Now, it was nothing to her beyond a bit of an ache in her left hip, and that more the joint than the muscle.

Vincen sat at his tent with Captain Wester and the priest beside him. Kit and Vincen both rose when she approached. Marcus only nodded to her, as he would, she thought, to anyone, regardless of their station.

"What news, then?" Wester asked.

"Reinforcements have arrived. They're building with straw in a windstorm, but they're here."

"Something's better than nothing," Wester said.

"I suppose it is," Clara said, then turned to Vincen. "I believe it is time to gather our things."

"Are you going somewhere, lady?" the priest asked. She knew that he was an ally, and that he had never done anything to undermine her efforts or Cithrin bel Sarcour's. Still, the similarity of his face and skin and hair to those of the others who haunted Camnipol made it hard for her to keep from pulling away from him.

"Yes," she said. "Back to court. I followed the army in

hopes of bringing it to Antea's true defense, and I've done it. There is no more I need do here."

"And there is in Camnipol?" Marcus asked.

"One may at least wait for catastrophe on more comfortable beds," she said smartly.

The captain laughed. "That may be the wisest thing I've heard said all week."

"I find I shall miss your company, Lady Kalliam," Master Kit said. "But I also hope we are not driven to meet again too terribly soon. When we come again to Camnipol, I pray that it is in peacetime."

"That would be lovely, wouldn't it?" Clara said, surprised to find a sudden grief rising in her. It seemed her hopes were as low as Daskellin's. And like him, she would not say it.

One of the unexpected lessons she'd learned on the road concerned the speed of small groups and the slowness of great ones. The army of Elassae, even un-harassed, would have taken weeks to reach Camnipol. For her and Vincen on fast horses, the journey took four days. She arrived at Lord Skestinin's manor having sent a runner ahead to give Lady Skestinin and Sabiha time to put anything in order that needed to be put. There might by an enemy army at her back, but that didn't make an avoidable rudeness polite. When she arrived, the servants fought not to look shocked and Lady Skestinin's usual reserve seemed deeper than Clara had become accustomed to. It wasn't until she reached her rooms and for the first time since leaving Carse encountered a mirror that she understood.

"Vincen, I've gone brown as an *egg*."

"You've been walking from dawn to dark for weeks, m'lady. Months."

Clara sat at her private table and flapped her hands at the

powders and kohl. "Everything I have is the wrong color. If I use any of this, I'll look like someone dipped a cake in sugar! It all has to be replaced. You'll have to find Sanna Daskellin or Kieran Shoat and ask what they have that I can borrow until—" She put her hand to her mouth, a sudden horror passing through her. "My dresses."

"Your dresses?"

She rose from the table, marching to the dressing room. A simply cut yellow silk gown with pearl beads and complexly embroidered sleeves came first to hand. She stripped off her traveling cloak and leggings, at first by herself and then— distractingly—with Vincen's wide hands to help her. For a moment, she considered dropping the yellow gown as well, but anxiety won out. She pulled the silk over her head and twisted. The cloth swirled around her. She didn't sit down so much as fold.

"Clara?"

"They don't fit," she said. "None of them will fit. They'll all have to be taken in. I have literally nothing I can wear to court. Nothing. Stop that, it isn't funny." She put a hand to her head. "The sun's bleached my hair, hasn't it?"

"Well, it's a bit travel-worn at the moment," Vincen said. "We can wash it, and then we'll know better, but likely so."

She took a deep breath, let it out slowly, and slapped the floor. She felt tears of frustration and embarrassment stinging her eyes.

"*Fuck,*" she said.

Vincen slid down to sit, his back against the wall. His eyes were alight. "You are the most amazing creature in the world."

"I know I'm being silly, but knowing doesn't help."

"That's what makes you amazing," Vincen said. His voice was warm and soft, and there was laughter in it, but not at her. She balled the silk in her fists and tugged at it. And then she laughed too.

"This is trivial, isn't it?"

"No, it's not," he said. "How you look to them is important...and not even that. You could come before the court dressed as a swordsman or a beggar and not be ill at ease if you'd chosen it. It's not being able to control what they see of you that leaves you feeling at sea. I understand it. I do."

She felt her own smile growing to match his. "Then why are you laughing?"

"Because you will be more beautiful now than any of them, and more so by standing out proud. I'll go fetch you new powders, and Sabiha will have gowns from before she had the baby that we can use until the tailors come."

"I can't wear those," Clara said. "They're cut for a girl half my age."

"Then you can go naked and be even prettier," Vincen said.

"Oh," Clara said. "Now you're only trying to distract me."

"I am alone with you for the first time since we left Porte Oliva," Vincen said. "I'm surprised I can still use words."

She shifted, pulling her legs out straight before her, sitting across from him like they were two children exhausted from too much play. Vincen's skin was sun-darkened as well, his hair longer than he usually wore it and shaggy and light. With all the time they had traveled in company, it had become easy to gloss over him. To think *Yes, Vincen is here* and take comfort in his presence and move on. She had managed somehow to forget that he was beautiful. And if he was, then perhaps she might be as well, in her own way. She reached out, touching the sole of his left foot with the toes of her own.

For a long moment, she didn't speak. And then she did.

"I love you, Vincen. You make everything in this mutilated world a bit better."

"Only when I'm with you," he said. "When you're gone, I sulk."

"Come over here," she said, and he did.

Later, she sent a Dartinae girl out to the perfumers for new powders and appealed to Sabiha for aid with gowns. Between the constraints of color and size, the options were few. Clara chose a pale-green ensemble with a fairly conservative cut, though it was more daring than she would have affected on her own. When the time came to go out for the evening and make her return to court known, Vincen was among the guards and footmen, standing a little apart. His hair was combed and freshly trimmed. His borrowed uniform had bright glass buttons down the sides for decoration. She didn't stare, but she appreciated. When he saw that he'd caught her attention, he made the faintest bow and a smirk that matched it. The boy was taking entirely too much joy in teasing her. Someone would notice. She couldn't find it in her to chide him.

The affair was only in the middle of the scale of court events. Lady Emming had opened her garden, which meant that Clara hadn't needed a specific invitation. There was neither music nor a dance, which signaled what sort of guest was expected, and no one was so forward as to barge in where they were unwelcome. In her absence, the style of court had shifted to the positively macabre. Cerrina Mikillien was actually wearing a cloak decorated with rabbit skulls, but she was only the most extreme of a larger trend. Clara in her new-leaf-green gown and glowing skin became a fashion of one and as difficult to overlook as a rose on snow. When asked, Clara admitted she had spent some time in the company of the army. When the questioning grew too specific, she mentioned Dawson and got teary and her interrogators were forced to leave the issue aside.

There was, after all, gossip enough to go around. Geder Palliako, it seemed, had all but retired from courtly life. He'd gone off on some little campaign to Asterilhold at the beginning of the winter. Another apostate, another splinter cult, another small slaughter of the sort the spiders engendered. Some ascribed his withdrawal after returning from it to the rise of the Timzinae in Elassae. Others to the slaughter of the hostage children. The general wisdom was that he was in council with Basrahip, planning the brilliant endgame for the nations-wide war he'd begun.

Clara left not quite as early as form permitted, but nearly so. The other women of the court—and with as many armies as still were in the field, it was a court overwhelmingly of women—would spread word of her arrival and outlandish appearance before morning, she was sure. Well, it was awkward, but it would give her a new opportunity to find which members of the court were her allies now. And she was mother of the brilliant Lord Marshal who'd swooped in from the west to parry Elassae's blow. That was some protection. At worst, she expected to be called eccentric. If Jorey hadn't enjoyed his current grace, the word would have been *cracked*. A bit of drama, a few uncomfortable probings by women of equal dignity, a few people laughing down their sleeves at her. A minor scandal at worst. A small loss, and easily born.

She was mistaken.

Hornet, the actor friend of Cithrin bel Sarcour and Master Kit, arrived in the morning dressed as a courier. She met him in the withdrawing room that overlooked the garden. Sabiha was resting in the shade, nursing her daughter, while Lady Skestinin chided the gardeners. Vincen stood discreet guard in the hall to keep them from being overheard. Hornet stood at attention, playing his role to the hilt. He seemed to be enjoying himself in it.

"Cithrin bel Sarcour is in Camnipol?" Clara said. "With Lehrer *Palliako*?

"Yes, Lady Kalliam."

"Has she lost her *mind*?"

"No, m'lady. I've traveled with her a fair bit, and she's always like this," Hornet said. "Yardem Hane's come as well, though he rode off south to fetch Master Kit and the captain when he heard you'd made it close."

Clara sat on the divan, waiting for panic or outrage to overwhelm her, but they didn't. She felt the same anxiety and bright, breathless excitement that she remembered from when she was a child steeling herself to jump into a cousin's swimming hole from too great a height. "Has she a plan, then?"

"Yes, ma'am, and she was hoping for your help. It's a little gathering of friends and family that needs arranging. Only it's going to decide the fate of the world, so we'd like to get it right."

Marcus

Karol Dannien's army was on the road, stretched out north to south, braced for their attack. Marcus made something like fifty sword-and-bows protecting the supply wagons. Jorey sounded the approach, and their little force moved forward, approaching the vastly larger enemy's vulnerable flank.

"Watch for it," Marcus said under his breath. "Careful. Don't over-commit."

But the young Kalliam had been through the exercise enough now. The ripple in the Timzinae ranks as the order went out, the soldiers shifting to the counterattack. Jorey lifted his hand, and Marcus and the others slowed, inching toward a battle they couldn't win.

The reinforcements from the north had been telling. Old men, sickly boys. Half a dozen women with shoulders as broad as a man's and expressions that dared you to question their presence. These were the defenders Camnipol had to offer. The story of the vast dark empire with unstoppable armies defeating city after city, sweeping across the world like a dark tide, had been a sheet over a more prosaic story: an inexperienced war leader had overreached and left himself as vulnerable as a naked man in a dogfight. If the armies of Elassae reached Camnipol, Marcus didn't give the city good chances. The best scenario was a sack as vicious as any he'd ever seen. The worst was Antea's capital set on fire as an example to the next petty tyrant who thought to invade Timzinae cities.

Except that wasn't the worst case. The worst case was more like this, all the time, forever.

The Timzinae counterattack came. The column parted, and riders poured out, streaming toward Jorey's force. The boy barely had to sound the retreat that they'd all known was coming. Marcus and the Anteans spun their horses and rode away, loosing arrows back over their horses' rumps as they fled. The Timzinae followed them almost half a mile this time before turning back to their own column, careful not to be drawn so far out that they left a vulnerable flank.

Jorey and his force regrouped. It would take the Timzinae something like an hour to put themselves in order and be ready for the march north. So in something just more than half that, another group of riders would appear on the top of another hillside, renew their threat on the supply wagons, and they'd do the same dance again, over and over and over until one side or the other went so mad with impatience that it made a mistake—waited too long to retreat or pursued too far and exposed a weakness. If it was Dannien's mistake, Jorey would pick off a few supply wagons. If it was Jorey's, Dannien would slaughter as many of the Antean men as he could and leave fewer to slow his progress toward the butchery to come.

The previous day the army hadn't made it farther than a mile and a half from breaking camp in the morning to building its cookfires at night. That had been a very good day for Jorey. The chances were thin that they'd manage to slow the army that badly for long.

"We can't win," Jorey said.

Marcus swung down from the saddle and gave the poor,

exhausted nag he'd been burdening a cup of water. "We're not trying to."

"I don't know if I can stand this." He almost made it a joke.

"Well, I think of it this way. Every hour they spend moving their defenses around or chasing us through the grass or playing stare-down on us is one more that the people north of here get to watch their kids grow older. Every day is another morning they have the privilege of waking up next to their husbands and wives. Feeding their dogs. Living in the houses they were born in. The ones their parents died in. Because when Dannien's men get to them, all that ends."

"But there's no victory for us. There's no ending to it. It just goes on."

"There will be an end," Marcus said. "Chances are it won't be one we like, but this doesn't last forever."

Jorey let that sink in. When he looked out toward the horizon, it was like he was seeing all the way back to Kiaria, Suddapal, Inentai. All the way back to the beginning of the war, whenever that had been. "This is what we did to them, isn't it?"

"And what you'll do to them again, if you get the upper hand," Marcus said.

"Never again. Not if I can help it."

"No? Well, good luck with that, but we'll have to visit the question when we're not down a well and drowning. Everyone loves peace when they're losing the battle."

Canl Daskellin's scout arrived an hour later, just as Jorey was preparing to lead his men back out to harass the Timzinae column again. The scout didn't come alone. Marcus would have recognized the Tralgu riding high in the saddle beside him if there'd been a blanket thrown over him. He spat, turned his mount out of the formation, and trotted over.

"Captain," Yardem said when they drew alongside.

"Can't help noticing you're here, Yardem."

"Yes, sir."

"This isn't Carse."

"Isn't."

"I left you in Carse with Cithrin."

"Did."

"This won't make me happy, will it?"

"No, sir."

"All right. Report?"

"Magistra's put together a scheme against the priests. She's in Camnipol, and she needs Master Kit to make her argument."

"You let her do that?"

"Stopping her wouldn't have worked," Yardem said. "And the situation's desperate."

Marcus twisted to look over his shoulder. Cithrin was in Camnipol working another of her mad plots. Of course she was. And when the city fell, she'd be in it. "How is it we've managed to be on both losing sides of this war?"

"It's a talent, sir."

"You might as well take Kit. Karol Dannien knows the trick of him, and Kit's all but confessed to the men that it's all hairwash anyway."

"Be good if you came as well, sir."

"That's not going to happen," Marcus said. "The Kalliam boy's good enough, but he's still green as grass. I'll hold these bastards off as long as I can, but when it fails, get Cithrin away safe. If she'll let you."

Yardem flicked his ear, the rings jingling. "If you say so, sir."

"It's how it has to be," Marcus said.

The poisoned sword across his back felt heavier. Or as

heavy as always, only he was more aware of it. The sun slanted down from the afternoon sky, baking his skin and narrowing his eyes. The world all around him had a sense of being only half-real that came from having been too long on campaign. Depending on how he counted it, it was either since the march from Birancour or the caravan contract out of Vanai. Or since Merian and Alys died. It was hard to say when exactly one fight stopped and the next one began. That wasn't just him, either. It stretched from the nursery to the history books.

"Should I ask who she's trying to convince that they're better off standing against the Lord Regent?" Marcus asked. "Or will it only make me anxious?"

"She's approaching the Lord Regent."

A hot breeze snaked off the wastes, carrying a breath of dust and salt. Far above, a hawk circled, hardly more than a dot against the pale-blue sky.

"Geder Palliako?"

"Yes, sir."

"She's talking Geder Palliako into fighting on our side? Against the priests?"

Yardem didn't answer.

Marcus cleared his throat. "All right," he said. "You get Kit, then. I'll need a minute to tell Kalliam he's on his own."

The promontory on the south of Camnipol made it seem like the bones of the earth itself had lifted up the city wall. The land sloping out to the east and west almost glowed with springtime green, and an orchard they passed at sunset caught the orange light on millions of pale petals—the promise of a good harvest in autumn if the people tending them still lived. If the orchard hadn't burned. Oxen worked the fields, digging furrows in rich valleys. They passed a slave master driving a line of Timzinae men linked neck to neck to neck with a dull iron chain. The slaver was Firstblood with a wide, friendly smile, bright, shallow eyes, and red cheeks. He looked confused when Yardem drew his blade and held the man down as Marcus and Kit undid the chain. Likely, they'd all run off to Dannien and join the march, so Marcus made certain they all remembered the names of the men who'd freed them. At least he could give Dannien a moment's confusion.

Apart from that distraction, they rode hard enough that there wasn't much opportunity to talk during the day, and at the simple camp they put up at night, Marcus fell into a torpid sleep, like a man recovering from a fever or else still in its grip. He slept to the sound of Kit and Yardem talking at their little fire about love and war and the spiritual consequences of violence, so probably it was better. Kit's worn, gaunt look softened a little on the journey. The role of army priest hadn't suited him anyway. Hearing his genuine laugh again was like seeing a friend who had been traveling a long time and only just returned.

They reached the base of the promontory in the late afternoon of the second day's travel and began moving up the weird, looping path of dragon's jade as it made its way up the cliff face. If there was any hope of keeping Camnipol whole, it was likely this. A company of slingers and archers could hold the dragon's road and force Dannien's army to go around to the east or west and find some other path up. Camnipol might be taken, but not from the south.

The southern gate was preparing to close when they reached it, but Kit talked their way through. Likely his appearance was enough. As they passed through the slit of a gate and along the passage through the stone, Marcus had the sense that the guards shied away from the priest.

The twilit streets of Camnipol bustled with men and women of half a dozen races hurrying home before the final darkness of night. Yardem took the lead, moving through the alleys and squares with an air of passive boredom that Marcus recognized as deceptive. He matched it, and Kit— better practiced than either of them—practically blended into the stonework. At every corner, Marcus was ready to see the robes of the priesthood waiting for them. For him to come this far and die in a street brawl would be just the sort of humor the world seemed to enjoy.

The compound they reached was small. A grey stone wall surrounded it. A lantern hung from a black iron sconce by the gate. Yardem paused there.

"Should I know where this is?" Marcus asked.

Yardem pounded on the gate, three times, then two, then two again. "No, sir. It's the compound of the Baron of Ebbingbaugh."

"I don't know what that means."

"Geder's estate," Yardem said as the gate opened. "Took it from a man named Feldin Maas back before he was Lord Regent. Supposed to retire here when the prince takes the throne. Meantime he lets his father use it."

An ancient-looking Jasuru woman ushered them in with an air of anxious confusion that suggested she hadn't welcomed guests to the house often enough to be quite sure how it was done. The gardens were large, but from what Marcus could make out in the dying light, poorly tended. A small paved area flickered with light, and night air carried the scent of flowers and the sound of voices. Marcus recognized them.

Cary caught sight of them first, and she walked from the light into the shadows, falling into Kit's arms as he fell into hers. Then Mikel, then Hornet and Sandr and Charlit Soon, and Lak, still uncertain of his place in the company. They stood together, heads pressed to each other's shoulders, their eyes wet with tears, and Kit in the center, beatific joy on his face. Marcus had seen it before. After so many partings and reunions, some part of him expected it to become rote or common or insincere, but it never was.

However often they came together, the troupe always felt it deeply. Even when the players themselves had changed. It was, Marcus thought, part of walking a stage and calling forth the emotions of the crowd. To do what they did, they had to feel deeply and authentically and without reserve, just the way that doing what he did—overseeing the death of men both under his command and on the enemy line— meant falling back into step with Yardem despite months or years apart as if they'd only walked into adjacent rooms for a moment.

A thick-bodied man with white hair and a smile that looked as if it didn't get used much came out of the house and spread his hands to them.

"Welcome to my son's house. Come in, please. Come in. I broke out the good wine. It's a celebration," the older man said, but his voice had the high drone of anxiety and fear beneath it.

Marcus followed him down a hall to a well-lit drawing room with panels of thin mesh fit into frames instead of one wall. It let the breeze through, but discouraged the insects. And there, sitting side by side on a silk divan, were Clara Kalliam and Cithrin bel Sarcour. Cithrin's smile was part rueful and part defiant. She rose to her feet and walked to him.

A traitor lump knotted Marcus's throat. Something that felt like sorrow and pride and fear.

"Magistra," he said.

"Captain Wester," she said fondly, but casually. As if they had only walked for a moment into adjacent rooms. Yardem coughed once, in a way that meant *I see it too*. Cithrin wasn't his daughter. Had never been his daughter. And still, a hell of a woman they'd raised, he and Yardem and the players. A long way she'd come. "I assume you'd like a private word?"

"Several," he said.

She turned and nodded to Clara, who returned the gesture. Cithrin led the way into the garden. Nightfall had called up a fountain of moon lilies. The gentle scent soothed like the murmur of a river. Moonlight refashioned the leaves in silver and black. Cithrin sat on a low stone bench, and glowed in the moonlight herself. He lowered himself beside her, fighting the urge to take her hand. For a moment, he envied Kit.

"Didn't expect to find you here," Marcus said. "Last I'd heard you were safe in Carse."

Cithrin chuckled. "Last you heard I was in Carse, anyway. There's no place safe. Not now."

"Got Barriath Kalliam to carry you here?"

"He's back north with the ship now, in case we need a way out. I think he may have soured on my company."

"Yardem told me some hairwash about you confronting Geder Palliako and...I don't know. Turning him sane and good with the power of your kiss? What is the plan here? Because all I can see looks like a particularly gaudy kind of mad."

"Don't raise your voice," Cithrin said.

"Apologies. I'm bone-tired and scared as hell. Every hour you spend in this place puts you and all those back there at risk."

"I agree we should move quickly," she said. "But this is our best hope."

"Then our best hope is shit," he said. "Listen to me, Cithrin. You cannot change Geder Palliako."

She turned sharply. "I don't want to. I need Geder, and more than that I need Geder to *be* Geder."

"The man is evil, Cithrin. We can put bows and bells on it and dance ribbons into maypoles—"

"Stop that," she said, annoyance in her voice.

"Stop what?"

"Making him into the story about him. He's not Orcus the Demon King. He's not war incarnate. He's just a person, and my job is to judge people and risk and what losses are wise to hazard in return for what rewards."

"He's a person with a history of hacking people to death if he feels betrayed by them," Marcus said. "And not to make the knife too sharp, but he feels betrayed by you."

"Yes, I am putting my life at risk. And yours and Clara's and Barriath's. All of us will be killed if I'm wrong. But the return if I'm right will be everything, and…"

She turned away, her lips pursed like she'd tasted something sour.

"And?"

"And I'm right," she said.

Marcus wove his fingers together over his knee. From the house, Charlit Soon laughed and Sandr's grieved voice floated behind it, the words less clear than the tone of them. Everything in Marcus's body was screaming to throw Cithrin over his shoulder and run. Find a way to get her away from the city and the little kings who threw children to their deaths as a kind of political punctuation mark. The urge was larger than oceans, vast and powerful, and he recognized it from a lifetime of nightmares. It was the same thing he felt when he wanted to draw Merian and Alys from the fire. The want to save her was as complete as for his own wife and daughter, and it was as impossible. It left him trembling.

But then, he hadn't understood her when she wanted to turn gold into paper either, and everyone had seemed to think that terribly clever. So maybe he just didn't see what she did. Faith in her was as good a bet as anything.

"What's the job, then?" he asked.

Her face took on a calm seriousness that was better than a smile. "In the short term, see to it that we aren't interrupted. Especially not by any of the priests. I've arranged a bit of a theater piece. I believe that having his father with us gets us past the first barrier, but there will be some dangerous spots."

"Glad we agree on that, anyway," Marcus said. "Care to tell me what you expect they are?"

A bell sounded, dry and clanking, but with a long rolling finish that seemed to cut the night in two: all the moments that had come before it, and all the ones after.

"We may have to learn those lines when we say them," Cithrin said.

"You mean?"

Cithrin gestured toward the garden gate. "He's here."

Geder

Geder's illness, whatever it was, seemed to be getting worse, or at least no better. He couldn't sleep at night or wake fully in the day. The business of the empire was as vast as it had ever been, but he couldn't even bring himself to address it. Letters and reports and requests came in each day, high nobles requested audiences on any number of concerns. Rates of taxation and disputes over land rights and slights of honor. Reports from the searchers he'd sent to Lyoneia and Hallskar, tracking the ancient wonders and threats of the world that he could no longer muster any enthusiasm for. Geder had a basket the size of a bed filled with invitations to one thing and another. The blessing of Maken Estellin's newborn granddaughter, a garden fantasia by Lady Nestin Caot, a tasting of brandy captured from Nus the year before at a private room of the Great Bear. Everyone seemed to want something of him, and the weight of it bore him down until even the simplest thing felt too much because it was attached to all the rest of it.

The death throes of the enemies of the goddess were growing stronger, which Basrahip told him was a good sign. Inentai and Nus and Suddapal were all in open revolt now, and a Timzinae army was pushing its way north with Jorey and Canl Daskellin doing all they could to hold it back. Written reports said the temple in Nus had been burned to the ground and the priests with it, but that was fine. It was *good*. Basrahip said it was good. And despite that one terrible haunting moment of confusion that Geder had seen in the huge priest's eyes, Geder believed him. He heard the man's voice, and he believed, but he was so tired. And the fog grew in his mind.

His study was warm with the light of sunset. A bird sang outside the window, three rising notes and a pause and the same three again, like a musician practicing a flourish. Geder plucked at the cuff of an embroidered jacket sent from Asterilhold in celebration of his glorious victory over the apostate. It was hard to remember sometimes that he'd done that.

A carafe of cool water sat on the edge of his desk, sweating. When the drops of water it called out of the air dried, a girl from the kitchens would come and replace it with another that Geder also wouldn't drink from. This was the third of its kind that had come since he'd sat down. It was strange that he felt he'd been working so hard but nothing, so far, had been finished or done.

The knock at the door startled him. A thin-faced Dartinae woman in a servant's robe bent almost double with her bow. He caught a glimpse of the tops of her breasts as she stood, but they excited neither lust nor shame. Just a kind of weariness.

"Lord Regent," she said, holding out a silver plate. A slip of butter-pale paper stood folded on it. He almost turned away, but the script was familiar. His father's. Geder felt a mix of pleasure and anxiety as he plucked it up and unfolded it, but at least he felt something.

I'm at your mansion here in the city, and I need you to come over right away. There's something we need to discuss. I love you very much.

Geder blinked at the words, his heart beating a little less

sluggishly than it had a moment before. It was the profession of love at the end that scared him. Something had happened. Something must have happened.

"Call a carriage," he told the Dartinae girl. "And tell the guard I need to go. Right away."

And still *right away* took the better part of an hour. The sun was gone below the roofs and city wall in the west by the time Geder's carriage surrounded by his personal guard clattered across the cobblestones of the darkening city. A fog was rising from the depths of the Division and creeping out into the streets that surrounded it, the bridges across the great urban canyon shifting and undulating like the surface of a slow, grey lake. Geder drummed his fingers against his thigh, willing the driver to push the horses faster. Lehrer Palliako wasn't a man given to appearing in court or sending mysterious messages. What if he'd fallen ill? What if something was wrong that Geder didn't have the power to fix? He wondered as they arrived at the gate whether he should have brought a cunning man with him, just in case.

As soon as his carriage stopped and before he'd even stepped out of it, the gate slave struck a bell. The clanking sound had a long, clear finish, and before it had faded to silence, Lehrer Palliako was walking out into the street to meet him. He was well enough to walk, then. Maybe it wasn't his health.

"My good boy," his father said. "My good, good boy." There were little tears in his eyes catching the torchlight. "I knew you'd come."

"Of course I would," Geder said. "Why wouldn't I?"

They hugged awkwardly before Lehrer tugged him forward to the dark gate and the garden beyond. "Come along. And leave the guard here. There's something we need to talk about in private."

"They can be trusted," Geder said. "They're my personal guard. Basrahip talks to them every morning. They're the most loyal soldiers in the empire."

"Leave 'em here," Lehrer said. His voice had taken on a rougher note. This was all very strange, but Geder motioned to the captain of his guard, and the swordsmen took up positions in the street and along the wall. If they weren't to guard him, they'd guard the house he was in. And it wasn't as if there were going to be anything dangerous. It was his house. His father.

Once the gate had closed behind them, his father's pace slowed. Geder walked at his side past a wide spray of moon lilies bobbing in the soft breeze.

"I want you to know," Lehrer said, "that I'm proud of you. Whatever happens, I'm very, very proud of you."

"Of course," Geder said with a tight, nervous laugh. "I mean I'm Lord Regent. Master of the Empire. We've almost doubled the size of Antea since I stepped in. Who'd ever have thought that we'd be this important?"

"That's not why I'm proud of you," Lehrer said.

"But it's still quite a thing. You must admit, it's quite a thing."

Lehrer didn't respond. They passed into a little courtyard and through a screen to a drawing room with pale screens that kept the worst of the bugs away. Clara Kalliam sat there on a divan. Her face was so dark and thin, he almost didn't recognize her at first, but when she rose to her feet, the movement was unmistakable. *Are they here to tell me they're getting married*? Geder thought. And then, *Would I be Jorey's brother then*?

"Lord Regent," Clara said, her voice warm and gentle.

"Lady Kalliam?"

Lehrer sat on a silk chair, bent forward, his hands clasped

between his knees. "I love you, my good, good boy. I love you, and I need to you listen. Don't...don't be afraid."

"Of course I'm not afraid," Geder said, though it wasn't true. "And I'll always listen to you."

"Not to me," Lehrer said.

"Then—" Geder began.

"To us," a voice said from behind him.

Cithrin bel Sarcour. Cithrin, in a pale dress. Geder heard a low grunting sound like someone had been punched, and realized afterward that it had come from him. In the light of the lanterns, she glowed like the wick of a candle that had just been blown out. Her expression was soft, her hands clasped before her. He had a vague impression of people at her side, but he couldn't care about them. His heart clattered in his chest like a kettle suddenly at the boil.

He'd imagined some version of this moment so many times. Cithrin throwing herself at his feet, weeping and begging his forgiveness. Or else haughty and dismissive, reveling in his humiliation. Neither version of her made sense now that she was here.

She was here. Why was she here? And she was so beautiful. And why couldn't he catch his breath?

"I didn't know you were here," he heard himself say, wincing even as he spoke the words. Of course he hadn't known. God, he sounded like an idiot. But she didn't laugh at him, only lifted her hand a degree. *And yet here I am.*

"Geder!" another voice said. Cary, the actor. She stepped out from Cithrin's side, her arms wide, and scooped him up in a vast hug. And then Hornet, grinning, and Mikel and Sandr. And a couple of new people Geder didn't even know. They all hugged him and clapped him on the back, grinning and laughing and greeting him like he was an old friend they hadn't seen in too long. And at the end of them,

Clara Kalliam took him in her arms too, pressing her cheek to his.

And then Cithrin was there, and she put her arms around him, embracing him gently. *Don't wake up from this*, Geder thought. *If this is a dream, die in it. Only don't wake up.*

"I don't understand," Geder said. And then, without being sure quite what he meant, "I'm sorry."

"There's someone else you need to talk to," Lehrer said, his hand on Geder's shoulder. "Before any of the rest of this."

The priest looked much like the others, only maybe thinner and more worn. Olive-toned skin and wiry hair, and an expression of gentleness and an indulgent fondness. "We haven't met," the man said, "but it seems we have a great number of friends in common. I am called Kitap rol Keshmet, or sometimes Master Kit."

He took Geder's hand in both of his. Amid the shock and confusion and joy, Geder felt a thread of fear. "Are you with Basrahip?"

"I knew him once, when he was a boy. But that was many years ago."

Geder felt a cool breath of fear. "Are you an apostate, then?"

The priest sighed. "I'm afraid you'll have to decide that for yourself."

Geder shook his head. His body felt weirdly separate, like he was watching himself from a distance. "For myself?"

Lehrer took Geder's elbow and guided him to a chair. Kit walked along with them and sat at Geder's side. A beetle that had escaped the frames and mesh floated in the air, its wings beating so quickly he couldn't tell they were there except for a soft buzzing.

"I think you are aware of the curious gifts that the spiders allow men like myself, yes? I hope you will understand, then, the position I find myself in."

"I don't think I do," Geder said. His father sat beside him, leaning in toward the priest. Cithrin put her weight on the divan's side, leaning casually against it. Her gown clung to her arm, draped from her shoulders and breasts. Geder couldn't focus clearly on anything but her. At least not until Kit spoke again.

"I believe you have been played for a fool, Lord Regent. *I* believe that, but you must make up your own mind on the matter. And because of my . . . condition, I find I must choose my words with you very carefully."

"What do you mean?"

"Everything you've heard about the goddess and her role in the world might be wrong," Kit said. "You will have to consider it, and come to your own conclusion. Knowing what you do of me, and Basrahip, and all the men who are like the two of us, you can weigh what you know of us and of the world, and decide for yourself what is true. It's possible that we will disagree."

Something in Geder's mind shifted. "Disagree?" he echoed.

"You can disagree," Kit said, his voice low and powerful as a drum. "To look at the world and doubt the stories you've heard of it is your right. Your responsibility, even. If something can be harmed by a question, I think it should be. Must be, even. And especially when it's said by someone like me."

"But Basrahip—"

"The things the Basrahip says may be wrong," Kit said. "You should look at the evidence yourself and see what sense you make of it. I understand you're something of a scholar."

"I was," Geder said. His hand was shaking. That was very strange. Why should his hands be shaking? "I am. I've translated text out of a dozen languages. Not always very well, but...I have...I have a collection of speculative essays."

"Then perhaps you understand already the importance of looking outside of a story for other bits of evidence that a thing is true."

"But written words are dead," Geder said. "They're just things. They can't be true or false. The living voice can carry intention in a way that written words can't."

"Possibly," Kit said. "But only possibly. Are you certain of that?"

"You're doing it to me now, though," Geder said. "You're using the power of the goddess to...to..."

"To open your mind to doubt," Kit said, "and to ask that you reevaluate the conclusions you've drawn. Not mine. Your own. If they are true, then considering them can do no harm. For example, you have heard—I did too when I was at the temple—that nothing written can be judged and those things which are spoken can be. Is that your experience?"

"Yes," Geder said, and looked at his father. Lehrer's expression mixed fear and pain and a fierceness Geder had rarely seen. "I mean, I think so..."

"Listen to my voice, Lord Geder," Kit said. "Some of the things the Basrahip has told you may be true. Others may not. You must judge them for yourself and decide whether the world he describes is the same as the one you know. You are permitted to disagree."

"But—"

"Listen to my voice, friend. *You can disagree.*"

Cary came to him, a cup of water in her hand. Geder sipped from it out of a kind of habit. He looked out past the pale screens to the moonlight on the roofs of Camnipol to the vast tower of the Kingspire. The banner of the goddess, red in the daylight, had faded almost to black. Lights glowed in the high windows where Basrahip and the other priests held their ceremonies. The great doors had been swung open to allow in the night's cool air. Geder felt like the tower himself. It felt as though the fog that had taken him for the past months was being stirred by a cold wind. The illness that no cunning man could identify, much less treat, began to resolve. The sensation of it was physical, and the words that it carried were *I can disagree.* He hadn't been ill. He'd been confused. Caught between two things that he couldn't reconcile until a kind of moral vertigo had consumed him. But he could disagree.

"They came to help, Son," Lehrer said.

Everything that Basrahip said, everything about the war and the goddess and the nature of the apostate...He could disagree. As soon as it was said, he knew that he did, and the force of it pushed at his throat like too many people rushing through too small a door.

"I don't know," Geder said, and the words were like a confession. "I don't know. I'm not...sure."

"Is there some question that's bothered you, my lord?" Kit asked.

"The fire years," Geder said, then stopped. His jaw felt almost stiff with the effort of saying it. He paused, tried to catch his breath. The words hurt in a way he couldn't quite explain. It wasn't physical, but if it had been, it would have been the bright, itching pain of tearing off a scab. "Basrahip said there were years after the dragons fell when the whole world was burned, but there's nothing about that in any of the histories."

"I see," Kit said, but Geder couldn't stop now. The words had begun and they wouldn't stop until he'd finished.

"And there are buildings in Hallskar with wooden perches. Either the perches would have to be a wood that doesn't burn or someone would have had to make them after there weren't any dragons left to use them. And there's not a layer of ashes under any of the ruins in the Division, and it just doesn't make *sense*!"

"Then perhaps there were no fire years," Kit said.

Geder's blood felt bright in his veins. Somewhere in his gesturing, he'd spilled a bit of the water from his cup. It dripped down his knuckles. Clara Kalliam put a hand on his shoulder and smiled down at him. His father nodded. His breath felt clean and clear for the first time he could remember. Across the room, Cithrin stood like a statue of some ancient hero, her chin high but her eyes kind.

What if it wasn't the death throes of the enemy, but just losing a war? What if killing the apostate in Asterilhold wasn't the final victory of the goddess? What if having a temple in a city didn't mean it would never fall?

Wouldn't it all make more sense?

"Tell me," he said. "Tell me what you know. And I'll say what I think of it."

"Yes," Cithrin said, as Kit cleared his throat.

"I think I might not be best suited to that," he said. "Do you think we should invite in Captain Wester?"

It took hours. The story of Master Kit's apostasy, the power he'd found in the word *probably*, and the price he'd paid for it was all told by Marcus Wester and a Tralgu called Yardem, presumably so that Geder wouldn't feel he was being influenced by the spiders in the apostate's blood. The trek through the wilds of Lyoneia and the ancient ruins guarded by the Southling tribes there. The sword and the temple, the attempt on the life of the goddess, and the discovery that she was no more than a statue and a story. And

then the search that Geder himself had begun with Dar Cin-
lama, and the discovery of the last dragon.

Then Cithrin came and sat by him, her voice low and serious, her pale eyes on his in a way he'd thought would never
happen again. She didn't take his hand, and he didn't reach
for hers. She told what she'd learned from Inys. The prank
against Morade that had begun the last war between the
dragons, the invention of the tool that would strip the dragons of their slaves, the release of the spiders, and the fall of
the ancient world. Geder listened, enraptured. It was like all
the best histories and poems and speculative essays he'd ever
read, wrapped together with confirmation by sources who'd
been there.

All my time in power, he thought, *I could have been
doing this. I could have been having conversations like this
one and hearing stories and putting them together.* It made
something familiar and terrible shift in his gut that he didn't
think about. Not yet.

They came to the creation of the Timzinae—a race made
for fighting the dragon Morade—and he stopped them.

"But why did the Timzinae want to kill Aster?" Geder
said. "Why did they suborn Lord Kalliam?"

"They didn't," Clara Kalliam said. "Dawson would never
have taken direction from a foreign power or another race.
My husband did what he did because he felt the throne had
been usurped by a cult of foreign priests who were using you
and Prince Aster as puppets."

And, she didn't need to say, *he was right.*

For the first time, the implications of it all struck him and
left a vast and oceanic hollowness behind his breastbone. If
this was all true, if Basrahip's goddess was an artifact of the
dragons, if the Timzinae were only another race of humans
fashioned from the Firstbood as they'd all been, if the war

was not about bringing the light of truth to the world, then Jorey's father had been right.

The cities they'd taken in the war were no more or less likely to fall than any other captured land in any other of a thousand wars. Geder had been tricked into throwing those children into the Division. Like a hand puppet stuck on the big priest's fist, he'd been telling Aster all the things Basrahip had poured into his own ear and none of it true.

He'd been played for the greatest idiot in history, and he'd brought Antea to the edge of collapse by it. The thing that had been moving in his belly came to life, lifting up into his heart, his throat, his brain.

It was relief.

Cithrin

It was working. The change showed in the way he held himself and the timbre of his voice. Geder Palliako sat on his divan like it was made from nails and he was determined to endure it. All around, the others sat and stood, spoke and were silent. Played their parts. Cithrin cared about Geder.

He looked . . . bad. His skin had taken on a strange sheen, like dust and oil. His eyes seemed smaller than she remembered them, and darker. When he first came in, his father had led him to Clara to create a setting of the familiar. The known. Geder's voice then had been tight and tense, his body braced as if against a coming blow. She'd feared what would happen when she spoke, and it made her speak sooner than she'd intended.

His dark eyes had widened when he saw her, but he hadn't called for his guards. When Cary embraced him, and then the other actors, each greeting him as an old friend, as if none of the atrocities that had come between the day he'd come out of hiding and now had ever been, he'd seemed dazed. The deeper change came with Kit, sitting at his side, opening the doors of Geder's mind the way she'd hoped he would. When the history of the spiders came clear to him, it was like watching a child see his first rainbow. The joy and wonder in it would have been beautiful if they'd been in some other setting. As it was, they were more unsettling.

What she had hoped for, what she'd come here to achieve—but unsettling.

Marcus spoke to him in professional tones, like a soldier giving a report of a battle, as he explained all that had come before. Disapproval showed in the corner of his mouth, but Geder didn't see it. He only listened. As Marcus tore away every story that Geder had lived by, every poisoned dream, Geder's breath deepened. The tightness in his voice smoothed gently away. As he grew calmer, she did as well. When her turn came, and she sat beside him, he seemed almost the man she'd known in the darkness, and she could at least remember the girl she had been.

They brought tea and coffee which Geder drank without seeming to notice he was doing so. She unfolded the story of Inys and Morade with all the skill and grace Cary and the players had been able to teach her, and Geder listened to it all. His eyes were on her, but seeing the deep past and the grand sweep of history. *He could kill me*, she thought, *but he isn't going to*.

The idea felt like victory.

"But why did the Timzinae want to kill Aster?" Geder said. "Why did they suborn Lord Kalliam?"

Cithrin looked for the words, for the gentle way to say it. Clara Kalliam answered before she could, and her voice was hard as stone.

"They didn't. Dawson would never have taken direction from a foreign power or another race. My husband did what he did because he felt the throne had been usurped by a cult of foreign priests who were using you and Prince Aster as puppets."

Geder's eyes went flat, his expression terribly still. His eyes flickered from side to side as though he were reading some invisible text written on the air. Cithrin felt her belly tighten with excitement and fear. It had all gone so well, and now they were at the crisis point. Everything depended on the next few seconds. If he heard the woman's words as an insult, they would all be dead by morning. Cithrin felt a deep calm come over her. She didn't think he would.

At the edge of the room, Yardem started and blinked, his ears flat against his head.

"I see," Geder said, the syllables gentle as a fawn. His eyes filled with tears that he wiped away with the back of one hand. And then, a moment later, "I understand. Thank you."

He rose to his feet, and his father came forward. The elder Palliako's face drew a picture of regret and resolve. "Are you well?"

"I think," Geder said, his voice artificially calm, "it might be better if I could stay here tonight? I don't think I want to go back to the Kingspire right now. And if it's not too much, will you stay? Will you all stay too?"

"Of course," Lehrer said. "You never have to ask."

"Thank you, Da."

They embraced. A tear tracked down Lehrer's cheek. For a moment, Cithrin wondered what it was like to have a mother or a father who would take you in no matter what you had done. It was here before her, and she still couldn't imagine it. When they parted, Geder could not look in his father's eyes. His hands were at his sides in fists, his face dark. His lips moved as he talked to himself, too quietly for her or any of them to hear, and he shook his head.

"You are the only one who can stop them."

His eyes found her like he was peering through a fog. "What?"

"You can stop them. You're the only one who can put an end to this. Call them together, all of them. A conclave like the Council of Eventide, only for the priests. You can tell them it's because of the rise of the apostates. It won't be telling them the whole truth, but it won't be lying."

"And then what?" Geder said.

Kit cleared his throat. "There is a play called *The Archer King*. The king, betrayed by his ministers and lords, calls them all together for a triumph, then locks the doors of the common house and floods it." The actor shook his head. "The nearest convenient river would be in the depths of the Division, of course. So I can't recommend that."

Geder didn't speak for a moment. When he did, his words were cool. "We'll find something."

Clara Kalliam left shortly after Geder and Lehrer Palliako retired. Staying away until daybreak would, she said, excite comment, and she'd already done more than enough of that for the time being. The players and Master Kit went to the servants' quarters where there were cots enough for them all. Lehrer Palliako's hospitality meant that Cithrin had her own bed in a small chamber of its own that opened into a narrow courtyard of ivy and lilac, an honored guest in the house of her enemy. A thin mesh over her window let in a breeze thick with the scent of the flowers and, beneath that, of the city. Perfume and shit. She didn't take off her dress, only lay on the mattress and pretended that sleep would come.

Her gut was a single knot, hard as stone. Her body was wretchedly tired. She trembled with it. But each time she closed her eyes, her mind sped away from her—where was Geder now, what was he thinking, would destruction of the priests mean her own transgression against his pride would be forgotten, what would she do if he came to her chamber now in the night—and without noticing when it had happened, she realized her eyes were open again.

Outside, birds that had been silent began their raucous choir. She saw no sign of the coming dawn, but they did. She forced her eyes closed again, again found them open, and surrendered to the inevitable. Even if she'd had enough wine to bring her down to sleep, it was too late to begin it now. And in her present situation, she wouldn't have. Miserable or not, she needed her wits. She rose, washed her face in the basin, combed out her hair, and prepared herself as best she could to face the new day and the dangers she'd created for it. When she opened the door to the hall, ready to call for a servant to bring her food or else lead her to it, Marcus Wester was waiting. He sat with his back against the wall opposite her door, the poisoned blade on the floor beside him. His hand rested on its hilt.

"Captain?"

"Magistra," he said, and the tone of his voice made it half a joke.

"Are you . . . all right? What are you doing?"

"The job, as I understand it," he said, levering himself up with a grunt. As he rose, she caught a glimpse of his shoulder where the sword usually rested. The skin there was red and peeling as from a sunburn. "With the present factors at play, I thought having one of our guard outside your room was literally the least we should do. I also considered killing our hosts and slipping out the back, but it seemed rude."

"Have you been here all night?"

"No," he said, brushing his sleeves with open palms. "Yardem took first watch. I caught a little sleep."

"I didn't hear you."

"We're good."

Outside, the birds all went silent at once, then burst forth again even louder. Marcus glanced down the hall, one way and then the other. When he spoke, his voice was low and disapproving. "I saw what you did back there."

"Back where?"

"With the Lord Regent."

Cithrin's mouth pressed thin and she nodded back toward her room. Marcus followed her through it and out to the little courtyard. The sky had gone from black to charcoal. A single high cloud held a delicate pink color. The lilacs nodded in the little breeze like holy men sprinkling blessings out over a crowd, filling the air with a sweetness that was almost cloying. Marcus found a low stone bench and sat. Cithrin crossed her arms.

"How does this go?" Marcus said. "In your head, how does it play out? Everyone comes and gives Palliako a hug and rubs his little belly and suddenly he's our dog? Is he going to come running when we whistle now?"

"I've given him the chance to look at his world from a different perspective," Cithrin said. "What happens next depends on what he sees." Weariness sharpened the words more than she'd intended. It felt as though she'd spent her life with all her decisions being questioned by Marcus Wester. He could afford to have a little more faith in her. More than that, she wished she'd rested as well in her bed as he had in her hallway.

"You played him as much the fool as the spiders have. Damned near drowned him with how much everybody liked him," Marcus said. "Everyone there touching his shoulder and taking him in their arms and smiling at him like he's always been their favorite."

"Love is what he wanted. What he still wants. I only pointed out that we are a way it could be supplied."

"But we aren't. The truth is everyone in that room hates that man. We'd each of us have thrown him off a bridge if there was a way to."

"Not everyone," Cithrin said. "His father was sincere."

"And what happens when someone lets slip? Geder

Palliako's head is a bag of snakes. If he decides we're the one plucking his strings—"

"Then we're very nearly no worse off than we were before we came," Cithrin said. "We'll die a bit sooner, and the world we leave behind won't be worth living in anyway."

His half-coughed laughter surprised her. "Well, that's true enough, I suppose."

"Here's how it plays out. Geder does as he has always done. He sees that he's been made a fool of by the priests. He gets angry about it, has them all brought together, and we kill them." She spread her hands.

"It won't work."

"It will," she said. "Geder's *predictable*. Yes, we'll need to be careful with him, but we have the thing he needs, and he will trade it for it. Love for dead priests. This will—"

"That's not the hole in it." The little rosy cloud had faded to white. The grey sky had brightened into blue. She could see Marcus's face better now, the lines and wrinkles around his eyes and mouth. The yellowed ivory of his eyes. "You say you can have him call the dinner bell and have the priests come running, and so I believe you can. Makes me nervous as hell, but anyone else's battle plan besides my own has that effect. The problem's the trap."

She wanted to yell at him, to tell him that he was trying to find ways that she'd failed. That he didn't want anyone to win if it wasn't through him. It was the voice of her fatigue. "Go on," she said.

"We have to build the thing. There have to be people at the palace ready to throw boards over some banquet hall's windows or rain burning oil through a false roof or . . . something. And this while as near as we can manage it all the lie-sniffing priests there are swarm around the court like flies on a shit heap. This conspiracy of yours is too big already.

Throw in builders and servants? The people who supply the oil and the boards? Even if it were Geder's own guard, it's too many people to keep the secret."

"So we find a better way to build the trap. Simpler."

Marcus made a thin grunt and scratched his head. "All right."

"You have an idea?"

"No, I don't," he said. "But if you need one, I'll find one. Someplace. Yardem, maybe. He's always impressed by his own wisdom and clarity. But we will have to be clever about it. And there's the problem of getting all the priests here when we've got two armies making their way toward us. If we wait too long, Camnipol will have already fallen when the bastards get here."

"Can it be saved?"

"The city? No. If Camnipol's not a ruin by winter, it'll be because Karol Dannien decided to let it live. We can postpone the thing, but we can't stop it." He coughed out something like a laugh, and looked out to the east. The tower of the Kingspire was barely visible above the courtyard wall. "That temple of theirs. That's a long way up, isn't it? Well… ha. All right, I may have a way."

But Cithrin barely heard him. The exhaustion in her body, already crippling, doubled. The army of Elassae was coming, and she should have been delighted. Not so long ago, she would have been. They were the wronged, the people crying out for justice that they deserved. That she and Magistra Isadau and Marcus—and Clara Kalliam in her way—had all risked their lives to achieve. She had seen the body of the Timzinae priest hung from his own church. She had seen the children ripped from their families, their parents shipped away as slaves. Many of those children were dead now. How could she want those to go unavenged? And yet

what would killing the bakers and groomsmen, street clean-
ers and taproom servers of Camnipol achieve? No depth of
violence ever retrieved a single person from the death they'd
already suffered. More dead were only more dead.

"I don't know what justice is," she said.

"That's because it isn't the sort of thing you discover. It's a
thing you make." She looked at him, and he shrugged. "There
are things you find out in the world. Rocks and streams and
trees. And there are things you make. Like a house, or a
song. It's not that houses and songs aren't real, but you don't
just find them in a field someplace and haul them back home
with you. They have to be worked at. Made."

"Like war gold," she said.

"Wouldn't have been my first example, but why not?
That's about as made up a thing as I can think of."

"Antea's crimes can't be paid for," she said, testing the
thought for the first time even as she spoke it. "They could
fill the Division with the dead twice over, and it wouldn't
rebuild Suddapal or bring their children back to life."

"That's true enough."

"It's another debt that can never be repaid. That's..."
Marcus's head snapped up to look at her, but she only shook
her head. It was there, at the edge of her understanding, but
she was spread too thin to grasp it now. It would come if she
gave it time. If she had enough time to give it.

She walked through the house only half seeing it. Tapestries hung along the walls, telling the tale of House Palliako or else merely showing the skill of the weavers. A few
servants scuttled along before her, staying out of her way
as they'd been told to do. War was a debt paid with a debt
that left both sides poorer. It was always that, and never
anything else no matter what the songs and stories claimed.
That was what Morade had seen and embraced. The mad

dragon emperor had tried to drown the world in an acid that would eat away everything. But he'd failed once.

The dining hall was smaller than Maestro Asanpur's café had been. Two long wooden tables stood at an angle to each other, platters of eggs and beans, bread and jam standing ready to be eaten. At the smell, Cithrin's stomach lurched awake, and a vast appetite filled her. At the end of one table, the farthest from her, Lehrer Palliako and Geder sat across from each other, talking and gesturing and laughing. A father and a son, taking pleasure in each other's company. Seeing them was like looking down a cliff; it left her a little dizzy. Or maybe that was only hunger and lack of sleep.

"Magistra!" Lehrer said, rising to his feet. "Please, come sit with us. There's enough room, God knows. Isn't there enough room, my boy?"

Geder nodded, but his eyes were on his feet and a wild blush was pushing up his neck and out to his cheeks. When his gaze did flicker up to meet hers, he tried a smile. She returned it, and the artifice was easier than she'd expected. And then she remembered how many lives had been spent by his misplaced affection and she looked away. Marcus shifted behind her.

"Thank you, my lord," Cithrin said, "but the captain and I have business we should see to. I've only come for a moment."

"Well, eat. Eat before you go," Lehrer said, gesturing toward the expanse of food. "This is all for you and your people, after all."

Cithrin took a plate of sausages in her hand. The first one popped between her teeth, flooding her mouth with grease and salt and the sweetness of roasted garlic. "You're too generous," she said.

"Not generous enough," Lehrer said.

Clara

"I am reconciling myself to the idea that I will never see my husband again," Lady Skestinin said.

"Oh you mustn't say that," Delliah Kemmin said around a mouthful of sweet bun.

The garden party was at Lord Emming's estate. A pavilion of colored canvas decorated with banners of colored silk had been raised over a wide paved square at the garden's center. A trio of Dartinae slaves wearing glittering robes that matched their glowing eyes stood on a dais not far away from Clara's table, their voices mixed in a careful harmony. They kept the song quiet enough not to interfere with conversation. The air was thick with the scents of turned earth and flowers and freshly brewed tea. The overall effect was to leave Clara shifting with a barely contained impatience.

"It has been too long without word," Lady Skestinin said. "He was lost in Porte Oliva before the city fell. And I've been seeing a cunning man on it."

"No," Rielle Castannan said. "Which one?"

"The Jasuru woman that Lady Caot recommended," Lady Skestinin said. "She's been lighting fires for me and reading the flames. She's seen his body in them, she said. Killed and buried under the plains of Birancour." Her voice broke at the last. Clara put down her teacup too abruptly. It rattled.

"Before you give up all hope," she said, "I would recommend being sure your cunning man is what she claims to be."

Lady Skestinin's lips tightened and her shoulders slid back a degree. "I'm not certain what you mean, Lady Kalliam."

"Ask her something you have the answer to," Clara said. "See whether she can learn what you do know before you put too much trust in her ability to know what you don't."

Because, while *the plains of Birancour* was a pretty phrase and rich with connotations of lost love and exotic locations, she'd been there. There were any number of Antean dead in that ground, but Lord Skestinin was in a decent if uncomfortable cell in Carse. Not that she could say that. It was only that watching another woman's grief be exploited upset her, even if it was Lady Skestinin's.

"Or take one of the priests," Lady Kemmin said.

"Or that," Clara agreed, sourly.

A dozen women or more had arranged themselves around the garden, each according to their own dignity and position. Depending upon who spoke to whom and where the apparently casual traffic of social exchange went, their status would be ratified by the women around them or else denied. Clara watched it with a practiced eye for the occult significance of it all: Lady Emming had taken the chair with its back to the house, and so commanded the best view of the gardens; Canl Daskellin's youngest daughter had arrived slightly before her older sister; the ladies whose houses extended to Asterilhold weren't deferring to the purely Antean houses the way they had been when Clara had left to follow Jorey. All of it had meaning.

Including—*especially*—Nickayla Essian's dress.

It was simply cut, and flattered her figure. The cloth was a gentle green set off by more vibrant ribbons at the spine and woven into the skirt. During King Simeon's reign, it would have been an acceptable if unremarkable choice. Among the black leather jackets and unsettling ossuary cloaks of the present fashion, she stood out like a single live blossom on a burned field. The context made it bold, even brash. And more, it announced an allegiance to Clara. The borrowed green dress she'd worn to Lady Emming's previous, smaller garden party had begun a new fashion. Nickayla Essian's statement was the boldest, but once Clara knew to look, there were others. Dannie Sennian had a pale-green ribbon woven in her braids. Lauria Caot, while still sporting a fringe of bones along the cuffs of her sleeves, had a choker with a single new leaf as its pendant.

None of them knew or could know the depth of the conspiracy in which she'd involved herself. She felt tired because she'd spent a fair portion of the previous night with the Lord Regent and the banker who was his mortal enemy and unhealthy obsession. Most of them would have been horrified to find out that she had camped at the edges of Jorey's army with the whores and merchant carters, much less that she'd helped to engineer a fundamental realignment in the forces of the war. For them, the struggle was still very much the Severed Throne and the spider goddess standing against the draconic and inhuman Timzinae. But Nickayla had seen something in the accident of Clara's appearance, and she'd grabbed on to it.

It wasn't hope, but it might be the desire that there be hope. A shoot of new growth in the decadence of black jackets and bone robes. That the potential existed at all meant something, and Clara suspected it would be something good. Unless the two armies in the field against Jorey did their work and everyone here faced the blades and arrows of Elassae.

It seemed impossible that Camnipol could fall. Even with the men of court scattered for the most part to the army, everything was too familiar, too regular. Catastrophe would surely announce itself more clearly. Simply by having garden parties and dances, feasts and performances of poetry, they affirmed the normalcy of the world. Surely if the end were really coming, they wouldn't have sweet buns and tea, and so sweet buns and tea were a kind of armor against what they all feared. The laughter that covered the shriek.

She imagined Suddapal had felt much the same before their own army had come to it.

Her mind turned to Hoban, the cunning man who'd saved Vincen Coe's life once. She wondered whether he still worked out of the little house in the low quarter of the city. Alston, who had been her servant when she'd been Baroness of Osterling Fells and kept a compound of her own, and was now... she didn't know. She'd been so careful to keep track of all her old servants. Now that she'd come back from her tour with the army, she needed to find them all again. Tomorrow. She would do that tomorrow, unless the enemy came. Unless Geder decided to execute them all as traitors. Unless Lady Skestinin discovered that Clara had...how had Lord Skestinin put it? *Betrayed the kingdom?* Well, if the world didn't find some way to collapse before the next morning, she would put in the effort to find her old servants and go to the Prisoners' Span and renew her old acquaintances there.

Oddly, the idea cheered her. It would be good to see them all. And, now that she thought of it, there might be other connections within the court that it would be wise to renew. The problem of the Timzinae children in the prison and their parents working as slaves on the farms, for instance, might be something that—

"Don't you think, Clara?" Rielle Castannan said, and Clara realized she'd utterly lost the thread of the conversation.

"I am making a concerted effort not to think at all," she said, and the others chuckled politely.

The commotion in the house was small at first: a raised voice, and movement in the doorway. Clara hardly noticed it. It was only when the others began to rise from their seats that she turned back to look. Geder Palliako stood on the stone-paved walk with a too-cheerful smile and cast his gaze across the gardens. Lord Emming trotted out from the house, his shirt and hair in disarray. He looked like a man half wakened from a nap, which he likely was. Clara stood, either in respect for the Lord Regent or through the animal impulse to run. Discerning between the two was not straightforward. If Cithrin bel Sarcour had failed, this would be Clara's last moment as a free woman. She tried to savor it.

Her mouth set in a tight smile, Lady Emming came to where the two men were speaking. Neither priests nor guards accompanied the Lord Regent, so that was something. Clara chanced a look around the garden. Not all the guests were standing, but most were. Not all looked frightened, but more than didn't. So at least she wouldn't stand out.

Lady Emming nodded to the Lord Regent and gestured toward Clara's table. Geder's gaze shifted to her and grew brighter. He trotted toward her, waving to the other women as he came, like the parody of a carefree man. "Please don't let me interrupt," he said as he reached her. "I only need to borrow Lady Kalliam for a moment. You don't mind, do you?"

"No," Lady Skestinin said, but too late. Geder had taken

Clara's arm in his and was already leading her off to a corner of the garden where rosebushes formed a little grotto
of thorns and buds not yet in bloom. Geder looked back at
the party, playing his grin over the ladies of the court like a
searchlight in the darkness. When he spoke to her, his voice
was low and conspiratorial.

"We're meeting tomorrow night," he said. "The Ebbingbaugh compound, just before sundown. Can you be there?"

"Of course I can," she said.

"Good, good, good. I'm putting a plan together, and I
want you all to be part of it. You're the only people I can
trust anymore."

I have betrayed you as deeply as I could manage, Clara
thought. *I stood by and watched you slaughter a man I love
with your own hand. And yes, I see that you trust me.* Her
heart was complicated by pity and hatred and a hope of
her own.

"I will make my way there," she said. "Discreetly."

"Yes. Important that we be discreet," he said, with the
eyes of the garden party on him. He appeared unaware of
the irony. "There are going to be a lot of things we need to
manage if we're going to fix all this. A lot of things to be
done."

"That's true."

"And I wanted . . . I wanted to thank you. For what you've
done. For bringing her back to me." He nodded, his gaze on
the roses, as if by nodding he could convince her to agree
that Cithrin bel Sarcour had been brought back as a gift
for him.

"If I helped the throne, I'm pleased," Clara said.

When he looked up at her, his eyes were as bright as a
fever. "I'm going to show her it wasn't me. She'll understand. Better than anyone. Don't you think?"

"I think we'll all need to be careful," she said, not answering the question, though he acted as if she had.

When she returned to her tea, Geder made a show of shaking Lord Emming's hand and escorting him back into the house as though it had been him the Lord Regent had come for and meeting Clara had been only a happy accident. It was overacting of such scale that it would, she expected, be inscrutable to the court. They would see the change, though. The Lord Regent had returned to public life. His energy and optimism of form would mean something to those seeing it. What exactly they would think, she couldn't guess.

"Preparations for Jorey's triumph?" Lady Skestinin asked. An undertone of jealousy sharpened the words.

"Something like that," Clara said mildly.

Not all men of the court had left Camnipol, but those who remained fell into distinct categories: the old and infirm, like Jaram Terrinnian, Earl of Attenmarch, who had outlived three kings in his time and hardly ever left his gardens; the very young, like Daunan Broot, toddling now after his mother and unlikely to see his father in this world; the highest leaders of the empire, like Geder and Aster and the bull-huge Basrahip; and the disgraced. It was to this last category that Clara turned her attention.

Curtin Issandrian's home shared the street with the one Geder had claimed from Feldin Maas. From its gate Clara could see the vast and unruly hedge where she'd hidden once from her cousin's husband's guards. Where a wounded huntsman had stolen a kiss, long before her own husband had died. She supposed that with so many lives packed so close together, all the city must be like this. The architecture and streets recurring in people's lives, meaning something a bit new every time, but echoing all that had come before.

Or perhaps that wasn't the city. Perhaps that was the whole world.

The courtyard outside Curtin Issandrian's house had fallen into disrepair. The cobbles themselves showed holes where the cold had shattered stones that had not been replaced. The hedges had the yellowed look of distressed plants, and the flowers within showed more stem than blossom. The door slave was a Kurtadam man with a greying pelt and a limp, who seemed astonished that anyone would come to the house. Company at Issandrian's compound was clearly an exceptional thing.

The years had been kinder to the man himself than she would have expected. His once long hair remained short-cropped as she had seen it last, but he also sported a thick mustache and beard that suited him better than she would have guessed. His whiskers, like his gardens, were in need of some trimming, but the potential was there.

"Lady Kalliam," he said, walking with her into his withdrawing room. "It's been too long. I hadn't expected to see you again."

When she'd been there last, it had been to filch letters from his study. She recalled it now with a combination of shame that she'd taken advantage of the man's good nature and pride that she'd gotten away with it. She sat on the divan now and he sat across from her, his legs crossed.

"I'm afraid events have conspired to keep me away from court more than I might have liked," she said.

"I can't say you've missed much of consequence," Issandrian said. "Or at least, if you have, I've missed it as well. I made an unfortunate friend in Alan Klin once, and I'm paying for it still. The Lord Regent isn't a man who easily forgets a grudge."

The Lord Regent, she thought, *is a man who will easily*

forget whatever it pleases him to forget and recall what he
wishes to recall. It's what makes him most like the rest of us.

"Well, the wheel of the world hasn't stopped turning yet,"
Clara said. "There may be changes of fortune ahead still."

"I don't see much hope of it," Issandrian said.

"I do, but I stand upon a slightly different stair."

A Cinnae man in a servant's livery knocked at the door,
bowed his way in with a carafe of steaming coffee, served it,
and bowed his way out. Clara took her pipe from her sleeve
and packed it with fresh leaf.

"I wondered," she said, "whether you might still have
friends among the farmers?"

"Some, yes," Issandrian said, and sipped at his cup.

"Have you a sense of whether there is a common opinion
on the Timzinae slaves?"

"They're a godsend," Issandrian said, without hesitating.
"There's not a farm in the southern empire that hasn't lost
at least one son to the army. Near Sevenpol there are farms
running that have lost four or five to it. Without the slaves,
we'd be eating clouds and drinking raindrops."

"I see," Clara said, drawing on her pipe. The smoke
tasted rich, and the coffee better. Issandrian's gaze was a
question. She let the smoke seep out through her teeth
while she considered what she wanted to ask, and how
she wanted to ask it. "Between the two of us, and purely
as speculation—yes?—purely as speculation, what do you
imagine your friends among that stratum would think of
setting the Timzinae free?"

Issandrian laughed, but it was from shock, not conde-
scension. That was good. "I can't think why they would."

"Say as speculation it was required to make peace."

"Peace? Peace with who?"

"Elassae. Sarakal. Everyone."

Issandrian put down his cup. His skin, already pale, had gone a shade paler. She gave him the moment, drinking her own coffee. It wasn't quite pure, she thought, but she couldn't identify what the extender was that he'd used. Something about the kind of bitterness it carried made her suspect it was a root of some sort. Issandrian folded his hands on his knees.

"I thought we were winning," Issandrian said. "Everyone says that we're winning."

"We're not."

Issandrian pressed a hand to his chin. His distress would have been comic if it hadn't been so sincere. "I can talk with them about raising more troops. I don't know that there's many to be had, but if it's that or lose the war—"

"The war cannot be won. Only prolonged," Clara said. "It may come to a place where prolonging it is worth the effort and blood, but that isn't what I need to know of you now. I believe there is a change coming upon us rather quickly. If I'm right, it may give us a chance to save something of the empire, but we would need to be ready to act."

"Lady," Issandrian said. The poor man. He'd started his day as an outcast, ill-dignified and shunned by polite company. Now here he was listening to half riddles from a woman with the most complex and uncertain status in the history of the court. In his position she wouldn't have known if she was being asked to defend the throne or conspire against it. Which, in fairness, hadn't been clear to her either, these last few years. It was a problem, she supposed, of trying to use the tools of another time as if nothing had changed. This war was not like the last one, this kingdom was not the kingdom it believed itself to be, she was not the woman she had once been, nor Issandrian any of the versions of himself that had come before. Hardly a surprise that he felt a bit dizzy with it all.

He gathered himself. "I will do what I can," he said. "What are you asking of me now?"

"Should we require that the Timzinae be freed, it will need to happen quickly and uniformly and without any of the farms demanding that they be excepted."

"That won't be easy," he said.

"Not if it's demanded without any return," Clara said, then laughed. "I sound like a banker, don't I? Well, regardless, if you could use what contacts you have to sound them out, we might be able to recompense them for their loss."

Issandrian shook his head. Somewhere in the world of the dead, Dawson turned his head away. Poor ghost.

"It may be time," Clara said, "to revisit the idea of a farmer's council."

Geder

Geder slept through the night and woke rested in the morning. He lay in the wide bed, looking up at his ceiling, the blankets a nest around him and over him. Outside his room, servants went about their morning routines. The sounds of voices were like music just at the edge of his hearing. Outside, a bird sang and another answered it. His belly growled, pleasantly empty, and he stretched his arms above his head until his muscles felt tight enough to sing if someone took a viol's bow and struck them.

He smiled without having a particular thing he was smiling about. Only everything at once. A servant rapped gently at the door, brought in a washstand and fresh cloth, then retreated, careful not to speak or look at the Lord Regent in repose. Geder stretched again, sighed, and hauled himself up from bed. He washed himself in privacy, chose his own clothing for the day, and prepared himself.

The euphoria wouldn't last forever. He knew himself well enough to know that at least. Just now, not feeling ill was enough to make him feel well. The buzzing, cottony sensation of a mind at war with itself had gone, and he felt clearer than water in a fountain. All the joy in his body just now came from that. The rage—and oh, there was rage—lay below it. Rage and humiliation and the overwhelming conviction that the men who'd misled him were going to suffer. There were only two ways this story could go. The world would either remember him as the greatest dupe in history, or it would tell the story of what a terrible mistake it had been to cross Geder Palliako. He'd been Lord Regent long enough to know how it felt to put his enemies on their knees, and it felt very, very good. He was looking forward to it.

And then there was Cithrin. She was there, in his city. In his house, even if it wasn't the one he'd lived in most. Her face was as beautiful as he'd remembered. When she'd touched his hand, it had been like his skin was in a cunning man's fire—bright and alive and unburning. All the fantasies he'd had about her—her mocking laugh, her mewling and naked shame—paled when they were faced with the actual woman. She'd come to him, to help him. And together they'd do what needed to be done and save the world. He was already imagining sitting with her after it was over, taking her hand again, pressing it to his chest. He'd tell her that he understood now why she'd fled Suddapal, that he forgave her.

What had happened between them during the insurrection had been between a man and a woman of equal dignity. It had felt almost like that again when they'd seen each other now, and likely would be even more so at the meeting of the conspiracy tonight. And once Basrahip and his lackeys were done with and Aster took the throne—

"Lord Geder?"

"Not yet," Geder snapped, and returned to pulling on his clothes. "I'm not ready yet. Give me time."

The workings of the Kingspire—the functions, in fact, of the whole empire—seemed clearer to him now. The effort it had required to look at the maps of the war and see victory in them only became clear now that he was able to stop.

That he could trace his fingers along the paths the armies had taken and would take, count up the numbers of the men he'd sent out and the reports of the dead, and not be forced into finding one particular message in them was like being released from prison. The empire was crumbling, and that was a terrible danger that had to be addressed. But he saw it now, and the truth alone gave him peace.

It did not, however, make him want to spend more time at the Kingspire.

The late-morning light slanted down out of a bright sky. Blue arced above the city, unbroken by clouds. Camnipol shifted along its streets and bridges, the commerce of human activity rushing through it like blood through veins. The birds of winter were still there, but with them, brighter ones. Finches among the sparrows. Robins with the crows. Geder watched out the carriage window as he ate dried apples and boiled oats.

There was a beauty in Camnipol he felt he hadn't seen for some time. The city bore its ages well, the ruins of what had come before making the foundation of all that had come after and above it. The curving streets with their dark cobbles felt familiar and dignified. The Tralgu beggar at the corner singing in his low and broken voice was ignored by the passersby, but his song was part of the grandeur of the empire. The occasional unfortunate wind that brought up a curl of the rot and shit in the chaos at the base of the Division was a part of the city, part of what made it unlike anyplace else in the world. And the Kingspire, with the red banner he'd been tricked into placing there.

But more than that, there were the city's fresh wounds. The compounds of the families who'd risen in revolt against him had been torn down or burned or given to loyalists from Asterilhold or lesser families promoted by Geder's favor. The lane he passed now had once been travelled by Mirkus Shoat and Estin Cersillian, whose houses were broken now for rising against Geder and the throne. There was still a plaque at the Great Bear in honor of a poetry contest won by Lord Bannien, Duke of Estinfort, in deference either to his wit with a rhyme or the power and wealth he'd commanded. All of which were only memory now. Camnipol, like the world, was drawn in scars and violence, and for the most part beautiful despite that.

Geder pressed at the thought of those fallen houses like he was scratching at a wound. Technically, he was responsible for those dead. However much he had been made the puppet of Basrahip and the so-called goddess, he had been the one to give the final commands that ended the men whose grandeur he'd once admired. He tried to feel guilt for their deaths, but had to make do with a kind of peace. Almost forgiveness. He saw now that they had been as much tools of the conspiracy as he had been himself, and in a sense, it put them all on the same side now. He wished there were some way that they could know it. He'd been their enemy once—even their executioner—but he would avenge them now. He couldn't imagine they'd be anything but grateful for that.

The Great Bear was empty. With so many gone to war and so early in the season, it would have been nearly so anyway, but Geder had made his wishes clear. The rooms were vacant, what servants there were kept away in their corridors and kitchens until he called for them. With Canl Daskellin in the field and Mecelli retired to his holding, only Cyr Emming, the last of his inner councilors, waited at the wide oaken table. His war room. Not the miniature maps built of glass and dirt in the Kingspire. Nothing so near to the temple as that. He'd chosen his own space now, and this—this, where the great minds of the kingdom had come together for generations—was his. The old man's face broke into a smile when Geder walked in, but it was a smile that meant nothing. There had been a time when Geder might have cared.

"What news?" Geder demanded.

"Reports are...ah...still coming in, Lord Geder. It seems certain that Nus has in fact been taken up in the death throes of the enemy. The unrest hasn't spread further."

Because it isn't unrest, Geder thought. *It's a military campaign reorganizing after a conquest.* He leaned on the table and squinted down at the maps, making what sense he could of the marks and scratchings.

"How likely is it that they'll come to Kavinpol before the end of the season?"

Emming laughed, then, when Geder didn't follow suit, sobered. "Cross into Antea proper? It can't happen, my lord. This is the poison of the dragons being purged from the world. There was never any poison here to begin with inside Antea. No, I expect Nus and Inentai will return to order before the summer is done."

Of course lifted toward Geder's lips, but he didn't say it. He even believed it somewhat. The habit of seeing all the marks of the war through the story of the goddess and the purification of the world wasn't gone from him. Its back was only broken. Nus and Inentai might return to the empire by the end of summer, but he didn't have to agree that they would. He could dissent. And because that option existed, the freedom to consider his own opinion did as well.

And his opinion was they were fucked.

The thinner thread at the south of the map was the greater issue. The army of Elassae pushing its way north from Orsen would reach Camnipol long before the forces in

Nus could fight their way through Kavinpol to reach him. If it hadn't been for Jorey coming back with the Antean men over the winter, the Timzinae might already be at the gate. He needed time. They had to find a way to give the priests scattered across the map time to reach Camnipol. Anything else that mattered would come after.

"How much gold do we have?" Geder asked.

"Lord Regent?"

"Coin? How much coin do we have? Can we hire mercenaries in the south to slow the Timzinae? Or pay the mercenaries who're with them to abandon the campaign? There's got to be some nomad prince in the Keshet who's looking to grab a bit of glory. We could make the Timzinae pull back to protect Suddapal."

"Is there any need?" Emming said.

Was there any *need*? Geder looked into the man's swimming eyes and saw the confusion there. It was like seeing someone walking in their sleep. Emming literally couldn't see the world because he was trapped in someone's dream of it. Geder felt a surge of impatience and then, to his surprise and confusion, a vast and terrible grief. Hot tears filled his eyes and spilled down his cheeks, smearing the ink that was Camnipol. It lifted him like a storm wave hoisting a ship and brought him down to shatter on rocks hidden under the surface of his heart.

Cyr Emming flapped his hands and looked about at the empty halls as they rang with Geder's sudden sobs. Was there any need? There was *all* of it, and it was his fault. From the start, it had been him. *He* had brought Basrahip back from the Sinir Kushku. *He* had let the priests poison his mind and through him the minds of all Antea. Anyone who might have had the strength of will to stand against him, he'd exiled or killed. The stupidity of it washed him away until he could only sit, his knees drawn to his chest, bawling like an infant. Emming patted his shoulder like a dog pawing at his wounded master.

There was nothing—*nothing*—Emming could do. No insight left in the man's pithed mind. He was dead already, as Geder had been before Cithrin had come and brought him back to life. Geder bared his teeth and screamed, the sound echoing through the chamber. It was like a beast larger than himself stalked the hall. The Great Bear forcing its way into the world through Geder's throat.

And then laughter that had nothing to do with mirth, everything with rage. He had been fucked. Basrahip had fucked him and broken everything he held sacred and dear. He'd poisoned Aster's mind and his friendship with the boy along with it. He'd taken away Geder's *books*. Geder stood now, taken in a glorious madness, and tried to tip over the oaken table and its maps, only the thing was too heavy. He had to make do with scattering the papers to the ground.

Cithrin had cracked the egg; the small, still part of himself that watched him suffer saw that. She'd opened him enough to blow away the fog that had taken him. Now, he couldn't stop ripping open from the same hole. And he would not be silent until there was blood in the streets for what had been done to him. He grabbed Emming's cloak, pulled him close, and screamed in the sleeping bastard's face. Spit flicked the man's cheeks, bright as froth. Geder screamed again, and again, and again, louder each time.

And then it was gone. The wave had passed. Geder felt worn. Wrung out. Emming was weeping a little now too, in fear and confusion. There was nothing Geder could do to wake him. Not yet, anyway. Later perhaps. Geder took a long, shuddering sigh and sat back in his chair. The rage was still there. The humiliation and the anger and the grief. Like an infected wound, it would fill again and be drained again and fill. But for now, he was empty. He used his fingers as combs. Gathered himself.

"I think," he said, in a calm, level voice, "we should do whatever we can to reinforce Kalliam and Daskellin in the south. If there are standing garrisons in Sevenpol and Anninfort, we should call them south. Even if they're small."

"L-lord Regent," Emming said.

"Every little bit will help. And it's important, I think."

"Yes," Emming said. When Geder clapped him on the shoulder, the man flinched.

"Sorry about that," Geder said. "I'm sorry."

Prince Geder," Basrahip said through his vast, placid smile. "You honor me by your presence."

I can disagree with that, Geder thought. *I might honor him with my presence. I might not. I might have no effect on his dignity at all. I'll have to decide that myself.*

"Thank you," he said, and sat.

The high priest's cell was as simple now as it had been in the Sinir Kushku. A lantern. A brazier, unused now in the warmth of spring. A censer with a few smoking twigs of incense. Outside the cell, a half dozen priests stood at the open doors, hauling up the blood-red banner so it could be washed and mended and set out again in the morning with rites and chants imported from the caves east of the Keshet. The vast stretch of the city spread out beyond them, and the horizon past that. The wide bowl of the sky seemed wider up here, higher than the birds and trees below.

Geder considered all he'd planned to say and how he'd planned to say it. Perhaps he should have waited to see

Cithrin again, to consult with Master Kit and Captain Wester, but he couldn't. Waiting was too hard, and there wasn't time. And this wasn't their fight. Not really.

"You always say I am the chosen of the goddess, yes?"

"You are such," Basrahip said with a dumb certainty. "The goddess has chosen you to lead us out to the world, and through you her truth has spread through the world."

I don't have to agree. Geder clung to the thought like a castaway hugging a bit of wood. *I can disagree.*

"Can you say it?"

"Prince Geder?"

"Say it. Hear your own voice. Hear the truth in it. Geder Palliako is the chosen of the goddess."

Basrahip's shrug was vast, his shoulders rolling like cartwheels. "Prince Geder, you are the chosen of the goddess, precious to her and blessed."

"Good. Do it again."

Basrahip shook his head this time, but complied. "You are chosen of the goddess."

"You know that's true, then."

"Of course."

"Good, now listen to me. Listen. We have a problem. The apostate we killed wasn't the only one."

"He was—"

"No. To me. Chosen of the goddess?" Geder said, pointing to himself. "Listen to me. We still have a problem. You've felt it troubling you, but you haven't been able to think about it. Am I right? But I know it's going on. And I know how to fix it."

Basrahip shuddered. It wasn't a motion that came from anger or confusion. It was like a man twitching in his sleep or in a fever. He swallowed.

"Listen to my voice," Geder said. "We have a problem, and I know how to fix it. Am I lying?"

Basrahip's voice came slowly now, creaking like a bad hinge. "You. You speak the truth, Prince Geder."

"I do. And you *know* I am chosen of the goddess. You know it because you said it."

"I know this"—still slowly—"to be true."

"I have been visited," Geder said. "Truths have been revealed to me, and I will reveal them to you. Listen to my voice. Am I lying?"

Basrahip only shook his head this time. No, Geder wasn't lying.

"I will reconcile every schism. I will bring every apostate to a place where there is no dissent and no confusion and no lies. Do you hear me?"

"I hear you," Basrahip said, and there was wonder in his voice. "I hear the truth in you."

"Damned right you do," Geder said. "Call all of them. I'll give you the best couriers in the empire. The fastest birds. All the cunning men we can use. Send the word to every priest there is, everyone who carries her in his blood. Bring them all here. To me."

"Prince Geder...."

"Am I the chosen of the goddess?"

"You are."

"I know how to fix this. Bring them here, and I will. Do you believe me?"

Basrahip moved forward, wrapping his vast arms around Geder's body in a massive embrace. Geder thought of the swarm of spiders pressing against him, kept away by a thin veil of human skin. It made his flesh crawl.

"We are blessed to have you, Prince Geder." The priest's

breath was warm against his ear. Something damp touched Geder's temple and for a second he was certain it was blood, but Basrahip was only weeping. There were no tiny black bodies in his tears.

"You bring them here," Geder said, "and bring them quickly, and I'll see all of you reconciled forever."

And that's true, he thought. He wasn't lying. *Because there's no room for dissent in the grave.*

Marcus

Rain came in the north starting on their second day. Mornings were pleasant enough apart from the damp of the day before, but shortly after midday the few white puffs of cloud coalesced and joined together into great angry pillars with grey veils at the bases. They crept across the Antean landscape like giants, unaware of humanity and its little wars. Marcus envied the storms a little. There was a great deal about humanity he'd prefer not to be aware of himself.

When the hard grey clouds passed over them, Marcus and Yardem plucked up their hoods and rode on. The little mules that carried them were as unimpressed by the wet as they were by everything else. If the downpour became too great, they took what shelter they could or, if there was none, stopped where they were and suffered until it abated. By sundown, the cloud giants began to decay into great swaths of red and gold and peach that faded to ash as the light failed, and the midnight sky was clear for the stars.

The going was slow. They kept off roads and tracks, making their own trail as they went. Solitude itself was the goal, and anywhere they could find it would do. Only it had to be complete. If it worked—and there was every chance it might not—being observed at it risked everything. The stakes justified the effort.

Marcus called the halt at the ruins of a small fort by a

clearing in the heart of the wood. The tumbled stones showed no sign of human use. Thick moss hung on the tie-posts. A black mat of rotten leaves choked the half-tumbled fire stand. The clearing was a little narrower than the courtyard of a small inn, and showed the marks of a lightning-struck fire a year or two old. New trees thinner than fingers were already competing to choke the grasses with shade again. Like all places of light and openness, this one was temporary.

The only tracks were of deer and rabbit, wolf and bear. No horses and no humans and no dogs. Even poachers and huntsmen had left this place behind. Whoever had built the fort and whatever danger they'd built it against were forgotten. The only exceptional thing they found in the search before making camp was a bronze statue of a Jasuru woman that had been half engulfed by the trunk of an ash. Marcus stopped there for a moment, trying to make out the features on the statue's face. Whether it had been martial or serene, it was a tree now. Marcus moved on.

The second meeting at Palliako's compound had, for Marcus, been the test of Cithrin's scheme. Not whether it would work. Only God knew that, and that was the same as saying no one. No, the second meeting was the proof of whether Cithrin and Kit and Geder's father had managed to sway the Lord Regent into forsaking his own reign out of spite. As it happened, the little man had arrived on time and without a regiment of guards to haul them all to the gaol or throw them down Camnipol's throat. More than that, Geder Palliako had seemed pleased. Almost excited. Marcus couldn't begin to guess what sludge was flowing behind that man's eyes, but Cithrin's take on him seemed solid. His anger had turned toward the priests, and if it fixed there long enough for the rest of the plan to play out... Well, that was more than Marcus would have hoped for.

Geder had listened to the schemes that might slow down the invasion and open corridors to let the wide-scattered priests come home with a seriousness and intelligence that were more than a little surprising. When Marcus laid out his own plan for the trap, there'd been a spark in Geder's eyes. He'd even called for paper and pen and written out letters of passage for Marcus Wester and Yardem Hane. The pages, signed with Palliako's private chop, were still folded in an envelope of oiled parchment sealed with wax in Marcus's little mule's saddle pack. If they were stopped by soldiers and questioned, they had the Lord Regent's protection. It wasn't a shield he'd try against an arrow, but it was more than nothing.

He'd expected nothing. Or worse than that.

They'd sent out a bird for Northcoast the next morning. Clara Kalliam was a past master of sneaking messages to Paerin Clark in Carse. Her couriers were fast and well practiced. Lehrer Palliako even thought he might know a cunning man who could be put upon to drive the message through his peculiar talents. It didn't matter what channel the word went by, only that it arrived.

There was more than enough dead wood under the canopy of trees, and Marcus had a small fire crackling by the time Yardem emerged from the wood with the corpse of a rabbit he'd hunted down for their dinner. Marcus cleaned and dressed the animal and set it on a thin, improvised spit. The smell of roasting meat was pleasant and a little melancholy too. Until today, the animal whose body was crisping on a stake might never have seen anything more human than these ruins, and tonight, it had learned—however briefly— what humanity was.

That wasn't fair. Not really. The world was filled with people who did things more noble than killing in order to eat. Artisans who fashioned tools of great utility and beauty. Poets who made songs that honored the living and the dead, or only made people laugh for a while. Brewers and bakers and all the puppeteers from the streets of Porte Oliva. Some of them probably didn't even eat meat. It was just Marcus and Yardem weren't among that number, and the rabbit whose haunch he carved had had the ill fortune to run into them.

"Ever think about what we look like to the dragons?" Marcus asked. "Well, the one, I mean. Isn't like there's a wide choice of dragons to compare among."

"Sometimes, sir."

Marcus bit into the rabbit. The flesh was a little gamy, but after a long day of nothing but dried fruit, nuts, and some twice-baked bread, it was decent enough. That or else carrying the poisoned sword had numbed his tongue past the point of knowing good from bad. Yardem was eating it too, though. It couldn't have been that wretched.

"Draw any conclusions?"

Yardem flicked his ears thoughtfully, the rings jingling. "Hard to say. Inys isn't human. I am. It's a wide gulf to cross."

"You think that? I don't know. He's seemed fairly explicable to me, one way and another. Lonesome, self-indulgent, convinced that he's a monstrosity and also the only hope for the world. Well, his version of the world, anyway."

"Hard to say how much is there and how much we're putting there."

"Meaning you still think I'm using the great bastard as a mirror."

"Wouldn't say so, sir."

Marcus popped open a waterskin and took a long, tepid drink. They'd want to find a spring tomorrow if the dragon hadn't arrived. "So what would you say?"

Yardem was quiet for longer than Marcus had expected. He'd almost thought the Tralgu wasn't going to reply at all when he finally spoke. "We only understand other people by imagining what we would do in their position. What we would have to feel to do what they have done. If we can't put ourselves into that place, then we can only guess."

"That's not only dragons. That's anyone."

"It is."

"Palliako and Inys would get along if they didn't hate each other."

"If you say so," Yardem said so mildly that Marcus looked at him again to see if it was mockery. Yardem's expression was so polite, Marcus laughed. He handed his friend the waterskin. They waited.

Inys appeared in the late morning, four days later. He began as a thin line of black high in the western sky, easy to overlook. Then he was a hawk riding the high air, only with something odd about the shape of his wings. Marcus could imagine people on the roads looking up at the wide blue-and-white expanse and never seeing the predator in it, and wondered whether the rabbits he'd been eating had noticed Yardem.

When the dragon descended, he came down fast, folding his wings and dropping toward them like a stone. Marcus felt a pang of unease shift in his chest—would Inys be able to stop in time? Had he chosen this particular moment to die suddenly of whatever the hell killed dragons?—before the great wings opened. They caught the air with a sound like a tree snapping in half or a vast canvas sail bellying suddenly out in a high wind. The wings themselves were ragged. Bits of blue shone through here and there where the scars of Porte Oliva would never entirely heal. The fall slowed, and as he came nearer the earth, Inys flapped the wide, ruined wings to slow himself further. It was like storm wind aimed straight down. The boughs of the trees nodded with it until it seemed like the forest itself was bowing to the fallen king of the world.

When Inys's claws sank to touch the grass of the meadow, it was with the lightness and grace of a dancer. The dragon lifted his wings out again, stretching them, then folded them in against the shining scales of his body and stood still as stone for a moment. A smell like burning pitch and fortified wine filled the air and left the birds silent. The wilderness might ignore the presence of two men, but a dragon set the world on its best behavior. Every sane animal in the wood was still and quiet and hoping against hope not to be noticed. And so, it being the job, Marcus strode forth.

Inys turned his head, considering him with a wide, dark eye, then hunkered down, crushing the young trees of the meadow with his belly or ripping them with the casual motion of his tail.

"Marcus Stormcrow," Inys said, his voice a deep rumble that seemed to come up from the ground as much as the beast's vast throat. "You *sent* for me, and I, like your servant, have come. Do not insult me again."

Well, God smiled, Marcus thought. *Baby's in a sulk.*

"Thank you for this," he said aloud. "I'd have come the full way myself, but there may not be time. And the roads you travel have fewer enemies on them than the ones I have to hold to."

Inys grunted. His massive eye blinked. Marcus took it as permission to go on.

"We're gathering all the priests together in a place they feel safe, and then we're killing them all. But for it to work we need to keep the number of people who know what we're up to low, the trap we kill them with simple and effective. That's why we need you."

"Go on," Inys said and laid his head on the turf like a child bored by their father's lecturing.

"They moved the temple to the top of the Kingspire after some rioting and insurrection a few years back. That's where we're bringing them."

"Kingspire?"

"Tower in the north of the city. Only one like it, and it has the banner of the goddess hanging out of the temple proper like a dog's tongue. It'll be hard to overlook. You'll have to be near enough by we can get you the signal but not so close you'll be seen. We'll bar the door so they can't get out and run like hell for the bottom. You come in, burn them all to the bones and the spiders with them, and they're through."

"The war ended," Inys said. "After so long. And at such cost."

"It's got some holes in it," Marcus said. "There's at least one army, possibly two, headed in the general direction of Camnipol, which might make bringing them all in one place difficult. The priests are moving in pairs and small groups. They'll go quicker than a fighting force, and we're doing what we can to speed them up and slow the other down, but—"

"My brothers gone. My people turned to ash. Our perches drowned and lost forever. This is the fruit that war brings forth."

Yardem flicked his ear, scratched his arm, and looked back at Marcus. No help there. "Yes," Marcus said, guessing at what the dragon wanted to hear. "It's rough. But it's almost over. And look at all you did."

"I killed them all," Inys said. "I drowned the city and sent my allies and friends...my love...to death while I hid in darkness. Like a coward. Ah, Erex, what have I done?"

"And you're striking the last blow," Marcus said. "You're the one who made it to the end, where you can crush Morade's invention for the last time." Inys sighed. Marcus bit back a shout and tried again. "And think of the other things you've managed. You carried the secrets of the spiders and what they are and how to defeat them when the world had lost all knowledge of them. That isn't nothing. And the Timzinae. You made a race of warriors who right now are—"

The dragon roared in anguish, thrashing his massive tail into the trees and stripping away the bark with his violence. His claws ripped into the ground, clenched in what looked like pain. *Something's wrong with him.* Marcus thought. *He's wounded.*

"I did not," Inys sobbed. "I did not."

Marcus waited a long moment as the dragon shook his head and bared his teeth, but no more words came out. "Didn't what?"

"Asteril, my brother, made the Timzinae. They are *his* children. When I claimed them, it was a lie. This is what I am. What I am reduced to. Dishonoring myself to court the approval of slaves."

"No one cares," Marcus said, his voice sharp. "None of us ever thinks about which dragon made which race. It's not a thing that matters, unlike the chance to kill the priests that're tearing the world apart. That matters. So why don't we come back to it?"

Inys reared back like the words had stung him. Violence filled the dragon's dark eyes, bare as a taproom drunk about to take a swing. Marcus fought the impulse to take a step back. Instinct told him that any show of weakness now was the same as death. Fumes leaked from between Inys's scaled lips, poisoning the air with the threat of fire. In his peripheral vision, Yardem had gone very still. If there was a way to get between the dragon's shoulders—someplace where his head couldn't reach—and find a break in his scales before he flew up into the clouds or rolled on his back and crushed any attackers...

Inys's roar filled the world. There wasn't room for the noise and thought both. The trees shuddered, their leaves flickering pale undersides like a wind was passing through them. Marcus scratched his nose, pretending that his heart wasn't ticking over in his chest fast as a stone rolling down a mountain. The dragon bared teeth as long and cruel as knives. Then visibly deflated.

For a moment, they were all silent, and the forest too. Somewhere to Marcus's right, a particularly stupid bird sang out, as if its small, bright trill could answer the dragon. Stupid or brave. Or both.

"I will do as you ask, Stormcrow," Inys said. "Bring me my brother's work, and I will end it, scatter its ashes, and bury the grievance between us forever. When the time is right, light a torch of sage and pitch like the funeral pyres of emperors, and I will come. There will be a kind of honor in that."

"All right," Marcus said. "It is going to be important that no one notices there's a dragon in the vicinity, though. You can't be near the city. Will a torch be enough to—"

"Do not question my ability again. I am not a child fresh from his first kill."

"Pitch and sage then," Marcus said.

"And once we have finished, then the work will begin. I have smelled remnants of a workroom far in the south. Little more than a hint of old herb and vivarium, but it will be a start. Yes."

Inys turned, his head snaking up and to the north. There

wasn't anyplace on his back a swordsman could be that head couldn't reach. But maybe if there was a way to grab on to the back of the neck itself...Inys launched himself into the sky with no word of farewell. The scarred wings commanded the air, graceful and strong and the image of power. The last dragon rose toward the sun until he was smaller than a sparrow. Marcus lost him in the light.

"Could have gone worse," Marcus said.

"Could."

"That workroom bit at the end was a little disturbing, though."

"Was."

Marcus walked to their little camp and started to pack it away. "I believe our great scaly friend up there is still think-ing about repopulating the world in his image and keeping us as pack animals and pets."

"Problem for another day, sir."

"Maybe," Marcus said. He tied the leather thongs of his pack and swung it over the shoulder that didn't have the sword on it. The meadow looked like a badly tilled field: ripped grass and churned earth. Long, dark wounds marked where Inys's claws had torn the forest, and the smell of sap from the ruined trees competed with the lingering stink of dragon's breath. He'd come and had a short conversation, and the place would bear the scars of it for a century. Maybe more.

"Those big toys we had to leave in Birancour?" Marcus said. "The ones Jorey used to knock our scaly friend there down in Porte Oliva?"

"Yes, sir?"

"We should see if Palliako's got any more of them."

Entr'acte: The World

The summer sun punished the Keshet, but the messenger ran on. The green of Antea and Sarakal were behind him, the trailing mountains on the north of Elassae as well. He'd moved fast, traveling by night as well as day, avoiding the well-trodden paths and dragon's roads. Where he could buy or steal horses, he did, riding them until their exhaustion left them of no use, then setting them free. It was not a journey but a sprint that stretched out behind and before. The Lord Regent and the high priest had chosen him for the task because he was the best tracker in the kingdom, and of all the journeys in this nightmare summer, this would be hardest.

In the sand-colored hills of the Sinir Kushku, he had to slow. Consult maps and diagrams that he carried in his pack. Here were the fallen pillars, here the hidden spring that only the men who'd lived here knew. He found the mountain where men who looked to be the Basrahip's cousins led sheep across barren-looking ridges. He found the chieftain and said the words he'd been told to say.

The gate to the temple towered as high as the western gate in Camnipol. A machinery of gigantic gears rumbled and clanked as it opened. Banners like the one hanging from the Kingspire adorned the walls, though in all the wrong colors. Ruined statues stood in audience or else as guard, worn to nothing by wind and time. Words stood in iron, each letter as tall as the messenger. KHINIR KICGNAM BAT. He didn't know what they meant. The priests who came out wore darker robes than the ones in Camnipol, belted with chains. The messenger rubbed his chin and nodded to them as they came close. The lead one was a tall, thin man with dark eyes and a scar on one cheek like someone had laid him open with a rock at some point and it hadn't healed quite right.

It was to him the messenger addressed himself. "I have a message from the Basrahip. He said I should invoke the third oath."

The scarred priest's thick black eyebrows rose and his eyes narrowed.

"What do you know of the third oath, traveler?"

"Nothing except that I was supposed to invoke it. And he said you'd hear it in my voice if I told you true. Figure as I have, so you know I'm not farting out my mouth here."

"What is his command?"

"You're all to come to Camnipol now. Like pack-some-water-and-let's-be-off now. The goddess is making her voice known direct in the temple there, and you're all meant to be present when it happens. I'm to guide you back."

The scarred priest flushed, his eyes brightening like a babe seeing a sweet gum. "I will gather our elders to join you—"

"Everyone. Lord Regent was very particular on that. All those touched with the power of the goddess've got to be there. It's what he said." The scarred priest nodded, though some struggle was clear in his eyes. The messenger leaned forward and tapped him once on the shoulder. "Everyone."

"I will bring all of the faithful together. In the morning, we will take leave with you."

What's wrong with right now? the messenger thought, but didn't say. "Good enough, if it's all you've got."

"Will you take rest with us?" the priest asked, gesturing to the vast iron gate that stood open behind him.

"I'll camp here," the messenger said. "Not much one for being cooped up."

"As you prefer."

That night, the messenger slept in the lee of one of the statues, looking up at the vast carved dragon that covered them all. The best part of the journey was over. Now it was all going to be sheepdogging the priests back the way he'd already come. He'd do it, but he wouldn't like it. You didn't become the fastest tracker in the empire by enjoying the company of people.

Porte Oliva in the summer fell on Kurrik's shoulders like a smothering blanket. It wasn't the heat. He'd grown up in the Sinir Kushku. It was the steam-thick air and the stink of the sea and the unbearable smugness of his alleged brother Vicarian Kalliam. Of the three, the last was worst.

"The tide goes out before nightfall," Vicarian said. "If we aren't at the docks, we'll miss the launch."

"Thank you, brother," Kurrik said. "I intend to return in time, and I will be vigilant."

He ducked out the door and down the hall of the cathedral toward the square and the sun before Vicarian could find another way to say *If you're not right, you'll be wrong.*

The streets of the city were thick with people. Claiming the city had cut the number of streets and houses almost in half, but it hadn't killed nearly half the people. Now they lived stacked one atop the other, two and three families in rooms that had before housed only one. Buildings were rising up over the ashes of the battle, but small ones. Shanties that might one day grow to dignity but had none now.

Vicarian, who claimed to have great knowledge of the world because he'd lived so many years in decadence and lie, didn't see how the locals scattered before them. They were frightened even now of the power of the goddess, and Kurrik knew it. And he sensed the same fear—the same taint—in Vicarian's yammers of Cleymant and Addadus. He was careful to couch all his words such that there was no essential lie, but Kurrik sensed it lurking at the back of all their conversations. It had been an error to believe that men new to the priesthood would comprehend what they had been given. Without the lessons learned from boyhood, the habit of deception and lie ran too deep. Vicarian and all the new priests like him were flawed at the base.

And now it seemed Kurrik might not have to be the one to resolve the matter after all.

Shandor Paan lived in a shed near the waterfront. He was a thin man, hunched at the shoulder and slow of speech. His loyalty to the goddess was based in fear more than faith, but it would do. If it had to. Their meeting place was a dark corner in what was called the salt quarter where they could speak without being seen, and Kurrik found the man waiting for him there.

"You took my message?" Kurrik said.

"I did. I did," Shandor said. "How long are you gone for?"

"I do not know. The Basrahip called us, and so we go. I believe he has seen the same flaw that I have. If so, we may not need to go forward."

"That's good," Shandor lied. Of course he did. His wish now was not the elevation of the goddess but of Shandor Paan. It pained Kurrik to see men so lost to lies that they forgot they were telling them, but there was no denying that Shandor was one such.

"If it is not that," Kurrik said, "I will approach the

Basrahip myself, so that when we move forward with the correction of our error, it will be with his blessing."

And if it turns out that the Basrahip has also fallen into error, we will find another, purer way to remake the temple in her image, free of the corruption of the fallen world. He could already imagine taking the children of Porte Oliva into a temple of his own, conducted as they had the first temple, the *true* temple, before they'd been led out to the world and astray.

"So we'll still kill the other one?" Shandor said, hope lighting his eyes. It took Kurrik a moment to understand what he was saying.

"If the need is still there, the need is still there. I will know more when I return."

"Yeah. It's only..." Shandor ducked his head like a bird.

"Only what?"

"What if the city rises up with you gone, eh? What if those letters that keep coming down from Carse make people think they can go back?"

"They will never go back," Kurrik said. "The goddess is here whether you feel her presence or not, and once you have been touched by her grace, you will never fall to error."

"But...the other one...*he's* in error, yeah? So sometimes..."

Kurrik's blood surged with impatience and anger. Having the city all around him was like living in a pile of rotting meat. The ignorance and the lies were worked into the skin of the place, and it would never, never be wholly clean. That was why men like Vicarian and Shandor should never be granted her gifts.

"It won't fall," Kurrik said. "Listen to my voice. Porte Oliva will be loyal to the goddess forever. The fighting here is over unless I am the one who brings it."

*   *   *

The priesthood of the goddess left Asinport under a flow-ered archway with the local children singing the praises of the goddess in chorus. Girls in summer gowns with ivy braided into their hair strewed light-pink petals along the jade road before them. They were seven men in robes rid-ing the best horses the city could offer. A train of servants followed, and a cart draped by the blood-red banner whose cousin hung above the temple.

Where the dragon's road leading south widened, Sir Rail-lien Morn had set up a little stage. He stood on it now. He'd oiled his scales, and they glowed like metal in the morning sun. The men and women of court were all of lower families. Most were Firstblood, though there were a few of his own family present as well. The merchants present were more varied. Kurtadam with formal beads tied on their pelts. A pair of Cinnae men standing with the goddess and the empire in defiance of the banker girl who, they said, soiled the name of their race. There had been a Timzinae quarter in the city once, though of course none of it remained now. The lowborn who crowded the road were of any number of races, all equally unbathed and uneducated. They had come for the spectacle and the distraction, as if honor were a the-ater piece.

The priests paused before him. Sir Raillien lifted his hand to them in formal greeting.

"Since the coming of the goddess to Asinport," he declared, "we have known nothing but peace and prosper-ity. While the world itself has shaken and struggled, our city has known only blessings and joy. This we credit, as is right, to our newest and best-beloved citizens. We wish you speed in your journey and safety on the road that you will return to us soon and with the further blessings of her truth. In her honor and in yours, I pledge a week of feast and celebration beginning upon whichever day you return to us."

The eldest priest rode forward. When he answered, his voice carried as loud as if he'd held a speaker's trumpet, and Sir Raillien felt himself washed by the words.

"You do yourself honor by this," the priest said. "And you will not be forgotten by us or by her. We leave only briefly and look forward to our return to this, our right and proper home. Asinport is blessed by the Righteous Servant, and taken into her protection now and forever."

The crowd cheered and waved small paper banners, red and pale and black. Sir Raillien took to horse, riding south with the priests. Both sides of the road were thronged. Every man, woman, and child in the city or the lands nearby had come out to watch.

A mile past the city's southern gate, they came to the place where the prisoners had been executed. The bodies were nailed to poles set in the earth. Apart from a few scraps of white, the leaflets the dead men and women had been found with couldn't be seen sticking out from between their rotting lips. But Sir Raillien knew they were there, as did the priests. And everyone else as well.

Morn stopped there among the righteously punished and the dead. The priests and their train rode on.

Strange not hearing them," Coppin said, leaning on his spear like it was a walking stick.

"That's truth," Jerrim said, then chuckled. "Strange not hearing the truth is truth. Funny, that."

Kavinpol stood in the fragrant sun of the summer evening, the guard looking down both sides of the wall. On one, the city streets slow in the heat. On the other, the traffic along the road and the river docks. Carts filled with early harvest crop, and lambs and pigs carried in carts or led on ropes, heading for the slaughterhouses and the butchers and the fires and the tables. Flatboats waited at the water gate where a team of men like Coppin and Jerrim took the tax, let in who could pay, negotiated with who couldn't. Sometimes the rules bent, sometimes they didn't. A farmer who'd brought Timzinae slaves, for instance, might be looked at more carefully than one who'd brought real Firstblood help. Having the roaches inside the gates at all made some people jumpy, and for a reason.

Twice in the last week, the forces in the south had come looking for resupply and cunning men. Daskellin's once, Kalliam's the other time. Seeing what the roach army was doing had sobered more men than Coppin and Jerrim. Lost legs and fingers and eyes. Men half-gone from fever. Lady Flor had set aside her personal ballroom and filled it with cots for the injured and the dying. They said you could smell the pus two streets away. Others had come down from Sevenpol and Anninfort. Boys and women now bearing whatever weapons they could scrounge, coming to defend the empire.

Coppin, leaning on his spear, clumped along the wall, and Jerrim followed after. Coppin had lost three toes off his left foot to an axe when he was ten. His arm was good enough to pitch spears down the wall if it came to it, or else he'd have been on the road with the others. Jerrim had fits, sometimes three a week, and the captain of the guard said he'd be more trouble than he was worth in the fighting. It didn't matter. They had their part, and that was enough. They manned the walls, they kept the peace, they showed the roaches and traitors that Kavinpol had teeth enough to bite if it had to. And they waited for the war to get done with. The priests came along every day or two and gave a talk about it, and they always left feeling better after. It didn't matter how things looked. It mattered how things were. Truth would carry them through.

And the truth was that the goddess was alive in the world. No city that had her temple had ever fallen. Even if one was occupied for a time, that wasn't the same as fallen. The roaches hated her because they were made by the dragons to seem like they were human, but they were really the servants of the lie. It didn't count when you killed them.

Coppin stumbled and Jerrim steadied him. A voice called from behind: Coppin's name, then Jerrim's. Drea was climbing up the rope ladder to the wall's top, a basket bouncing against her hip. She was a small woman, brown as a nut with bright eyes and a gap in her teeth when she smiled, and everyone know that she and Jerrim were in love except for her and Jerrim. Coppin, for instance, didn't have doubts.

"Brought some bread," she said when she reached them, holding out the basket. "Had extra."

"Thank you," Jerrim said, taking it from her carefully so that their hands brushed each other's.

"You can bring me back the basket later," she said.

"I will."

She smiled, nodded once to Coppin like she was agreeing that yes, he was there too, and went back down the ladder. Jerrim watched her go with a longing that was almost palpable. Coppin took the basket and opened it. The bread was fresh anyway. So that was good.

"She's what we do this for," he said around a mouthful of the stuff.

"What?" Jerrim said.

"This," Coppin said, and held up the spear. "Being guard. Risking our lives to protect people like her. The whole city of them. Truth is, I've got nothing against the roaches as roaches go. Until they crossed the Severed Throne, I didn't care about them one way or the other."

"Me too."

"If they all just went back where they came from and didn't come back, I wouldn't chase after them. Would you?"

"Not me," Jerrim said. "Heard the other army's left Nus heading this way."

"They've been saying that for weeks. It hasn't been true yet."

"But what if it is?"

"We'll kick 'em in the nuts and send 'em to work the farms, same as we always do," Coppin said. It was what he always said, and Jerrim gave his usual chuckle in reply. Both the bravado and the appreciation of it felt different this evening, though. Thinner somehow. It reminded Coppin of the feeling at the back of his throat before he got sick. Not the actual illness so much as the announcement that something unpleasant was coming. It wasn't in his throat, though. The whole city felt like that. Maybe the world.

"Think they'll come this far?" Jerrim asked.

"Elassae they or Sarakal they?"

"I meant Sarakal, but either, I guess."

"Maybe. Yeah, probably before the end of summer. It won't matter, though. They're roaches. We're destined to win."

"Yeah."

They reached the station house, a room the size of a tool-shed bound to the inner face of the wall. Arrows and bolts were stacked there in cylinders of twenty each. Hand axes for cutting lines if an enemy tried to climb. Long spears with hooks at the bases of the blades for pushing back ladders. The pair looked at it all for longer than they usually did.

"Strange not hearing them," Coppin said again.

"Yeah."

Marcus

"I believe that history is a listing of atrocities and horror," Kit said, gesturing widely with a cup of wine, "not because we are evil, but because history is itself a kind of performance. And we are fascinated by those events and characters which are most unlike our essential selves."

"Wait," Marcus said. "Just wait. You're saying...are you saying that the whole blood-drenched history of the world—war after murder after war—says something *good* about humanity?"

Cary's voice came from outside, lifted in a simple melody. Lak's rougher, less practiced notes rose up around them to an odd but pleasant effect. The smell of nearby coffee and distant stables harmonized as well. Like a single green meadow in the ash fields after a forest fire, Palliako's estate had become a small place of calm in a vast and implacable chaos.

The peace was an illusion created in the gap between understanding that trouble was coming and the appearance of banners on the horizon. Anytime the approaching enemy arrived even an hour later than expected, there was a limn of hope that maybe something unlooked for but not unwelcome had happened. Maybe this time the storm would turn aside. That the hope was doomed didn't make it less precious.

"The truth of history, I can't speak to, but the *version*

we tell? I think yes," Kit said. "I can't see how any history could be complete and accurate. To be told at all, it must be simplified, and every simplification means something, yes? What we leave in, what we leave out, and how we choose tells, I suggest, a great deal about the teller."

"*I* suggest you're drunk," Marcus said, laughing.

"It seems to me that what makes us human is our ability to create a dream and live within it. History, I think, is storytelling that begins, 'Here is a thing that actually happened,' but after you've said that, you're constrained by all the same rules of technique and structure that a playwright or a poet labors under. Which was why I said that history itself is a kind of performance. Consider." The actor held up a finger. "Why do you suppose there are no plays about good people being kind to each other? Thoughtful lovers who, in the face of adversity or misunderstanding, have a conversation between them?"

"Because they'd be terrible stories," Marcus said, laughing.

"I agree," Kit said, "and why is that?"

"Because nothing would ever happen."

"It would, though. People would be thoughtful and kind and gentle and resolve their hurts and confusions with consideration and love. Those are things. They happen. And they *seem* like nothing. Thoughtfulness and kindness and love, I contend, are so much the way we expect the world to be that they become invisible as air. We only see war and violence and hatred as *something happening*, I suggest, because they stand out as aberrations. In my experience, even in the midst of war, many lives are untouched by battle. And even in a life of conflict, violence is outweighed by its absence."

"That's going to be a hard apple to sell all the men and women who've died hard in the last few years," Marcus said. "Seems more likely to me that violence and strife catch the attention because ignoring them leads you down a short road. I've walked a lot of battlefields that had boys who'd have lived another few decades watering them. I've made my gold working at war and death, and I haven't often gone hungry."

"But war's not the same as death, is it?"

"The one involves the other, Kit."

"I disagree. War, I think, only involves a particular *manner* of death. Everyone always dies. It's the price of being born."

Marcus laughed. "All right. I don't know anymore if you're drunk or I am."

Kit scowled, his beard bunching at the cheeks, as he stared into his cup. "I can't judge you," he said, "but I'm fairly certain I am." A fly buzzed past them, and then away. Cary began her song again, and Lak joined in more gracefully this time. "I am afraid, Marcus. I've come to love the world, and I feel we're on the edge of losing it. We won't, will we? We can't have come all this way through so many fires only to lose, can we?"

"If you knew this was going to fail, would it change anything you did?"

"I don't know. Perhaps."

"Either we're about to end the dragons' war for the last time, or go down to unremembered deaths in a world condemned to constant and unending war. However it comes out, what we've got to do is the same. So it doesn't make any difference whether we win or lose. It's the job."

Kit rubbed a hand over his forehead. There was more grey in his hair than Marcus thought of him having, and it caught the sunlight. "It may be wrong of me," Kit said, his voice melancholy and warm, "but I do wish you'd just told me you were sure we'd win."

"You'd have known I was lying."

*   *   *

The Kingspire stood in the northern reaches of Camnipol, close enough to the Division that it seemed the great height of the tower and the depths of the pit were commenting on each other. Marcus walked through the streets and alleys surrounding it, Yardem at his side, considering the great tower from every angle. The thing had been built to impress more than as a means of defending against attack. Unless it had been built for something else.

It didn't look good.

From the east, after ambling among the tombs and mausoleums of generations of the noble dead, they reached the wall separating the grounds of the Kingspire from the streets of the city, too long and too low to effectively man. From the south, where the compounds of the most favored of the high families stood shoulder to rose-scented shoulder, the gardens and houses, servants' quarters and kitchens and stables looked more like a medium-size village than the palace of a king. To the west was the Division, to the north the city wall. Marcus found a narrow stone-paved square and sat at the base of a bronze statue. Pigeons cooed and trotted to him, hopeful of crumbs or corn.

"I don't know," he said. "Two hundred men, maybe?"

"To take it or to hold it, sir?"

"I was thinking hold it. Taking it . . . twice that."

"Plausible."

"Problem is, we've got you, me, a baroness, a banker, and a handful of actors. Hard to make that work for two hundred."

"Is," Yardem said. And then, "Do have the Lord Regent."

"That's Cithrin's plan, but I was trying not to count on him," Marcus said. "I have the feeling this will be the last time anyone will be able to put all the spiders in the same place at the same time. If they scatter after this, it'll be the work of generations hunting them down. If it can be done. That's not something I want to enter into without a fallback plan."

Yardem nodded. "Do you have a fallback plan?"

"No."

"Do you expect to find one?"

"Doesn't seem likely. You?"

"No, sir."

The puzzle of the thing was still shifting in Marcus's mind, pieces of their conspiracy moving against each other, trying to find where one thing fit another. Geder Palliako hadn't turned against them yet, and his visits to his compound were still rare enough they could pretend that he was coming for something other than the chance to moon over Cithrin. He hadn't seen the dragon since their meeting in the forest, but Marcus had worked up enough pitch and sage to fill a brazier, and he thought he'd found a good place to put it. Clara Kalliam had started bringing more people into bits and pieces of a broader plan, aware that each new person who smelled smoke in the wind was another thousand chances for things to turn to shit. The foundation of the thing was all as stable as a drunkard, but it hadn't fallen over yet. And the problems that bit at Marcus now weren't the strategy, but the tactics.

The priests were arriving now in pairs and clusters. Basrahip apparently kept a complete record of them all in his broad head, and, according to Geder, greeted each of them by name when they appeared. As more and more came, their simple density was going to make keeping the plot a secret difficult. Putting them all in the temple at the Kingspire's top shouldn't, he thought, be too hard. Keeping them there until Inys arrived might be more of a trick, but what had to be done had to be done. Those plans were made, and if the details were still being tapped into shape, even that didn't bother him deeply.

No, the splinter in his ass was all the things that they had to think wouldn't be today's problem. What Inys would do once he'd snuffed out the last of his brother. What Geder Palliako's play would be once it was ended. Whether it was possible any longer to bring the scattered priesthood together and not have them each fall on the others with clubs and swords.

The spiders were engines of chaos, after all, and they'd been generating schisms and apostasy for months already. If they all wanted to be reconciled, they might all keep their blades sheathed. If they were already past that, Cithrin might be blundering into a half dozen dramas she knew nothing about. The moment when four assassins all arrived at the same garden was only funny when it happened on a stage.

And it wasn't as if Marcus didn't have some betrayals of his own to plan out.

"The smith?" Marcus asked.

Yardem shrugged and stood, as near to a yes as made no difference. Marcus sighed, rose, and turned his back to the Kingspire. Not carrying the poisoned sword left him feeling a little naked, but blending into the city was a better defense now than trying to cut his way through it. And he had his old blade at his side, in case trouble of the more usual kind arose. He made the attempt to fall into the flow of men and women in the streets and yards of the city, to be so much a part of the mood of Camnipol that it accepted him without noticing that it had done so. Two aging fighters on business of their own, and nothing more.

The street life of Camnipol was a strange and disjointed

thing, though. Hard to fit into. There was a brightness and energy all around. The beggars capering on the street corners and the women rushing past with cages of live chickens slung over their shoulders, the old men of half a dozen races sitting in the cafés with pipes pinched in their teeth. Everyone had an air almost of celebration, and all of it echoed like thumping a hollow tree. Camnipol knew it was in danger, and was bent almost double with the effort of pretending otherwise. Smaller banners of the goddess hung from windows and over doorways, bright red and white and stark black, and as loud as a coward claiming bravery.

As they made their way to the southeast of the city, the stink of smoke slowly growing as they came near and the wind shifted, Marcus tried to imagine what it would have been like living through the dark years here. How many people had Palliako taken away to his little magistrate's chamber to question? How many of those had come back? It was no surprise that the city was a tissue of false gaiety and desperation. None of them knew what was happening now, and no one had any idea what would happen next. For all that the girl selling cups of roasted nuts in the square knew, Geder Palliako would reign over Camnipol and Antea and the world under the spiders' banner for the rest of her life. Or the Timzinae would come from the south and hang them all from their own windows. None of them guessed the goddess was false, or if they did they'd become expert at keeping the thought to themselves.

The only ones untouched by the keen madness of the times were the children and the dogs. And the dogs seemed a little nervous.

The smith's yard belonged to a massive Jasuru named Honnen Pyre. It sat near the city wall, where the smoke from the forges turned the air white and foul. When the servants

announced them under the false names Geder Palliako had
given them, the smith loomed up out of the depths of his
shop. His arms were thicker than Yardem's thighs and his
skin stretched so much by the muscle that lines of pale skin
made a lacework around the bronze of his scales. He shook
their hands gently, like it required conscious effort not to
break them.

"Come back," the Jasuru said. "I'll show you what we
have."

The smith's yard went back farther than Marcus had
expected, opening into a private courtyard with the forges
off to one side. A pair of women were hauling out double
handfuls of bright metal and arranging it on the paving
stones. Marcus looked back into the shadows. All Pyre's
apprentices seemed to be women. The men, he assumed,
had all been pressed into the army, and he wondered what
would happen when they came back and tried to retake
their places by the fires. The women stacking the weapons
looked broad enough across the shoulder he wouldn't have
wanted to pick fights.

"This is what the Lord Regent was asking after," Pyre
said. "We've got a half dozen of these ready to put on carts
if the army had a need, and we can make more. Take time,
though."

Marcus walked slowly around the metal. It was like a ballista, but built on a base that could shift and turn, tracking
the vast body of a dragon through the sky. The bolts were
light, but barbed as a fishhook, with a small pulley built
into the shaft. The line that it carried out with it was finer
than yarn and laid out to tug back on the bolt as little as
possible, then tied to a braided cord. He imagined firing up
into the dragon's wings and belly and then trying to pull
the line through enough to drag the great bastard out of the

sky before it turned the weapon and everyone using it into slag and ashes. If he hadn't seen the scars from it on Inys's flanks, he'd have thought it wasn't possible.

"Six of them is all?" Marcus said.

"All the rest went out," the smith said. "They're beautiful, but they aren't fast work."

"Fair enough," Marcus said.

The smith crossed his arms and glanced nervously from Yardem to Marcus and back. "Should I put them on carts?"

Marcus shook his head. Honnen Pyre was asking if the dragon was likely to attack the army. That was his fear: the Timzinae and the dragon joining forces to destroy Camnipol. If Marcus told him to have the things delivered to the Kingspire, what would he make of that? And what were the chances that he'd keep his speculation to himself? If the priesthood found there was a secret shipment of weapons designed to slaughter Inys being installed around their temple, would that tip Cithrin's hand or reassure them?

"Have them ready to move," Marcus said. "We'll send word where to take them when the time comes."

Pyre nodded sharply and motioned to his apprentices. Marcus and Yardem made their way back to the street. Their rooms were halfway across the city from here, and Marcus's feet felt sore. When they crossed the oiled and arching wood of the Silver Bridge, Yardem turned toward the courtyard of a taproom there without having to ask Marcus whether he wanted to stop.

The building was three levels tall, each narrower than the one below, with benches and tables on each. The walls were an unlikely yellow that caught the sunlight and made the whole place seem more cheerful. Beyond, the Division gaped, a canyon that was also a city. A Firstblood boy with black skin and hair brought them cider and took their coin.

It was decent enough drink, but the pleasure of just sitting still was better than the best alcohol. At least for the time being.

"We're going to need to a way to move through the Kingspire without drawing notice."

"There are servants there," Yardem said.

"We can't use them. The more people we involve, the more likely someone's going to step wrong."

"I meant we could hire on," Yardem said.

"Oh," Marcus said. "Yes, there's that."

"Only?"

"It's nothing. Just sits wrong to be a servant in Geder Palliako's house."

"Could see it as playing the role," the Tralgu said.

"I'm too old to start worrying about dignity. You think Cary and the other players will be able to pass too?"

"Imagine so," Yardem said. "They've done worse before now. But I can't see them crewing the weapons to kill a dragon."

"They won't need to kill him. We just have to hold him in place until the locals can join the fray. This whole thing would be simpler if we could actually bring Karol Dannien into it on our side. There's a perfectly capable army not a full day's ride from here, and I can't put it to use."

"Life's rich irony, sir."

Philosophically, Marcus spat. "It strike you as odd that we're looking to bring about peace in the world by killing a great bunch of people?"

"Think the peace part's supposed to come after, sir."

"That's always the story. Ten more, a hundred more, a thousand more corpses, and we'll be free."

On the street, someone shouted. Another voice shouted back, and the people paused, shifting to the side to let a carriage ride past with the banner of the goddess jouncing at its side. It clattered onto the Silver Bridge and out across the abyss.

"More priests arriving," Yardem said.

"Ah," Marcus replied, dryly, "I guess that means we're doing well."

Geder

When it was over, Geder decided for the hundredth time. When Basrahip and the other priests were burned bones and ashes, *then* he'd kiss Cithrin.

It would be a moment of shared joy, after all. And it wasn't as if she'd never kissed him before. They'd done much more. And there wouldn't be a better time to bring her back to him. He'd have proven himself. He'd have saved the world. He'd be a hero. And in the wake of that, he would put his arm around her waist and pull her close to him, and...

It was so strange knowing she was close. That he could, if he chose, go to her anytime he wanted to, and there she would be. All his day's work took on the feeling of dreams. He attended the wedding of Perrien Veren and Sanna Daskellin, sitting on a chair set aside for his own honor while the priest intoned a version of the rites, but Cithrin was in the city. He sat the long hours of the grand audience, listening to complaint and petition while it was really Basrahip that stood in judgment, and the hours didn't bother him because he was borne up by his secret. And the promise of the time very soon when he'd proved himself to her.

Even apart from Cithrin's presence, there were other little and unexpected joys. Basrahip, for example. From the moment he'd delivered his message, Geder had made a point of avoiding the great priest as much as he could. It had begun simply enough as an effort to keep his newfound secrets secret. But with every meeting he cut short, with every meal he ate away from the great bastard's company, Geder saw something more than curiosity rising in the priest. There was a need there, a longing to know what it was that had been revealed to Geder. For the first time, Geder had power over the priest. It wasn't Basrahip's world any longer. His connection to his imaginary goddess had been undermined, and in a way that put him at Geder's feet for once. And Geder's mind was clear now. Clear and cool as river water. He'd hardly had any more moments of killing rage like the one in the Great Bear, and the few he'd had were justified.

There was a pleasure, he thought, that came from being outside a group. Looking back, he saw that he'd always really been like that. Before his journey to the Sinir Kushku, he'd been excluded from the charmed circle of Alan Klin and Feldin Maas and Curtin Issandrian. It had ached for him only because he'd wanted so badly to be accepted, not because belonging gave him anything worth having. The moments of authentic pleasure he'd had in his life had all come from being apart. Reading alone in Vanai, for instance. Or the dark days after Dawson Kalliam's insurrection, hiding with Aster and Cithrin, being protected by her friends who—through that—became his own. He'd always been at his best when he was his own man. Funny that it had taken him so long to understand it. He had been—still was—the Lord Regent of the greatest empire in the world. His commands, life and death. And what made him happiest in the whole time he could remember was that Cithrin was here, and Cary and Hornet and Mikel. Jorey's mother and the bank's mercenaries. And among them, with *them*, him. It was as if Lord Regent Geder Palliako had ceased to be, and he was only playing the part now.

His real friends were with him at last, and he hadn't even known how much he'd missed them until they appeared.

Marcus Wester, dressed in the bright tunic of a servant, walked across the kingdom, stepping carefully over the dragon's road between Kavinpol and Camnipol, then looking to the south and the markers of Jorey Kalliam and Canl Daskellin and the approaching Timzinae army. The man's expression was a strange combination of amusement and despair. Geder found himself trying to imitate it. The Tralgu—Yardem Hane—stood with his feet in the blue glass beads of the northern sea, his arms crossed before him. The news of Kavinpol's fall hung in the air between them like smoke.

"That's going to make things harder," Wester said, then turned to Geder. "We're sure about the numbers?"

"No," Geder said. "We aren't sure about anything. But it's what Daskellin wrote, and I don't have a better source."

Wester grunted. "All right. The next question's whether Karol Dannien's going to turn east to join them or keep pressing north."

"North," Yardem said.

"That's what I figure too."

"Is that bad?" Geder asked.

"It's different, anyway," Wester said. "We're hard-pressed for good in any of this. We've slowed him to a crawl, but that was with support coming from the east. With that cut, Kalliam and Daskellin...well, I don't see a way to keep Dannien in the field. Better to have them pull back to the city. The road up the cliff on the south's a nightmare. We could hold it with two legless men and a slingshot. The question's whether we want the siege to come in from the east or the west. He'll go to one of them."

"There are still priests coming in from the Keshet," Geder said. "All of them from Asterilhold are here already."

"And Birancour?"

"Soon," Geder said, hoping it was true.

"Better to have Karol dancing out west of the city, then. So draw Jorey and Daskellin here"—he pointed to a hill to the east of Camnipol, where the landscape of Antea grew rough—"and here." A small lake halfway between Kavinpol and the city.

"But the traditional families…"

"They won't set foot out of Kavinpol," Marcus said. "They've taken themselves a city, and they know better than to push on past their strength."

He spoke the words with a bland matter-of-factness, but Geder felt the sting of them anyway. They would know better how to fight a war than he had. Well, that was fair, after all. They didn't have Basrahip pouring poison in their ears. It wasn't his fault the spiders had tried to ruin everything.

"I'll send out the orders," Geder said. "Anything else I should tell them?"

"No," Marcus said. And then, "There hasn't been any word from Magistra Isadau, has there?"

"There hasn't," Geder said.

"All right, then no. Just have them set up where I showed you and we'll see what comes next."

Geder made his way out first. So far as the court was concerned, he was planning out the rest of the war by himself. With Mecelli lost in his own despair and Daskellin in the field, the only one of his advisors left was Emming. And he'd been happy enough to leave Geder to himself.

He walked out to the gardens and the private house where King Simeon had spent his last days. Geder understood the sense of keeping rooms outside the Kingspire. Walking up numberless stairs for the pleasure of looking down over city and empire could get wearisome, especially for a man in failing health. He'd have been tempted to use the house himself just for the convenience of it, except that he'd been thinking of Basrahip's comfort. Holding the royal apartments where he had given the big priest a way to come only halfway down from his temple. Geder didn't care a wet slap about that anymore. Let the huge cow of a man puff his way up and down a dozen flights of stairs and have his priests haul him the rest of the way on a rope. It didn't matter to Geder.

But the other reason not to was Aster. These wooden walls with their carved shutters, this fountain with its verdigris-taken statue of what was supposed to be a dragon, were the place Aster's father had belonged. Better, Geder had thought, to leave it behind. Sitting with the sorrow would only make the boy sad.

And so, when Geder walked in and found Aster sitting beside the little fountain, it surprised him.

The prince wore a dark leather cloak, full cut in the style that Geder had started years ago, with a green sash that had only come into fashion this season. His hair was slicked back and dark with the water, and his face was terribly still. When Geder cleared his throat, announcing that Aster wasn't alone any longer, the prince stiffened.

"Didn't think to see you here," Geder said.

"I can go if you want," Aster said, and the raw hurt in the words felt like a slap. Geder paused.

"Is something wrong?"

"No," Aster said. "Everything's fine."

The water chuckled and murmured to itself as he came nearer. He more than half expected Aster to rise up and storm away, but he didn't. The prince only kept his gaze fixed on the water and scowled. It was an expression Geder knew well, though from the other side of it. He'd worn it enough himself.

"Is it something I did?" he asked, gently. "If it is, I'll apologize. If it's someone else...I don't know. Maybe we could think of some way to make me useful?"

"It's not you. It's not anyone," Aster said. And then, a moment later and softly, "It's me."

"Feels like that sometimes, doesn't it?" Geder said, his words pressing gently to see where the hurt was and trying not to make it worse. "You don't have to say if you don't want to. But if you do want—"

"Then what?" Aster shouted. "You'll take time out of your busy schedule to nursemaid me? Put a rag in some warm milk so I can suck on it? Why would you suddenly start caring about me?" The pain in the boy's voice was like violence.

"I've been thinner on the ground than I should be," Geder said. "That's truth. I'm sorry for it."

"Why be sorry? You're busy doing all the things that I should be. If I could. Trying to keep everything from falling apart because I can't. And all the armies and the dead men and..."

When Geder took the boy's hand, Aster tried to pull away. He wouldn't let him. By main force, he pulled Aster close, wrapped his arms around the boy's shoulders, and held him. Aster struggled for a moment, trying to break free, and then the sobbing came in earnest and he held tight to Geder instead.

He'd been a fool to forget Aster. All the effort that Geder had put into avoiding Basrahip and the other false priests had also kept him away from the boy, and that was a cruelty he hadn't intended. He thought of all the confusion and pain he'd suffered before Cithrin came. The sense of wrongness that had filled the world and his heart and everything in between. Of course Aster felt the same things, only more so because he was young and fatherless and doomed to spend a lifetime on the throne that Geder had the chance to walk away from. In Geder's mind, Aster was still a child, and what you didn't point out to him he wouldn't know. Likely he'd been wrong about that last part even when the first had been true.

"I don't know why I feel this way," Aster forced out between sobs. "The war. And you calling all the priests back. And spending all your time away. I know everything will be all right, but I can't *feel* it. I can't feel it that way."

Geder shushed the prince gently, and rocked him back and forth the way he remembered his own father rocking him.

"It's my fault," Geder said. "I'm so sorry. This is my fault. I thought it would be easier for you not to know, and I was wrong. And I'm sorry. This was my fault."

"I don't *understand*," Aster said. A life's burden of long- ing fell in the last word, and Geder kissed the boy's temple.

"Come with me," he said, "and you will."

Watching the reunion of Cithrin and Aster was like getting to live his own moment over again. The boy's shock and confusion and then Cary and the others sweeping him up in their arms, grinning and laughing and telling Aster how much he'd grown and changed. Aster's smile was more the blank look of a man stunned than actual joy until Master Kit led him to the garden to explain.

In the withdrawing room with its screens and lemon candles, Cithrin looked like a picture of herself painted by an artist who loved her. She wore her white-pale hair braided back and a thin summer dress with loops of silver at the shoulders that caught the warm light of the sunlight and remade it. The murmur of voices—the apostate priest and the crown prince of Antea—drifted in on the evening's breeze. His father came in briefly and then made a pointed show of being needed elsewhere and left them alone again.

Geder couldn't tell if the silence between them was comfortable or charged. He wished more than he'd ever wished anything that he knew Cithrin's mind. A summer beetle tapped against the screen, trying to reach the candle flames, then gave up and buzzed away into the afternoon sun.

"I wanted to . . ." he began, and then found he didn't know what he was going to say next.

Cithrin shifted to look at him. In truth she looked older than he remembered her. Her Cinnae blood meant she would always be unnaturally thin, unnaturally pale. He could trace the veins beneath her skin. Her smile seemed genuine, though. Encouraging, but the way she'd have encouraged Aster. To speak, perhaps. Not more than that. When the time came to do what he'd promised himself he would do, pull her close to him, enfold her in his arms, kiss her again as he had once before, it was going to take more courage than anything he'd ever done. He could feel himself balking at it even now. He found himself breathing shallowly and made a point of not glancing at her breasts. He wasn't going to embarrass himself. He wouldn't do that.

Through main force of will, he kept his voice from shaking. "I wanted this, you know."

"This?" she said, the smallest lilt making the word glide a little.

"All this," Geder said. "I wanted to be someplace nice, with you. Where we weren't worried that someone was going to try and kill us at any moment. With a little breeze and the smell of flowers. Aster somewhere we could hear him. That's silly, isn't it? Like having a little family. I'm Lord Regent of Antea. I could have anything I want, but this . . . this is nice."

"It is," Cithrin said.

"I was thinking of kissing you," he said, "but I was afraid you'd laugh at me."

The air in the room seemed to go solid. Nothing moved. He looked down at the floor. Someone had tracked in lumps of mud and grass. He might have doen it. He couldn't be sure. The brightness and excitement faltered in him, and settled into a kind of peace. He'd said it. It was done. He'd jumped off the bridge, and there was no taking it back now. Either he'd fall or he'd fly.

He glanced up at her. Her gaze was on him, her face expressionless. The candles danced in the pale blue of her eyes, sparks living inside ice.

"It's stupid, I know," he said. "But there it is. Every time I think of it, I remember coming to Suddapal thinking you'd be there. Rushing through the streets like an idiot. And then..." He pressed his lips together, as if the pressure could keep the memory at bay. Humiliation shifted in his heart like a snake in darkness. He gestured vaguely, trying to explain something to her, show something to her.

Her voice, when it came, was perfectly calm. "Do you think about the people you've killed?"

Geder blinked, thrown off by the change of subject. "Who? You mean Dawson?"

"Dawson Kalliam," Cithrin said. "The others who fought with him. Lord Ternigan. The people of the court who weren't loyal enough. The men and women in Elassae and Vanai. Sarakal. Birancour. The hostage children. All of the thousands who would be alive if things had gone a little differently. Do you think of them?"

For a moment, he saw the little Timzinae girl in his memory. The one he'd had called back from the edge. And the silhouette of a woman against the flames of a burning city. "I do sometimes," he said, and sighed. "I don't like to, but I do. Why do you ask?"

"I have never laughed at you."

Outside, Aster said something and Kit responded. A bell rang from somewhere deeper in the house, and a man's voice called out. The door slave, most likely. Geder couldn't look away from her. So many nights, all he'd thought about was her mouth, her body, the look in her perfect eyes. His heart felt full and heavy with her presence, like it was the only real thing there was about him.

"Thank you," he said softly, and she nodded. Footsteps hurried toward them from the house. Geder didn't know if he wanted them to turn aside or hurry to him. The moment was perfect and painful and too rich to stand for long. When the knock came at the door, Geder looked deep into Cithrin's perfect eyes and said *Come in* as if the words meant *I love you.*

His father entered the room, his eyes bright with excitement. He held a scrap of paper in his hand, yellow and black in the light of the candles. "There's a message come, my boy," Lehrer said. "From the Kingspire. A message."

Geder rose as his father pressed the paper into his hand. The script was Basrahip's. He recognized the shapes of the letters even before he read the words. It said a great deal about where Geder and Basrahip had been and what they had become that the priest used these dead words he so much despised to seek Geder out.

"They've arrived," he said. "The last of the priests have come to the temple. Basrahip wants to know when I want them to gather so that I can share my revelations." Cithrin made a small noise at the back of her throat and closed her eyes. It might have been joy or fear or something of both. He tucked the paper into his belt. "What should I tell him?"

"Tomorrow, midday," Cithrin said. "That will give us time to arrange everything we need."

"Tomorrow then," Geder said with a sharp nod. *I will kiss you tomorrow.*

Cithrin

The day moved quickly and quietly as a rat in a dining hall. Marcus brought the actors out to the gardens, drilling each of them in turn, Yardem at his side. Geder, thankfully, went back to the Kingspire to make a full night of preparations there. As many of the servants and guards as could be sent away from the great structure would be. Even the royal guards were to be stationed outside the royal quarter, their backs to the Kingspire ready to fend off some imagined attack from the streets. And Geder had taken Aster with him, which cut Cithrin's heart a little. Seeing the boy, she'd realized she'd missed him. Or if not quite him, at least the thought of him. In a better world, she'd have known Aster more.

The little drawing room by the garden became a war room. Or no, not that. Something like it, but dedicated to something different. As desperate, as dangerous, as likely to end in sudden death, but different. She had to believe that.

"We'll need to have the letters out to the farms as soon as the couriers won't get cut down by the Timzinae," Cithrin said.

"We could send them to the south," Clara suggested.

"They won't leave the south road open. The main body of the army will swing to the west, but they can't have a siege with an open route to the south."

"No," Clara said. "No, of course not."

The siege of Camnipol that would mean the end of the Antean Empire. The death of Clara's friends and family, the sacking of her city. It was the war they were trying to stop, it and all the wars after it. Or as many of them as Cithrin could.

"The gaol will be the first thing," Cithrin said. "And after that..."

"I have...friends ready," Clara said. "I've sent word. When we go out the gates, we'll be well accompanied. There's a baker I used to frequent near the Prisoner's Span? I have him devoting himself to raisin cakes and lemon bread. And there's a footman who used to serve at my house. Back when I had a house. He's gathering up toys. Dolls, you know. Little things for the children."

Cithrin took Clara's hand, and the older woman's head bent forward. Wet tracks slid through the powder on her cheeks, and Cithrin felt tears of her own coming up in answer. She didn't know what they were for. She thought Isadau would have understood.

"I feel as if I've been playing at making peace my whole life. Only playing. Now I look at all my nation has done," Clara said, "and I think we're going to defend ourselves with children's baubles and ribbon. A knife will cut through that so quickly, and so deep."

"It's how peace gets made," Cithrin said. "At least I hope it is."

"It is *when* it is," Clara said, "but I wonder whether we deserve mercy."

"It isn't mercy if you deserve it. Mercy justified is only justice."

Clara laughed once and mirthlessly. "That has all the virtue of being true and none of the comfort."

"It wasn't mine. Someone told me it once. I don't remember who."

"Someone with more mind than heart," Clara said, and looked at the candle on the little table by the wall. It had already burned a third of its length. "I should go back now. It would be strange if I weren't at Lord Skestinin's home." Her voice carried a burden of dread, and she wiped at the tears angrily.

"Is there something happening there?" Cithrin asked.

"Yes, dear. My son the priest has come home from Birancour. Vicarian is no doubt waiting for me."

And you will let him go to his death, Cithrin thought. The two women were silent for a long time before Clara rose, placed her hand briefly on Cithrin's head as if passing her a blessing, and left. Cithrin sat alone after that, listening to the patter of moths against the screens and the voices of Sandr and Lak, Charlit Soon and Cary, Marcus Wester and Yardem Hane and Lehrer Palliako. Her chest hurt, just between her breasts and up a little, and she tried to remember if she'd been hit there. It felt like a bruise, but she came to the conclusion it was only sorrow and nothing to be done about that.

She was in her room near midnight, a third bottle of wine on its way to ignominious death by her hand, when the soft knock came at the door. She rose, sat, and rose again more carefully. The little twinge of shame she felt at being drunk was easy enough to push away. Without the wine, she'd have been sick hours ago. She opened the door, her chin already lifted in defiance. Marcus Wester stood alone in the corridor, not even Yardem at his side.

He looked old. Still strong, but old. His hair had gone whiter since the first time she'd seen him on the caravan from Vanai. His skin had a transparency despite a lifetime of being roughened by the sun. His eyes were the same, though, and the way he held himself.

He nodded to her. "You sent for me?"

"Hours ago," she said. "I assumed you'd chosen not to come."

"Lost track of time. Night before an action, I'm always worried."

She held the bottle out to him. "So am I."

He hesitated, but only for a moment. He sat on the little stool beside the washbasin and she sat on the bed. He was a handsome man, well bruised by the world. He wore his scars and weariness gracefully. She wondered whether, when she was as old, she would do the same. He wiped the mouth of the bottle with his sleeve and drank. Smacking his lips, he passed it back to her.

"Not bad," he said.

"I didn't see call to save anything for a better occasion."

"Well, there'll be a better one along shortly or else not at all," he said.

"Call this a hedge, then. If we lose, at least I won't have spared the good wine."

"Thanks for sharing it."

"And," she said, and then faltered. She looked at her feet. The room wasn't spinning. She wished that it were. If her mind had lost a little more of its clarity, this might have been easier. "Thank you. For being who you've been to me."

"Not sure what you—"

"Don't. Not now. Not tonight."

It was the mercenary captain's turn to look away. "Right. Night before the battle. Sorry."

"I met you when I was a child who thought walking outside the city walls was like jumping off a cliff. I have taken terrible risks with myself and the people around me, and

I've won more than I lost. And you have done everything you could to keep me safe. We don't talk about it. We don't say it. But it's true, and I want you to know that I appreciate it. All of it."

"It's the...Hell. Yeah. All right." Marcus took a deep breath and held his hand out for the bottle. This time when he took it, he nearly drained it. "You're near the age my daughter would have been. A little younger now than my wife was when I met her. You're not them, but you fit in that part of my head for a time."

"I'm sorry I couldn't be them."

"No, not that. Be sorry for something else if you have to, but not for that. I did what I did because I thought it wanted doing. That's all. And I knew you weren't my daughter. Yardem kept pointing it out, for one thing. It's been...it's been the longest, strangest job I ever took. I always thought of bankers as being dull."

She laughed. "We want you to think that."

His sheepish grin made him look younger. She could see who he'd been as a boy. "Picked up that part. Took me long enough, but I see it. You...you didn't know your parents, yeah?"

"I remember remembering them, but nothing more than that."

"For all this? They'd be proud of you, scared as hell, I expect, but proud."

"They don't care," Cithrin said, taking back the bottle. "They haven't cared in decades. They're dead."

She drank the wine to the dregs. There had been a bitterness in her words that surprised her. If someone else had said it, she'd have said they sounded hurt, but she didn't feel it. To her surprise, Marcus laughed. "You're one ahead of me, then. Fine. I'm proud of you, then. Proud to know you, proud to work for you. Proud of all you've done, though God knows I don't understand half of it."

"If we die tomorrow..."

"Then we do," Marcus said with a shrug. "If it's all the same, I'd prefer to go first. Bad for my reputation if you die before me, and it's hard enough to get jobs when you won't work for kings."

"I'll try to survive, then."

"Do that," Marcus said. He looked up at her from under lowered brows. "What are the chances I'll be able to keep you from coming to the Kingspire?"

"Poor," Cithrin said.

"I'll be there to call Inys. Yardem's going to run sheepdog on Palliako. Chances are decent that the dragon'll follow up killing the priests by turning everyone else there to slag. Not sure how having you present's going to improve things."

"You might get your wish and die before me," Cithrin said. "If you fall, I'm picking up your damned blade myself."

The last morning—she couldn't think of it as anything else—dawned without a moment of sleep behind it. The day came early in the high summer, and rich with birdsong and the clatter of carts in the streets. Cithrin washed, changed into the robes that would let her pass as a servant, and tried to prepare her heart for what was to come. She could as easily have willed herself to fly.

The sunlight slanted in from the east when they set out through the cobbled streets. Lehrer Palliako led them, riding a tall black horse and bright clothes like a man heading for a festival. Or, less charitably, performing at one. He was there to be seen and to draw any casual attention to himself and away from the motley train of servants behind him.

For the first few streets, Cithrin felt her heart in her

throat. But with every corner they passed, every tradesman who pulled aside to make way for the Lord Regent's father, every street cleaner waiting with barrow and shovel for them to pass, every beggar and child and half-wild dog that saw them without any light coming into their eyes, she felt a strange elation growing in her.

No one knew, and so no one saw. They were disguised as much by their improbability as by their robes. The grey-haired Kurtadam woman selling wilted cabbages in the square lived in a world where the question was how the goddess and the Lord Regent were going to defeat the roach army. If she even thought of that. More likely, she wasn't even concerned with that so much as whether she'd be able to get rid of her produce before it started to rot. The baker's boy with his handcart piled with sacks of flour didn't see a suspicious bunch of servants trailing after an anxious-looking nobleman so much as an obstacle in his morning errands that he had to track around. Cithrin walked among them unrecognized either for herself or the change she was about to bring upon them all. Or try to, at any rate.

Geder waited at an ivied archway, the entrance to one of the royal gardens. He wore a light summer tunic with braiding of gold down the sides, and the crown of his regency on his head. His personal guard stood along the edge of the garden, facing out, and created the sense of a wall even in the stretches where no actual wall existed. When the guard stood aside to let the grooms help the Lord Regent's father off his mount, Cithrin had to bite her lips to keep from laughing. She was fairly certain that once she'd started, it would have been hard to stop, and it wouldn't be the sort of laughter that promised sanity.

After the press and noise and stink of the streets, the royal quarter seemed too quiet and sparsely peopled to be part of the same city. No gardeners tended the deep-green hedges and breeze-shuddered flowers, no slaves sang at the little hidden corners to sweeten the summer air for the court. It was expected, of course. She'd told Geder to send as many people as he could away. To see it all in motion was eerie all the same.

Once they were out of sight of the guard, Geder stopped pretending to walk with his father and came to her side. His eyes were bright and he bounced on the balls of his feet with every step, like a boy excited for cake.

"The pieces are in place?" Marcus asked even before Geder could speak.

"The blacksmith delivered them this morning," Geder said.

"The priests?" Cithrin said. Something passed through Geder's expression that she couldn't read, a flicker here then gone that reminded her of the day she'd seen him cut down Dawson Kalliam. She was almost pleased to see it.

"Gathering. It isn't like it was before, but I don't know if it's because they've changed or I have. It seems like there's more fighting now. They rub each other the wrong ways all the time. Basrahip's been going to all of them and promising how they'll all be reconciled and I have seen her plan."

"Both true," Cithrin said, "if not the way he means it."

"He keeps asking to see me before the gathering at the temple, but I've put him off. Better not to have the chance for things to go wrong."

Cithrin made a little sound of agreement.

When they reached the entrance of the Kingspire, the wide doors stood open and the great halls beyond empty. From so near, the banner of the goddess was only a shifting darkness that clung to the walls high above her. A shadow the light couldn't dispel. The sun had risen higher than she'd expected, the morning more than half-gone already.

Master Kit and Cary huddled for a moment with the rest of the players, bowed their heads together the way they sometimes did before a performance. Marcus stood at Geder's side, ignoring the Lord Regent's almost palpable annoyance. Rough cloth wrapped the poisoned sword on his back, too valuable to discard and too dangerous to expose, especially here where so many of the priests might know it for what it was.

A sparrow flew past, its fluttering brown wings loud in the air.

"Torch ready?" Marcus asked.

"On the dueling ground," Geder said, nodding to the west and the great chasm of the Division. "All that needs is lighting. How...how long will it take before the dragon comes?"

"Damned if I know," Marcus said. "Great bastard may not show up at all."

He clapped Geder's shoulder and walked away. Geder glanced from Cithrin to Yardem to the captain's sword-crossed and retreating back. "He's joking, isn't he? The dragon's coming. It's going to be here."

"There's always some element of improvisation in the plan," Yardem said mildly, and flicked his ear. "Looks a long way up. We should go. You staying here, Magistra?"

Cithrin clasped her hands behind her back so tightly that her knuckles ached. Everything in her body was stretched so tightly that she felt the way a viol string sounded. Clara and Aster would be waiting by the path to the gaol, ready to go with her as soon as Geder returned. There was so much to do and so much doubt. She closed her eyes.

"Yes," she said. "I'll be waiting when you come back."

Geder surged forward and took her hand in his. His eyes were intense and dark, his mouth in a scowl that was meant to be heroic. "We will return," he said, then turned to Yardem and spoke with a false lightness. "We'd best get started. As you said, it can be a long way up."

Yardem nodded to her and smiled his placid canine smile that might have meant anything: *He's green* or *Don't worry, it will all work out* or *It's been good knowing you.* Cithrin felt the urge to take the Tralgu man in her arms, but she was afraid that Geder might take it as a precedent. "Thank you, Yardem," she said.

She watched them walk into the vast mouth of the tower. A moment later, the high priest joined them. She watched as the huge man traded words with Geder that she could not hear, and then walked away. She stood for a moment, her heart a complication of elation and fear and a vast antici-pated grief.

When she walked away into the gardens, the actors were setting the weapons at the ready on the rough gravel paths. The bright steel looked wrong in Sandr's hands, and she realized she'd become so accustomed to seeing mock weap-ons in their hands that the bright steel of the real thing seemed wrong. Cary's laughter seemed to echo the birdsong. Sandr and Hornet and Mikel snapped and argued like they were trying to put together a stage.

Marcus strode to the knot of men, Lak at his side, and pulled Sandr and Mikel away from the weapon. He shook his head in an amused sort of disgust and strode off toward the dueling yard. It was all so familiar and also so estranged from all she knew. A dream she couldn't wake from. The minutes stretched, time bending itself like a fiddler's arm to make her nerves ring.

"You look thoughtful," Kit said.

"If I am, I don't know which thoughts they are," Cithrin said. "I can't tell if I'm stuffed so full of them I can't tell one from the other, or if I'm emptied of them."

The old actor put a hand on her shoulder. His smile consoled her.

"When I was a child," she said, "I had a nurse called Old Cam. She wasn't really my nurse, but she took the role on as no one else was doing it. I remember once I was climbing a wall that I wasn't supposed to. I was...eight years old at the time. Maybe nine. And I was afraid she'd catch me and punish me, and I hoped she would come and give me a reason not to go further."

"Hoping for someone to rein us in?" Kit asked.

"Astounded that no one has," she said.

"It's been my experience that the world is often—"

"*Cithrin!*"

Aster's voice cut through the warm air like a blast of winter. Had someone heard him? The prince sprinted out of the Kingspire, his eyes wide and his mouth a gape of horror. She found herself running toward him before she saw him. His chest worked like a bellows and he grabbed at her sleeve, shaking with distress.

"What is it?" she said, willing the boy to catch his breath and dreading what he'd say.

"Basrahip," Aster said. "He *knows*."

Clara

It had gone so well for so long, it was hard to believe how little it took to destroy it.

Clara had left Lehrer Palliako's house after conferring with Cithrin bel Sarcour, knowing she'd stayed too late. She'd arrived at Lord Skestinin's manor irrationally certain that by being tardy, she'd given the game away. Instead, laughter had greeted her at the doorway. The door slave nodded to her happily as she went in, and the footman led her to the largest of Lord Skestinin's drawing rooms. The thing that had been her son sat on a divan dressed in priestly white. Sabiha and Lady Skestinin sat with him, and little Annalise cooed in his lap, reaching up toward his chin with thick, innocent fingers. The impulse to snatch the baby away was too much to resist, but she was able at least to make it seem like greed for the babe's company more than fear.

"Mother!" the thing that had been Vicarian said, putting his arm around her. "Here I was afraid you'd taken off to fight in the war again."

"Don't be clever, dear," she said, and kissed his cheek because it was something she would have done. "I'm certain Jorey has no need of me at the moment."

"And he did before?" The mockery in his voice was gentle and warm and familiar. It was how he would have spoken before the spiders had taken him.

With her son, she could have laughed or lied or done whatever she pleased. With this one, every comment was an interrogation, every answer an evasion desperately trying not to seem evasive. "The need might possibly have been my own," she said, matching the lightness of his tone. "I see you've met your niece."

"Indeed I have," Vicarian said. "She's more charming than she has any right to be, given the hour."

"She's always stayed up late," Sabiha said. "Ever since she was born."

Clara put the child in her mother's arms, took Vicarian by the wrists, and led him back to the couch and away from the baby. She imagined that his skin moved under her fingers. Tiny bodies crawling through the veins like living clots. Like a man already dead and worse than dead. She could picture too easily one of the little things slipping out of Vicarian's mouth and stealing into the baby's. She didn't let go of him, even as her own flesh crawled. "Jorey was just the same," she said. "He was always brightest when everyone else was half-dead from exhaustion. By *everyone else*, of course, I mean myself and his wet nurse. What was her name? Idrea, I think. Something like that. Lovely woman, though of course I haven't needed a wet nurse for something near twenty years now, and even if I did, I can't think she's still in that line of work. One's body cannot last forever, after all, and don't look like that, dear. You're in a house of women now."

"I consider myself warned," he said.

"But tell me everything," she said. "What news from Porte Oliva?"

It wasn't so hard from there, prodding him to speak about himself. Vicarian had always had a bit of the showman in him, and he enjoyed taking even so small a stage as this. The coffee in Birancour was better than in Camnipol. Porte Oliva was already starting to regrow after its difficult year. Trade ships from Lyoneia had begun negotiating fresh contracts. He'd had a report of Korl Essian, off on a treasure hunt for Geder Palliako and the throne, that made some fairly outlandish claims about tunnels passing under the depths of Lyoneia and a buried machinery deep underground that connected in some obscure fashion to dreams. He'd brought the report with him, ready to deliver to Lord Regent Palliako tomorrow.

Tomorrow. When Vicarian, who didn't realize he'd been killed long ago, could finally be put to rest. Her throat ached and her eyes fought tears the whole night. Lady Kalliam left first, and then Sabiha and the child. When Clara rose to go, Vicarian rose with her and put his arm over her shoulder as they walked down the hallway together.

"Jorey's a lucky man," he said. "This Sabiha seems a genuinely good woman."

"I've become quite fond of her," Clara said. It was true. She could say it. Everything now she had to judge before it left her mouth. Was it true, did she believe it, would it give away more than she meant it to? Vicarian tipped his head to the side, resting it against her even as they walked, just the way he'd done before.

For a moment, she was taken by the transporting memory of a five-year-old Vicarian bringing her a sprig of lilac, his hands and feet caked in the garden mud. She'd knelt beside him, torn between amusement and annoyance. He'd pressed it in her hand with such solemnity and then touched his forehead to hers. It had been a gesture of such simple love from a boy to his mother. She'd thought then and for years after that it would be among her most treasured memories. Now it hurt.

"Good night, Mother," he said, stepping away. "Will I see you in the morning?"

"I was hoping to walk to the Kingspire with you," she said. "I have some business there." True. All true.

"I would be honored, my Lady Kalliam," he said with a flourish and a bow. Then, in a more prosaic voice, "We really do have to do something about getting Jorey the family title back. He's earned it, that's clear enough. And it feels odd not being able to call you *baroness*. *Lady*'s too general. Could mean anyone."

"It would be *dowager baroness* now," Clara pointed out. *You were such a good boy. Such a good man. I am so sorry that I've lost you.*

"Near enough," the thing that had been her son said. "Good night, Mother."

She could not say good night in return. It wasn't a good night. It was a terrible one. Instead, she made herself ignore the things lurking under his skin and kissed him lightly on the cheek.

Vincen waited in her apartments, sitting by the window as faithful as a dog. As a husband. They didn't speak, he only held her as she wept, muffling her sobs with his shoulder and the enfolding comfort of his arms.

As they rode through the city streets together in a small and open carriage, Clara's gaze kept drifting to the Kingspire. The bloody banner of the goddess hung almost motionless and dark, heavy still with dew. This is the last day I will see it there, she thought. Tomorrow, it will be gone or I will. The fear and excitement and grief and rage all fused together in her body. Like metal in a forge, she became an alloy of herself, stronger than anything pure could be. Or so, at least, she hoped. Vincen rode behind, but not too close.

"You're quiet this morning," Vicarian said. Clara smiled.

"I'm tired," she said.

"Can I ask you something?"

Her heart began to tumble in her chest, but Vicarian's demeanor hadn't changed, or if it had it was only a bit embarrassed. She saw no malice in him, or no more than she ever did since the change. "If I may reserve the right not to answer, I don't see why not," she said, forcing a lightness she did not feel.

Vicarian nodded more to himself than to her. He rubbed his palm against his cheeks. It was a gesture he'd learned from his father, and seeing it here felt like an omen. Not a good one. "Mother, did you think no one would find out?"

"I don't know what you mean," she said. She lied, and she saw in his face that he knew. But he hadn't revealed the plot yet, had he? Surely if he'd told anyone, she'd be on her way to the gaol in chains, and Cithrin and the others beside her. The gaol or the Division. Perhaps there was something in him that was still her son, Dawson's son. She held her breath.

"He's my age," Vicarian said. "Or if he's older, not by more than a few years. And he's a servant. A huntsman? What would Father think?"

Clara lowered her head. Bright relief ran against shame. It wasn't the banker and the dragon he'd discovered. It was Vincen.

"I hope your father would understand," she said. There was no point in denying it.

"Jorey has done everything he could to return the Kalliam name to dignity," Vicarian said. "I love you, Mother. Never doubt that. But you'll become a joke in the court. Chasing after the army was peculiar enough, but at least there was a way to tell the story that you did it from bravery and love of the throne. Spending your nights with your dead husband's huntsman?" He shook his head. "You know this has to stop. If not for your own dignity, for Jorey's. And Sabiha and Annalise. Can you imagine what that little girl's life will be like if the name she took from you comes to carry the reputation for fucking the servants?"

The truth was, she hadn't. Now that she did imagine it, she didn't like the picture. She didn't ask how he'd found her out. It didn't matter.

"This has to stop," Vicarian said, "before someone else finds out."

"You've made your point."

They were almost at the low wall and the wooden gate that led to the paths of the royal quarter. The huge priest, Basrahip, stood by the open gate, embracing another man who looked much like him. One of the original priests come from the Keshet, she supposed. She was a fool. An idiot. A randy old widow like the jokes all painted, and it had taken her monstrous son to show her how she looked through other people's eyes.

"It has to stop," he said again.

"I said you've made your point."

He turned away with a grunt, and the carriage stopped. She heard Vincen's horse clatter to a halt, but she couldn't look back to him. She stepped out of the carriage, her legs unsteady beneath her. Did Lady Kalliam know? Did Sabiha? Did Jorey? And if it did stop, if she did send Vincen away as she'd always known in her heart she should, what of her would be left?

"Brother Kalliam," the huge priest said, wrapping his arms around Vicarian's shoulders.

"Minister Basrahip," the thing that had been her son said, returning the embrace. "You remember my mother?"

"Of course," Basrahip said, bowing to her. "The fearsome Lady Kalliam and the swordsman who fights at her side."

Did he know too, then? Only, no. Basrahip and Vincen had met each other before. Had faced Feldin Maas together once in some long-vanished world. God. How had she ever thought that any part of her life could be kept safe from any other? Everything mixed. Everything bled into all that surrounded it.

"Are you well, my lady?" the priest asked.

"Fine. Or, no. I'm not. But I'll *be* fine, Minister Basrahip," she said. "I find I need to refresh myself."

"There are no servants or guards to lead you," he said, apology in his voice. They were all so goddamned polite. She hated that. "The Kingspire today is the temple of the goddess first. Tomorrow, it will be the seat of the empire again."

"I believe I can find my way," she said, and walked away briskly before anyone could stop her. She was weeping again, and bitterly. The humiliation had flanked her, and now the full edifice of her composure was crumbling. She marched toward one of the smaller buildings whose use she neither knew nor cared. She prayed that Vincen would not follow her. Or that he would. She turned and found herself in a stables. A dozen horses stood calmly in their stalls, considering her with huge, soft eyes as she sat on a wooden stool and quietly cursed.

It was his voice. It was the spiders in Vicarian's voice. The power they held to make anything seem plausible, to seem true. He'd as much as called her a foolish old slut, and she couldn't help but believe it. It was his curse and his magic, the venom of dragons still deadly after thousands of years.

"It isn't true," she said. "It isn't true." Except that maybe it was. Some part of her had already thought or feared to think everything he'd said. That the spiders had said it didn't mean it wasn't also true. In the distance, she heard voices fading in the direction of the Kingspire. She had to get up. She had to find Cithrin and the others, prepare herself for Geder's return. She heard footsteps and wiped her eyes with her sleeve, ready to put a brave face on whatever indignity came next.

"Lady Kalliam? Are you all right?"

"Prince Aster," she said. "I would say I'm well, but that might be overly simple."

"I saw your son going to the tower, but no one knew where you were. I asked Basrahip, but he didn't know. I was afraid that maybe..."

"All's well," she said, biting the words as she said them. "The plan is still intact."

"It will be over soon," Aster said, taking her hand, offering her comfort and perhaps asking some in return. "They'll be dead and we can put it all right."

She saw the shadow in the doorway even as the last words passed the prince's lips. She thought for a moment it was another horse wandering loose, but of course it wasn't.

Minister Basrahip was come to see if the prince had found her, if she was well, if there was anything he or his false goddess could offer. He stepped in among the animals as Aster finished speaking and stopped, as stunned as if he'd suffered a hammer blow. His huge eyes blinked, his mouth gaped, and then, as understanding blossomed in him, he flushed.

There could be no explaining their way free of this.

"Go," she said, pushing Aster behind her. "Find Cithrin. Tell her."

"But—"

"Go!" Clara shouted, and with that, Aster fled.

She stood before the priest, her hands at her sides but in

fists. The priest's gaze shifted from side to side, as though
he was seeing more than only her. His jaw clenched until
she could hear his teeth groan, and his voice was raw with
anger. "What is this?"

It didn't matter what she said now. There was no deceiving her way out from under it. So, then, she was ready to
be damned for what she was. "There is no goddess," Clara
said, speaking each word clearly and sharply. "You have
spent your life in service to a deceit."

He roared, surging forward, and the world seemed to narrow to her body. The sounds all around her stuttered into
silence, and she was on the ground, her face pressed against
the hay and filth. Her cheek bled where he had struck her,
but she felt it only as a rivulet of wetness, both warm and
cool. In their stalls, the horses shied and kicked, frightened
by the violence. She rose to her feet, but Basrahip was gone,
running on tree-thick legs toward the Kingspire.

She neither thought nor hesitated, only lowered her head
and ran. She was a woman, and older than the priest, but he
had spent his winter sitting in a temple worshipping a lie while
she'd marched through snowbound mountains, and she was
half his weight. She had no doubt that she could catch him.

"Vincen!" she shouted as she ran. "Vincen! To me!"

*To me, to me, and burn anyone who says otherwise. To
me, damn it, before he gets away.*

Basrahip reached the tower before her, pushing open one
of the servants' doors. Behind her, a welcome voice called
her. "My lady!"

"Stop him, Vincen," she shouted, and ran on. Her knees
hurt, her feet hurt, a sharp pain stung her back, and she felt
none of it. There was only the chase. The perfect focus on
the bastard huffing his way along before her, and the desperate need to stop him.

The Kingspire was a maze to her. Halls and corridors, stairways and servants' passages. If she lost sight of him, he would be lost. Everything would be lost. She spared nothing, and Vincen Coe, his sword drawn, ran at her side.

They found him before a wide, sweeping stair. She threw herself at his legs to slow him as Vincen looped around to block his way. The huntsman's blade shone in the light. Basrahip lowered his wide head, shook it like a man recovering from a blow.

"You think," Basrahip said, "to cut me?"

"This far," Vincen said. "No farther."

Basrahip laughed. "Would you draw my blood? You wish to feel the goddess's kiss? I can do this for you."

Clara cried out, crawling away from him. With the sprint done, her lungs felt in flame. Her heart might burst at any second. Vincen moved forward, putting himself between her and the priest.

"You end where you are," Vincen said.

"I continue forever," Basrahip said, and Clara knew it was truth. He wasn't a priest, nor even a man. All unknowing, he was the voice of dragons. Of war and death and violence that bred violence that bred violence, in a fire that burned on bodies from the dawn of time to the death of everything. "You have already lost. Listen to my voice. You dare not hurt me. You and your filthy sword. Everything you love is already lost. Everything you hope for is already gone. You cannot win."

The words burst against her like storm waves. Jorey would die on the field, cut down by Timzinae blades. Sabiha, Annalise, Lady Skestinin. All would die. Vicarian was gone. Dawson was gone. And if Vincen turned his blade, if he drew the enemy's blood, the spiders in it would come for them as well.

"No," she said. "You have to let him go."

"You have already lost," Basrahip said. "You cannot win. You will *never* win."

Vincen's blade shifted, its point drifting down as a terrible comprehension filled his eyes. Tears of horror streaked his face. Basrahip stepped forward and took the sword from Vincen's hand.

"You cannot win," Basrahip said, and pushed Vincen to the ground. She crawled to him, took his hands in hers as behind them the great priest mounted the stairs, his fist making Vincen's blade seem a table knife. "Everything you have is already gone."

It was the spiders, she thought. It was only their power; there was still hope. But her heart knew otherwise.

They'd lost.

Marcus

Marcus's left foot hurt. A mild ache down in the joints at the ball of his large toe. He tried to stretch it as he walked the three-sided dueling yard, leaning back a little into each step. It didn't seem to be helping. The sword strapped across his back chafed, and he was getting an annoying little twitch near his eye. Likely he wouldn't have noticed any of it, except that he was tense as if he were leading a full army into the field, with nothing that he could do but pace and wait to light the signal torch.

He'd planned it out with Yardem. If Inys came too early, the priests wouldn't be gathered in their sacrificial temple. Too long, and they'd have noticed they were trapped and devised an escape. As soon as Geder and Yardem reemerged, Geder could call in his guard, put them in place. Be ready when the dragon came. Any of them that jumped, he'd be at the bottom with the sword to kill whatever spiders splashed out of the corpses.

Only being anxious tempted him to move too fast, so while the thing he wanted most in life was to take the little torch from beside the wide iron brazier they'd set out on the gravel of the yard and push it into the lump of sage and pitch, he waited instead, cataloging the ways his body hurt and watching the shadows shift with the sun. He looked toward the Kingspire, waiting for Yardem and the Lord Regent. They weren't there.

The buildings around the base of the Kingspire felt empty as a burned city. The pathways seemed to miss the servants and courtiers that normally walked them. The windows stood shuttered against the summer sun. Geder's private guard manned the streets at the edges of the grounds, keeping any attacker, the story was, from interrupting the priestly conclave. He had to think their eyes were as much on the tower as the streets. The goddess was the center of the empire, after all. The enemy was nearly at the gates. He'd been in enough cities facing attack to know how deeply a people consumed by fear could long for the miraculous— a cunning man's vision of victory, a child's imagined portent, anything that promised a future that could be known. Geder and his priests had spent so much effort pruning away everyone in the city who didn't have faith, the ones who remained had to be certain that this was the moment that would save them.

And maybe it was, but it would be an ugly surprise for them all the same. If their salvation came today, it would be dressed like defeat. He squinted up into the sky, tested the air with his upstretched palm, and wondered again how long the dragon would take to arrive. *I will come* had sounded near to immediate when Inys had said it, but even the thickest smoke needed the wind to carry it. Flying might be faster than the swiftest horse, but it still took time. Why wasn't Yardem back yet? This was all taking too long. Or he was more impatient than he thought? Marcus stretched his foot again. It ached.

When Inys came, there would be a moment when he was just in front of the great opened doors of the temple, bathing the enemy in flame. The eyes of Camnipol would all be on him, including the harpoons and lines that would encumber him and bring him down so Geder and his guard could end both threats to humanity in a single day. Marcus made it an even bet that the little bastard would be hailed and remembered as a hero for it. The world wasn't fair that way, but so long as the dragons' war was well and truly ended, Marcus didn't care. That everyone who deserved credit claimed it and blame stuck where it belonged was too much to ask for. Winning would have to be enough. If Yardem would just *get back*.

Aster came running down the path, head down, arms and legs pumping. Cithrin sprinted just behind. All of Marcus's aches and complaints were forgotten. His mouth went dry. He took two steps toward them, looked toward the torch, the tower.

"Basrahip knows," Aster gasped. "He heard me. He heard Lady Kalliam. He knows."

"All right," Marcus said, his voice calm despite the copper taste in his mouth. Cithrin came, her lungs working like a bellows. The distress in her eyes said more than words. If he left the torch, Cithrin could light it, provided Yardem came back down. Or Geder. Or him. Or anyone. He squinted up at the tower, and past it to the sky. No great wings marked the blue. There wasn't time. In two long strides, he reached the torch and tossed the living flame into the brazier. The dry sage spat and the stink of burning pitch billowed up and out into the wide and empty air.

"Marcus," Cithrin said. The word carried more questions than he had time to answer.

"Rally the guard," he said. "If I don't come back, finish the job."

"But—" she cried, and he was already running. The Kingspire had a dozen ways in at the base, but only one direction: up. The great priest would try to stop Geder and Yardem, and that meant climbing the endless flights of stairs. Marcus moved through the empty hall, ignoring the wide and airy archways, the statues of thousands of years, the tapestries and censers and images of worked gold. For him, there was only the hunt.

He took the stairs two at a time, reaching back as he did and tugging the wrapping away from the blade. They were past all disguises now. His footsteps echoed. Far away to his left, he heard something like a woman's wail, but he didn't have time or attention to spend on it. He didn't know where the priest was, how far the man had gotten, how much of a head start he'd had. It didn't change anything. The worst that would happen was Basrahip would reach the temple, sound the alarm, and Marcus would have to hold as many of the priests from coming down as he could before they slaughtered him or the dragon came. He felt himself grinning with the effort of the run. Or maybe it was just grinning.

As the tower rose, the walls sloped gently in, each level a bit smaller than the one below, the rooms and corridors a bit less grand, the stairs to the next level up narrower and fewer. The nearer they got to the temple, the more the tower itself would push them toward each other. He'd known a butcher once, and had the sense that slaughterhouses worked in much the same way.

The priest knew the path, and Marcus was finding it as he went. The priest had a head start. The urge to sprint, to push himself up as fast as he could go, tempted him. The sense that the enemy was just beyond his reach, and that if he pushed himself a little harder, he might catch him in time, sang in his blood. Instead, he kept to a brisk, steady pace. He focused on the architecture, finding his way through the halls and corridors like it was a deer path in the wood.

Outside, beyond his senses, the signal smoke was rising.

The dragon was on his way. He couldn't think about that. Just where was there more wear on the carpets, where had steadying hands left smudges along the wall. He couldn't hurry. If he went too fast now, he'd exhaust himself. He'd fail. If he drew the sword—and he wanted badly to feel its weight in his hands—it would cost him speed and add to his fatigue. He found another curving stair, and went up. His footsteps echoed weirdly against the jade.

Only no, they didn't. The sound he heard complicating his steps came from above. He paused, his hands stretching wide and then tightening into fists. Footsteps retreating above him. The feral grin stretched his lips wider, and Marcus let himself run. Up the flight to a hall with half a dozen corridors converging on it. The sound was louder here. There was labored breath as well. He was close. A narrow window looked out to the southwest, offering a view of the grounds, the gaol, the Division, the sprawling city. But not a dragon. Not yet. Marcus closed his eyes, listening. The footsteps and breathing grew a degree quieter as he turned slowly, but he found which of the hallways it came from. He ran again with the long loping stride of a scout and a soldier.

The chamber at the hallway's end was low-ceilinged and wide. Carved wooden tables stood discreetly against the walls under portraits of kings long dead. A thin white carpet covered the floor like fallen paper, and the spill of light from the shuttered window drew bright lines across it. The priest labored his way across it toward a half-open door and a fresh flight of stairs.

"Hey!" Marcus shouted as he drew the poisoned sword.

The priest turned. He was a large, broad man with flushed face and rage in his eyes. Marcus had known others like him, naturally strong even if he didn't train. It wasn't the only hint of Yemmu blood in the man's history. The shape of his jaw had a bit of it too. Marcus drew the poisoned sword, holding it in a double-handed grip. He saw Basrahip understand what it was, and what it meant.

The priest held a bright steel blade in his right fist like it was a stick. Not much technique, Marcus guessed, but plenty enough power. In case it was easy, Marcus lunged, his blade cutting fast and low.

The priest parried him. A little technique, then. That was a shame.

The priest's breath was fast and hard. It might have been the exertion of the run or mind-blanking rage. Basrahip bared his teeth and shouted in wordless, animal aggression. Marcus took an involuntary step back. Even absent meaning, the sound of his voice held power. The gift Morade had given him and his kind along with their world-killing madness.

Basrahip swung his own blade in a short, hard arc. Marcus danced back, and the priest surged forward, shouting again. The poisoned sword stank with fumes that left a foul taste in Marcus's mouth, but the priest ignored that, striking out artlessly with his own steel blade. Marcus parried and countered. Basrahip pushed the attack aside like he was clearing weeds. Marcus felt the impact of blade against blade in his wrists and shoulders.

"Strong bastard, aren't you?" he said. "How's your stamina?"

For that, he thought, *how's mine?* But the priest was hammering at him again, the raw fury of the attack driving Marcus slowly back. The shuttered windows was behind him. If this went on too long, he'd be driven against it. Marcus imagined himself being tossed out, spinning head over feet to the path below. It would be a stupid way to die.

The priest used the moment's distraction. His vast howl

came again, and the blade with it. Marcus shifted away, but the tip of the priest's sword touched his arm as it passed. The pain was bright. Blood pattered against the perfect white of the floor and Marcus drew himself into a guard position and countered, driving the priest back toward the stairway. The injured arm felt numb, but it wasn't weaker. Or not much so. As far as he could tell. There was a lot of blood, but no muscle cut through. He only needed one solid hit, and the venom would do the rest. If it meant letting Basrahip open his guts for him, it wouldn't matter. The priest would still be dead. He wouldn't raise the alarm. Where the hell were Yardem and Geder anyway?

The priest's laughter began as a deep sound, like someone chopping wood, and grew.

"Something…funny?" Marcus gasped out.

"Cannot," the priest said. "Cannot win. You cannot win."

In Marcus's belly, something gave way. Not fear, not despair—not yet—but the awareness of how he was vulnerable. He struck forward, pushing the priest, but Basrahip was laughing now, even as he avoided the envenomed blade.

"You have already lost," the priest said. "Listen to my voice. Everything you love is already gone. You cannot win."

"Heard that before," he said, as if defiance would rob the man's voice of the dragon's power.

"There is no reason to go on."

Marcus tried to pull his attention away from the words. Tried to focus on the weight of the blade in his hand, the stance of his opponent. The brightening pain in his arm, the sound of his blood pattering onto the floor like raindrops. But the words pressed through it all, taking him by the throat.

"You have lost," Basrahip said, and even as he knew the trick of it, Marcus felt the deep, familiar darkness rising up from his mind to meet the man's voice. "You cannot win. Everything you love is already gone. Listen to my voice. You *cannot* win."

For a heartbeat—no more—he was holding Merian's body against his. The smell of fire and death filling his nostrils, the fumes rising up from her corpse and changing who he was forever. Merian. Alys. His wife and his child, dead because he'd been loyal to the wrong man. Cithrin was already the same. Already doomed because he hadn't been strong enough or wise enough to turn her from the path she'd chosen. Yardem was as good as dead. Kit and the players. Because he hadn't done better.

"You cannot win. You have already lost. Everything you fight for, everything you care for, all of it is already gone. Your failure cannot be changed. You have lost!"

The priest's voice rang out in the narrow space, and Marcus felt the poisoned sword growing heavier. It sank lower, dropping out of defensive stance. Tears familiar as old enemies filled his eyes, and his chest ached with every failure he'd dragged behind him all through the wide, empty world. The priest stepped closer, as Marcus had known he would. Basrahip's blade was stained at the tip, red with Marcus's blood.

"You can *never* win. You have lost everything. Everything and *forever.*"

The vast and familiar ocean of sorrow in Marcus's chest opened, blooming out endlessly. Other people healed, other people mourned and moved on. But he would feel the pain fresh every time, every moment without Merian and Alys would be as bright with grief as the first one. And nothing could ever undo it. The priest took another step nearer. His eyes were bright and certain. The blade in his vast hand was ready. Marcus blinked away a thick tear.

"Listen to my voice," Basrahip said. "You cannot win. You have lost, now and always. Everything you love is lost to you. Everything you do is doomed. Empty. *Meaningless*."

"Old news," Marcus said, and sank the poisoned sword into Basrahip's gut.

The priest's eyes narrowed in what looked like confusion as he stepped back. Dark, thick blood poured out of his belly onto the pale floor. Spiders ran a few skittering inches from where they fell, tracking pinpoints of inky blood behind them, then stilled and died. Basrahip put a hand to the wound, astonished and confused. Already a thick white foam was forming where the blade had broken the big man's skin. A smell like heated wine and fresh shit filled the room, but Marcus didn't gag. Basrahip's breath stuttered and became harder, gasping.

"What have you done?" he demanded through clenched teeth.

Marcus shrugged and nodded toward the flowing, spider-clotted blood. "The job."

His own arm was slick with his brighter blood, and the pain from it was getting worse. He stepped back, waiting for the priest to fall. Instead Basrahip's eyes filled with rage, and he bulled forward, swinging his sword before him like a farmer's child at his first reaping. Marcus moved back, his center low, the two-handed blade shifting to turn every blow. The priest was strong, but with each breath, his attacks grew weaker. Less precise.

Something was happening under the priest's skin; a dark mottling covered his hands, his neck, his wide face. His eyes lost their focus on Marcus, found him for a moment, then wandered again.

Slowly, Basrahip sank to his knees, trembling, but he did

not drop his blade. The blood on his belly was so dark now, it looked black, and the spiders that fell from the wound were dead before they found the floor. Marcus watched, unmoved and unmoving, as the last vestiges of life left Basrahip and his empty body slumped to the side. Marcus drove the poisoned sword through the stilled chest, leaning until the blade came through the dead man's back, just to be sure it was done. He didn't intend to sit so much as he simply found himself, legs crossed, on the floor. The fresh red blood from his arm pooled around him, mixing with the darker spatters, and it occurred to him for the first time that the injury he'd taken in the fight might be more serious than he'd thought.

He should bind it. Slowly, like a man half-asleep, he pulled his belt from around his waist and cinched it around his arm above the wound. He felt borne up on a soft relief. It was done. He'd stopped the priest. He was done. It was over. He realized he'd closed his eyes when he opened them. The poisoned sword rose from the corpse like a flagpole. Or the marker for a grave. He'd carried the damned thing so long, and at such cost. It was good he'd gotten some use from it.

He needed to get up. Find Yardem. Warn him. The dragon was coming, or had already come. Marcus opened his eyes again and had to concentrate to keep from closing them. He wanted to rest, wanted to let sleep take him, and maybe something deeper than sleep. Basrahip's empty face was turned toward him, still as stone. The stench from him was awful, but Marcus didn't mind it. Death shouldn't be pretty. It shouldn't be dignified. Better that it come ugly and brutal and true. If you could love it then, you'd be sure you were ready.

He closed his eyes, and waited for Merian to come. For

Alys to take his hand. For all the shit and sorrow of decades to go away forever. When none of that happened, he sighed and levered himself up to his feet.

Some other day, then.

"Yardem!" he shouted. "Are you still here?"

Geder

I'll be waiting when you come back," Cithrin said.

Geder's heart ached at her fragility and her strength. What he wanted was to take her in his arms and swear he'd protect her and that she'd never want for anything again. Instead he looked at her, his expression serious, and promised the next best thing. "We will return." It meant a hundred things more than the words themselves. He hoped she understood. He turned to the Tralgu guard. Yardem, his name was. "We'd best get started. It can be a long way up."

The guard smiled vaguely, and Cithrin said, "Thank you, Yardem."

Geder turned, and they walked toward the Kingspire. Geder felt her eyes on him, or imagined that he did. He held himself a little taller in case he was right. When they stepped through the main doors of the Kingspire, Geder hesitated. Something felt wrong. Then he realized it was only that the great tower was quiet where usually it echoed and rumbled with the voices of servants and slaves and the business of the crown.

"Prince Geder!"

Basrahip lumbered toward him from the shadows. Geder's smile went still. The great priest wasn't supposed to be here. He was supposed to be up in the temple. Cithrin bel Sarcour wasn't fifty feet behind him, and here was Basrahip looking at him. It was oddly thrilling. *Which one of us is the dupe now?* "Basrahip."

"We have all come to your call," Basrahip said, hunching forward in unconscious deference. "The last of us are making their way up to the temple even now."

"Just going there myself," Geder said. Because it was true. He had to be careful to say only things that were true. Things were going well, but they were still on a knife's edge.

"I will join you in a moment," Basrahip said, and looked back over his shoulder.

"Is there anything wrong?" Geder asked.

"The Lady Kalliam said she wished to refresh herself and that she would be well, but..." He shook his great head.

You can deal with it when you come back, Geder almost said, then stopped himself. Basrahip couldn't deal with it when he came back because he would never be coming back, and Geder knew it. No lies. He could mislead, but he couldn't lie. He'd almost given the game away, and the nearness of the mistake chilled him. "All right, but don't take long. I really, *really* want you up there."

Basrahip's smile was broad and grateful. "I shall be there in a moment, Prince Geder. I long to hear the voice of the goddess in yours."

Do you? Geder thought. *Well, don't wait underwater.*

Basrahip turned and lumbered off. Geder made for the stairs, the Tralgu guard at his side.

"That going to be a problem?" the guard asked.

"I'm sure it's fine," Geder said.

What's taking him so long?"

The temple hadn't been made as a temple. Geder had had it dedicated to the spider goddess, the Righteous Servant, after Dawson Kalliam turned Camnipol into a battlefield.

There was a large room with an open window almost as wide as the wall itself that looked out over the city and past it to the haze of land in the south. Ropes as thick as Geder's arm held the great red banner draping down from here. Far below, the tops of the trees shifted in the wind, their soft green billows echoing the shapes of the white clouds above.

Beyond the main room, the temple was only corridors and rooms that had been pressed into the goddess's service. Cells for the priests to pray in, an altar where they carried out their rites. A pantry somewhere that servants stocked with bread and soup and wine. A privacy closet that they cleaned five times in the day. Old sconces with the black soot halos that marked where generations of torches had guttered and burned. Iron rings in the walls and ceilings whose use Geder could only guess at. The stones were older than the empire, and generations of footsteps had worn the floors smoother than glass. There was a beauty to the rooms, and a sense of age and dignity.

Geder scratched his arm and glanced back at the great doors. The ones that led to the stairway that they would escape down. The doors he and Yardem would bar and block just as soon as Basrahip arrived.

If he would only *come*.

"Might be a problem for another day," the Tralgu man said.

"No. No, he has to be here," Geder said.

Yardem flicked a jingling ear. "Any reason?"

Because he was the one who lied to me, Geder thought but didn't say. *He was the one who made me look like a fool.* "He just does."

The rooms of the temple were loud with the rush and crash of priestly voices. The air stank of incense and bodies. Geder hadn't known really just how many priests there were. Between all the cities of the empire and the men still tending the original temple in the mountains east of the Keshet, hundreds had come. Most Firstblood, but at least one Jasuru and what looked to be a handful of Cinnae men, pale and reed-thin. He didn't know when they had been brought into the fold. Tainted by the spiders.

The priests walked through the rooms of the temple, segregating themselves into groups that eyed one another warily. There were so many, it was hard to see where one group ended and the next began. The divisions were there, though, marked out in the motion of bodies and the suspicious glances.

The group standing nearest the great doors were all Antean, inducted into the temple in the last years. Jorey's brother was among them, talking and laughing. They were too near the doors. What if they stepped out? What if they found the bars that were going to turn the temple first into a prison, and then into a kiln? How would he explain that?

"Don't," Yardem said.

"Don't what?"

"Don't stare at the door. They're watching us."

Of course they were. Geder was their savior, after all. The man who had called them all into the reach of his living voice to reconcile all their differences and schisms. To end forever the wars between them. And he would, he would, but Basrahip needed to be there. He turned away, looking out over the city without seeing it. His chest felt tight, and between the heat of the room and the smell of it, little waves of nausea were starting to crawl up the back of his throat. This wasn't what it was supposed to be like. This was his moment of vengeance, and all he wanted was for it to be over.

So many things in his life had been like that. Everything

he'd expected, everything that was supposed to be good and wonderful, had actually been sour and sad. He'd ridden off to war expecting camaraderie and friendship, but except for Jorey, he'd been the butt of jokes and pranks. He'd been protector of Vanai, but only because he'd been set up to fail. He'd had a triumph thrown in his name, been given the regency, and none of it had brought the satisfaction he'd expected. None of it had carried any lasting joy.

Well, that wasn't fair. There had been moments. His time with Cithrin and Aster in the ruins, of course. But others as well. Undermining Alan Klin had been a pleasure, and that had been before he'd met Basrahip and everything had been tainted. That one time, when Klin had sent him into the winter mud of the Free Cities hunting for the fleeing wealth of Vanai, he'd actually found it, made his own little fortune, and let the smugglers go rather than hand Klin the glory. The memory of the chest filled with gems and jewelry, half-sunken in ice and snow, of pouring double handfuls of the treasure down his shirt before anyone could see him, filled him with a soft, nostalgic glow. Of all he had done in all his life, *there* had been a good moment.

Something plucked at the back of his mind. The smugglers had been in a caravan guarded by some famed mercenary captain. He couldn't remember the name. But...

"Were you ever in Vanai?" he asked.

Yardem answered with a noise deep in his throat. He put a hand on Geder's shoulder.

"Now," he said.

"Now? What now?"

"We have to do the thing now."

"We can't," Geder said. "Basrahip—"

"The signal torch is burning," Yardem said.

For a moment, it was as if the words were in some

unknown language. He couldn't make sense of them. Then, slowly, the air left him. He looked down toward the dueling yard. The iron brazier there glimmered like a star in the night sky. A thin cloud of smoke billowed up from it. Geder's chest tightened more. He couldn't breathe.

"No," he said. "No, that's just the sunlight. That's just a reflection of the ... of the ..."

Yardem steadied him with a wide, strong hand. His voice was low and conversational. Nothing in his tone suggested that their lives were suddenly at risk. "We'll be all right. But we have to go now."

"We have to go now," Geder echoed.

He gathered himself to walk, but his limbs suddenly felt as if they were made from wood. He'd become a puppet with an impatient child yanking at his strings. He forced his mouth into a smile that felt grotesque and false. The urge to run pricked him, and he had to pretend he didn't feel it. Yardem padded calmly at his side, as if the distance from the great open windows to the door at the temple's far end weren't the difference between life and death. Geder tried to match the Tralgu's stride.

The priests turned to watch him. Of course they did. That didn't mean anything. He'd called them here. He hadn't explained what he was doing. They were curious. Of course their attention was on him. It wasn't because they *knew*.

The doors seemed to come closer, even through it was really him moving toward them. A wire-haired priest in a black robe with a belt of chain nodded to Geder. He nodded back, but didn't speak. He couldn't speak. They were thick doors. Hard to break through. Now he wasn't sure of that. There were so many priests, after all. But the dragon was coming. All they needed to do was pass through the room, close the doors. There were iron bars waiting there in the shadows.

He'd hold the doors closed while Yardem fit the metal across the brackets, and then they'd run. Geder could already imagine himself running down the stair so fast it felt like falling.

His heart stopped. What if they met Basrahip on their way down? How would he explain what was happening?

"We can't," he whispered, hoping the priests weren't close enough to hear.

"Going to have to, my lord," Yardem said.

The doors came closer, and Geder's heart beat again, harder now for having lost its rhythm. It fought against his ribs like a panicked bird killing itself against the bars of its cage. He couldn't quite believe the priests didn't hear it. His own ears were roaring with his pulse. A dozen more steps to the doors, then the stairs...

"Remembered something important, Lord Regent?" Vicarian Kalliam asked, his voice light as a joke.

Geder nodded, acknowledging him without answering. He couldn't answer.

"Prince Geder?" another priest said. "You look unwell. Are you leaving us?"

"I—" Geder said, and stopped.

The room was silent now. All the priests—there were hundreds of them—had shifted to face him. There were too many. He couldn't fight his way free. He had to say something. He had to tell them everything was all right, but it wasn't, and they'd know. He had to tell them he wasn't leaving, but he was leaving, and they'd know. He had to lie, because if they knew the truth, they'd rip him to shreds with their hands and spill out into the world again, and Cithrin would know he'd failed. And Aster. Only he couldn't lie.

There had to be a way. A turn of phrase and intention that would get him free, but he couldn't think of anything. The seconds stretched, and fear with them.

He looked up into the Tralgu's warm, dark eyes. *We're going to die here*, Geder thought. *I've done all this, come all this way, and I'm going to die here because someone asked me a question I couldn't answer.* The monstrous unfairness of it was like a torch in his belly. It hurt and it filled his nose with the scent of smoke. The anger flowed into him, an old ally come in his hour of need.

He had to say something.

It had to be true.

Fine.

"No," Geder said. "I'm not leaving."

The Tralgu blinked, but if there was any surprise in his expression, Geder couldn't see it.

"I'm not leaving," Geder said, his voice ringing out. "Hear my voice? I'm not...I'm not leaving."

Because if I were, you bastards would know it. And if you knew, it would all be over. And I'm not *losing to you again.*

Yardem nodded. "I'll let her know."

The sense of loss was less terrible than he'd thought it would be. It wasn't even grief, precisely. Only a profound disappointment. There were going to be days and nights in Cithrin's company. He was going to read poetry to her, and watch Aster become king. He was going to go out to Rivenhalm with his father and spend a long day fishing at his side, the way he'd always meant to. He'd see Sabiha and tell her himself how Cithrin bel Sarcour had come and saved the empire with him, and everything was going to be all right. Only no. He wouldn't. He was going to do this instead.

"Yes. Please tell her," Geder said. "Tell them all."

Then he stood silently and watched while the Tralgu walked out the doors and closed them solidly behind him. Briefly, something in Geder's mind shrieked. *This is the moment. Change your mind again. Run!* But then the low growl of the iron bars came, and all hope died.

He looked around at the men staring at him. Dozens of different faces. Some were confused, some sullen and angry, some lit with hope. He smiled. It felt real this time. It was as if everything he'd ever seen had been through a dirty window, and now the glass was clean.

He was done. Nothing mattered.

"Well," he said, rubbing his hands together. "All right. Why don't we get started? Can all of you come here, please? Everyone from the back rooms too? Yes, good. Everybody. Come out here where you can get a good look out at the city."

Like a nurse with too many children to care for, Geder made a show of putting them all in lines and rows. They shuffled and pushed under his guidance, jockeying for position without knowing it was their own pyre. Geder found a bleak and terrible joy in it all. *Here, you're taller, so stand at the back. Make sure everyone's got a good view. This is important. This will be amazing. You've been looking forward to this, haven't you? I can tell.*

They stood in ranks, facing the open sky, and Geder took his place behind them. Their heads blocked the blue. It was fine. There, almost too small to see, but high in the open air, something was gliding. A hawk above the city walls, perhaps. Or something larger and farther away, but coming close.

"All right," Geder said, his voice a cheerful singsong. "I want everyone to close their eyes. Everybody, now. You've come all this way to hear what I have learned about the goddess. So close your eyes, and relax. I want you all to feel her power within you. I want you to feel the comfort she gives you all. Can you do that for me?"

A murmur of gentle assent rose all around him.

"Think about all that you have sacrificed for her," Geder said. The wings were larger than a hawk's now, but not yet, he guessed, within the city. With every heartbeat, they seemed to grow just a bit wider, just a bit thicker. Like someone had drawn a pen across the clouds, and the ink was still seeping in. "Think about the trust you have put in her. The faith. You have all given your lives for her. Died out of the life you had before in order to carry her voice into the world. Without your dedication to her, you might have had wives. Children. You might have written songs or brewed beer or any of a thousand different things, but you are the servants of the Servant because you knew in your heart that this was better. Am I right? Do you deny it?"

Another wave of voices, now in negation. No, they did not deny. No one could deny the power of her voice. Some of them were swaying now. Someone was weeping, and it sounded like joy. The wings were no longer like a hawk's. They took a shape more like a vast and ragged bat. Not quite that, but more like. It was a beautiful creature. He could make out the dragon's head now, and it might have been only his imagination, but he thought he heard a roar rising in the city. A thousand throats shouting in a chorus of fear.

"Think of the promises she made you," Geder said. "The golden glow of truth. The knowledge that you were better and purer and more right than everyone else. Take a moment, and feel all the love in that promise. Take comfort in it."

Someone in the group moaned in something like religious ecstasy. Geder bounced on the balls of his feet. His grin was so wide, it ached.

"My voice doesn't have that power. But it can carry truth.

And the truth I have for you—the one you have been waiting for and searching for, the one that will end all dispute
between you, has come. Take a breath, open your eyes, and
hear my truth. You don't get to *fucking* laugh at me."

One opened his eyes, then a handful, and then all of them
together. They looked around in confusion, reared back,
cried out. They surged for the doors, but to no effect. The
iron held. The dragon's approach shrugged off the illusion
of floating gentleness. It drove toward them all like a falling stone. The great mouth opened, and Geder could see its
teeth.

Inys slammed into the tower, his vast head blotting out
the city, the sky, the future.

For the first few seconds, the flames felt cold.

Cithrin

Inys hit the Kingspire with a sound louder than thunder. Cithrin felt it in her chest like a blow. Massive claws dung deep into the tower's flanks, leaving marks so wide she could see them from the gardens where she stood. His body filled like a bellows, and the roar of the fire was an assault in itself. Flames blew out, bathing the dragon's head. They lit the windows of the Kingspire. Black smoke billowed up, rising into the sky. An announcement of tragedy. The violence of it staggered her.

Aster, unthinking, pushed himself in front of her as if his body would offer any protection. She put her hand on his shoulder. All around the grounds, the others were gaping up at the spectacle. Other voices raised in alarm came from behind her. Geder's guards. The city watch. All the men and soldiers that Geder was supposed to have summoned making their own approach, alarmed and unsought. She didn't know if this was a blessing, and she didn't turn to see. The banner of the goddess fell toward them, but slowly. It burned as it fell, and seemed borne up by the heat of its own unmaking. It rained ashes below it and belched smoke above.

The dragon drew another vast breath, and the fire came again. A cracking sound, sharp as a board snapped across a knee, but a thousand times louder, came from the Kingspire.

She wanted to call out to Marcus, to Yardem. To anyone.

But there was only her and the prince, and the actors who were the nearest thing to her family. The dying tower at the heart of a dying empire. The terrible grandeur was more than she'd expected. Marcus, Yardem, Geder...they'd been meant to escape the tower first. This wasn't what was supposed to happen. Either the ground was shaking or she was. She couldn't tell which.

The banner reached the trees, draping over the broad and leafy branches. New smoke rose up. New flames to echo the ones still glowing in the tower.

We have to get water, she thought. *We have to put the fires out before they spread.* It wasn't enough to spur her into motion.

The horror and awe that consumed her shifted, and a new thought slid brightly into her mind. This was it. This was the moment she'd aimed herself toward. If they'd been in the temple, the spiders were gone now. The war that had spanned all human history was rising in the smoke above her. She wanted to see it as a victory, but she couldn't see it as anything but an act of breathtaking destruction. That peace could come from *this* was an article of faith. A thing she believed because she had to.

Someone called her name, the voice almost drowned out by the sound of the flames. It took her a timeless moment to find him: Sandr waving his hands and pointing at the mechanism beside him. Cithrin shook her head, confused. The actor yelled something and pointed up, at Inys. The serpentine tail wrapped the tower.

Oh. He was asking whether they should loose the bolts and try to pull the dragon down. She turned to find Marcus, only he wasn't there. She'd known that.

They should wait. They could deal with Inys another time, when Marcus was back. If he came back.

If you fall, I'm picking up your damned blade myself.

Humanity had driven the spiders to the edge of the world once. But it had also thrown off the yoke of the dragons. Defeating one without the other now would only be half the job. If it meant betraying Inys, it was also being true to Marcus. And the royal guard was coming near.

"Do it!" she shouted over the roar and cacophony. "Bring him down!"

Sandr nodded and turned back to his mechanism. From all around the garden, splinters of bright metal arched up toward the dragon's glittering scales, trailing gossamer. When the first two hit, Inys shifted, swiveling his massive head in confusion. Clinging as he was to the side of the burning tower, he didn't have the freedom of movement he might have. It was why Marcus had chosen this moment.

Inys ripped out one of the barbs as two more hit. The gossamer on the first looked like it was growing thicker as thread drew up string to draw up rope, to pull Inys down. Geder's guards rushed past her as if she weren't there, bows drawn. More shouts came from behind them. Camnipol rising in terror and rage, as Marcus had hoped and intended.

Inys ripped another barb free, shifted his head toward them, and opened his mouth, but the gout of fire that came from him wasn't strong enough to reach the ground. For the space of a heartbeat, the lines burned and turned to ash. Embers in the shape of spider web, crumbling, and then gone. The dragon's roar was louder than the fire had been. His face, even from so far away, was perfectly readable— confusion and pain, followed by a vast indignance.

More people rushed forward to the gardens. Not only guards now, but the servants Geder had ordered back. Some brandished swords and bows, but others rakes and horse-whips, stones plucked off the garden's paths, or only raised voices and balled fists. For a moment, she loved them all. Aster pressed himself closer to her, but whether to protect her or be protected, she couldn't say.

There was a strange nobility about it. All these people, faced with catastrophe, and running toward it. Any one of them would have been wiser to turn and flee, but instead they came together. By instinct, they would do together what none of them might have managed alone.

Inys rose, leaping up into the wide sky, his wings beating the air. The wind blew the fires brighter, and the dragon rose high above the reach of their weapons, spiraling up toward the clouds and then diving back down. Screams filled the air, and bows were drawn, ready to meet the attack. But Inys pulled out, swooping around to hit the highest point in the tower with all his weight. The burning Kingspire shook.

"It's coming down!" Cithrin shouted. "Get out of the way! He's pushing it down!"

Fire and stone fell together, coming faster than the banner had. It was only the highest part of the great tower that tipped over and tumbled down toward them, but it was still larger than her countinghouse in Porte Oliva had been. It hit the ground, spewing fire and dust. The screaming hadn't stopped, but it had changed its character. No longer defiance and horror, but pain.

The dragon, hovering in the high air above the city, screamed. Cithrin thought there were words in it, but she couldn't tell what they were. Inys spread his ragged wings and flew away to the south, far beyond their reach. They hadn't brought him down. He'd gotten away.

"Well," she said, her voice sounding as if it belonged to someone else, "that could have gone better."

The royal quarter looked like a city after a sack. Stone and ancient wood burned hotter than a forge, scattered across the gardens in heaps taller than buildings. The people of Camnipol, guards and servants, divided themselves among fighting back the flame, tending to the wounded, and staring in open horror at the destruction. Cithrin found herself weeping with them, and didn't know how many of her tears were sorrow, how many fear, how many relief.

Clara Kalliam stumbled forward out of the haze of dust and smoke, her huntsman close behind her. She came to Cithrin, and for a moment, each tried to find something to say. They fell into each other's arms, embracing like mourners at a pyre. Cithrin felt other arms around her. Aster was with them, sobs wracking his body. And then Cary as well. And Kit. And Sandr, his hair singed and a thick burn over his right eye. And Charlit Soon whom Cithrin barely knew, holding her now like a sister in the wreckage. In the heart of the terror, they made a knot with each other, and the simple animal comfort of being held by others who shared her distress was the nearest thing Cithrin had ever felt to love.

"Is it done?" Clara asked. "Are they gone?"

"I think so," Cithrin replied. "Probably?"

Cithrin felt the movement in the group, a shifting that filled her with dread before she understood it. Master Kit, his expression gentle, stood back. His hair was whiter now than it had been when she'd met him on the road from Vanai. The age in his face more pronounced. But the kindness and amusement and sorrow with which he embraced the world still glowed in his eyes.

"No," he said. "There is one more."

"Kit?" Cithrin said, struggling free of the others. Behind him, a vast structure within the rubble shifted, throwing out black smoke and embers like a thousand fireflies. Tears streaked Kit's ash-powdered face.

"Don't cry," he said. "I have been thinking of this moment for some time."

"No," Cary said. "No no no."

"Yes," Kit said, lowering his head.

"You can't," Cary said. "We've just *won*. We did everything right. It isn't fair."

She took a step toward Kit. Her mouth was a slash of grief. Cithrin came to her side.

"It isn't," Kit said. "The world has never been fair. Often beautiful. Sometimes kind when kindness was not deserved. But never fair."

"What are you thinking, Kit?" Cithrin said.

He stepped back, his arms rising at his sides as if he were only walking a stage, and the flames and devastation behind him were just a clever set piece.

"As long as I am in the world, the danger is as well. I am known to too many people, and the power I carry is too great. No, no, please. Don't cry. This is victory too. I love you all. It has been an honor traveling with you."

"Kit!" Cithrin shouted, but he was right. She felt it in her heart like a bruise too deep to touch.

The old actor turned his back to them and walked toward the fire, his steps steady and sure. His head held high and bravely. A dead man, choosing his own pyre.

Cary shrieked and surged forward. Sandr leaped for her, grabbing her shoulder and half spinning her. Cithrin took her arm, but the woman shrieked louder and fought. Clara came as well, and her huntsman, and even Aster. Cary lowered her head, pushing madly against them as the other actors came. It was a cruel parody of the embrace they'd just shared. Or else it was the same. Just the same.

When Cary's knees gave way and she buckled, the others sank to the wounded grass with her. Cithrin's world stank of fire and soil and dust and tears. When she looked up, Kit was gone among the flames. She closed her eyes again and looked away.

Time moved strangely for a while. The guards came, eyes wide, swords drawn against some enemy that they imagined they could cut. When none such appeared, they took position around Aster but then seemed not to know what they should do. Eventually, the boy prince ordered them to help contain the fires. A rose garden was in flame to their right. The rubble and debris from the Kingspire scattered like bones to the left, falling out over the edge and into the Division. If something caught flame down there, Cithrin didn't know how they'd extinguish it, or if maybe it would find its place in the layer upon layer of ruins that were the earth under Camnipol, and set the whole city up like an endless torch. It didn't matter.

As the fires moved, Aster joined the soldiers and servants in hunting through the wreckage for any who might still live. A sweep of well-tended grass became a makeshift cunning man's tent, the wounded and the dying laid out in rows. There were more than Cithrin had hoped, but fewer than she'd feared. The cunning men moved through them, chanting and calling forth angels until the air seemed to bend from their petty magics.

She found Marcus on a gravel path by the edge of a burning pavilion. Blood caked his side, and his face was pale with its loss. It seemed almost certain that he would have collapsed without Yardem at his side, supporting him. The evil green blade in its scabbard was across Yardem's back now. A soldier in the livery of House Caot stood before them, a naked blade in his hand.

"You can't find an axe?" Marcus said.

"No," the swordsman said. "This is all I have."

"It'll have to do. Get to the north side, up by that fountain. We need to clear all that brush. What you cut down,
bring *to* the fire. Burn it where we can control the flames.
Clearing the ground doesn't do shit if you're building up a
pile of kindling on the far side of it."

"Yes, sir," the enemy soldier said, and sprinted away.

Marcus sagged, shaking his head.

"All their best men are in the field, sir," Yardem said.
Then, with a nod, "Magistra."

She wanted to run to them, to fold her arms around them
as she had with Clara, with Kit. But somehow, it felt wrong.
That wasn't who they were to each other. Or perhaps to
themselves.

"Kit's dead," she said.

"How?" Marcus asked. She made her report—what Kit
had said, holding Cary back as he walked into the flames—
with a calm that sounded like shock even as she said it.

The pain that flickered across Marcus's eyes was real, and
more terrible for being so little expressed. "Sorry to hear
that. Liked him. I'm fairly certain we got all the rest. I took
the big one. Yardem locked the others in the tower before
Inys came."

"Inys escaped," Cithrin said. "I...I tried."

"You did fine. It's the best plan I could find in the moment,
but was long odds even before we started improvising."

"Still..."

"You stopped the world from falling into an endless war
of every man for himself," Marcus said. "One asshole got
past you. Still makes for a damned good record."

"The asshole was a dragon."

Marcus shrugged gingerly, flinching when the pain struck.
"Didn't call it perfect."

"And Geder?" she asked.

Yardem flicked his ears and looked thoughtfully up at the ruined tower. "Dead, ma'am. He stayed behind so that the priests wouldn't be alarmed. He wanted me to tell you."

Cithrin frowned, waiting to see what emotions rose up in her. A bit of relief, a bit of confusion. "What did he want you to tell me?"

"That he died a hero, I think. That he sacrificed himself for your plan. For you."

"Ah," she said. "Not sure what to think of that."

"We'll put it on his tombstone," Marcus said. " 'Here lies a vicious, petty tyrant who damn near broke the world. He did one brave thing at the end.' "

"It's the thing he hoped to be remembered for," Yardem said.

"I can hope for the clouds to rain silver," Marcus said, "but it's not going to happen."

"No," Cithrin agreed. "It isn't."

Her mind was already racing ahead. With Geder gone, the rest of the plan had to change as well, but possibly in ways that made things better. There wasn't time for the Anteans to appoint a new Lord Regent. The city was wounded and under threat. The mark of their power was broken both in the city and in the world outside it. But there was a symmetry—the new saving the new—that might help sell what she needed sold now.

"Come with me," she said.

"Where are we going?" Marcus asked, already falling into half-carried step behind her.

"We need Aster."

At the base of the Kingspire, the worst of the fire had exhausted itself. Here and there, great beams still burned like tree-thick logs in a Haaverkin common house. The tower stood smoking, its top jagged as a broken tooth.

A severed monument to match the Severed Throne. The players were gone except for Mikel, Lak, and Sandr, who were moving with a group of the palace servants, carrying shovels to bury the little fires that still burned. Clara had been joined by several of the other women of the court, and was bringing water from some palace pump or well, not to stop the conflagration but to soothe the throats and clean the eyes and burns of those who did. Cithrin lifted an arm to her, and Clara nodded. She understood. It was time.

Aster stood amid the royal guard, staring up at the ruin that had been his home. Tear tracks marked his soot-dark face, but he was not weeping now. He only looked emptied. She couldn't help wondering what this was like to him. So many years of believing all that Basrahip and the priests had said. She wasn't sure even Kit's words could have untied all of that knot. Would he still hate the Timzinae, even knowing that there was no call to? Would he still believe in a great spirit in the world that promised to slaughter all lies, when it had itself been proven false? Or would he reject everything, and live his life in the desolation that comes after betrayal? She didn't know what to hope.

The guards closed rank to keep her from him, but Aster ordered them back. She walked to him. Her clothes were as filthy and smoke-stinking as his. Her body was shuddering with weariness. He smiled at her with a sorrow that belonged on a much older face.

"He's gone, isn't he?"

"He is," she said.

He lowered his head, mouth twisting for a moment in grief. "I thought so. He would have found me before this. If he could."

"That's true," she said, because she believed that it was.

"I'm so terribly sorry. About all of this. But I need you to come with me. With us. I need you to take Geder's place."

Aster shook his head. When he spoke, his voice was thin and lost. "I can't."

"You have to. This isn't over," she said. "And you may not be crowned yet, but you're king."

Entr'acte: The Dragon

Inys flew. The fallen, empty world passed beneath him like a bad dream from which he could never wake. His mind drifted as effortlessly as his body. He ached in both. Steel barbs still dug in his flesh, his blood sowing the fields he passed over. His wings were more torn and ragged. Even now, he carried the funereal scent of pitch and sage in his nostrils like a memory. There had been a poem he'd heard once about flames being the beginning and end of all things. He tried to remember it now, but it slipped away from him. And if he forgot it, it was gone forever.

The sun slid to the west and vanished. The forests below him turned to waves. Far beneath the sea he could follow the ghost lights of a great pod of the Drowned as they met for their slow council, even as they had done when they were a race new-made. He felt something at that. Not pleasure, but a nostalgia so steeped in longing as to grow poisonous. Near a great rocky island, he found an updraft and spiraled in it, rising up until the moon seemed as near as the ocean below him. The air grew thinner and colder until the draft could carry him no higher, and he only turned in a wide circle watching the moonlight play across his own outstretched wings. Silver against the black.

Marcus Stormcrow had betrayed him, but Inys bore no anger. Later, he might. Or he might not. There was no wisdom in blaming a flawed tool for shattering. His Storm-crow here was too feral. Untrained. If anything, the blame for the attack lay on Inys himself. He should have spent the time to better manage his slaves. So long as they valued their small, petty wills over his own, they would be dull knives for him, and he had a world to unmake and stitch back together.

He would be more careful next time. Whatever else, he had learned to respect the low cunning of this new gener-ation of slaves and their untamed violence. The long ages through which he'd slept had changed them. The races were as they had been before, or at least nearly so, and he'd let that lull him into thinking that the men and women within the races were likewise unchanged. And perhaps some were. Perhaps it was only a few like Marcus Stormcrow and the half-breed girl whose willful natures had gone unchecked.

It didn't matter. He knew now. He would do better next time.

He made one last lazy turn, and sloped down to the south. The bones in his back where his wings locked fast creaked and ached. The promise of rest plucked at him like a drag-onet begging for food, insistent and endearing and annoy-ing all at the same time. But there was no land wide enough for him yet. There would be. By morning, if not before. The wind of his own passage whispered in his ears until he could almost imagine voices in it.

And still, despite everything, the Stormcrow had helped him. Clinging to the side of the great tower, he had smelled again the coppery tang of his brother's flesh as the last of Morade died. Each of the tiny creatures and the corruption they'd carried had burned and the fumes from them had felt like a promise. Morade had meant to steal away the use of the slaves, and he had done, once. Nearly did again. But Inys had won the battle against his dead brother. Yes, through unstable alliance. Yes, through subterfuge and lies. Yes, despite his own grief and despair. What mattered was only that it was done. Had the spiders spread, the slaves of the world would have been tainted forever. Untamable. Now Morade's influence was gone, they could be made use of in a more systematic way. That credit belonged to the Storm-crow. For that, Inys resolved not to kill the treacherous servant. But he wouldn't breed him. Mercy had limits.

The ache in his body grew worse slowly. That was fine. Pain was nothing. It was a message he could choose to ignore. He watched the jungle canopy below him until he scented the animals that made their homes beneath the nighttime green, and found a place where he might not be disturbed. With a shrug, he unlocked the bones of his back and canted his wings to cut the air. His descent felt like the long slow fall into sleep made physical. He was not only tired, but weary.

He landed harder than he'd intended, belly thumping against the ground, claws digging into the soil as he tried to slow himself. He came to rest against the trees and lay still, his eyes closed and the wounds in his flesh shouting in new pain. The emptiness of the world overwhelmed him. No air carried the scent of another of his kind. No water carried their taste. And he, like a fool, had allied himself with slaves. He could as well have expected loyalty from fish and pigs. An animal that could speak and write was still an animal. He had lowered himself to treat them with dignity. It was only that there was no one else.

He lifted his head in the air, opened his mouth to breathe more fully. For an hour, he stayed still, waiting, tasting, longing with a fervor worse than physical pain. And then— for a moment—he caught the scent. Cloying and musky and gone again even before he was certain it was there. It opened a vault of memories. His mother's workshop in the South Tower, the air hot and rich with the smell of blood and iron, salt and sand. He remembered being so young he could do little more than perch and watch as she took her turn fashioning wonders for the court. He had thought little enough of it all then. He could wish now he'd been a better student. Now that all had been lost, and everything depended on how he could remake it.

Another workshop. Stale and empty, perhaps. Unused for ages come and passed, without doubt. Or a figment born from desire and the ability to lie to himself. It didn't matter. It was all he had left, and so he would reach for it. At worst, he would die in the attempt. No one would mourn him. No one remained.

The steel barbs of the Stormcrow's betrayal still clung to him like well-forged thorns. He plucked them out. The blood that came from them drew flies and scavengers, but Inys had more than enough flame now to keep them away. The trees here were so lush and heavy with water that no fire they took would spread for long. There were maggots hearty enough to live under scales, though, so he burned his wounds closed before he slept. The blood on his scales charred and flaked away, leaving him bright again. Scarred, but bright. It was the nearest he had to honor in a world where no other voice could ratify him. He was the highest of his kind and the lowest. Purest and most debased. It was the lack of community in which he might place himself that would eat his mind. If he wasn't more careful. He had to be more careful.

When he closed his eyes, he dreamed of battle. His wounds and exhaustion must have taken more from him than he'd known, because he didn't sense the hunter's approach until he was already upon him.

He was young and alone with the pale skin and huge dark eyes of the Nightswarm. The race the others called Southlings now. He held a sling in his hand, but did not threaten Inys with it. His stillness was abject, and his scent all but covered by the paste of leaves and talc that decorated his skin. The animals he hunted would not know he was there until the blow came, but he had nothing that could harm Inys.

The hunter, aware that he'd been seen, did not flee. He took a single, tentative step nearer, and then, when Inys did nothing, another. The wide black eyes glimmered slightly with trapped moonlight. Inys caught the smell of fear now, and it reassured him. Good that the young one should fear. A dragon, even one as worn and broken as he was, deserved fear. When Inys shifted his head, the boy froze but did not retreat. For a time they considered each other. The only sounds were the ticking of leaves, the calls of night animals, the distant drum of thunder from a storm too far away to see. The hunter sank slowly to his knees and made a sign in the air with his two hands. It looked like the pantomime of a bird in flight, but Inys took it as a mark of respect. A self-abasement before something deserving of the Nightswarm's awe.

Inys moved gingerly as much to keep from crushing the boy as from fear of reopening his own wounds, drawing himself up. He felt a moment's pleasure at the hunter's fear.

"You have a name, little one?" Inys asked.

"Amin," the hunter said. His voice was deeper than his body suggested. Older. Perhaps Inys had misjudged him. "Amin of Emissir Large."

"Your people are nearby?"

Amin pointed to the west. "Two nights. I am...I am no longer with them. I was cast out. I did something bad, and so I live here now."

"An exile?"

"Yes," Amin said, defiance in his voice. "I am."

"What were your crimes?"

Amin's eyes closed and he swayed for a moment before he opened them. They were full of tears. "Am I dreaming this? Are you my vision?"

"No. But if you seek a judge, I am it."

The answer appeared to satisfy the Nightswarm. He sat and bowed his head. When he spoke, his voice was softer, but clear.

"There was a beast killing my people. I tracked it to its den, laid in wait, and I killed it. Myself. But when I brought it back to my people, my friend said he'd helped. He'd done nothing, but he said he'd been my equal and more than that. I...was angry. I didn't mean for him to die. I would take it back if I could."

Inys felt a rush of sorrow. "You cannot. None of us can. Not even me."

The Nightswarm was quiet for a long moment. "You're hurt?"

Inys glanced at himself. He'd been cut and healed and been cut again. The edges of his wings looked like ribbons and made his control muddy and rough. *No*, he wanted to say. *This is nothing. No slave can hurt a dragon.*

But what point was there in lying? He'd debased himself once by caring what they thought. By acting as though their good opinion of him mattered. Better to learn from his errors. Better not to repeat them. "I am."

"I was a healer once. For my people, and for others. Perhaps..."

Inys shrugged and spread his wings. *Do what you can.*

Amin came close. Inys smelled the fear in him and heard it in the hummingbird-fast beating of his heart, but it did

not affect the boy's movement. The slave slowly cataloged
the insults to Inys's flesh, new and old both. The rips in
his wings, unhealed since the battle in the south. The new
burns and pricks still raw under the bandage of char. The
long swaths where his scales had once been smooth as water
and were now rougher than unfinished stone. An odd peace
filled Inys. He recalled long baths of water and oil, tended
by a dozen slaves. The gentle vibration of the rasp as teams
of slaves sharpened his talons. It had been years ago, before
the war started, when he'd lived in his cousin's house and
dreamed of besting his brothers...No, not years. More
than that. More than centuries. Even Marcus Stormcrow
had only addressed Inys's body as a thing of convenience
and need. To feel cared for, even in so small a way, called
forth an ache deep in Inys's breast.

And then the chanting began. Amin's hands brushed his
scales, his wings. A warmth radiated out from the slave's
fingertips, and Inys felt an energy answering it. As if his own
ability to heal had been sleeping and now roused, the dragon
felt the rough scales shift and realign. The torn fabric of his
wings knit together. The aches of his newest wounds and his
oldest scars eased, even where they had been for so long he'd
forgotten the ache was there. But that was not the greatest
gift the chanting carried.

Against all hope, the melody was one Inys knew. He
didn't realize it at first, lost in the bliss of his remaking, but
soon he realized he was anticipating the song, expecting
the rising trill, the falling cadence, the near resolution that
danced away again. It was one he had heard from Asteril
when they'd been young and fresh as a first flight. The syllables were foreign and unfamiliar, but when he turned his
attention to it, there were even fragments of the old languages. Bits of human words that echoed and carried all

unknowing the power of humanity's masters, even in the masters' absence.

And that, Inys thought, his heart lifting in joy, was more than a lone healer's cantrip. That was the whole of the world. He had thought the dragons gone, apart from himself, but it was true only in one sense. Yes, he was, unless another sleeper lay buried in the world, the last to lay claim to his own whole body, his own complete mind. But like the shards from a broken glass, the dragons were still everywhere. In the bodies of the races they'd made, in the poems and magics that their cunning men passed down through the generations, in the slave paths they had imposed on the changing face of the earth.

He remembered a little thing his first teacher, Myrix, had shown him. A sheet of crystal with a moment's light captured within it, so that the paths of it shaped any new raw light into the form of it. As the surface of a pond alive with ripples and then suddenly frozen held the pattern of all the cooperating and annihilating waves, even a sliver of the crystal was formed of all that the full stone knew. With a sense of comprehension deeper than love, Inys saw that the world was the same way.

The shards of the dragons were in the laws that humans enforced upon each other. In the shapes of their bodies and the functions of their minds. The way their cities grew and the melodies of their songs. To bring the dragons forth again into the world wouldn't be an act of creation, but of reassembly. He shuddered with pleasure. And with hope.

The chanting stopped. Amin stepped back. How long it had been, Inys couldn't say, only the sun was in the sky now, pricking at the Nightswarm boy's too-large eyes. Amin's skin was covered in a sheen of sour-smelling sweat, and he trembled. His heart was calm, though. The fear was gone.

Inys took stock, and was pleased. Even with the char fallen away, his wounds no longer bled. The scars of his old battles had faded or vanished away. Even the tatters and holes of his wings had been repaired, the membrane thinner where it had ripped, but whole again. When he stood and stretched his wings out, his bones didn't ache. He was astonished at how much of himself the slave had offered up.

Inys folded himself down to consider the boy. The Nightswarm blinked and made the curious gesture again. This time it seemed less the motion of a bird and more that of a dragon's wings.

"I am on a desperate journey," Inys said. "I will remake my kind and redeem my errors, but the path I seek is long and terrible. You have already done me great good. Greater even than you know. I name you Amin Stormcrow, first among my servants and destined to command all those who follow after, three upon three upon three."

The boy fell to his knees. "I...I am yours," he said.

"Swear to me now that you will never act against me. That you will never betray me."

"I swear I will never betray you, higher-than-mothers. What you wish, I shall wish. Now and always."

Inys shifted back a degree. He sensed no duplicity in the boy's words, but neither had he in Marcus Stormcrow or the half-breed banker girl. Better to learn from his errors. Better not to repeat them.

"I don't believe you," Inys said, and killed him.

The Nightswarm's blood had a strange, almost peppery taste, and his flesh was tough. Inys ate until his belly was full, then launched into the wide, open air, testing his newly-healed wings and leaving the rest of the body behind for the flies and jungle scavengers. Within the hour, he found the coast—huge waves breaking on a beach of perfect white sand. He landed in the high surf gently, delicately, and washed the last of the boy's blood from his scales. Then, for a time, he lay on the sand-strewn beach, his neck stretched out. The sun warmed him and the sound of the water lulled him until, half dreaming, he felt he could hear a choir of dragons, their voices raised in song, in among the waves.

Refreshed, renewed, and confirmed in his task, he would fly to the south until he unearthed the workshop or discovered it definitively to be a mirage. He would gather all that he could of dragon-nature from the world, distill it, and call it forth to its true and purer form. He would redeem his error. All his errors.

Only first, he would sleep a while. Not for long, though. Not again.

Marcus

They left the permanent green of the dragon's road behind them in the middle morning, where it curved north along the track toward Kaltfel and Anninfort. The little villages that clung to the jade path, making their keep from the traffic of merchants and farmers and all human trade like ticks on a dog's ear, vanished quickly behind them. The roads turned to gravel or mud or two strips of crushed grass running parallel across the fields, a cart's width apart. The last march of the war was to be on human paths. That seemed like an omen, though Marcus was damned if he could say if it was a good one or bad.

The farmhouses and stream-run mills they passed weren't only Firstblood homes. The men and women and children who came out to gawk as they passed were also fur-pelted Kurtadam shaved to the skin for summer, Jasuru with scales that looked more like a dragon's now that he'd seen a dragon up close, reed-thin Cinnae, even a family of tusk-jawed Yemmu. No Timzinae, though. Or at least none the company hadn't brought itself.

The land itself was lush with the high summer. Tall grasses hummed with insect life. The sun's heat would have been stifling if a breeze hadn't stirred the air. The trees had traded the peapod-green leaves of spring for deeper, more mature foliage that, in ten weeks or so, would shrivel and brown and fall. There were no flowers on the branches and few on the bushes, but green nuts and acorns, ripening berries and seedpods. They rode through a deep scent of growth and decay, the complex perfume of every summer ever. They weren't a day outside the city, and already the jays and sparrows here were unaware there'd been a war on. Would have been astonished to hear it.

Jorey's scouts met them in the early afternoon; bone-thin men whose eyes registered neither grief nor wonder at seeing them there, hearing the news of the Lord Regent's death and the slaughter of the spider goddess. They only nodded, accepting what they heard because the strength it would have taken to feel anything was beyond them. They wouldn't be called heroes when this was done. Just soldiers, and maybe not even that. It didn't seem right.

Aster rode at the column's head on a silver mare that might have been bred to the task of looking regal and being calm. The boy himself sat his mount like he'd been born to it. Maybe he had. Marcus didn't know much about the tradition of horsemanship in Antea, but it was a common enough way to make a leader seem greater than those around him. And Aster would need all of that he could muster. Someone had convinced him to shave off the peach-fuzz moustache he'd been attempting and Cithrin had reminded him a bit of how to seem older than he truly was. *Better to look youthful than young,* she'd said. Odd, the way tricks and skills once learned cycled back to be useful again in strange circumstances.

And, as if in echo of the boy at the column's head, the Timzinae children rode behind, tended by Clara Kalliam and a dozen other women of the court. Eight carts of girls and boys, most too young for heavy labor, and each with a fresh new toy to cling to, each fed with raisin cakes and lemon bread. Each in bright new clothing that had belonged to a Firstblood child not long ago, or else had been newly sewn for the occasion. The contents of Geder Palliako's gaol. The ones who'd survived. They'd wrapped them up like wedding presents, as though acting as if it were a celebration could forgive the gaps in their lines. The ones who wouldn't come home.

For himself, Marcus tried to ignore the pain. A young Southling cunning man had done her best to patch his opened arm back together, and all in all she'd done a serviceable job. Apart from a hole the size of a coin near his shoulder, he wasn't bleeding anymore, and even that was only weeping. The poisoned sword was back in the city, which likely helped as well. It was hard to believe that any wound, however well tended, would mend in that thing's presence.

Yardem rode at his side, and by the time they reached the little confluence of streams that was their goal, he'd almost stopped checking whether Marcus was about to fall off his horse every third breath. Not that the concern wasn't appreciated in spirit. It was the practice that annoyed. In the end it mattered that his armor fit him, which it did well enough, that the soldiers who rode with him looked more an honor guard than a fighting force, and that Cithrin rode by Aster's side. Cithrin bel Sarcour of the Medean bank, who'd risked life and fortune for the Timzinae in occupied Suddapal, and was about to trade her reputation and eight cartfuls of children for peace. Assuming she could find a buyer.

God knew she looked the part. She didn't wear mail, but she managed to make a well-cut dress and a hunter's leathers seem as imposing. Her Cinnae mother's blood left her seeming elegant more than frail, her Firstblood father having given her a strength about the spine and shoulders. Or maybe that was unfair. Maybe Cithrin was only Cithrin, and her virtues and flaws her own. She was old enough to have earned them. If he could still see the amateur smuggler called Tag when he looked at her, it didn't matter. How she seemed to him wasn't the point. What mattered was how she—how all of them—impressed Karol Dannien. Or failed to.

The field of parley wasn't actually a field this time. Low, sharp hills marked the path like the landscape stuttering. The curve of one made a natural amphitheater, open to the south so that when Dannien and his men arrived, Lord Emming, Cithrin, Aster, and Marcus himself were all waiting at the table. It was the kind of staging Kit would approve of. Or no. Would have approved of. Marcus still couldn't quite believe the old actor had walked into the flames that way . . .

The banner of Antea and Aster's personal sigil hung above them. The blood-red banner of the priests was absent. The carts stood a little apart, but not so far that the opposing force could overlook them. The presence of children alone argued against violence, or Marcus hoped it did. Seemed rude to slaughter anyone else where the little ones could see, but worse things had happened in the world. And he could tell from the way Dannien walked that he was angry.

Cep Bailan strode at Dannien's side bare-chested, rolls of blubber shifting as he walked and his ornate blue tattoos brightened by sweat like stones in water. Summer in Antea couldn't be a pleasant place for a Haaverkin, but Bailan had chosen to take work in the south. And if the heat exhausted him, maybe he wouldn't talk much. The man was an ass. Behind them, Timzinae soldiers stood in ranks, swords at their sides, and stared across the gap at the children. Even at this distance, Marcus saw the focus—as strong as hunger—that fought against their discipline. How many of those men there had children among the hostages? Nephews, nieces, daughters, and sons. As many as Geder had hauled up north, it didn't seem any family in Suddapal could have gone untouched.

Dannien sat at his chair, his gaze roving across the opposing group, lingering on each in turn. Bailan only collapsed onto his stool and panted, waving a hand at his face like a fan. Aster's expression was calm. Either the boy didn't understand he was facing a man who'd sworn to kill not just him but everyone who served him or else he had the makings of a better-than-average king. Ignorance and bravery could be hard to distinguish with only one experience to judge from. Dannien's gaze skipped over Emming like he wasn't there, but lingered on Cithrin and stopped at Marcus with a nod.

"Ran away last time," Dannien said.

Ignoring Aster was a calculated rudeness. Taking offense was the first step down a path they didn't want, so Marcus chuckled. "Wouldn't count on it again. It's not a trick that works twice."

"Be drinking on it the rest of the season, though. Karol Dannien, the man who made Marcus Wester sneak away in the night." Despite himself, Marcus tensed. Dannien smiled and turned to Aster. "So, are we here for terms of surrender?"

"This isn't a surrender," Cithrin said. "Your enemy's already conquered. We've come to bring the happy news and offer you our help as allies. You know who I am, yes?"

"I do," Dannien said grudgingly. "And I'm as surprised to see you on the other side of this as I was to see Wester. Figured he'd got his head folded by these priests, now maybe you have too."

"They're dead," Emming said. "We killed them all. *We* killed them. Prince Aster and the others here. Our nation has been through a nightmare. Nightmare!"

Cithrin hid her annoyance well. Not perfectly, but well. "It's true. The spider priests were an artifact of the dragons, built to make war between—"

"I know," Dannien said. "I read the letters. I've been getting updated from the council and your Magistra Isadau damn near since I went on this campaign."

"Then you know this wasn't Antea's fault," Cithrin said.

"That I do not," Dannien said. Cep Bailan wheezed and leaned forward, his head on the table. Dannien kicked him, and he sat back up. "So how's about you tell me the whole story of how Antea could slaughter thousands, burn villages to the ground, put free men and women in slave collars, and throw *babies* off *bridges*, and still have clean hands."

It wasn't the best reception they could have hoped for, but it wasn't the worst. Cithrin leaned forward, her chin high the way Kit and Cary had taught her once, years ago. She spoke clearly, cleanly, without flourishes or rhetoric. She laid out the story like she was a scout bringing a report. Every time Emming tried to insert himself, she cut him back.

Through Geder Palliako, the priests had taken root in Camnipol, subjugating it long before Antea's aggressions in the east. The priests had spread lies and fear, and those who'd stood against them had been killed or exiled. Camnipol had been as much under a conqueror's thumb as Nus or Inentai or Suddapal. The forces that had resisted it had been met with ruthless slaughter, not the least of them Dawson Kalliam, who had been the first to stand against Palliako and his priests.

But it was over now, the priests destroyed, Palliako dead, and Aster—the rightful king—returned to the throne. The way she told it, Dannien and his men had been in alliance with Aster even as they invaded his lands, only they hadn't known it.

It was a vast simplification, and like all of its sort, it erased what Cithrin wanted gone. Geder had been working with her as well at the end, but no call to point that up. Evil, false rulers were easier to understand. The children thrown to their deaths hadn't been ordered so by the priests. The slaves whipped and abused on Antean farms hadn't suffered because of Basrahip, but because of the instinctive cruelty of people in power over those they controlled. Her story ignored generations of Antean wars in the Free Cities, the suppressed revolt of Anninfort, the whole long history of battle and conquest, blood and fire and sword that was human history even without the dragons to spur them into it. To hear Cithrin speak, war had been created by Morade and hidden in a box that Geder opened. It felt to Marcus like a lie. But a necessary one.

"So that's it?" Dannien said when she finished. "Tyrant's dead, rightful king's on the throne, and now all's made right in the land? That how it's supposed to work?"

"You can come back to the city with us," Emming said. "Send your emissary or come yourself. You can see it's all true."

"What do I care if your tower won't stand up?" Dannien said. "I've been walking for a lot of weeks now with people who've lost homes and family. Who didn't do anything but be born to the wrong race. And if you think for half a minute there won't be a reckoning for what's happened, you're mad and stupid too. Even you, Magistra."

"There will be," Cithrin said. "There will be a reckoning. There has to be. But it will be in coin and land. Trades, treaties. Compensations. Not blood. There'll be no reckoning in blood. Here." She took the little golden cask from under her chair and put it on the table for Dannien to take. "It's letters to every farmhold in Antea. It frees every Timzinae slave, whether they were taken in the war or indentured before then. All of them."

"Really?" Dannien said. "Going to feed me my own food next? I can free anyone I see fit and put any farmers that disagree in with the pig slop. What do I need your word for to do it?"

"It's a gesture," Cithrin said.

Cep Bailan, recovered from the heat, grinned. He had an ugly grin. "I know another gesture. Wanna see it?"

"Fuck's sake, Karol," Marcus said. "They're trying to end this."

"So they don't get their own noses bloodied," Dannien snapped. "Let 'em see what losing a war feels like, and maybe they won't be so damned fast to start the next one."

"Didn't slow you down," Cithrin said, and the frustration and contempt in her voice were like a slap. Dannien stood up. This wasn't going well, and Cithrin wasn't done. "Elassae learned a lot about war and how much good it does, but you're still here turning aside the opportunity to stop it. Why should they learn something from being hurt? You didn't."

"Elassae didn't start this, and you don't get to tell me when to end it. If I want to kick Antea's balls until I'm bored with doing it, that's mine to choose. I'll go back to camp now," Dannien said, his voice low and dangerous. "And I'll confer with my men. If we decide to accept your *surrender*, I'll let you know. Meantime, you guarantee the safety of all the hostages. All of them. Tomorrow, maybe we'll talk."

Cithrin nodded crisply, Emming less so. When Aster spoke, it surprised them all.

"No," the boy said. "You take them. I won't make them go back to Camnipol. They need their parents, and their parents need them. I didn't bring them as hostages."

"Ah," Dannien said, suddenly on the wrong foot. "All right, then."

Aster rose to face the mercenary captain. His eyes were clear and his voice stronger than Marcus had expected it to be. He was maybe a third of Dannien's mass, and damned little of it muscle. He hardly looked older than the Timzinae children in the carts. Marcus felt his gut clench and had to fight the urge to push the boy king back, to put himself between Aster and the enemy soldiers.

"This is my fault," Aster said, "because this is my kingdom. When my father died, I was too young and too weak to rule. I should have protected Antea. And Elassae as well. I didn't, but I'm older now. And I'm stronger. If the council feels that there has to be more blood, say so. You can kill as many of us as you need to make it right. Give me a number, and I'll bring them to you. I only ask that you start with me."

Cep Bailan shrugged and put a hand on the hilt of his sword, but Dannien was the one who mattered, and he shifted his weight, confused.

Aster said, "I'm sorry I wasn't strong enough to stop this sooner."

Dannien pressed his lips together until they went white. "Well," he said. And then, "Shit."

The coffeehouse looked out over the Division toward the ruin that was the Kingspire. For that matter, the ruin that was Camnipol. The whole city—carts and carters, beggars and bakers, everyone from the highest lord to the mange-hatted dog sulking at the alley's mouth—had the half-stunned look of a man trying not to faint. But when Marcus glanced down into the chasm of the Division, past the bridges of wood and stone to the rope-and-chain contrivances below, he could see the ruins of other Camnipols. The city had been broken before, collapsed, and been rebuilt. This present stumble wasn't the worst it had seen.

Cithrin, sitting at his side, drank her coffee and sighed. Yardem, sitting across from them both, stuck to beer. Marcus only wanted water. Since he'd stopped wearing the sword, an acuity was returning to his tongue that left it easily overwhelmed. He hoped that stage would pass too.

The staff of the little house walked around them like they were lions, as likely to claw the help as ask for bread. He supposed that was fair. Cithrin bel Sarcour, who had humiliated and ultimately destroyed the beloved or despised Lord Regent. Who had thrown down the false goddess or else brought the world into a new age of lies. Who had saved Camnipol or else debased it before the Timzinae. Aster had made it clear that she was under the protection of the Severed Throne, but Marcus kept at least one guard with her wherever she went. It was a little odd to realize that, killer of kings and hero of Wodford and Gradis, he wasn't the most storied person at any table where he sat with Cithrin.

"Jorey Kalliam's called the disband," Marcus said.

"I heard," Cithrin replied. "But I don't think he's planning to throw a triumph."

"He should," Marcus said. "If people pretend there's a reason to celebrate, it won't be long before they convince themselves it's truth."

Cithrin's chuckle wasn't much more than a low noise in her throat. It sounded like satisfaction. Marcus found himself smiling as well. Yardem...well, he seemed amused, but it was hard to tell with him sometimes.

Most of the morning had been spent in what they were calling a business meeting. For the most part, it was the same thing that came after any battle. Relief and fear and anger and more relief coming out in stories and jokes and fights. And the weird melancholy that came at the end of a contract. He'd never understood why the end of a war should carry that sense of rootless mild sorrow, but it did. Something about endings, even when what had ended, was awful.

Yardem had told the story of Geder's death again. Marcus, his minimal description of killing Basrahip. Cithrin retold the attack against Inys, the death of Kitap rol Keshmet, the only good priest in the history of the world. Or maybe that was only Marcus being cynical. Hard to say. With every story, the sense that they'd actually come to a place of relative calm and safety grew. Yes, Dannien was leading the men south. Yes, the Timzinae slaves were freed, and their children—the ones who remained—were going back to Elassae. Yes, the spider priests were dead. And Geder Palliako with them. The bravery of Aster and their hopes for his reign. Jorey's return. Clara Kalliam's role in rallying the court. All the things that had happened and were happening and would come in the future, as certain as kittens in springtime. And then, like a child before sleep, Cithrin would ask a question or clarification that really meant "Tell me again," and Yardem would. And Marcus would listen. And at the end, they'd begin again.

Though there was one part that kept catching on his mind like a splinter too small to see. Invisible still, but present...

"So that's done," Marcus said, lifting his cup toward the serving boy to call for more water. "What's the plan from here?"

Cithrin smiled. "I'd thought that was obvious," she said.

"We won't get a better opportunity. I've already written the letters to Paerin and Komme. We have to open a branch in Camnipol."

"Of course you do," Marcus said.

"The only way Aster will ever be able to pay reparations to Elassae and Sarakal is war gold," Cithrin said. "And it'll help build trust back with Northcoast and Birancour once they're all part of the same system."

"A temple," Yardem said, "in every city she conquers."

Probably, he was joking.

Cithrin

The war was over.

The thought couldn't quite find its resting place in Cithrin's mind. It rattled through her like the last dried pea in a jar. The war was over. The priests were gone, the goddess killed, Morade's vengeance wiped from the world. Geder was dead. The war was over. No one was going to die at the edge of a sword today, or at least no one more than the usual. Her heart should have been all songs and celebrations, and perhaps it would have been, except she couldn't sleep.

Now that'd she'd come out of hiding, the world around her had changed. She took rooms at the moral successor of the inn Paerin Clark had brought her to her first time in Camnipol. A lifetime ago. The new place was on the ruins of the old, and the halls still stank of fresh wood and paint. The rooms were larger, and the one she'd taken had its own little balcony that looked down on the street, a table for her to work at, if she had any work, an anteroom where her guard could sleep and make sure no one slipped in during the night to slit her throat. The keeper was an elderly Dartinae woman whose glowing eyes reminded Cithrin of the sun behind clouds. The keeper's husband treated Cithrin and her guards like ambassadors from a powerful country, as perhaps they were. The morning sun greeted Cithrin with coffee and eggs, the night with wine and salt crackers. And more wine after that, without any hesitation or hint of disapproval. Despite all that, Cithrin felt like a six-legged pony trotted out for the amusement of the crowd.

The city and the kingdom—and perhaps the world— seemed in a moment of stillness, like the pause between breaths. They were between what had happened before and what would come next, and she was that uncertainty made flesh. Cithrin bel Sarcour, once the deadly enemy of Antea, and now confidant of Prince Aster and Clara Kalliam, her son Jorey. She was welcomed in the imperial court because Aster insisted on it, and because everyone there was shaken and frightened and ready for the world to be something different than it had been. So long as Cithrin held her head at the best angle, so long as she walked with authority and spoke with confidence, she would be assumed to have power. And so perhaps she did.

She traveled under guard always. Geder had stripped the court of any dissent or disloyalty. If he'd survived the plan, they might have been able to use that to steer the court. Now there would be some who still believed in his cause, since he was no longer there to disavow it. People would still call the Timzinae roaches, as they had before the priests had come. They would still look down upon them, as the Yemmu disdained the Tralgu; the Cinnae, the Kurtadam; everyone everywhere, the Drowned. The war was over, but humanity was still itself. The hatred might last forever. The injustice. The petty cruelty and moral blindness.

There was no call to believe that wars would not come again, and for reasons as obscure or justified, as they had without Morade's spiders. Blood and innocent lives were still the currency of empires, as they had been in the absence of the priests.

But the spiders wouldn't spread, and Cithrin was not yet done.

During the day, she made herself present at court and among the merchant class of Camnipol. At night, she sat in her room and drank until she fell into a stupor not so unlike sleep. Or walked the night-black streets in the center of a protecting square of swordsmen. Or sat in the taproom, beer in one hand, and watched the players there put on another version of *The Butcher's Daughter* with the part of PennyPenny played by a sweet-faced Jasuru who seemed all too happy to mock his own race.

Her players—Cary and Sandr and Mikel, Charlit Soon and Lak—were gone. As gone as Kit. As gone as Smit. As gone as Pyk Usterhall and Opal. They'd left without saying goodbye to her, leaving only a note saying that Camnipol was too rich in sorrow for them anymore. That their tour had begun in tragedy, and that they would follow it until there was a comedy again. Or a romance. Or an adventure that they could bring themselves to smile at. Cithrin didn't blame them, but she felt their absence like a wound on some part of her that she could touch.

And so when Wester had said he was leaving as well, it had been doubly hard.

He'd brought his bad news in the afternoon. The high Antean summer was announcing its end with bright mornings and hard rains. Cithrin, on her way back from an informal gathering with Clara Kalliam and a nobleman named Curtin Issandrian, had paused in a baker's shop while the clouds dropped a small river onto the city. The roar of the water would have been frightening if the men and women of the city hadn't shrugged it off quite so calmly. Along with the lemon tea and the plate of flaky butter bread, Cithrin took comfort in the way the baker and her son treated the downpour as an inconvenience. She sat at the front, suffering a little mist for the pleasure of watching the streets flow like little streams, the filth and wreckage that came from humanity simply going through its day being washed away. Marcus, sitting across from her, had cleared his throat in a way that meant something.

"I've sent for Enen," he said. "She's a solid lead, been with us since Porte Oliva. She's bringing a full company of guard with her. As long as you're here, you'll want watching, and I don't recommend hiring local talent. Too many people in this city have been asleep for too long. Can't trust they'll all wake up just because it's morning."

"You think we need more guards?" she'd said, but there had been a tightness in her chest even then.

"Different's more the issue," he said. "There's some things Yardem and I need to take care of."

As the baker had made little of the rain, Marcus said the words like they only meant going off to visit an aunt or having a contract signed. She surrendered to understanding, and must have reacted, because Marcus took her hand.

"Inys?" she said.

"Among others," Marcus said. "Just some things that want attention."

A hundred questions had swirled through her, each clamoring to be the one that passed her lips first: *How can you track a dragon? Do you think the danger from him's real? What if Camnipol rises again in revenge for Geder and the Kingspire and the end of the war? What if Elassae changes its mind and marches back in force?* Her world was a labyrinth of uncertainties, contingencies and barely restrained chaos. Which, in fairness, it had always been.

"Will you be coming back?" she asked. She cared about all the information, but this was the only question that seemed critical.

Marcus's smile was as much an answer as his words. "Hope to, but you know how the world is."

"I do," she said. He'd nodded, and that was the last they'd spoken. When they got back to the inn, Yardem had horses ready for the two of them. The Tralgu had folded her in a vast, warm embrace, his chin resting on top of her head while she wept a little, and then they were gone.

She'd spent the evening on the roof of the inn, sitting on a stool and watching the carts hauling debris away from the royal quarter in the north to drop into the Division. The sun, setting behind her, had lit the high, ornate clouds in gold and orange. And then grey. She'd drunk a full bottle of wine by herself on that roof and had come back down steady as a stone.

And so she was a little drunk and a little maudlin three days later when, without warning, Magistra Isadau arrived.

Cithrin caught sight of her from the balcony as Isadau and her guards walked toward the inn from the public stables. She wore a dress the color of gold with a lacework shawl blacker than her scales, but no armor that Cithrin could see. Her guards were Firstblood men and Yemmu women, all in mail, with swords and axes at their sides, and the glowering expressions of people who'd taken up that kind of work because they enjoyed hurting people. Even in the relative darkness of the summer twilight, a crowd lingered at the margin of the group. A Timzinae woman walking in Camnipol. A sign that, welcome or not, change had come. The mix of pride and joy and apprehension was not made simpler by the dead bottles of wine at Cithrin's feet.

The urge to wave and call and maybe crawl out the window and slide down the tiled roof to where she could lower herself down to the courtyard fought with the sense that she should behave as if she were already the voice of the Medean bank in Camnipol. Which meant clearing away the bottles and skins and chewing a handful of mint fairly quickly. She wiped away the tears she'd been crying, threw the evidence of her dissolution into a sack under her bed, and washed her hands and feet before the scratch came at the door.

"Yes?" Cithrin said, her heart racing.

"It's a Magistra Isadau," the guard's voice said.

And then Isadau's. "I've come to speak with you about... about the peace, I suppose."

Cithrin opened the door. The older woman stood there like a vision from a dream. Her smile was calm and amused, her hands folded before her. Only the flickering of the nictitating membranes in her eyes, opening and closing without ever blocking her gaze, gave any sign of the strength of Isadau's emotions. For a moment, Cithrin was frozen, filled with the powerful and irrational fear that anger was shaking the Timzinae woman. That by saving Camnipol from the armies of Elassae, Cithrin had lost her respect.

And then Isadau stepped into the room and opened her arms. Cithrin fell into her the way she imagined a sister might. Isadau smelled of earthy perfume and sweat and the open air.

"I've missed you," Isadau said.

"You too," Cithrin said.

Cithrin led her to the little table and sat with her, their two hands touching like a priest offering comfort to a mourner.

"How are things in Suddapal?" Cithrin asked.

Isadau's laugh was low and rueful. "Complicated. Very complicated. But improving. After Kiaria, the fighting all through Elassae was vicious. It was only the Anteans at first, but after they'd been driven back, there was more. The occupation undid some of things that kept the five cities playing nicely with each other. In the last year, I've been brokering armistice agreements between the oligarchs as much as helping with the war against Antea."

"Ah," Cithrin said, and her mind caught at the fact. Found a toehold. "Is that why they had Dannien leading the army and not a Timzinae?"

"Yes," Isadau said. "The mercenary was the compromise everyone hated least. And he was good, which was a blessing. He sent word of his victory along with the children. The ones who survived."

"I'm so sorry," Cithrin said. "How bad was it?"

Isadau's smile was wistful. "Jurin lost one of his sons in the fighting. Kani is fine, though our mother is gone. She left the world last winter. It wasn't violent, but I think it was the war. Seeing her world tear itself apart was an injury, if not a physical one. War always has more casualties than we see. All the things that we might have done instead are lost as well."

"Could have made a glorious world with what we spent on this one. Or at least a few decent roads," Cithrin said. She felt as though she were speaking in Wester's voice, and the pang of loss came again. "Wait. Salan? Is he...?"

"Wounded in the battle that broke the Antean army. It went septic, but it didn't carry him off. He still has fevers sometimes, and the cunning man says he will have for the rest of his life."

"That's terrible," Cithrin said.

"Only give him so much sympathy. He's been known to play the crippled patriot more than once for the joy of the role. The way he's living now, he's more likely to die from an angry lover than an old wound."

"Still," Cithrin said, her hands rising to her throat. She undid the necklace there, pulled the pendant of the little bird from her chest, and held it out for Isadau to take. The older woman looked at it, shifting the necklace in her hand so that it caught the light. "He wanted me to keep it until the war was over."

"And it is," Isadau said, and tucked the bird away, "isn't it?"

Cithrin smiled and wiped her eyes with the back of her hand. Isadau's frown was so slight it barely seemed to exist. Cithrin still felt it like a thorn.

"How are you?" Isadau asked.

"I'm fine," Cithrin said, lightly. And then, "I'm not fine. I don't know how I am. Everything I had, everything I thought or felt, was bent toward getting here. All the plans brought me here, except the ones about how to handle Geder afterward, and those don't matter anymore."

"You've won."

"I have, but I now that I see it, I don't understand what victory is at all. Somehow, I thought it would mean an ending. That we'd cut away Morade's priests and all they'd done, we'd stop the armies and the fighting, and then...I don't know. It would be over. We'd all be together and everyone would be all right. Only that isn't how it works, is it?"

"It's not," Isadau said. "There's only one utter ending for each of us, and it isn't one we reach toward. Until then, it's the next change, and the next change, and the next. And profound change, even when it's the one you prayed for, is displacing."

"I didn't think I'd have to mourn my victories."

"And now you know something you didn't."

Out in the street, a dog barked in excitement and a woman shouted back in anger. In the distance, a murmur of thunder. Cithrin rubbed her hand across the table, feeling the grain of the wood, listening to the sound of her own skin hushing. They let the moment sit with them quietly like a third person until, gently and politely, it left.

"Have you thought about where you want to be next?" Isadau asked.

"I'm not sure. We need to open a branch here, and I'm either the perfect person to do it or absolutely the wrong one, and I'm not sure yet how to tell which. And then there's Porte Oliva. I know Birancour wasn't part of the bank's long-term plan, but my branch there made money. With the damage to the city, there are going to be opportunities."

"And I think you may not technically have finished your apprenticeship," Isadau said.

"You must be joking."

"I am, and I'm not," Isadau said. "I don't think anyone can argue that you're inexperienced at this point, but there are some advantages that another decade of life might offer. A shared branch, for instance. Chana Medean is drawing up proposals."

"Is she?"

"Between us? I think Komme would be willing to make accommodations with you just from fear you'd start your own competing company. You have a strong position. You should think about where you would be happy."

Cithrin blinked. *Where I would be happy.* It was like a language she didn't know.

"I've come for two reasons," Isadau said. "There's an ambassador coming from Elassae as soon as the coronation's done. The common wisdom has it that the bank is the ideal intermediary for forging a real treaty. We're respected on both sides, we're seen as neutral, though not by everyone, and the war gold in the west has become something of a fashion. They see promise in it. I've been asked by my country to confer with you and bring back anything that would be useful to them."

"Do they really think you will?"

"They aren't wrong," Isadau said. "I love my people, and I will go a very long way to find justice for them."

"Sorry," Cithrin said. "That's fair."

"The other reason is more complex, but not unrelated. Something strange has happened with the war gold."

Cithrin felt herself shift forward on her chair. A glimmer in Isadau's eyes said the other woman had noticed. "What is it?"

"The merchant guilds in Stollbourne have started valuing debt in Carse above debt from Herez. They're calling it a confidence discount."

"What?"

"A cargo valued at fiftyweight of gold," Isadau said, "is being paid with forty-eight if the notes are against King Tracian's debt. The full fifty if it's from the Herez contract."

Cithrin sat back. "But it's the same gold. Or not-gold. War gold. Why would—"

"Herez is relaxing tariffs on its blue-water trade. Komme isn't certain yet if Stollbourne's decision is an attempt to keep Northcoast's trade where it is, or to call Herez's letters into question. Either way, a weight of gold isn't a weight of gold any longer, depending on who it belongs to."

"Well," Cithrin said. "That's...interesting."

"Komme is thinking of how to stop it, but—"

"No," Cithrin said. "No, wait. We should look at that first. There may be an opportunity in there. What happens, do you think, when you trade money for money?"

"I'm not sure I even understand the question."

"I'm not either," Cithrin said. "Let's talk this through..."

Cithrin had dinner brought up to them after the first hour passed. Roasted chicken with lemon and rosemary, underripe apples in honey and spice. A bottle of wine that for once she didn't crave particularly. They talked about money and wealth and value, and how each term meant a different, if related, thing. How the war gold could disconnect them, or make the relationships more flexible. What the bank could accomplish, and what it risked by trying.

When, near midnight, Isadau pled exhaustion, Cithrin walked her to her rooms. Her mind felt like morning light and cool water, and she was sure she wouldn't sleep. But when she did lie down on her bed, the breeze of the Antean night slipping in at the window like a cat, she found her body relaxed and the pillow comfortable. She played scenario after scenario out in her mind: what would happen if the bank declared that debt couldn't be transferred between nations; what would happen if it could only be traded at values they set; at values the merchants themselves set; if the bank charged one on the hundred for making the transfer; if the crown did.

As the versions became less and less real, the half logic of dreams spinning out along lines of debt and credit, the phrase came back, as clear as if it had been spoken. And, oddly, it came back in Marcus Wester's voice, not Isadau's.

Where would you be happy?

It isn't where, she thought. *Here or in Porte Oliva or Carse. I'll be happy. Or else I won't. Even when I'm miserable, I'll be doing the work I'm best at. That's* better *than happiness, and there's not one person in a thousand who can claim it.*

I'll be fine.

She smiled before she slept.

Clara

On the first day of King Aster's coronation ceremony, they burned an empty pyre.

It wasn't something done as part of the ceremony proper. There was precedent for it when someone had died in a way that their body couldn't be found or brought back for the family, so it was known generally as a sailor's pyre, but it wasn't for seamen this time. In an abundance of tact, no one said outright whose absent body the fires consecrated. *Those who have fallen in defense of the empire* was the phrase most often used. It might have meant the soldiers who'd died in Asterilhold and Sarakal, Elassae and the Free Cities and Birancour. It might have meant the bodies left unburied in the snowdrifts and ice west of Bellin or the governors and protectors of Nus and Inentai and Suddapal, lost now in the uprisings there.

To Clara, it meant the men who'd died the day the Kingspire broke. Vicarian, the other priests, and Lord Regent Geder Palliako.

Lehrer Palliako's presence at the burning made the point without anyone's having to speak. Aster was there too, his eyes red from tears or smoke. Clara sat with Jorey and Barriath, present as the mother of her sons. Her remaining sons. Sabiha and Lady Skestinin sat with her as well, and all of them wept, though not for Geder. And in the court, the grey

rags of mourning were tied around the arms and throats of
the representatives of all the great houses. But the sleeves
beneath the armbands were green, the cloths that people
used to dab away their tears had leaf-shaped embroidery,
and no one had the unutterably poor taste to wear ossuary
on their jackets. The currents of the court might not have
found their channel yet, but if fashion was anything to judge
from, Geder Palliako had fallen from grace with history.

Clara wished in her heart that she could feel some pang of
sympathy for him. Already, he was being painted in the stories and gossip of the court as at best an incompetent and at
worst a traitor. The man who'd delivered the nation to dark
wizards and foolish wars. The worst steward the Severed
Throne had suffered since Lord Sellandin, eight generations
back, and likely worse than he'd been.

A priest in white robes chanted in the smoke of the pyre,
calling on the traditional cult gods of Antea. After the rite
was done, the fire under the empty structure still burning,
Clara and the others murmured their respects and retired to
a wide rose garden for a light meal. The blooms were long
since gone from the bushes, of course, but the leaves were
bright and lush and the thorns seemed somehow appropriate.

Clara walked confidently among the groups, aware that
she was being observed. The coronation would take almost
a week to trace its arc from its funereal beginning through
the formal ascension of Aster to his father's throne and then
back down to celebrations and feasts. It wasn't the most
important series of court events of the year so much as of
the generation. Alliances made and broken here would set
the course of the empire for decades to come. Certainly for
more then her own lifetime. Clara was curious to see which
groups would be most open to her, which cool and polite,
which unwelcoming.

Her expectation was that her association with the army and the bankers, the return from exile of Barriath, and the suspicion—well founded, it was true—that she'd somehow carried on Dawson's vendetta against the spider priests after his failure would give her the whiff of brimstone that would keep all but the most adventurous from her company. She was prepared to be politely shunned.

She could hardly have been more mistaken.

"Is it true, my lady," Lord Emming said, "this nonsense that Lord Issandrian's spouting about the farmer's council?"

Curtin Issandrian's nod to her was a thing of subtle gratitude. As if she alone had engineered his return to polite society after the joint catastrophes of Feldin Maas's conspiracy with Asterilhold and Geder's rise to power.

"Excuse me, Lord Emming," she said. "Which nonsense precisely?"

"Emming here was arguing that the farmers would have released the Timzinae slaves out of loyalty to the crown," Issandrian said.

"We can't begin to lower the dignity of the throne," Emming said. "Especially now. Farmers? Your good husband was against it, I think."

My good husband, Clara thought. God, how strange the world could be. Geder had become a lord of darkness, and Dawson's name resurrected as a champion of virtue. How little any of it had to do with the truth.

"I'm surprised that you feel loyal servants of the crown lack dignity," Clara said, smiling. "With all that's happened, I think it's clear that loyalty to the Severed Throne is the highest of virtues."

Emming's smile widened. His gaze flickered about as if to see who might have heard her words. "Well said, Lady Kalliam. Very well said."

She nodded to Issandrian and then to Emming, then stepped away, her heart strangely light. Her opinion was being sought by the counselors of the throne, and in public? She paused for a cup of white wine and a bit of twice-baked bread with melted cheese on it. She sat alone on a stone bench that overlooked the milling group as she ate.

Jorey and Sabiha stood at the end of the garden, arm in arm, speaking with a group their own age. She had to remember not to think of them as children. All were adults now, married and with children of their own. Jorey had the too-thin look of a man still recovering from desperate illness, but his smile was warm, and when he glanced at Sabiha, it was with a tenderness that Clara could only see as a good omen. Barriath was there too, wearing a uniform of naval cut, though without any markings to show his rank or position. He stood with Canl Daskellin, whose hair had gone entirely white since King Simeon's death. They were smiling, and if she was reading Barriath's hand gestures rightly, he was telling the story of how he and his impromptu pirate navy had bested Lord Skestinin. Lord Skestinin, who even now was making his way back from Northcoast, no longer an honored guest of King Tracian. Or, more accurately, of the Medean bank.

Everyone, it seemed, was anxious now to have been against Geder Palliako all along. Or at least to appear to have been. She expected that over the course of the season, the tales of who had been conspiring to carry Dawson Kalliam's legacy would spread and elaborate. It would be difficult to argue her away from the center of the story, though. Her and her boys. Her fallen house. Her husband. That little of it was true and what was hadn't seemed at all as clean and clear at the time only meant it was history, she supposed. Playing the loyal traitor would be a fashion for a year or two, until the next thing came along. Or the people who despite everything still believed in the spider goddess felt safe enough to show themselves again.

Barriath laughed, shook Daskellin's hand, and made his way over to her. Clara lifted a hand to him, and he kissed it as he sat at her side. His cheeks were flushed and his eyes bright.

"You've had some news," she said.

"A bit," Barriath said. "Just a bit."

Barriath grinned at her, barely able to control himself but enjoying the chance to tease her curiosity. Clara lifted her brows and batted her eyelashes, a parody of a young coquette, and her son laughed. "Daskellin's been in with Aster and Mecelli these last few days. Part of the coronation's going to be a formal amnesty."

"I'd hope so," Clara said. "If there wasn't an amnesty, half the men here would be honor-bound to kill you."

"Not for me. For Father. This time next week, I'll be Baron of Osterling Fells."

Clara felt the air go out of her lungs. She put down the wine. "Barriath. That's…that's…" *Wonderful. Absurd. Utterly confusing.*

"We'll have the holding by winter," he said, "and the mansion here in the city. You won't have to stay in that tiny place of Skestinin's."

"Or a boardinghouse," Clara said, and her son laughed as if it were a joke. As if that weren't something she'd done. A woman she had been. He went on, and she listened with half an ear. With the barony restored, Jorey would be expected to go to the priesthood, but with a military career already behind him and all the local cults in disarray after the disaster of the Righteous Servant, it seemed more likely he'd retire from service. At least until the next war came.

It was such exceptionally good news that Clara couldn't understand why it landed on her heart with such weight. Her family restored. Her status regained. Her sons in places of honor and respect in the court. Her remaining sons. Her sons besides Vicarian.

You'll become a joke in the court.... Can you imagine what that little girl's life will be like if the name she took from you comes to carry the reputation for fucking the servants?

"Ah," she said, the implications of Barriath's news unfolding in her mind like a poisonous bloom.

Barriath's brows knit, but only a little. "Ah?"

"Remembered something," Clara said, putting a hand on his shoulder. "Nothing you need be concerned about."

He rose and kissed her head, a gesture more informal than the gathering, but almost certainly it would be overlooked. "It's a bad day for our enemies," Barriath said.

"It is," she said. *For our enemies, and for others.*

The sorrow and regret and deathly dread lay in her breast like a dead thing. Vicarian had been spider-ridden, but he hadn't been wrong. Her dignity wasn't only hers any longer. And Vincen...

She found quite suddenly that the company of the court was more than she could suffer. It wasn't the others. They walked and ate and gossiped and fought just as they always had. It was only that she couldn't do it. Not now.

Beside the garden, a thin artificial creek ran along its sculpted bed. Clara walked its murmuring length, pretending to admire the stonework and the statuary. She took out her pipe and filled it with leaf, struck it alight. The smoke tasted good. Familiar, at least. She would always have tobacco among her little pleasures.

The stream ended in a narrow grotto with benches around

a rough stone god of some sort with several arms and two faces on his head. She didn't know what it was meant to represent or who might have worshipped so odd and awkward a figure. She'd meant to sit alone for a time and gather herself there, but when she reached it, the benches were not empty.

Lehrer Palliako sat hunched forward, his elbows resting on his knees. The white-salt tracks of dried tears striped his cheeks, but his eyes were dry now. Dry and fixed and empty. Clara thought of retreat, stepping back unnoticed to give the man room for his grief. Before she could, he spoke.

"He was a good boy," Lehrer said. "They don't say it now, but he was a good boy. Smart. The books I have that he translated? There are some that don't exist anywhere else in the world except for him. I never told him how proud I was."

Clara came forward and sat at the man's side. "Losing a child," she said.

"Fuck losing a child. People lose children all the time," Lehrer said. "I know that sounds small of me, but it's true. People have lost their babies all through history. Fevers and fights and stupid accidents. No one's ever lost *my* boy before. No one will again. It's not the same."

"It never is."

"Never is," he echoed. "Never."

Clara took his hand, and for a moment, it was like holding a dead thing. Then his fingers twitched. How odd, she thought, that everyone, whatever they were, whatever wounds they left on the world, had someone who would mourn them. Someone who loved them and felt their loss.

"He died a hero," Lehrer said. "Died saving the throne. Not that you'll hear any of them say it."

"I know," Clara said. "It isn't fair." *And,* she didn't add, *I don't know what would be. I'm not even sure that fairness is something we need more than mercy. Or forgiveness. Or freedom from the past.*

Lehrer turned to look at her now. The whites of his eyes were marbled with red, and he swayed like a drunkard or a man collapsing from fatigue.

"I'd kill every damned one of them if it would bring my boy back," he said. "Even you." For a moment, she saw his son in him. She squeezed his fingers gently.

"I know," she said.

Winning carried its own costs. She saw that now. Even when all went well, there were consequences. She could celebrate their success and still regret the price of it. To her, and to Vincen.

She dressed well to do the thing, as if her clothing were a kind of armor of the heart. As if the wound would come from outside her. She chose a cream dress in a formal cut they called *old empire*, though in truth it was hardly more than a generation old. It had been tailored to her new body, and it seemed too slight until the servant girl fastened the stays. Then she had her hair plaited into an ornate braid that pulled back and showed the grey at her temples. Her face had been roughened by the wind and the cold and the sun, by a season spent as a soldier. She sent the girl away and applied her powder and rouge herself. War paint for her final battle. The one she could only lose.

She ended by putting on jewelry. Bracelets and a ribbon choker. Not too much. She wanted elegance. Formality. She wanted to make a mask of herself that would carry her through doing what had to be done. Not for her sake, but for the family's. For the honor and status that had been restored to them. For fear of being a stupid old woman made foolish by an inappropriate lover. She turned away before tears could ruin the paint.

If it was to be done, better it should be done quickly. No wound was ever made less painful by going slowly.

She met him in the little drawing room, where she sat on the divan while he stood. His hair looked like raw honey in the light. His expression held the mixture of amusement and affection that had come to fill her world like the scent of flowers in springtime. She ached already with what she had to do.

"You called for me, Lady?" he said. Formal where they might be overheard. She felt herself drinking in the syllables. She would not be hearing his voice again after tonight.

"I did," she said, heavy as lead weights. "Close the door."

"If you like."

She rose. She hadn't meant to. In her mind, she'd conducted the whole bloody affair from her seat with the cold dignity of a queen, but here she was. Up and pacing the back of the room. Worrying her hands until the knuckles ached.

"What's the matter, love?" he asked softly, and she coughed out something like a laugh. Love *was* the matter.

"Vincen Coe," she said. "I have—"

Oh, God *damn* it. A sob choked her. She swallowed it back.

"I have to release you from service. You can go. Tonight. And if any of the things you've ever said to me were true, I will not hear from you again."

He was silent and still. She chanced a look at him, unsure what to expect. Rage, surprise, heartbreak to echo her own. The smile was gone from the corners of his mouth, but nothing else had changed. She knew better than to go on, but she did it anyway.

"My son is going to be given his father's title, you see?

We've...we've returned to the good grace of the court, and I can't...We will be found out, you and I. If we haven't been already."

"I see. And would that be so bad?" he said. "You've done other scandalous things, if I recall."

"It's not about me," she said. "I have a granddaughter who carries my name. You don't know how cruel the court can be, especially to a girl. If I'm known for taking a lover—"

"Below your dignity?" The words were spoken gently, and still they cut.

"A lover who is half my age, I'll look a fool. And no, I don't care for my own sake. If it was only me, I'd take you and retire to the holding and let them all say whatever they pleased to say, king and court and my sons besides. But it's *not* only me. I have Annalise to think of."

Vincen nodded slowly, a deep furrow marking his brow. "I'll go if it's your choice. I'll make no trouble, but...why do you want your granddaughter to live her life with less courage than yours?"

Clara opened her mouth.

Closed it again.

Something in her heart shifted, slipped away. *You'll become a joke in the court.* Well, and she had been. A joke and an embarrassment. A curiosity. A noblewoman who chased after her boy's army like a nurse chasing a wandering child. She'd been the kind of woman polite society turned away from. And she'd saved her family. Her kingdom. She'd ordered men killed before her eyes and engineered the slaughter of a general. She'd been carried by a dragon. Who she chose to share her bed with was almost literally the least interesting thing about her.

She took one slow, shuddering breath. Then another. Something uncurled in her. They stood in silence for a moment, and then, to her own astonishment, she chuckled. It was a low sound, earthy and rich. Vincen tried a smile, and watching him find it was a pure pleasure.

"Are you dressed for an occasion?" Vincen asked, all trace of her attempt to break off their affair gone from his voice.

"No," she said.

"So... your evening's open?"

"Why? Are you looking to take advantage of my fragile emotional state?" she asked, wiping back her tears.

"Only if you will it, my lady," the huntsman said with a sincerity that asked whether he was welcome.

She was shaking, not a great deal, but noticeably. It was like the feeling of looking over a precipice until the dizziness came, and then—at the last instant—stepping back. After a long moment, she rose, walked to the door, impressing herself with the steadiness of her stride, and called for the house girl.

"Do you need something?" Vincen asked.

"I'm going to start with a glass of wine and a pipe while you tell me of your day," she said. "We'll see whether anything comes from that."

"And if the girl spreads rumors that we're meeting in private?"

"Well," Clara said, her head still spinning, but less. Much less. "Then I suppose she does."

Epilogue

The Last Apostate

In Herez, the summer rose and then broke as it always did. The vineyards in the low, rolling hills of the north gave their season's crop of thick, black grapes, and the Kurtadam women walked with the fur around their feet stained red for a week. In Daun, seat of the kingdom, ambassadors came and went. Couriers and cunning men and merchant caravans as well. As week by week it became clear that the war which had lit two-thirds of the world on fire had burned itself to ash and embers without coming to Herez, King Cyrian became more expansive. A taproom story made the rounds that he'd had to be talked out of a plan to announce his personal responsibility for keeping Herez above the fray, but that might have only been a story. It was foolish enough that the people who heard it wanted to believe it true. There were other rumors that were more plausible, if less entertaining.

The pirate fleet that Callon Cane had led to occupy the bays and smugglers' coves of Northcoast had fallen into mutiny when Cane was discovered to be an agent of Antea. Or else it was regrouping now with patronage from Narinisle. Or Cane had been the secret name of a cabal of Tralgu and had been found out. The truth that mattered was only that some of the pirates were coming back to their old waters in Cabral, but not so many as had been there before.

Porte Oliva remained under the yoke of Antea, but the signs were clear. With the fall of the regent, the empire's focus on conquest had waned. The wisest bettors had it that Birancour would reclaim the port by spring, though whether it would pay Antea a ransom for it or extract payments from the Severed Throne in exchange for peace wasn't at all clear. The Free Cities, led by Maccia, were threatening to band together against raiders crossing the Inner Sea from Lyoneia's northern coast.

The high princess of Princip C'Annaldé had taken a Jasuru lover because the chances of an embarrassing pregnancy between the races was so small, but she hadn't been seen in weeks, so maybe it wasn't so unlikely as she'd thought. The sailmakers' guild had come to an agreement with King Sephan of Cabral. In the next year, they would see the blue-water trade to Far Syramys out of the ports west of Daun triple. At least. Maybe more, if the treacherous strategies of Stollbourne could be countered...

Which, so far as Kitap rol Keshmet—once known as Master Kit, but now going by Duvit Koke—was concerned, showed as clear as water that the business of the world was once again flowing between its proper banks. He sat at a little tin mirror, brushing paint into the wrinkles at the corners of his eyes while Sandr and Mikel threw the last stitches on the new costume. It was the first time Kit had played Orcus the Demon King in years. Sandr was already dressed as Allaren Mankiller. The sharp reports of hammers assembling their temporary stage rang in from the yard, but the horses in the stalls ignored the players and the noise magnificently.

"Can't see why it would cost so much to keep the stage," Sandr said, not for the first time.

"Far Syramys is a long way," Cary said from the loft

where she was fitting Charlit Soon for her new gown. That Sandr wasn't craning his neck in hopes of catching a glimpse of the girl's bare flesh was a good sign. With luck, those two had burned themselves out of each other.

"I know," Sandr said.

"It's why they don't call it Near Syramys," Mikel said.

"They don't call it Far Syramys once you get there," Sandr said. "That would be stupid. Distant shores aren't still distant when you're standing on them."

Mikel put on the empty, wondering smile he used to tease Sandr. "You think they call this Far Herez over there?"

"I don't know what they call it," Sandr said. "We can ask once we get there, the same time we try to find a decent stage to replace the perfectly good one Lak's banging on out there."

"I have heard many tales of the lands across the ocean sea," Kit said. "I've heard the Raushadam walk on riverbeds, carried down by the stony weight of their skins, and that the Haunadam have wings like bats and butterflies. That the Tralgu who live there have fox ears, and the Southlings speak in languages no one but they can comprehend. There are even tales of a great hive where bees make gold from the flowers instead of honey."

"Cary!" Sandr called. "He's monologuing again!"

"It's your fault," she shouted back. "You started him on it."

"But among all the wonders," Kit said, ignoring them, "spread through even the most exotic and dream-soaked of lands, I'm fairly certain they'll have trees."

"I'm not saying they don't," Sandr said. "I just..."

"I believe the cost of putting it in the hold for the journey would be four times what it will cost to build a new one when we're there."

The hammering stopped, and Kit heard Hornet's voice, speaking to someone.

"It floats, you know," Sandr said. "All we'd need to do is tie a rope to it and drag it along behind. We wouldn't need space in the hold."

"Fair certain it doesn't work that way," Mikel said as a Tralgu man stepped out of the yard and into the stables. Kit turned, looked up into the wide, deceptively gentle eyes looking back at him. Kit's gut went tight. Sandr and Mikel were silent. Even the horses seemed to sense that something ominous had happened.

"Kit," Yardem Hane said as Marcus Wester came in at his side. The sickly green hilt rose over the captain's shoulder, ready to be drawn. Kit heard Cary's alarmed yelp and the clatter as she and Charlit Soon clambered down the ladder.

"Yardem. Marcus," he said. "I hadn't expected to see either of you again."

"Picked up on that," Marcus said.

Kit put down his brush with a click. "I think it might be best if the company gave us a moment in private."

"Not going to happen," Cary said, stepping between Kit and the two swordsmen. The others moved forward too, slow as the Drowned. Yardem flicked a jingling ear.

Kit put a hand on Cary's shoulder. "Please," he said.

The moment balanced on the edge of a blade. He felt Cary deflate under his palm. She walked forward, making her way between Marcus and Yardem without looking back. Charlit Soon followed her, and then the others together. When they were alone with only the horses, Yardem leaned against the wall. Marcus sat on Sandr's abandoned stool.

"Are you still working for the bank?" Kit asked with a casualness he didn't feel.

"Hard to say, exactly," Marcus said. "Now that we've hunted you down, I think the next thing's Inys. There's been talk coming up from Lyoneia of him. Sightings. Something about a tower rising up out of the sea. But it's going to mean going south until it starts getting cold again, and by the time we get there..."

"Dragon hunting. What a romantic and adventurous life you lead, Captain."

Marcus chuckled, recognizing the humor. He leaned back on the stool. "I don't do any of this because I want to, Kit. I do it because it needs to get done."

It didn't sound like a threat, though Kit knew it could be interpreted that way. Whatever meaning the captain intended, Kit knew he believed it to be true. Whatever happened between them now, it would only be from necessity. There was some comfort in that.

"May I ask how you knew I was alive? What did I do wrong?"

"Hm? Oh, that. You made it a theater piece. A grand sacrifice with everyone looking on, right to the moment that Cary pulled their eyes off you. You talked about doing more or less the same thing in the transformation scene in...ah damn it."

"*The Tragedy of Crellia and Somon,*" Yardem said.

"Yeah, that one," Marcus agreed. "Shifting attention to the far side of the stage while you switch out the actor for the puppet? Only this time, I figure it was more hiding behind a rock or some such."

"I had a servant's robe too, under my own," Kit said. "The tower's collapse complicated things. In the first version, I was going to cast myself into the Division."

"That would have been good too," Marcus said.

They were silent. There was no more hammering from the yard. Kit imagined the troupe standing together, waiting to see how this ended. Whether they would need to cast a new Orcus. *As long as I am in the world, the danger is as well.* He'd written the line for its single performance, and he'd believed it then as well. Only there had seemed a way out. A chance to see a bit more of the humanity. Taste a few new dishes, hear a few more songs, perform on stages he had not yet tried. Kit didn't think it had been cowardice on his part, though perhaps the fear of death had been part of it.

At least, he thought, *I can have a bit of dignity now.*

"Did you tell Cithrin?" he asked.

"That you'd fooled her? No. Wasn't sure it was truth until we tracked you all down, after all. And now that we've found you..." Marcus shrugged. "I don't know. What would the advantage be for anyone? Girl's got enough on her plate as it stands, trying to remake all of civilization or whatever it is she does."

"Thank you," Kit said. "I would rather she remember me as I appeared, rather than as I was."

"That's not just you," Marcus said. He rose, taking the poisoned sword off his shoulder. The scabbard shone green as a beetle's shell even in the dim light. The nearest of the horses blew out her breath as if she sensed something malign without knowing quite what it was. Marcus held it out. "If you want my advice, keep this under the beds when you aren't sleeping. Turns out the other thing it's useful for is keeping the lice down. All the time I carried it, never had so much as a nit. That's the only thing I'm going to miss about the damned thing."

Kit reached out, confused but understanding in a general

sense what seemed expected of him. Then he took the sword, and Marcus nodded.

"I don't believe I understand," Kit said, holding the blade. "I thought you'd come to finish me."

"Can't see it's come to that, yet." Marcus said. "Understand the confusion, though. I did offer to kill you once, didn't I?"

"You did," Kit said. "And I appreciated it at the time."

"Offer still stands," Marcus said. "If once this Inys thing's done, I start hearing about some actor who's turned Far Syramys into his own massive stage for the honor of the god of taproom dramas or some such, I can still track you down. Only you did save the world and everyone in it. Seems rude to kill you for the effort."

"I'm surprised you feel I saved the world," Kit said, hanging the scabbard from a nail beside his little tin mirror. The two aspects of his life on a single splintered pole. "I'd have called that more a group effort."

"Can't put on the play unless you've got the players," Marcus agreed. "But you've lived a lot of years in the world without letting those eight-legged bastards spread. There's still the risk, though, so you should have the blade with you. I won't need it anymore."

Kit swallowed down the lump in his throat. "Thank you, my friend. I don't know how to tell you how grateful I am for this. For all of this."

"No need. Look, I know you and this one"—Marcus nodded at Yardem—"think the world means something. I don't. As far as I can tell, life's just one flaming piece of shit after another, except when it's a bunch of them all at once. But I do believe in justice. Not the world's, but the one we make—"

"Technically, you are a part of the world, sir," Yardem said.

Confusion crossed through Wester's expression. "Your point?"

"Your justice is the world's. You were its path of justice unfolding itself."

"I'm the justice of the world?"

"Well," Yardem said. "Say you're *a* justice of the world."

"You're going to hold by that hairwash?"

"Just pointing it out, sir."

"Now I've forgotten what I was going to say. No, wait. I have it. I did what I did because I think it's the right thing. There's risk in it, but there's risk in everything. Keeping you in the world seems worth the chance."

The things in Kit's blood told him that it was true, and that if anything made it deeper. "I want you to know that traveling in your company, even during the worst of this, has been an honor."

"Yes, well," Marcus said. "Let's not get sentimental about it. We aren't twelve."

"Of course," Kit said, bowing.

"Until next time, then," Marcus said, turning. Once he'd left, Yardem returned the bow.

"You'll take care of him?" Kit asked.

"As much as he allows."

"I can still hear you," Marcus called from the yard. Yardem's wide, canine smile warmed Kit's heart. For the last time, the Tralgu man clasped his hand, and then he was gone as well. The players came back in, Cary first and then the others. The relief on their faces echoed his own.

"We're all right?" Mikel asked.

"I think we're fine," Kit said. "Except possibly that we have a performance and the stage half-together."

"Costume's not finished either," Sandr said.

In the event, Lak, Hornet, and Cary finished putting together the boards well before sundown. Charlit Soon's costume, while not of the most flattering cut, was done. And the Orcus costume was decent as well. In the last hour, the stable became a well-practiced chaos as each of them went through their lines again another time, Sandr and Hornet walked through the staging of the battle scene, and Cary and Lak marked out their places among the crowd to lead the reactions.

"You're ready?" Cary asked. Kit took a deep breath and let it out slowly. However many times he did this, there was always the little thrill of fear that came from stepping on the stage again.

"I believe that I am."

"That's as good as being true, then," she said.

The stage stood at the raised end of a little plaza, near a fountain, but not so close that they'd have to compete with the noise of the water. The men and women walking past were Kurtadam for the most part, but Firstblood and Cinnae as well. Yardem and Marcus stood across the way, eating meat and barley from rented cups. Kit found his place, raised his arms. A Kurtadam girl not more than eight years old with a pelt the color of wheat paused in her path to gawk at him. He nodded to her gravely.

"Stop!"

His voice went through the crowd like a ripple in a pool. The man selling wine by the fountain hesitated. The woman striding away toward the docks paused, looked back. Yardem lifted his ears.

"Stop now, and come near! Hear the tale of Allaren Mankiller and the Sword of Dragons! Or if you are faint of heart, move on. For our tale is one of grand adventure."

Marcus caught his gaze, nodded to him, and tapped

Yardem on the shoulder. Together they turned away into the streets under a wide and darkening sky.

"Love, war, betrayal, and vengeance shall spill out now upon these poor boards, and I warn you, not all that are good end well. Not all that are evil are punished. Come close, my friends, and know that in our tale as in the world, *anything* may happen..."

Dramatis Personae

Persons of interest and import in The Dagger and the Coin

IN THE GREATER WORLD

Inys, the last dragon

Marcus Wester, mercenary captain

Kitap rol Keshmat, former actor and apostate of the spider goddess

The Players

Cary

Hornet

Lak

Charlit Soon

Mikel

Sandr

Callon Cane, a convenient fiction

IN BIRANCOUR

The Medean bank in Porte Oliva

Cithrin bel Sarcour, voice of the Medean bank in Porte Oliva

Magistra Isadau, formerly voice of the Medean bank
    in Suddapal
Pyk Usterhall, notary to the bank
Yardem Hane, personal guard to Cithrin, also
Enen
Roach (Halvill)
Corisen Mout

Maestro Asanpur, a café owner

Mastién Juoli, master of coin

IN IMPERIAL ANTEA

The Royal Family

Aster, prince and heir to the empire

House Palliako

Geder Palliako, Regent of Antea and Baron of
    Ebbingbaugh
Lehrer Palliako, Viscount of Rivenhalm and his father

House Kalliam

Clara Kalliam, formerly Baroness of Osterling Fells
Barriath
Vicarian, and
Jorey; her sons
also Sabiha, wife to Jorey, and
Pindan, her illegitimate son
Annalise, her daughter

Vincen Coe, huntsman formerly in the service of
House Kalliam
Abatha Coe, his cousin

House Skestinin

Lord Skestinin, master of the Imperial Navy
Lady Skestinin, his wife

House Annerin

Elisia Annerin (formerly Kalliam), daughter of Clara
and Dawson
Gorman Annerin, son and heir of Lord Annerin and
husband of Elisia
Corl, their son

House Daskellin

Canl Daskellin, Baron of Watermarch and
Ambassador to Northcoast
Sanna, his eldest daughter

Also, various lords and members of the court, including

Sir Namen Flor
Sir Noyel Flor
Cyr Emming, Baron of Suderland Fells
Sir Ernst Mecelli
Sodai Carvenallin, his secretary
Sir Curtin Issandrian
Sir Gospey Allintot
Fallon Broot, Baron of Suderling Heights

and also Houses Veren, Essian, Ischian, Bannien,
Estinford, Faskellan, Emming, Tilliakin, Mastellin,
Caot, and Pyrellin among others

Basrahip, minister of the spider goddess and
counselor to Geder Palliako
also some dozen priests

IN ELASSAE

Fallon Broot, protector of the fivefold city
Carol Dannien, a mercenary captain
Cep Bailan, his officer
Salan, soldier and cousin of Isadau

IN NORTHCOAST

The Medean bank in Carse

Komme Medean, head of the Medean bank
Lauro, his son
Chana, his daughter
Paerin Clark, bank auditor and son-in-law
of Komme
Magister Nison, voice of the Medean bank
in Carse

King Tracian

IN HALLSKAR

Magra of Order Murro and
several of his compatriots

THE DEAD

King Simeon, Emperor of Antea, dead from a defect
of the flesh

King Lechan of Asterilhold, executed in war

Feldin Maas, formerly Baron of Ebbingbaugh killed
for treason

Phelia Maas, his wife dead at her husband's
hand

Dawson Kalliam, formerly Baron of Osterling Fells,
executed for treason

Alan Klin, executed for treason

Mirkus Shoat, executed for treason

Estin Cersillian, Earl of Masonhalm, killed in an
insurrection

Lord Ternigan, Lord Marshal to Regent Palliako,
killed for disloyalty

Magister Imaniel, voice of the Medean bank in Vanai
and protector of Cithrin

also Cam, a housekeeper, and

Besel, a man of convenience, burned in the razing of
Vanai

Alys, wife of Marcus Wester

also Merian, their daughter, burned to death as a
tactic of intrigue

Lord Springmere, the Mayfly King, killed in
vengeance

Akad Silas, adventurer, lost with his expedition

Assian Bey, collector of secrets and builder of traps, whose death is not recorded

Morade, the last Dragon Emperor, said to have died from wounds

Asteril, clutch-mate of Morade, maker of the Timzinae, dead of poison

Erex, lover of Inys whose manner of death is not recorded

Drakkis Stormcrow, great human general of the last war of the dragons, dead of age

Smit, a player lost in war

An Introduction to the
Taxonomy of Races

(From a manuscript attributed to Malasin Calvah, Taxono-
mist to Kleron Nuasti Cau, fifth of his name)

The ordering and arrangements of the thirteen races of
humanity by blood, order of precedence, mating combination, or purpose is, by necessity, the study of a lifetime. It
should occasion no concern that the finer points of the great
and complex creation should seem sometimes confused and
obscure. It is the intent of this essay to introduce the layman
to the beautiful and fulfilling path which is taxonomy.

I shall begin with a brief guide to which the reader may
refer.

Firstblood

The Firstblood are the feral, near-bestial form from which
all humanity arose. Had there been no dragons to form the
twelve crafted races from this base clay, humanity would
have been exclusively of the Firstblood. Even now, they are
the most populous of the races, showing the least difficulty
in procreation, and spreading throughout the known world
as a weed might spread through a rose garden. I intend no
offense by the comparison, but truth knows no etiquette.

The Eastern Triad

The oldest of the crafted races form the Eastern Triad: Jasuru, Yemmu, and Tralgu.

The Jasuru are often assumed to be the first of the higher races. They share the rough size and shape of the Firstblood, but with the metallic scales of lesser dragons. Most likely, they were created as a rough warrior caste, overseers to control the Firstblood slaves.

The Yemmu are clearly a later improvement. Their great size and massive tusks could only have been designed to intimidate the lesser races, but as with other examples of crafted races, the increase in size and strength has come at a cost. Of all the races, the Yemmu have the shortest natural lifespan.

The Tralgu are almost certainly the most recent of the Eastern Triad. They are taller than the Firstblood and with the fierce teeth and keen hearing of a natural carnivore, and common wisdom holds that they were bred for hunting more than formal battle. In the ages since the fall of dragons, it is likely only their difficulty in whelping that has kept them from forcible racial conquest.

The Western Triad

As the Eastern Triad marks an age of war in which races were created as weapons of war, the western races delineate an age in which the dragons began to create more subtle tools. Cinnae, Dartinae, and Timzinae each show the marks of creation for specific uses.

The Cinnae, when compared to all other races, are thin and pale as sprouts growing under a bucket. However, they have a marked talent in the mental arts, though the truly deep insights have tended to escape them. As the Jasuru are a first attempt at a warrior caste, so the Cinnae may be considered as a rough outline of the races that follow them.

The Dartinae, while dating their creation from the same time, do not share in the Cinnae's slightly better than rudimentary intelligence. Rather, their race was clearly built as a labor force for mining efforts. Their luminescent eyes show a structure unlike any other race, or indeed any known beast of nature. Their ability to navigate in utterly lightless caves is unique, and they tend to have the lithe frames one can imagine squeezing through cramped caves deep underground. Persistent rumors of a hidden Dartinae fortress deep below the earth no doubt spring from this, as no such structure has ever been found, nor would it be likely to survive in the absence of sustainable farming.

The Timzinae are, in fact, the only race whose place in the order of creation is unequivocally known. The youngest of the races, they date from the final war of the dragons. Their dark, insectile scales provide little of the protection that the Jasuru enjoy, but they are capable of utterly encasing the living flesh, even to the point of sealing all bodily orifices including ears and eyes. Their precise function as a tool remains obscure, though some suggest it might have been beekeeping.

The Master Races

The master races, or High Triad, represent the finest work of the dragons before their inevitable fall into decadence. These are the Kurtadam, Raushadam, and Haunadam.

The Kurtadam, like myself, show the fusion of all the best ideas that came before. The cleverness first hinted at in the Cinnae and the warrior's instinct limned by the Eastern Triad came together in the Kurtadam. Also, alone among the races, the Kurtadam were given the gift of a full pelt of warming hair, and the arts of beading and adornments that clearly represent the highest in etiquette and personal beauty.

The Haunadam exist to the greatest extent in Far Syramys and its territories, and represent the refinement of the warrior impulse that created the Yemmu. While slightly smaller, the tireless Haunadam have a thick mineral layer in their skins which repels violence and a clear and brilliant intellect that has given them utter dominion over the western continent. Their aversion to travel by water restricts their role in the blue-water trade, and has likely prevented military conquest of other nations bounded by the seas.

The Raushadam, like the Haunadam, are primarily to be found in Far Syramys, and function almost as if the two races were designed to act as one with the other. The slightest of frame, Raushadam are the only race gifted by the dragons with flight.

The Decadent Races

After the arts of the dragons reached their height, there was a necessary and inevitable descent into the oversophisticated. The latter efforts of the dragons brought out the florid and bizarre races: Haaverkin, Southling, and Drowned.

The Haaverkin have spent the centuries since the fall of dragons clinging to the frozen ports of the north. Their foul and aggressive temper is not a sign that they were bred for war, but that an animal let loose without its master will revert to its bestial nature. While they are large as the Yemmu, this is due to the rolls of insulating fat that protect them from the cold north. The facial tattooing has been compared to the Kurtadam ritual beads by those who clearly understand neither.

The Southlings, known for their great black night-adapted eyes, are a study in perversion. Littering the reaches south of Lyoneia, they have built up a culture equal parts termite hill and nomadic tribe worship. While capable of sexual reproduction, these wide-eyed half-humans prefer to delegate such activity to a central queen figure, with her subjects acting as drones. Whether they were bred to people the living deserts of the south or migrated there after the fall of dragons because they were unable to compete with the greater races is a fit subject of debate.

The Drowned are the final evidence of the decadence of the dragons. While much like the Firstblood in size and shape, the Drowned live exclusively underwater in all human climes. Interaction with them is slow when it is possible, and their tendency to gather in shallow tidepools marks them as little better than human seaweed. Suggestions that they are tools created toward some great draconic project still in play under the waves is purest romance.

With this as a grounding, we can address the five philosophical practices that determine how an educated mind orders, ranks, and ultimately judges the races...

Acknowledgments

I would like to thank Danny Baror and Shawna McCarthy for hooking me up with the amazing team at Orbit. The book would not exist in its present form without the good work of Will Hinton, Ellen Wright, Alex Lencicki, Anne Clarke, and Tim Holman.

Here, at the end of the project, I'd also like to acknowledge the people who helped me to launch it: George R. R. Martin, Walter Jon Williams, S. M. Stirling, Ty Franck, Ian Tregillis, Carrie Vaughn, Emily Mah, Melinda Snodgrass, Terry England, and all of the Critical Mass group. I'm glad none of you died when the lightning struck.

And, as always, my thanks to my family for their support during the hard parts.

The failures and infelicities are my own.

extras

orbit

meet the author

Photo Credit: Kyle Zimmerman

DANIEL ABRAHAM is the author of the critically acclaimed Long Price Quartet. He has been nominated for the Hugo, Nebula, and World Fantasy awards, and has won the International Horror Guild Award. He also writes as MLN Hanover and (with Ty Franck) James S. A. Corey. He lives in New Mexico.

introducing

If you enjoyed
THE SPIDER'S WAR,
look out for

SNAKEWOOD

by Adrian Selby

Once they were a band of mercenaries who shook the pillars of the world through cunning, alchemical brews, and cold steel. Whoever met their price won.

Now, their glory days behind them, scattered to the wind, and their genius leader in hiding, they are being hunted down and eliminated one by one.

A lifetime of enemies has its own price.

Chapter 1

Gant

My name's Gant and I'm sorry for my poor writing. I was a mercenary soldier who never took to it till Kailen taught us. It's for him and all the boys that I wanted to put this down, a telling of what become of Kailen's Twenty.

Seems right to begin it the day me and Shale got sold out, at the heart of the summer just gone, down in the Red Hills Confederacy.

It was the day I began dying.

It was a job with a crew to ambush a supply caravan. It went badly for us and I took an arrow, the poison from which will shortly kill me.

I woke up sodden with dew and rain like the boys, soaked all over from the trees above us, but my mouth was dusty like sand. Rivers couldn't wet it. The compound I use to ease my bones leaches my spit. I speak soft.

I could hardly crack a whistle at the boys wrapped like a nest of slugs in their oilskins against the winds of the plains these woods were edged against. I'm old. I just kicked them up before getting my bow out of the sack I put it in to keep rain off the string. It was a beauty what I called Juletta and I had her for most of my life.

The boys were slow to get going, blowing and fussing as the freezing air got to work in that bit of dawn. They were quiet, and grim like ghosts in this light, pairing up to strap their leathers and get the swords pasted with poison.

I patted heads and squeezed shoulders and gave words as I moved through the crew so they knew I was about and watching.

"Paste it thick," I said as they put on the mittens and rubbed their blades with the soaked rags from the pot Remy had opened.

I looked around the boys I shared skins and pipes with under the moon those last few weeks. Good crew.

There was Remy, looking up at me from his mixing, face all scarred like a milky walnut and speaking lispy from razor fights and rackets he ran with before joining up for a pardon. He had a poison of his own he made, less refined than my own mix, less quick, more agony.

Yasthin was crouched next to him. He was still having to shake the cramp off his leg that took a mace a month before. Saved his money for his brother, told me he was investing it. The boys said his brother gambled it and laughed him up.

Dolly was next to Yasthin, chewing some bacon rinds. Told me how her da chased her soak of a mother through the streets, had done since she was young. Kids followed her da too, singing with him but staying clear of his knives. She joined so's she could help her da keep her younger brother.

All of them got sorrows that led them to the likes of me and a fat purse for a crossroads job, which I mean to say is a do-or-die.

Soon enough they're lined up and waiting for the Honour, Kailen's Honour, the best fightbrew Kigan ever mixed, so the best fightbrew ever mixed, even all these years later. The boys had been talking up this brew since I took command, makes you feel like you could punch holes in mountains when you've risen on it.

Yasthin was first in line for a measure. I had to stand on my toes to pour it in, lots of the boys taller than me. Then a kiss. The lips are the raw end of your terror and love. No steel can toughen lips, they betray more than the eyes when you're looking for intent and the kiss is for telling them there's always some way to die.

Little Booey was the tenth and last of the crew to get the measure. I took a slug myself and Rirgwil fixed my leathers. I waited for our teeth to chatter like aristos, then went over the plan again.

"In the trees north, beyond those fields, is Trukhar's supply caravan," I said. "Find it, kill who you can, but burn the wagons, supplies, and then go for the craftsmen. Shale's leadin' his crew in from east an' we got them pincered when we meet, red bands left arm so as you know. It's a do-or-die purse, you're there 'til the job is done or you're dead anyway."

It was getting real for them now I could see, a couple were starting shakes with their first full measure of the brew, despite all the prep the previous few days.

"I taught you how to focus what's happening to you boys. This brew can win wars and it'll deliver this purse if you can keep tight. Now move out."

No more words, it was hand signs now to the forest.

Jonah front, Yasthin, Booey and Henny with me. Remy group northeast at tree line.

We ran through the silver grass, chests shuddering with the crackle of our blood as the brew stretched our veins and filled our bones with iron and fire. The song of the earth was filling my ears.

Ahead of us was the wall of trees and within, the camp of the Blackhands. Remy's boys split from us and moved away.

Slow, I signed.

Juletta was warm in my hands, the arrow in my fingers humming to fly. Then, the brew fierce in my eyes, I saw it, the red glow of a pipe some seventy yards ahead at the tree line.

Two men. On mark.

I moved forward to take the shot and stepped into a nest of eggs. The bird, a big grey Weger, screeched at me and flapped madly into the air inches from my face, its cry filling the sky. One of the boys shouted out, in his prime on the brew, and the two men saw us. We were dead. My boys' arrows followed mine, the two men were hit, only half a pip of a horn escaping for warning, but it was surely enough.

Run.

I had killed us all. We went in anyway, that was the purse, and these boys primed like this weren't leaving without bloodshed.

As we hit the trees we spread out.

Enemy left, signed Jonah.

Three were nearing through the trunks, draining their own brew as they came to from some half-eyed slumber. They were a clear shot so I led again, arrows hitting and a muffled crack of bones. All down.

In my brewed-up ears I could hear then the crack of bowstrings pulling at some way off, but it was all around us. The whistle of arrows proved us flanked as we dropped to the ground.

The boys opened up, moving as we practiced, aiming to surprise any flanks and split them off so a group of us could move in directly to the caravan. It was shooting practice for Trukhar's soldiers.

I never saw Henny or Jonah again, just heard some laughing and screaming and the sound of blades at work before it died off.

I stayed put, watching for the enemy's movements. I was in the outroots of a tree, unspotted. You feel eyes on you with this brew. Then I saw two scouts moving right, following Booey and Datschke's run.

I took a sporebag and popped it on the end of an arrow. I stood up and sent it at the ground ahead of them.

From my belt I got me some white oak sap which I took for my eyes to see safe in the spore cloud. I put on a mask covered with the same stuff for breathing.

The spores were quick to get in them and they wheezed and clutched their throats as I finished them off.

I was hoping I could have saved my boys but I needed to be in some guts and get the job done with Shale's crew.

Horns were going up now, so the fighting was on. I saw a few coming at me from the trees ahead. I got behind a trunk but I knew I was spotted. They slowed up and the hemp creaked as they drew for shots. There were four of them, from their breathing, and I could hear their commander whispering for a flanking.

I opened up a satchel of rice paper bags, each with quicklime and oiled feathers. I needed smoke. I doused a few bags with my flask and threw them out.

"Masks!" came the shout. As the paper soaked, the lime caught and the feathers put out a fierce smoke.

My eyes were still smeared good. I took a couple more arrowbags out, but these were agave powders for blistering the eyes and skin.

Two shots to tree trunks spread the powders in the air around their position and I moved out from the tree to them as they screeched and staggered about blind. The Honour give me the senses enough to read where they were without my eyes, better to shut them with smoke and powders in the air, and their brews weren't the Honour's equal. They moved like they were running through honey and were easy to pick off.

It was then I took the arrow that'll do for me. I'd got maybe fifty yards further on when I heard the bow draw, but with the noise ahead I couldn't place it that fraction quicker to save myself. The arrow went in at my hip, into my guts. Some things give in there, and the poison's gone right in, black mustard oil for sure from the vapors burning in my nose, probably some of their venom too.

I was on my knees trying to grab the arrow when I saw them approach, two of them. The one who killed me was dropping his bow and they both closed with the hate of their own fightbrew, their eyes crimson, skin an angry red and all the noisies.

They think I'm done. They're fucking right, to a point. In my belt was the treated guaia bark for the mix they were known to use. No time to rip out the arrow and push the bark in.

They moved in together, one in front, the other flanking. One's a heavy in his mail coat and broadsword, a boy's weapon in a forest, too big. Older one had leathers and a long knife. Him first. My sight was going, the world going flat like a drawing, so I had to get rid of the wiser one while I could still see him, while I still had the Honour's edge.

Knife in hand I lunged sudden, the leap bigger than they reckoned. The older one reacted, a sidestep. The slash I made wasn't for hitting him, though. It flicked out a spray of paste from the blade and sure enough some bit of it caught him in the face. I spun about, brought my blade up and parried the boy's desperate swing as he closed behind me, the blow forcing me down again as it hit my knife, sending a smack through my guts as the arrow broke in me. He took sight of his mate holding his smoking face, scratching at his cheeks and bleeding. He glanced at the brown treacle running over my blade and legged it. He had the spunk to know he was beaten. I put the knife in the old man's throat to quiet my noisies, the blood's smell as sweet as fresh bread to me.

I picked up my Juletta and moved on. The trees were filling with Blackhands now. I didn't have the time to be taking off my wamba and sorting myself out a cure for the arrow, much less tugging at it now it was into me. I cussed at myself, for this was likely where I was going to die if I didn't get something to fix me. I was slowing up. I took a hit of the Honour to keep me fresh. It was going to make a fierce claim on the other side, but I would gladly take that if I could get some treatment.

Finally I reached the caravan: smoke from the blazing wagons and stores filled the trees ahead. The grain carts were burning, so Shale, again, delivered the purse.

Then I come across Dolly, slumped against the roots of a tree. Two arrows were thrusting proud from her belly. She saw me and her eyes widened and she smiled.

"Gant, you're not done...oh," she said, seeing the arrow in me. I might have been swaying, she certainly didn't look right, faded somewhat, like she was becoming a ghost before me.

"Have you a flask, Gant, some more of the Honour?"

Her hands were full of earth, grabbing at it, having their final fling.

"I'm out, Dolly," I said, "I'm done too. I'm sorry for how it all ended."

She blinked, grief pinching her up.

"It can't be over already. I'm twenty summers, Gant. This was goin' to be the big purse."

A moment then I couldn't fill with any words.

"Tell my father, Gant, say..."

I was raising my bow. I did my best to clean an arrow on my leggings. She was watching me as I did it, knowing.

"Tell him I love him, Gant, tell him I got the Honour, and give him my purse and my brother a kiss."

"I will."

As I drew it she looked above me, seeing something I knew I wouldn't see, leagues away, some answers to her questions in her eyes thrilling her. I let fly, fell to my knees and sicked up.

Where was Shale?

My mouth was too dry to speak or shout for him, but I needed him. My eyes, the lids of them, were peeling back so's they would burn in the sun. I put my hands to my face. It was only visions, but my chest was heavy, like somebody sat on it and others were piling on. Looking through my hands as I held them up, it was like there were just bones there, flesh thin like the fins of a fish. My breathing rattled and I reached to my throat to try to open it up more.

"Gant!"

So much blood on him. He knelt next to me. He's got gray eyes, no color. Enemy to him is just so much warm meat to be put still. He don't much smile unless he's drunk. He mostly never drinks. He sniffed about me and at my wound, to get a reading of what was in it, then forced the arrow out with a knife and filled the hole with guaia bark while kneeling on my shoulder to keep me still.

He was barking at some boys as he stuffed some rugara leaves, sap and all, into my mouth, holding my nose shut, drowning me. Fuck! My brains were buzzing sore like a hive was in them. Some frothing liquid filled up my chest and I was bucking about for breath. He poured from a flask over my hip and the skin frosted over with an agony of burning. Then he took out some jumpcrick's legbones and held them against the hole, snap snap, a flash of blue flame and everything fell away high.

There was a choking, but it didn't feel like me no longer. It felt like the man I was before I died.

introducing

If you enjoyed
THE SPIDER'S WAR,
look out for

HOPE & RED

The Empire of Storms: Book One

by Jon Skovron

*In a fracturing empire spread across savage seas, two young people
from different cultures find common purpose.*

*A nameless girl is the lone survivor when her village is massacred
by biomancers, mystical servants of the emperor. Named after her
lost village, Bleak Hope is secretly trained by a master Vinchen
warrior as an instrument of vengeance.*

*A boy becomes an orphan on the squalid streets of New Laven
and is adopted by one of the most notorious women of the
criminal underworld, given the name Red, and trained as a
thief and con artist.*

*When a ganglord named Deadface Drem strikes a bargain
with the biomancers to consolidate and rule all the slums
of New Laven, the worlds of Hope and Red come crashing
together, and their unlikely alliance takes them further
than either could have dreamed possible.*

1

Captain Sin Toa had been a trader on these seas for many years, and he'd seen something like this before. But that didn't make it any easier.

The village of Bleak Hope was a small community in the cold southern islands at the edge of the empire. Captain Toa was one of the few traders who came this far south, and even then, only once a year. The ice that formed on the water made it nearly impossible to reach during the winter months.

Still, the dried fish, whalebone, and the crude lamp oil they pressed from whale blubber were all good cargo that fetched a nice price in Stonepeak or New Laven. The villagers had always been polite and accommodating, in their taciturn Southern way. And it was a community that had survived in these harsh conditions for centuries, a quality that Toa respected a great deal.

So it was with a pang of sadness that he gazed out at what remained of the village. As his ship glided into the narrow harbor, he scanned the dirt paths and stone huts, and saw no sign of life.

"What's the matter, sir?" asked Crayton, his first mate. Good fellow. Loyal in his own way, if a bit dishonest about doing his fair share of work.

"This place is dead," said Toa quietly. "We'll not land here."

"Dead, sir?"

"Not a soul in the place."

"Maybe they're at some sort of local religious gathering," said Crayton. "Folks this far south have their own ways and customs."

"'Fraid that's not it."

Toa pointed one thick, scarred finger toward the dock. A tall sign had been driven into the wood. On the sign was painted a black oval with eight black lines trailing down from it.

"God save them," whispered Crayton, taking off his wool knit cap.

"That's the trouble," said Toa. "He didn't."

The two men stood there staring at the sign. There was no sound except the cold wind that pulled at Toa's long wool coat and beard.

"What do we do, sir?" asked Crayton.

"Not come ashore, that's for certain. Tell the wags to lay anchor. It's getting late. I don't want to navigate these shallow waters in the dark, so we'll stay the night. But make no mistake, we're heading back to sea at first light and never coming near Bleak Hope again."

———

They set sail the next morning. Toa hoped they'd reach the island of Galemoor in three days and that the monks there would have enough good ale to sell that it would cover his losses.

It was on the second night that they found the stowaway.

Toa was woken in his bunk by a fist pounding on his cabin door.

"Captain!" called Crayton. "The night watch. They found...a little girl."

Toa groaned. He'd had a bit too much grog before he went to sleep, and the spike of pain had already set in behind his eyes.

"A girl?" he asked after a moment.

"Y-y-yes, sir."

"Hells' waters," he muttered, climbing out of his hammock. He pulled on cold, damp trousers, a coat, and boots. A girl on board, even a little one, was bad luck in these southern seas. Everybody knew that. As he pondered how he was going to get rid of this stowaway, he opened the door and was surprised to find Crayton alone, turning his wool cap over and over again in his hands.

"Well? Where's the girl?"

"She's aft, sir," said Crayton.

"Why didn't you bring her to me?"

"We, uh...that is, the men can't get her out from behind the stowed rigging."

"Can't get her..." Toa heaved a sigh, wondering why no one had just reached in and clubbed her unconscious, then dragged her out. It wasn't like his men to get soft because of a little girl. Maybe it was on account of Bleak Hope. Maybe the terrible fate of that village had made them a bit more conscious than usual of their own prospects for Heaven.

"Fine," he said. "Lead me to her."

"Aye, sir," said Crayton, clearly relieved that he wasn't going to bear the brunt of the captain's frustration.

Toa found his men gathered around the cargo hold where the spare rigging was stored. The hatch was open and they stared down into the darkness, muttering to each other and making signs to ward off curses. Toa took a lantern from one of them and shone the light down into the hole, wondering why a little girl had his men so spooked.

"Look, girlie. You better..."

She was wedged in tight behind the piles of heavy line. She looked filthy and starved, but otherwise a normal enough girl of about eight years. Pretty, even, in the Southern way, with pale skin, freckles, and hair so blond it looked almost white. But there was something about her eyes when she looked at you. They felt empty, or worse than empty. They were pools of ice that crushed any warmth you had in you. They were ancient eyes. Broken eyes. Eyes that had seen too much.

"We tried to pull her out, Captain," said one of the men. "But she's packed in there tight. And well...she's..."

"Aye," said Toa.

He knelt down next to the opening and forced himself to keep looking at her, even though he wanted to turn away.

"What's your name, girl?" he asked, much quieter now.

She stared at him.

"I'm the captain of this ship, girl," he said. "Do you know what that means?"

Slowly, she nodded once.

"It means everyone on this ship has to do what I say. That includes you. Understand?"

Again, she nodded once.

He reached one brown, hairy hand down into the hold.

"Now, girl. I want you to come out from behind there and take my hand. I swear no harm will come to you on this ship."

For a long moment, no one moved. Then, tentatively, the girl reached out her bone-thin hand and let it be engulfed in Toa's.

———

Toa and the girl were back in his quarters. He suspected the girl might start talking if there weren't a dozen hard-bitten sailors staring at her. He gave her a blanket and a cup of hot grog. He knew grog wasn't the sort of thing you gave to little girls, but it was the only thing he had on board except fresh water, and that was far too precious to waste.

Now he sat at his desk and she sat on his bunk, the blanket wrapped tightly around her shoulders, the steaming cup of grog in her tiny hands. She took a sip, and Toa expected her to flinch at the pungent flavor, but she only swallowed and continued to stare at him with those empty, broken eyes of hers. They were the coldest blue he had ever seen, deeper than the sea itself.

"I'll ask you again, girl," he said, although his tone was still gentle. "What's yer name?"

She only stared at him.

"Where'd you come from?"

Still she stared.

"Are you . . ." He couldn't believe he was even thinking it, much less asking it. "Are you from Bleak Hope?"

She blinked then, as if coming out of a trance. "Bleak Hope." Her voice was hoarse from lack of use. "Yes. That's me." There was something about the way she spoke that made Toa suppress a shudder. Her voice was as empty as her eyes.

"How did you come to be on my ship?"

"That happened after," she said.

"After what?" he asked.

She looked at him then, and her eyes were no longer empty. They were full. So full that Toa's salty old heart felt like it might twist up like a rag in his chest.

"I will tell you," she said, her voice as wet and full as her eyes. "I will tell *only* you. Then I won't ever say it aloud ever again."

———

She had been off at the rocks. That was how they'd missed her.

She loved the rocks. Great big jagged black boulders she could climb above the crashing waves. It terrified her mother the way she jumped from one to the next. "You'll hurt yourself!" her mother would say. And she did hurt herself. Often. Her shins and knees were peppered with scabs and scars from the rough-edged rock. But she didn't care. She loved them anyway. And when the tide went out, they always had treasures at their base, half-buried in the gray sand. Crab shells, fish bones, seashells, and sometimes, if she was very lucky, a bit of sea glass. Those she prized above all else.

"What is it?" she'd asked her mother one night as they sat by the fire after dinner, her belly warm and full of fish stew. She held up a piece of red sea glass to the light so that the color shone on the stone wall of their hut.

"It's glass, my little gull," said her mother, fingers working quickly as she mended a fishing net for Father. "Broken bits of glass polished by the sea."

"But why's it colored?"

"To make it prettier, I suppose."

"Why don't *we* have any glass that's colored?"

"Oh, it's just fancy Northland frippery," said her mother. "We've no use for it down here."

That made her love the sea glass all the more. She collected them until she had enough to string together with a bit of hemp rope to make a necklace. She presented it to her father, a gruff fisherman who rarely spoke, on his birthday. He held the necklace in his leathery hand, eyeing the bright red, blue, and green chunks of sea glass warily. But then he looked into her eyes and saw how proud she was, how much she loved this thing. His weather-lined face folded up into a smile as he carefully tied it around his neck. The other fishermen teased him for weeks about it, but he would only touch his calloused fingertips to the sea glass and smile again.

When *they* came on that day, the tide had just gone out, and she was searching the base of her rocks for new treasures. She'd seen the top of their ship masts off in the distance, but she was far too focused on her hunt for sea glass to investigate. It wasn't until she finally clambered back on top of one of the rocks to sift through her collection of shells and bones that she noticed how strange the ship was. A big boxy thing with a full three sails and cannon ports all along the sides. Very different from the trade ships. She didn't like the look of it at all. And that was before she noticed the thick cloud of smoke rising from her village.

She ran, her skinny little legs churning in the sand and tall grass as she made her way through the scraggly trees toward her village. If there was a fire, her mother wouldn't bother to save the treasures stowed away in the wooden chest under her bed. That was all she could think about. She'd spent too much time and effort collecting her treasures to lose them. They were the most precious thing to her. Or so she thought.

As she neared the village, she saw that the fire had spread across the whole village. There were men she didn't recognize dressed in white-and-gold uniforms with helmets and armored chest plates. She wondered if they were soldiers. But soldiers were supposed to protect the people. These men herded everyone into a big clump in the center of the village, waving swords and guns at them.

She jerked to a stop when she saw the guns. She'd only seen one other gun. It was owned by Shamka, the village elder. Every winter on the eve of the New Year, he fired it up at the moon to wake it from its slumber and bring back the sun. The guns these soldiers had looked different. In addition to the wooden handle, iron tube, and hammer, they had a round cylinder.

She was trying to decide whether to get closer or run and hide, when Shamka emerged from his hut, gave an angry bellow, and fired his gun at the nearest soldier. The soldier's face caved in as the shot struck him, and he fell back into the mud. One of the other soldiers raised his pistol and fired at Shamka, but missed. Shamka laughed triumphantly. But then the intruder fired a second time without reloading. Shamka's face was wide with surprise as he clutched at his chest and toppled over.

The girl nearly cried out then. But she bit her lip as hard as she could to stop herself, and dropped into the tall grass.

She lay hidden there in the cold, muddy field for hours. She had to clench her jaw to keep her teeth from chattering. She heard the soldiers shouting to each other, and there were strange hammering and flapping sounds. Occasionally, she would hear one of the villagers beg to know what they had done to displease the emperor. The only reply was a loud smack.

It was dark, and the fires had all flickered out, before she moved her numb limbs up into a crouch and took another look.

In the center of the town, a huge brown canvas tent had been erected, easily five times larger than any hut in the village. The soldiers stood in a circle around it, holding torches. She couldn't see her fellow villagers anywhere. Cautiously, she crept a little closer.

A tall man who wore a long, hooded white cloak instead of a uniform stood at the entrance to the tent. In his hands, he held a large wooden box. One of the soldiers opened the flap of the tent entrance. The cloaked man went into the tent, accompanied by a soldier. Some moments later, they both emerged, but the man no longer had the box. The soldier tied the flap so that the entrance remained open, then covered the opening with a net so fine not even the smallest bird could have slipped through.

The cloaked man took a notebook from his pocket as soldiers brought out a small table and chair and placed them before him. He sat at the table and a soldier handed him a quill and ink. The man immediately began to write, pausing frequently to peer through the netting into the tent.

Screams began to come from inside the tent. She realized then that all the villagers were inside. She didn't know why they screamed, but it terrified her so much that she dropped back into the mud and held her hands over her ears to block out the sound.

The screams only lasted a few minutes, but it was a long time before she could bring herself to look again.

It was completely dark now except for one lantern at the tent entrance. The soldiers had gone and only the cloaked man remained, still scribbling away in his notebook. Occasionally, he would glance into the tent, look at his pocket watch, and frown. She wondered where the soldiers were, but then noticed that the strange boxy ship tied at the dock was lit up, and when she strained her hearing, she could make out the sound of rowdy male voices.

The girl snuck through the tall grass toward the side of the tent that was the farthest from the man. Not that he would have seen her. He seemed so intent on his writing that she probably could have walked right past him, and he wouldn't have noticed. Even so, her heart raced as she crept across the small stretch of open ground between the tall grass and the tent wall. When she finally reached the tent, she found that the bottom had been staked down so tightly that she had to pull out several of them before she could slip under.

It was even darker inside, the air thick and hot. The villagers all lay on the ground, eyes closed, chained to each other and to the thick tent poles. In the center sat the wooden box, the lid off. Scattered on the ground were dead wasps as big as birds.

Far over in the corner, she saw her mother and father, motionless like all the rest. She moved quickly to them, a sick fear shooting through her stomach.

But then her father moved weakly, and relief flooded through her. Maybe she could still rescue them. She gently shook her mother, but she didn't respond. She shook her father, but he only groaned, his eyes fluttering a moment but not opening.

She searched around, looking to see if she could unfasten their chains. There was a loud buzzing close to her ear. She turned and saw a giant wasp hovering over her shoulder. Before it could sting her, a hand shot past her face and slapped it aside. The wasp spun wildly around, one wing broken, then dropped to the ground. She turned and saw her father, his face screwed up in pain.

He grabbed her wrist. "Go!" he grunted. "Away." Then he shoved her so hard, she fell backward onto her rear.

She stared at him, terrified, but wanting to do something that would take the awful look of pain away from his face. Around her, others were stirring, their own faces etched in the same agony as her father.

Then she saw her father's sea glass necklace give an odd little jump. She looked closer. It happened again. Her father arched his back. His eyes and mouth opened wide, as if screaming, but only a wet gurgle came out. A white worm as thick as a finger burst from his neck. Blood streamed from him as other worms burrowed out of his chest and gut.

Her mother woke with a gasp, her eyes staring around wildly. Her skin was already shifting. She reached out and called her daughter's name.

All around her, the other villagers thrashed against their chains as the worms ripped free. Before long, the ground was covered in a writhing mass of white.

She wanted to run. Instead, she held her mother's hand and watched her writhe and jerk as the worms ate her from the inside. She did not move, did not look away until her mother grew still. Only then did she stumble to her feet, slip under the tent wall, and run back into the tall grass.

She watched from afar as the soldiers returned at dawn with large burlap sacks. The cloaked man went inside the tent for a while, then came back out and wrote more in his notebook. He did this two more times, then said something to one of the soldiers. The soldier nodded, gave a signal, and the group with sacks filed into the tent. When they came back out, their sacks were filled with writhing bulges that she guessed were the worms. They carried them to the ship while the remaining soldiers struck the tent, exposing the bodies that had been inside.

The cloaked man watched as the soldiers unfastened the chains from the pile of corpses. As he stood there, the little girl fixed his face in her memory. Brown hair, weak chin, pointed ratlike face marked with a burn scar on his left cheek.

At last they sailed off in their big boxy ship, leaving a strange sign driven into the dock. When they were no longer in sight, she crept back down into the village. It took her many days. Perhaps weeks. But she buried them all.

———

Captain Sin Toa stared down at the girl. During her tale, her expression had remained fixed in a look of wide-eyed horror. But now it settled back into the cold emptiness he'd seen when he first coaxed her out of the hold.

"How long ago was that?" he asked.

"Don't know," she said.

"How did you get aboard?" he asked. "We never docked."

"I swam."

"Quite a distance."

"Yes."

"And what should I do with you now?"

She shrugged.

"A ship is no place for a little girl."

"I have to stay alive," she said. "So I can find that man."

"Do you know who that was? What that sign meant?"

She shook her head.

"That was the crest of the emperor's biomancers. You haven't got a prayer of ever getting close to that man."

"I will," she said quietly. "Someday. If it takes my whole life. I'll find him. And kill him."

———

Captain Sin Toa knew he couldn't keep her aboard. It was said maidens, even eight-year-old ones, could draw the attention of the sea serpents in these waters as sure as a bucketful of blood. The crew might very well mutiny at the idea of keeping a girl on board. But he wasn't about to throw her overboard or dump her on some empty piece of rock either. When they landed the next day at Galemoor, he approached the head of the Vinchen order, a wizened old monk named Hurlo.

"Girl's seen things nobody should have to see," he said. The two of them stood in the stone courtyard of the monastery, the tall, black stone temple looming over them. "She's a broken thing. Could be a monastic life is the only option left to her."

Hurlo slipped his hands into the sleeves of his black robe. "I sympathize, Captain. Truly, I do. But the Vinchen order is for men only."

"But surely you could use a servant around," said Toa. "She's a peasant, accustomed to hard work."

Hurlo nodded. "We could. But what happens when she comes of age and begins to blossom? She will become too great a distraction for my brothers, particularly the younger ones."

"So keep her till then. At least you'll have sheltered her a few years. Kept her alive long enough for her to make her own way."

Hurlo closed his eyes. "It will not be an easy life for her here."

"Don't think she'd know what to do with an easy life if you gave her one anyway."

Hurlo looked at Toa. And to Toa's surprise, he suddenly smiled, his old eyes sparkling. "We will take in this broken child you have found. A bit of chaos in the order brings change. Perhaps for the better."

Toa shrugged. He'd never fully understood Hurlo or the Vinchen order. "If you say so, Grandteacher."

"What is the child's name?" asked Hurlo.

"She won't say for some reason. I half think she doesn't remember."

"What shall we call her then, this child born of nightmare? As her unlikely guardians, I suppose it is now up to us to name her."

Captain Sin Toa thought about it a moment, tugging at his beard. "Maybe after the village she survived. Keep something of it in memory, at least. Call her Bleak Hope."